Also by Naomi Sawyer & Charles Sale

The Culling
Book Two
Chronicles of the Two Worlds

The Successor

Book One

Chronicles of the Two Worlds

Naomi Sawyer & Charles Sale

THE SUCCESSOR: BOOK ONE, CHRONICLES OF THE TWO WORLDS

This novel is a work of fiction. Any references to real people, events, establishments, organizations, or locales are intended only to give the fiction a sense of reality and authenticity, and are used fictitiously. All other names, characters, and places, and all dialogue and incidents portrayed in this book are the product of the authors' imaginations.

Cover design by Jeffrey Otto. Cover title design by Matt Scavezze. Cover photograph by Charles Sale.

EVENTS
Sawyer & Sale LLC can bring the authors to your live event. For more information or to calendar an event, email sawyersale@gmail.com.

PRINTING HISTORY
First softcover edition / 2016
Second softcover edition / 2017

ISBN-13: 978-1533379405
ISBN-10: 1533379408

FOR SHANNON AND ALL WHO DREAM OF OTHER WORLDS

Contents

The Successor

1   The Secret

Empires rise and fall. A dynasty flourishes for a thousand years and then becomes a story told by the native children. All the while the earth turns and we look up in wonder at the moon and the sun and the stars and all that lies beyond in the land of unknowing.

FROM *"HISTORY OF THE EXODUS" BY ANDRONIUS CALEDON*

D om André Du Bourgay emerged through a narrow doorway in the north wall of the abbey of Mont Saint-Michel. He filled his lungs with the cold maritime air, held his breath, and listened intently for any sound that might signal the presence of a watcher.

That is what he called them. He had never seen one, but he was certain they were about. They always accompanied the Guardian, and her arrival was not far off. He listened, but he heard only the cold, gray waters of the Atlantic lapping against the sea wall.

It was March twenty-first. Twilight was turning to dusk and a dense fog was settling like a shroud over Mont Saint-Michel. Sun, moon, and earth were in precise alignment and the moon's monthly rotation had brought it as close to earth as it would ever be. The gravitational forces were enormous, and the Atlantic Ocean was swelling beneath the fog. The tide's front water would soon pass over the sands of the estuary at a speed faster than a man could run, and its surges would rise as high as fourteen meters.

"Tide of the Century" people called it. A scientist at the Naval Hydrographic and Oceanographic Service explained that a supertide like this occurred once every 18.6 years. He said data from stations along the coast of Normandy and Brittany hinted that this tide would be higher and swifter than any on record. The scientist could not explain why.

Dom Bourgay, abbot of Mont Saint-Michel, knew why. The Guardian was using the tide for her protection. He could not imagine how she did such a thing. Divine intervention he understood; he was a believer. But he knew of no prayer to call up the tide. She could do it without a prayer, without God. The whole affair was an abomination, but he was bound by ancient contract to play a part in it.

Dom Bourgay left the concealment of the deeply recessed doorway, found the trail that switchbacked down to the north shoreline, and began his descent. The shoreline would provide a refuge from the witch and her watchers. He did not want to see her. He did not want to hear her voice. Even her voice had power, power that came from neither God nor Satan. God was God, Satan was Satan. It was a polarity that matched his beliefs comfortably. Something in between did not.

He pushed aside these thoughts. He had done his part. He had fulfilled the ancient agreement, passed down from abbot to abbot over the centuries. He had kept secret the hidden chamber at the top of the north tower of the abbey. He had done enough. He did not need to know by what magic they gained access to the chamber, nor did he want any part in the dark business that would be conducted there.

Bourgay heard the urgent sound of water against rock as he neared the shoreline. The wet gloom was heavier here than above. He groped through it to a familiar rock platform overlooking the sea. The water surged angrily against the wall beneath the platform. High tide usually brought the sea to a place some thirty meters below the platform, but tonight the waters were closer than thirty meters, much closer.

Bourgay peered through the fog at buildings set into the steep slope below where he had left the trail. There should have been three of them, but he could only see two. The third, the one furthest down-slope, was submerged by a tide higher than any he had ever witnessed in his forty years as abbot.

"Still rising, it is, *Père*."

Bourgay spun toward the voice that came out of the dark on the other side of the platform. He saw the vague outline of a man, in appearance a shadowy wraith blurred by drifting fog. He thought he knew the voice.

"Jacques?"

"No other," said the man, advancing a few paces toward him. "I've never seen it like this," the man continued. "Tide like this makes for good fishing."

Bourgay relaxed. Jacques Villedieu was an old friend who had a shop in the village below the abbey.

"The tide has made an ocean around us, Jacques. Everyone has retreated to the mainland. Where will you sleep?"

"My shop, if the tide don't sink it. I'll go upslope to the walls of the abbey if that happens. I've slept out before."

"Come inside the abbey. I'll prepare a place for you."

"No, no. Old sinner like me might be struck dead in there."

Both men chuckled.

"What brings you here, Father?"

"Contemplation, I suppose," Bourgay replied.

He could not tell Jacques the truth. He could not tell anyone.

"Ah, contemplation. The curse of the religious. I just fish. You can touch a fish, clean it, cook it, eat it. What can you do with contemplation?"

"It gives nourishment to the soul."

"Fishing does that too, feeds both places."

Bourgay smiled.

"Any fish?" he asked.

"*Oui.*"

Jacques held up a dirty bucket.

"The tide brings them in."

"A tide such as this will do harm, I fear."

"No doubt. Me included," Jacques replied. "God punishing the sinners."

Their conversation was interrupted by crackling and buzzing coming from the direction of the abbey. Both looked up, trying to see through the fog. A soft golden glow appeared where the abbey's roof should have been. The glow pulsed a few seconds and then was gone.

"What was that?" Jacques whispered.

"I think nothing sinister," Dom Bourgay said, smiling. "Perhaps static electricity, maybe something to do with the weather."

It wasn't quite a lie. Everything had something to do with the weather, and static electricity could be expected with the arrivals. The meeting would soon begin.

Jacques shrugged, not quite convinced by Bourgay's weather explanation. "Better check what's going on up there in your abbey. The devil vexes saints and sinners alike."

"I thought you didn't believe in either, Jacques."

"Didn't say that," Jacques grumbled. "Good night to you, Father."

Jacques collected his fishing gear and bucket, passed behind Bourgay, and stepped off the platform. The fog enclosed him as he started up the trail. First he was a man carrying a bucket and a fishing rod, then an apparition, then nothing.

Dom Bourgay gazed at the sea. It had covered the second building and was now only ten meters below the platform. Fingers of damp penetrated Bourgay's robe. He shivered.

The ancient secret envelopes me, he thought, *like this fog and the tide beneath it.*

2   Convergence

The Guardian does not know her powers. This is because they are shaped by her perception of necessity. We will manipulate her perception of necessity. She will become a tool in our hand, yet our hand will never touch her.

FROM A CONFIDENTIAL POLICY DIRECTIVE ISSUED BY AEDAN SHAW

The chamber at the top of the abbey's north tower was well hidden. There were no stairs, inside or out. There were no visible doors or windows or openings of any kind, and there was no passage to the chamber through the ceiling of the room below. The walls and ceiling were supported by four equally spaced buttresses. The chamber would have been without a photon of light were it not for a luminous sphere hovering at the base of each buttress.

The four spheres began to shimmer, then rise slowly in unison, each following the underside of its buttress. The spheres merged at the apex of the ceiling, where the buttresses met, and formed a cloud of blue vapor. The cloud descended, its vaporous center coalescing into a human being, a woman, tall and slim with thick silvery-blond hair. She wore an emerald-green traveling cloak fastened at the neck with a silver clasp. Her face was etched by time, but time had not robbed her of great beauty.

The woman's feet touched the stone floor. She steadied herself, held her breath, and listened for anyone or anything that might be lurking in the dark. Satisfied she was alone, she pulled a thin ebony wand from within the folds of her cloak. She pointed it forward, muttered a spell, and turned in a slow circle. Her spell ignited the wicks of fifty candles in iron stanchions surrounding the chamber. The spell also illuminated four stained-glass windows set into the walls between the buttresses. The windows (for that is what they appeared to be) were three meters high by two meters wide. They were not, of course, true windows, since there were no openings in the walls of the chamber, but the illusion was flawless, even to the touch, and it relieved the claustrophobic atmosphere of the place while not compromising its security.

The woman surveyed the magical windows.

Chapters in the history of the Two Worlds, she thought. *My history.*

She approached the first window. In it were images of grasses, trees, diverse flora, and all manner of earth-bound living things. Also depicted were the maneuverings of fire, water, and air to make mountains, deserts, jungles, lakes, and oceans. The grand landscape of the earth was before her, millennia captured and held motionless within the glowing glass.

The woman walked to the second window. Creatures of all kinds were depicted there in breathtaking color and light. Beasts of land, sea, and air were fixed in poses befitting their places in the fabric of life. No man or woman was among them.

She moved to the third window and gazed at the lifelike images of men and women. Farmers, seafarers, hunters, soldiers, prelates, kings and queens, mothers and fathers, children. The dominant theme was conflict. Flags were raised in triumph or cast down in defeat. At the center of the window were images of men and women being stoned, beheaded, hanged, or burned at the stake.

She turned away and walked to the last window. In it was

a wizard surrounded by smiling men, women, and children. The royal purple of the wizard's robe contrasted with his ivory cheeks. He held a wand. Sparks from its tip descended to flora that flourished in colorful abundance at his feet.

The woman felt the ancient reverence.

Andronius Caledon, Protector of All Magical Beings, Master of the Dimensions, and Creator of Second World.

Since childhood she had been taught to append his name to his accomplishments in precisely this way. This was his title and his legacy. It was he who had discovered the dimensions. It was he who had mastered passage between them, and it was he who had given these dimensions their names: First World for the dimension where Mont Saint-Michel existed on the coast of Normandy. Second World for the dimension she had just left, where there was no Mont Saint-Michel, and Normandy was called something else.

Andronius had opened a path for the exodus of magical beings from the persecutions of First World to the peace and protection of Second World. Not all witches and warlocks had joined the exodus. It was hard to leave kith and kin. The woman pondered the fate of those who had chosen to remain behind: Some ninety thousand executed for witchcraft from AD 1500 to 1660 alone. These numbers included thousands falsely accused and executed—thousands who died for what they were not and who knew nothing of a Second World to which they might have fled.

Will I undo here, today, all that Andronius accomplished sixteen centuries ago? Will that be my legacy, the legacy of the twenty-first century? Will I bring magic back to First World only to see a new pogrom launched against my people?

Outside, the alignment of sun, moon, and earth had pulled the waters as high as they would go. This was the last of her preparations. The tide would stay as high as it was until she released it.

It was time to bring the others across.

The woman directed her wand at the base of the west buttress. A luminous sphere appeared, rose along the underside of the buttress, became a shimmering blue cloud at the apex of the ceiling, and descended. The cloud transformed into a being, human in form but not human: a Nepenthian.

The Nepenthian's robes hung in layers, each layer a patchwork of multicolored leaves. The layers parted in front, revealing a graceful feminine form clothed in diaphanous white silk. Strands of her bright red hair moved randomly as though fanned by a gentle breeze. The Nepenthian's skin was the color of a fine pearl: soft white with the slightest hint of blue showing forth.

"Greetings, Guardian," the Nepenthian said, bowing to the woman who had summoned her. The title was spoken with reverence.

The woman nodded.

"Greetings, Nara. It is always good to see you."

"And you, Elizabeth, although I wish we were meeting under happier circumstances."

Elizabeth pointed her wand at the base of the north buttress. Again a sphere of light appeared, ascended along the buttress, turned a cloudy blue at the ceiling, and delivered a man of impressive physical presence.

"I don't enjoy traveling this way," the man said, "and I don't like meeting in this place."

Elizabeth smiled. Joshua always began with a complaint. It was his way of saying hello. He had been shaped in a sharp-edged mold. He was tall, solidly built, and handsome. He was rugged without being coarse, and had the masculine

magnetism typical of men like him in First World. He was in
his middle years and had the appearance of a man who
would forever be in his prime. He manifested unembellished
self-possession without the stain of haughtiness. His
countenance told a story, many stories, of having faced
danger, stared it down, and moved on. He wore a black
down parka over a gray fiber pile vest and maroon shirt. His
loose trousers were also black, with cargo pockets. On his
head was a black wool watch cap. Elizabeth knew he was
armed. He always carried a semi-automatic handgun in a
shoulder holster. Very First World, she thought. Almost
quaint by Second World standards.

Elizabeth pointed her wand at the base of the east
buttress. Again a sphere of light appeared, coursed up the
buttress, turned vaporous, and delivered a man. This man
was older than Joshua, but similar in bearing and demeanor.
The man nodded politely at Nara and Joshua before turning
to Elizabeth. His nod to her was a slower gesture,
accompanied by a slight bend at the waist: not quite a bow
but not merely a nod. The timbre of Elizabeth's voice altered
ever so slightly as she addressed him:

"Thank you for coming, General Borrington."

Andrew Borrington was commander of all Second World
armies. He was simply Borrington to his peers, and in the
stories told about him. To Elizabeth he was sometimes
Andrew, but not here, not in front of the others. Borrington
was close to her in age, and like her, he was undiminished by
his years. He looked at Elizabeth through penetrating amber
eyes that radiated calm self-discipline and a readiness to
command or obey without hesitation. His hair was thick and
white, worn long in the fashion of Second World military
men. He held his tall, lean body in a posture that was erect
without being rigid. He wore a midnight blue surcoat over a

white tunic and black leather leggings. The surcoat was embossed with the symbols of his rank and the coat of arms of Second World. A Norman sword was strapped to his waist. Borrington was Second World through-and-through, and this was much to Elizabeth's liking.

She took her eyes off Borrington and turned to the south buttress.

I must be careful with this last one.

She pointed her wand. A sphere of light coursed upward, repeating the transformation process, and a Lavertanian Unicorn appeared before them.

The animal resembled a well-conformed Arabian stallion except for the thirty-centimeter golden horn protruding from its forehead. He was large for his species, more than eighteen hands at the withers, and his coat was whiter than white.

The unicorn lifted his right foreleg and lowered his head in ritual greeting.

"Welcome, Sigvardr," Elizabeth said.

The unicorn snorted and jerked his head sharply upward. He was a being who communicated by thought emanation. Humans called this mental telepathy, but it was something more in unicorns. Sigvardr could filter his thoughts, like a human being whispering to another, or communicate to many at once, and over great distances. He knew the languages of humans, but, like Nara, he knew many other languages as well: the language of energy, of perception cleansed of opinion, of fight, and of flight—not as mere reflexes, but as carefully considered decisions that reflected uncanny prescience.

His response to Elizabeth was private:

With respect, Madame, let us get on with it, if you please. I am aware you seek some great change. I have not delved further in you. I trust you will reveal what you will reveal in your own good time. I wait upon you. But be quick, witch, if you please.

Elizabeth immediately blocked her thoughts. She took no offense. Unicorns in general, and Sigvardr in particular, were without social pretense. They believed pretense diminished discernment, and so made no attempt at it.

Elizabeth, Nara, Joshua, and Borrington took seats in tall-back chairs arranged around a large circular table on the west side of the chamber. Sigvardr stood nearby. Imbedded in the massive stained glass window above the table was the image of Andronius Caledon.

Elizabeth looked up at the image.

It's as though he presides here, she thought. *Sixteen centuries, and it is still his work we do.*

She looked at the others and began:

"A week ago, I accompanied General Borrington to a village in the foothills of the Andrian Mountains. He had received information that there would be an attack. He assembled available forces, and we set out immediately from Byrnhelen.

"We were too late. The smell of death was in the air as we approached the village. I shall not soon forget the sightless eyes of the dead, especially the children, their mouths gaping in silent screams of horror, their lifeless bodies twisted and broken, some still clinging to their dead mothers."

Nara nodded.

"I had heard something of this."

"I too heard rumors," Joshua said. "Uncharacteristic of your world, is it not? You have your squabbles, but I have been given to believe they are less...horrific than ours."

He turned to Borrington.

"How are you dealing with this?"

"Very carefully. These atrocities, while designed to appear random, form a slowly expanding pattern. Aedan is recruiting. Where enticement fails, he terrorizes. Where terror fails, he kills. His magical powers are growing. By what mechanism I don't know. We are working on that."

Elizabeth raised her hand:

"What we do know is the problem is growing and cannot be dealt with in the usual way."

"What does that mean, Guardian?" Joshua asked.

"We must cooperate more closely than we have in the past," she replied without hesitation.

"Forgive me for being a bit skeptical," Joshua said, "but I deal with First World atrocities every day. First World technology is a double-edged sword. So is your magic. We both have our share of madmen. I deal with mine; you deal with yours."

"This is different," Elizabeth said.

Joshua gave her a hard look and went on.

"It is your brother, Aedan, who is behind this. It is a Second World problem and, with respect, Guardian, a family problem. This is General Borrington's responsibility. He is Protector of Second World Human Kind and commander of your forces. I am Protector of First World Human Kind. We do not interfere with one another. I am unwilling to change this arrangement."

Elizabeth's jaw muscles tightened.

"And what if Aedan attacks the realms?"

"He won't do that. It's not in his best interests."

"You assume rationality, Joshua. My brother is mad, a nihilist of the most extreme type. Death and destruction fascinate him."

"As they do many in First World, Guardian."

Elizabeth looked down at her hands, and went on in a quiet voice:

"Separation of the Two Worlds has served us well, Joshua. It is the realms I am discussing at the moment. They must be balanced and unified. This is essential to sustaining the two dimensions. Without balance and unity within the realms, and synchronization between them, the dimensions would collapse, catastrophically. We depend on Nara and Sigvardr to prevent this. Nara for the earth, air, water, fire, and all flora; Sigvardr for the animals: marine, avian, and earthbound. These two realms, intertwined, are the platform on which we all stand."

"Factually correct," Joshua replied abruptly, "but not to the point. Aedan is a political problem, not an ecological one."

Elizabeth shook her head.

"He is both," she said. "He knows the realms form a tapestry woven across both worlds. He knows if the right thread is pulled, the whole tapestry will unravel, and with it our worlds. He searches for the right thread. When he finds it, he will pull it."

Joshua leaned back in his chair.

"With respect, Madame, I don't think the realms are as fragile as you suggest, nor do I think we are without the ability to respond effectively if Aedan tugs at a thread."

Hard and stubborn, thought Elizabeth, *and intelligent. These qualities are obstacles at the moment, but they will be quite valuable in dealing with what is to come. I must not destroy him in the argument.*

"You fail to comprehend," Elizabeth said, matching Joshua's bluntness.

"I don't think I do. Your brother has attacked his own people in his own world. Our rule has long been not to interfere. Aedan is a magical being, a power in Second World, but not in mine. He has no interest in us, and it is my duty as Protector of First World Human Kind to keep it that way. Preservation of the divide between the Two Worlds is sacrosanct. It protects us both. I am opposed to unification at any level."

"But this problem affects First World," Elizabeth responded.

"Not at the moment, and you have always depended on me to defend the interests of First World. I am doing so now. As you are aware, we in First World have problems of our own, many of them quite serious. That is why you left us centuries ago. This problem with your brother does not warrant abandoning a system that has worked so well to preserve our two cultures."

He argues the point well, Elizabeth acknowledged to herself, *and relentlessly. I will have to reveal all before this is done.*

Sigvardr read her thoughts.

He is open, you are not. In this, you are weak, and he is strong. Reveal what must be revealed, if you please. He makes his argument; you make yours. I will attend to both.

Elizabeth glanced at Sigvardr and forged ahead:

"I do not suggest this alliance lightly."

"Now it is an alliance," Joshua snapped. "Entangling alliances we don't need, for your sake and mine. Please, Guardian, remember your history."

"Stop!"

It was Borrington.

"You are speaking to the Guardian, Joshua. She is the preserver of the Two Worlds, not some petty adversary in your world. Your instantaneous rebuttals on each point delay our understanding of the whole. I have misgivings. We all do. Let courtesy accompany our misgivings. And let respect for the Guardian govern our tongues."

Joshua's eyes narrowed, but he kept his silence.

Moments passed.

Elizabeth broke the silence, speaking to them all:

"Aedan's ambitions and his growing powers impose an unprecedented necessity upon us all. We must form an alliance."

Sigvardr's mental response was immediate:

More revelation and less rhetoric would be a wise turn, Madame. You withhold, playing us like musical instruments. The tune does not suit. You are not in your fortress at Byrnhelen, where you are mistress of all you survey. Here you are merely first among equals.

Elizabeth's lips became a thin line.

Time to tell all, she decided.

The thought released her from doubt.

"If I die quietly in my sleep this very night, or if I am slain by assassins a week from now, it is the same. As things stand now, my brother Aedan will become the Guardian. He will assume all my powers and match them to the new powers he has gained. He will merge the technology of First World with the magic of Second World and unbalance the realms. He will turn everything dark and return the Earth to its primordial state. He imagines he will then arise and form a new world and create life upon it in his own image. He is poisoned by his own dark uses of magic and imagines himself to be a god."

Nara's eyes went wide. She opened her mouth as if to speak, but no words came. She stared at Elizabeth.

Sigvardr lowered his head slightly.

Borrington leaned back in his chair and folded his arms. He looked steadily at Joshua.

Joshua spoke.

"Your sister, Katherine, advances to the Guardianship in the event of your death, not that insane younger brother of yours. You have assured us of this, not once, but many times."

"My sister may be dead."

Joshua glared at her. "This is news! How long?" he demanded.

"Twenty-five years."

"Dead, twenty-five years ago? How could this be?"

"I said *may be dead*," Elizabeth replied. "She fled into First World that many years ago. We received occasional letters from her. They were vague, rambling accounts laced with fading nostalgia. She revealed nothing about her life in First World, certainly nothing that would give a clue to her whereabouts. Her letters always ended with a warning not to try to find her and a reminder she would never return to Second World. These letters stopped a year ago, about the time Aedan began intensifying his efforts to widen control over Second World."

"Twenty-five-years," Joshua said, emphasizing each word to communicate his disgust. "Twenty-five years you kept this from us, and now you want our help? You ask too much, witch."

Borrington tensed.

No one spoke for several long moments.

Nara's gentle voice broke the silence.

"Did your sister ever speak of children?"

"No," Elizabeth said quietly. "But her efforts to conceal her whereabouts would apply doubly to any child she bore. Katherine was a free spirit, a wanderer. She hated the thought of becoming Guardian. She hated the politics. She hated the trappings of power. She would not have wanted this life for her child—if indeed she bore a child."

Joshua looked around the table.

"Did any of you know of this?" he asked bitterly.

Nara shook her head, shock still registering in her face.

Sigvardr revealed nothing.

Joshua's gaze came to rest on Borrington.

"I knew," Borrington said.

"Of course, you knew; you are her man," Joshua sneered.

Borrington pushed back from the table.

Joshua raised his right hand, palm forward, and lowered his head in a conciliatory gesture.

"Do not take offense where none was intended, Andrew. I meant only that your first loyalty is to the Guardian. You are her general. In your role, I would have done what you did."

"Why did you not tell us?" Nara asked, speaking just above a whisper.

Elizabeth paused before answering.

"For the same reasons Joshua gives in opposing our alliance. It was a Second World problem. It was a family problem. I sought to solve it on my own. I hoped...I hoped Katherine would come back to us, especially when Father died and I became Guardian. But we had no way of telling her of these events. No matter, really. She probably would not have returned."

Joshua stared at the floor.

Nara closed her eyes.

"There is a perverse irony in our dilemma," Elizabeth continued. "We are here because my sister has spent her life in desperate avoidance of becoming Guardian, while my brother is gripped by a psychotic lust to assume that role. It is as you said, Joshua, a family problem, one I had hoped to keep from you, from all of you. I lied to you. I deceived you.

I have no right to come to you now for help, but I must. Can my mistake be corrected at this late stage? Perhaps not, but I must try. *We* must try."

"The genetic politics of your world are dizzying," Joshua said, not unkindly.

"I grant you that," Elizabeth replied with a faint smile. "The ancient Law of Succession protects the next in line from harm until he or she becomes Guardian or reaches twenty-one years of age, whichever comes first. Katherine would be past that age, and thus unprotected. That accounts for Aedan's eagerness to find and kill her. On the other hand, her offspring, if there be any, would have absolute protection because of age. In the politics of this matter, the child is therefore more important than the mother. Aedan has no power of life and death over the child."

"What a tangle," Joshua said unsympathetically.

"First World is not without tangles," Borrington snapped back angrily. "We have our ways; you have yours. Without our magic sustaining the divide, there would be no First World."

"And no Second World," Joshua added.

"Perhaps," Borrington said. "But First World technology has its dark side, just as magic does, and your politics are no less labyrinth than our own. But now comes a problem, and you, Joshua, become an idle commentator. This is not the time for commentary. We must decide and act on the problem presented to us. Mistakes have been made. So be it. Too much is at stake for us to be divided along the fault lines of our differences."

Borrington glared at Joshua.

Elizabeth continued in a soft voice:

"Aedan knows what we know. He searches as hard for Katherine as I do. His path is clear: He kills Katherine and then he kills me. The wild card is the possibility Katherine may have offspring. Dealing with that possibility is not so straightforward for Aedan. Control and ultimately abdication is the outcome he would have to seek with the child."

Joshua shook his head somberly.

The unicorn reared up, pumping his forelegs violently in tight circles above the others. He thundered down on his front hooves and stood stiff-legged. His horn glowed brightly. He lowered it to the horizontal.

Final argument, witch. The unicorn's thought fell over her like a wave crashing onto the shore of a cold northern sea.

She took a deep breath.

She made her final argument:

"The Guardianship holds powers you cannot imagine. I have kept the particulars of these powers from you, and you have never given me cause to use them against you. Aedan needs no cause; he is a cause unto himself. As Guardian, he will unleash these powers and others he has acquired. He will devastate the two realms and make of the Two Worlds a single dark universe ruled by Second World magic combined with First World technology, which in its most advanced forms is indiscernible from magic. At the moment of his choosing, he will end it all, with glee. He will do this and you will be helpless to stop him. This horror will surely befall us if I do not find my sister or, if she is dead, her offspring. Even if we unify against him in the meantime, as I pray we will, Aedan's success will be assured if we do not find my successor."

The thought transference that came next was so powerful it seemed the words were spoken aloud.

It is ended. The long-view is before me.

The unicorn stamped the stone floor once and made his

psychic pronouncement:

I am with you, witch. I will join in the search for your sister. If there be no sister, I will search for her child. You will no more be alone in this.

There was stunned silence for a moment; then Borrington spoke:

"I pledge with Sigvardr."

"As do I," Nara said.

Joshua gazed into Elizabeth's eyes, and his expression softened.

"You know what this could mean, for your people and mine?"

She nodded.

Joshua looked at the others.

"I see this must be," he said quietly. "I am with you, Guardian."

Tears welled up in Elizabeth's eyes. She knew he would keep his commitment with as much determination as he had earlier opposed making it.

The unicorn's head rose abruptly. The beast stomped his right forehoof three times on the cold stone floor and the history of sixteen centuries came to an end.

3   *The Alliance*

We must all hang together or, most assuredly, we shall all hang separately.

BENJAMIN FRANKLIN, FIRST WORLD POLITICIAN AND PHILOSOPHER

Joshua chuckled at the irony of his situation. He had been the one most opposed to the alliance, and now he was leading it. This made sense, of course: He was the Protector of Human Kind in First World, and Katherine, the next in line to succeed Elizabeth in the Guardianship, would be found in his world if she was found at all. If she was even alive.

He had embraced the necessity. If Aedan matched Second World weapons of the mind with First World technology, including nuclear weapons, the destruction of both worlds would soon follow. This possibility called for exceptional measures.

Joshua picked up the latest reports from Nara and Borrington (Sigvardr communicated by other means). He read each one, occasionally scribbling notes on a yellow legal tablet. He knew there would be nothing of singular importance in the reports. That would have been communicated immediately by other means. In the reports were the details, the tiny pieces of the puzzle.

He was good at puzzles.

***

Nara also was good at puzzles, but not in Joshua's way, not in the human way. As a Nepenthian, she did not solve, she discerned. She had the vicarious awareness of her species, honed to a sensitivity that could slice a molecule. She knew the dark floors of the great oceans and the airless reaches of space as humans know their living rooms. She and others of her kind did not interfere in the affairs of other species. They were the classic neutrals. Their mission was to balance the environment and oversee the earth processes that sustained all life. Nara risked all this by entering into a purposeful alliance with the other protectors and the Guardian. But she, like Joshua, was convinced of the necessity. If Aedan were not stopped, there would be nothing left to balance or sustain. There would be nothing left at all. She was confident in her decision, but realistic in her acceptance of the risks.

We've never done this before, she thought. *Shedding our neutrality could have dire consequences, unpredictable and potentially irreversible.*

Her concern had been echoed by her fellow Nepenthians, but they yielded to her judgment. They accepted the compromise of their neutrality, but insisted on playing only a support role in the alliance.

***

Sigvardr had a different set of concerns, and different powers. He held the long view better than any of them. He had listened carefully at Mont Saint-Michel. He had gazed dispassionately into the possible futures, and he had rendered his judgment. His judgment ended all argument.

He now stood alone at the dusty edge of a lush meadow, one of many hidden within the dense forest that stretched across the northern boundary of his territory. He pawed the earth with his right hoof once, twice, thrice, a physical preamble to setting his mental state for pure listening. He stood as still as a statue as the dust he had made settled back to earth.

He could hear them, all the sentinels he had assigned:

A Great Horned Owl in Alaska.

Another in Brazil.

A Condor in Baja California.

A White-tailed Eagle in northern Siberia and a Saker Falcon far to the south.

A Mountain Hawk-Eagle in Beijing.

An Egyptian Vulture in North Africa.

He used the raptors because of their visual acuity and ability to sustain flight above four thousand meters. He used the ancient Bar-headed Goose for surveillance above seven thousand meters. The smaller bird species gathered ground intelligence, the details.

Sigvardr used non-bird species as well, from the great whales to the solitary Demodex Brevis, a follicle mite that made its home in the human eyebrow. He listened to them all.

Out of this ocean of data, nothing distinguished the presence of the person for whom they were searching.

***

Aedan, meanwhile, was content to let Joshua conduct the search for him. His spy at Byrnhelen kept him informed of progress. If Joshua found nothing, the matter was simple: Kill Elizabeth and take power by straightforward right of succession. In the unlikely event Joshua found Katherine, or her offspring, the matter became more complicated. Aedan had a plan for this. It had more moving parts than assassination, and would require more time. But he had time.

4   Ashes to Ashes

No one discovers anything: We simply become aware. It is like going to a museum and staring at the same Rembrandt month after month, year after year, perhaps hundreds of times, and on your final visit, the one just before you die, you see a child sitting on a wall in the painting's background. You always saw the child. Your awareness simply changed on that last day. Out of the cloud of observed phenomena, the child introduced himself to you.

FROM "CHILD ON THE WALL" BY MASTER TOURIN ABDAL

L ook to how they honor their dead." This was the first time Nara had spoken at their meeting, and the other Protectors paid heed.

Borrington gave special attention to the Nepenthian's enigmatic pronouncement. Finding other Second-World expatriates was his part of the search, and he had made disappointingly little progress. Second World expatriates made every effort to blend in, to appear to be native to First World. They dispersed widely. They left no group footprint. Most changed their names. They seldom congregated because they feared discovery.

Joshua considered his role in light of Nara's suggestion. Up to now, he had focused on the cemeteries that appeared on maps, maintained records, and accommodated visitors. His team had made a thorough search of these, indeed of all known cemeteries. The team had poured over death records, obituaries, pictures of headstones, genealogical records, and related documents of all types, worldwide. Not a shred of evidence had emerged from this effort.

Look to how they honor their dead.

Borrington pondered how death was honored in Second World. Ancient tradition required that Second World dead be buried, not cremated, and that the grave be marked with the true name of the deceased. No one, however poor, was ever buried in an unmarked grave, and no one was buried without the presence of family and friends or surrogates for those relationships. The basest criminal was entitled to such a burial. Beyond this minimum, the dead were honored by the number of those present at the burial.

"She's right," Joshua said, looking at Borrington. "They would cling to their death traditions. They would not die in their alienation. They would honor their dead according to the traditions of the world of their origin."

Borrington nodded.

"A fair assumption," he said. "But where does it lead us?"

Joshua thought for a moment, then said, "We should concentrate on unrecorded headstones in unrecorded cemeteries that are small, remote, widely dispersed, and seldom visited."

"That is a great many cemeteries and a great many headstones," Borrington said.

"I can help," Nara said.

Sigvardr floated his thoughts:

As can I. Human beings die as we do, on schedule and with a certain tempo. Not all, but most. You say the expatriates would go to the forgotten places. I have means to observe these movements, these gatherings in such places. Nara has similar powers, and she can reach into the past. Joshua and Borrington have means to go to these places and search the headstones. Is the matter concluded?

Sigvardr had a way of pulling them out of deliberation into action.

"It is concluded," Joshua said.

He stood and pulled on his coat.

"Thank you all for coming," he added. "Please continue your regular reports to me. We should meet only when circumstances demand it. The risks are magnified when we meet, both in the prior arrangements and in our forming a single target when we are together."

No one disagreed.

5   Clues

All things are found in the last place you look.

ELIZABETH SHAW FROM "COMMENTARIES ON GOVERNANCE" BY
MASTER BRADYN ARISTARCHUS

Joshua stood in a graveyard on the outskirts of Shiatown, Michigan. He studied the plot map given to him by the team that had found the place. B14 was circled on the map. He walked along row B, counting the graves. At the fourteenth he stopped and peered at a snow-covered gravestone. He pressed his gloved hand against the face of the cold granite, brushed away the snow, and read the epitaph:

Katherine Shaw Grear. October 9, 1960 – November 19, 2006.

Devoted wife and friend.

This world is a better place for your having been in it.

Joshua considered the middle name. *Shaw* could be the woman's maiden name—a hopeful possibility—or it could be the given name or surname of a beloved relative or admired historical figure. This had yet to be determined. The absence of the word *mother* was disappointing. This Katherine had been a devoted wife and friend, but not a mother.

A gust of wind cleared snow from the face of the gravestone to the right of Katherine's:

Nathan Thomas Grear

February 26, 1949 -

The rest of the headstone was blank. No date of death. No

epitaph.

Could this be the husband? Joshua asked himself. *Same last name. The date of birth makes him some ten years older than she, a difference that allows for marriage. If Nathan is alive, he could be found. If found, he could...could what? I won't know until I find him. That's the next step.*

Joshua looked back at Katherine's gravestone:

Devoted wife and friend.

But not a mother, Joshua thought, *or if she was, she did not want it known.*

Joshua decided to wait to tell the others. Steady progress was necessary in a thorough search, not frantic jumping from clue to clue. The etchings on the gravestones were just clues. No firm conclusions could be drawn from them. Many questions needed to be asked and answered.

Joshua gestured with his right hand. A young man with long dark hair walked briskly to his side.

"Sir?"

"Bring me all you can find about Nathan Thomas Grear, date of birth February 26, 1949."

Joshua pointed to the gravestone and handed his assistant the plot map. The assistant took pictures of the gravestone, made some notes, and departed without further discussion.

The snow began to fall again, more heavily than before. Joshua stared at Nathan Grear's headstone.

What can you tell us, Nathan Grear? What secrets might you be hiding?

6   Birthday Surprise

Powers are not given, they emerge. Alexandra's powers emerged erratically, making them difficult to anticipate.

FROM "CHRONICLE OF THE SUCCESSION" BY MASTER BRADYN ARISTARCHUS

It would be a memorable day. John and Mary Ward regarded with pleasure the elaborate preparations they had made for their daughter's eighth birthday party.

"She will love it," Mary said, beaming.

John started to reply, but his wife pressed on, her enthusiasm, as usual, turning to concern:

"Oh, I don't know. Maybe we should have more ponies. Six may not be enough. And now that I look at the birthday cake, maybe it should be seven layers; four seems small. I just don't know. I want it to be perfect. Will it do, John? Am I being silly?"

"A little, my dear, but this is an important day. We are doing more with all this than celebrating a birthday."

Mary went silent, her store of doubts temporarily exhausted.

John Ward suffered no doubts. He smiled broadly, a bit too broadly for a man smiling to himself. He stood erect, hands on hips, chest raised, shoulders back. He rocked up on the balls of his feet, held, then settled back. Up, hold, back, up, hold, back. He radiated what on the surface appeared to be self-confidence. But a discerning observer (had there been one present) would have noted a certain smugness. There was about John Ward an air of superiority, of interest less in doing or being excellent than in being...above.

His too-big smile got bigger.

"Just look!" he said, making a sideways gesture at the three-acre rear yard. "We have the balloon castle, the riding ponies, games, exquisitely prepared food and drink that will be served up by an army of our servants, and a massive fireworks display after dark. All the right people will be here, with their children. Alexandra will acquire suitable friends today, just as we planned."

"I hope so," Mary said tentatively. "I really, really do hope so. You did make it clear to Mrs. Sutton that Daniel was not...that it was not appropriate for him to be here? You did it kindly, I hope."

"As kindly as I could, but I made myself perfectly clear."

Mary prattled on as though she had not heard his assurance:

"It would be awful if Daniel showed up. Alexandra would ignore everyone else. She would, you know. Such an embarrassment! What if the Horners, Van Tanners, Mattocks, and all the rest of our guests, and their children, were ignored by our daughter while she scampered around with that boy. I would be mortified!"

John put a hand on his wife's shoulder.

"We can manage this. Alexandra will grow up and take her place in the world, one quite apart from the boy. Young Daniel's world is not Alexandra's world. What we have arranged for her birthday is a small step in helping her see this. It will all work out, my dear."

"I know, I know, but I hate to hear you say it. He's not a bad boy."

"There are many not-bad-boys in the world, Mary, but that does not make them proper influences in our daughter's life. Mrs. Sutton did not seem distressed when I told her to arrange for her son to be elsewhere during the party. I think she understands. The matter is a practical one, and we are managing it with practical means. This party will be an important step. Alexandra will meet new friends. She will want to see them again. We will encourage this. Daniel will become less important to her. I guarantee it, Mary. Now stop fretting!"

They heard a door close behind them and turned to see Ellen Sutton approaching. She managed their household and served as their daughter's nanny.

"The Horners have arrived, Mr. Ward. Shall I bring them here?"

"No, no. The great room, please. We'll be right there."

John turned to his wife. "Just in time, my dear. Shall we go in?"

With affected formality, John offered his right arm to his wife. She took it and the two entered the house and made their way to their waiting guests.

Over the next hour, the who's-who of Connecticut society arrived. Laughter and merriment filled the Wards' expensively decorated Victorian mansion as guests wandered to and fro sampling the sumptuous culinary offerings.

John eventually herded the men into the library to sip Cognac and single malt Scotch and regale one another with commentary on business, sports, and politics. Mary joined the women in the sun room, where they drank tea from delicate porcelain cups and chatted about fashion and matters of local interest, indelicately referred to as gossip in less refined circles. In the background, servants busily replenished the food and beverage offerings and supervised the guests' children.

An hour past.

John announced the festivities were moving to the backyard. The children, excited and enthusiastic, led the way. Mary guided her daughter to the place of honor, a director's chair in the center of their large natural stone patio. In front of the chair was a mountainous pile of expertly wrapped gifts. On a long table left of the gifts was a multilayered birthday cake. It was a meter and a half high, covered with thick tan frosting and heavily accented with dark Brazilian chocolate filigrees. On top was a thirty centimeter bronze carving of the numeral eight. The carving was surrounded by eight large candles plated in fourteen carat gold.

Alexandra's gaze moved from the pile of gifts to the cake to the beaming faces of her young friends and their eager parents...and she knew immediately what, or rather who, was missing.

Alexandra turned to her mother.

"Where is Daniel?"

Mary exchanged a furtive glance with her husband. John leaned down and whispered into his daughter's ear:

"I'm sorry, dear. Daniel couldn't come."

Alexandra kept her voice low, like her father's. "It's my birthday. Why isn't he here?"

"Well, he had other things to do, dear. Now look at all those presents; which one are you going to open first?"

Alexandra was having none of it. Her voice rose steadily:

"Where is he? I know he'd want to be here. Why isn't he here?"

John and Mary glanced up at the faces of their guests. Mary then leaned close to her daughter:

"Sweetheart," she whispered, "you have your other friends here and many new ones. They are waiting for you. I promise that when the party is over, we will ask about

Daniel."

Alexandra felt her mother's breath on her ear, but heard her words as though from a great distance. Disappointment became confusion became anger, all in an instant.

"WHERE IS HE?"

Alexandra's voice was unnaturally deep, her face flushed, the pupils of her eyes almost black.

No one answered her question.

No one spoke.

Mrs. Sutton was standing nearby holding a large silver tray filled with deserts. She stared with a mixture of fear and compassion at the child she had raised. She knew, as no one else did, what was to come, and knew she could do nothing to stop it. The child's rage, and something else buried deep within it, had placed Alexandra beyond the reach of ordinary people, of First World people.

Mrs. Sutton felt her fingers being pried from around the handles of the tray. She looked down. No hands did the prying, yet her grip was being loosened. She looked up at Alexandra. Alexandra's eyes seemed to say to her alone, *Let go.*

She obeyed. The tray lifted out of her hands, rose up three meters, hovered, and began rotating—slowly at first, then faster and faster until it showered its contents over the crowd. Simultaneously, tiny tarts, miniature cakes, and other food delights leapt off plates held by the guests and smashed into their faces. Food platters held aloft by mingling servers rose up in the same manner as Mrs. Sutton's tray, spun in the air above the crowd, and dispersed the neatly prepared food over the heads of the partiers. Food and drink everywhere came alive, took flight, and targeted the guests, tangling hair, soiling clothing, and smearing faces.

Shrieks filled the air as party guests panicked and fled.

Some scampered under tables in a vain effort to avoid the barrage. As though possessed of intelligence, tiny hotdogs jammed their way up noses, into ears, and down clothing.

Some of the guests who had taken refuge under tables emerged and made a wild dash toward the house. As they ran, long red licorice whips began twisting around their ankles and whipping at the air as if driving cattle. The frightened guests stampeded across the grass, stumbling over upturned tables and leaping fences in their frantic rush to escape.

The entire backyard became a sea of confused humanity: people running, thrashing, rolling on the ground, and swatting at the air as they tried to beat off their bizarre attackers.

A small boy ran terrified and confused into the herd of German riding ponies. The six animals reared up dangerously and pulled against their loosely tied reins. The boy, swatting the air this way and that, stumbled backwards and fell into the ponies' drinking trough. All six animals broke free and galloped through the fleeing crowd. The ponies jumped over upturned tables and knocked down the decorative yard fences before disappearing into the woods.

Mrs. Nottingbatch, an exceedingly large woman, crashed drunkenly between two large tables, shattering glasses of punch and scattering plates and cutlery. She swung her cane at the tiny swirling tarts that filled the air around her. The pumpkin and pecan tarts attacked her viciously. They buzzed around her head like persistent bees trying to get at a delicious flower. The woman regained her footing and scrambled backward until her rather large buttocks collided with the corner of a table. She fell to the ground. The tarts assumed a unified formation and in a wide swoop smashed themselves into Mrs. Nottingbatch's face and upper body.

Now unable to see, she pushed herself up, stumbled forward, tripped, and fell against a large crystal punch bowl filled with pink lemonade. The bowl flipped over, dowsing the woman and nearby guests with a storm of sugary pink liquid and lemon slices before it fell to the ground and shattered.

Alexandra's father had lost all composure. He was yelling hysterically for his wife and daughter and screaming epithets at the flying food pummeling him. Finally he saw Alexandra and her mother crouched together near the shattered punch bowl. He ran to them while the last of his guests made good their escape. The screaming had stopped, replaced by occasional distant yells. The servants had fled with the guests. The previously malevolent food lay quiescent (as food certainly should), having painted with garish colors nearly everything in sight. The tents and tables and fences and playground equipment were flattened, utterly destroyed.

Mary gave her daughter a bewildered look.

"Alexandra," she whispered. "Are you OK?"

Alexandra's lips moved in a whisper.

"My dear, dear child. Please speak up just a little. Mummy can't hear you."

Alexandra paused and gazed steadily into her mother's eyes.

"Mother, you said Daniel could come as soon as the party was over. I do believe the party's over."

                                ***

Alexandra had readily accepted confinement to her bedroom after the party. She wanted to be alone, to be hidden, to think through the disaster.

What have I done? she asked herself.

She received no answer.

She surveyed the destruction from her second-floor

window. Jagged shards of the smashed crystal punch bowls reflected the late afternoon sun. Her once carefully wrapped birthday presents were scattered across the lawn, trampled by the fleeing guests. Tables and chairs were overturned, the legs ripped from them. Ten green-striped party tents had collapsed into twisted jumbles of lacerated canvas and broken metal. A once-towering air castle lay deflated on the grass. Food remains clung to every surface, including the entire back wall of the two-story Victorian mansion that was her home.

A random breeze brushed Alexandra's cheek. The breeze steadied and became a cold wind out of the north, scattering loose debris across the lawn and tangling her hair. The wind became increasingly wild and blusterous.

She willed the wind to stop, to be silent. It defied her for a moment and then collapsed into stillness. The sun continued its slow descent toward the horizon, gently beckoning the evening to come.

I thought all this, felt it before it happened...made it happen. What kind of freak am I?

Neither the settled wind nor the silently setting sun gave an answer.

7   The Child Who Never Was

*What motivated her was not simply distaste for politics
or for the poison of adulation. Katherine saw what was
coming.*

FROM "CHRONICLE OF THE SUCCESSION" BY MASTER BRADYN
ARISTARCHUS

The old man adjusted his fleece balaclava and cinched
the hood of his parka a little tighter around his head. His
moist breath came out in puffs of vapor through the porous
fleece covering his mouth. The vapor fogged his glasses. He
took them off. He didn't need them in the wild. He was a
little vain about the glasses. He thought he looked better
without them. His wife said she found him devastatingly
handsome either way. He knew she was not an impartial
judge.

"You keep going," she had said, "every day, just like
always."

He had promised her. The promise led him every day to
put on his mittens, gaiters, and down parka; shoulder his
daypack; and set out on the Mount Forester trail north of the
cabin. He marveled at how she filled his awareness, even
when she was absent. He never felt alone. Sad sometimes,
but not alone. She was always present, especially when he
climbed Mount Forester.

A large dog emerged from the woods and blocked the
trail in front of the old man. The neighbor's Akita always
met him here, about a kilometer before the trail turned steep.
He would stay with the old man to the top of the mountain

and back, about four hours, maybe five in the deep snow.

The animal licked the old man's hand and fell in behind. Man and dog continued on beneath tall, snow-covered evergreens. The trail's twists and turns blocked their view ahead, and the unique silence of winter surrounded them. The dog heard through the silence what the old man could not hear. He growled, stepped around the old man, and halted.

A tall, solidly built stranger blocked the trail about seventy meters ahead.

The Akita barked once and looked back at the old man.

"Sit, Beau."

The dog sat.

Where the old man lived was remote. The home of his nearest neighbor, Beau's master, was more than two kilometers from his cabin. The roads were dirt and minimally maintained during the most favorable weather. They were often impassible in winter, and the old man was certain last night's storm had rendered them so today. He had heard no snowmobiles. Perhaps the man had skied in. It would take a strong skier to make the trek from the nearest maintained road, some forty kilometers away.

The stranger waved the way men do: a single subtle gesture, a sort of nod given with the hand.

The Akita broke his sit, stared at the stranger, then back at the old man. The dog's tail didn't wag, it twitched.

"Stay," said the old man. He touched the dog's head with one hand and waved back with the other.

The stranger walked toward them.

The dog took two steps forward.

"Better hold there, friend. Dog's a bit protective. I'll come to you."

The old man and the dog approached the stranger. Beau

sniffed the man, circled him cautiously, then sat between them.

"No need to pet him. He don't much like petting."

"Understood," the stranger said.

The old man pulled his balaclava down under his chin, revealing his face.

"How'd you get here?" he asked.

The stranger gestured toward a tree a few meters away.

The old man saw a set of skis and poles leaning against the tree. The skis were fitted with skins.

"I'm impressed," the old man said, smiling a little for the first time.

"Got an early start."

"I'm still impressed."

They studied each other for a few moments, as men do in the wild.

"I'm looking for someone," the stranger said. He saw the old man stiffen just a little.

"Not many possibilities out here. What's the name?"

Joshua looked into the old man's dark brown eyes.

"Nathan Thomas Grear," Joshua said.

The old man blinked.

Joshua extended his hand slowly.

"It is a pleasure, Mr. Grear. I am Joshua Turner, and I have come a long way to meet you."

***

The two men sipped brandy before the fire in Nathan's cabin.

"Nice place," Joshua said.

"Yup. Not quite off-the-grid, but out of the way enough to..."

Nathan paused.

"To what?" Joshua asked.

"To enjoy peace and quiet," Nathan replied.

"And avoid visits from people like me," Joshua added wryly.

"I didn't say that."

"You didn't have to. I know why you live in a place like this. Peace and quiet doesn't cover it, not by half."

Nathan gave Joshua a hard look.

"I've done nothing wrong," Nathan said.

"Didn't say you had. I'm not here about you."

"Then who?" Nathan asked.

"Your wife."

Nathan took a sip of brandy and stared into the fire.

"She died a year ago," he said. "Cancer."

"I know," Joshua said. "I saw her grave."

Nathan continued to stare into the fire as his thoughts turned back to earlier this morning. She would have relished the crisp cold, the new-fallen snow, the feel of Beau's wet nose on her hand.

Gone only a year, Nathan thought, *but it feels like ten, like a lifetime really*.

He had heard people speak of soul mates. It did not seem right to him, what people said. She had been his soul mate, but it was not like what people said or what he read in books. It was simpler, more natural, more real, just the way things should be between two people who meet and marry and use up their lives together. That is why he felt her presence even now as he sat with this stranger before a warm fire. She was here. She was everywhere. She walked with him as she always had along the backcountry trails, over the talus fields, through the swollen streams of spring, and across the frozen lakes of winter. His soul mate would walk with him until his days were over. Then she would greet him on the other side. She would take his hand and he would hold her again, smell her hair, feel the light pressure of her head on his chest as she lay beside him, feel again her soft lips on his.

"Nathan."

Nathan heard the voice. It was not hers. It was the stranger, Joshua.

"Are you alright?" Joshua asked.

Nathan continued to stare into the jumble of glowing embers beneath the flames.

"Fine, just remembering," he said, speaking softly.

His eyes glistened. Tears streamed down his cheeks. He did not sob. His face did not contort. His expression remained relaxed, peaceful.

He mourns but he does not mourn, Joshua thought. *He misses something of her, the physical, but she is present. I can feel her presence in him. Some essence of her resides in him.*

Joshua leaned back in his chair and stared at Nathan.

Nathan continued staring into the fire. A smile spread across his face.

"She is here," he said to no one.

Joshua's breathing became shallow and quiet. This was not at all what he had expected. He knew affection, even love, but he did not know this.

***

A half hour passed.

Neither man spoke.

Nathan turned to Joshua finally:

"There were no children."

"Why do you tell me this?" Joshua asked.

"Because that's why you came."

"You don't know that, Nathan."

"Yes, I do. You said it was not about me. You said it was about Katherine. Yet you knew she was dead. I'm not stupid.

I was married to her for twenty-four years. Do you think she did not speak of this day, of you or someone like you finding us?"

Joshua made no reply.

"There were no children," Nathan repeated.

Interesting, the way he states it, Joshua thought. *Not, "we had no children," the way one might admit to having no offspring, but rather, "there* were *no children," the way one might describe a community consisting only of adults or a circumstance in which children were simply absent.*

"Do you wish there had been?" Joshua asked. It was a trigger question. Joshua fixed his attention on the man's face, watching for a sign.

Nathan looked away abruptly. He stared out the window. The snow was falling more heavily now. He would have to share his cabin overnight with this stranger, maybe days if the storm grew stronger.

"Yes," Nathan replied without looking away from the falling snow. He kept his face averted. He stared into the storm outside while one arose within him, an old storm of hard necessities and regrets.

Joshua saw all this and knew Nathan's "yes" lay at the bottom of a bucket of tears. There was or had been a child. Was the child dead? No, not dead, for Nathan would have no reason to deny a dead child. Aborted? Perhaps. Given up for adoption? More likely. There is reason to hope, Joshua concluded.

The two men sat in silence as the storm grew in intensity, winds howling and snow swirling in chaotic funnels outside the protective walls of the cabin.

"Do you have animals that need tending?" Joshua asked.

"No," Nathan replied.

"What about the dog?"

"The neighbor's. Just walks with me. He'll be fine," Nathan said. He turned back to the fire, cupping the side of his face in his hand, concealing whatever wetness might still be there.

"I have no children," Joshua said, "but if I did, I'd want to know them. To be an unknown to my own child...that would be intolerable."

I make a cruel suggestion, thought Joshua, *but perhaps, in the long run, I do him a kindness.*

Nathan leaned forward, elbows on knees. He held his head in his hands.

"I miss her so," he whispered.

The words caught in his throat and he began to sob.

"Katherine?" Joshua asked, knowing it was more.

"You know the answer to that," Nathan replied.

"I do, but you must say it. Free yourself. It is time."

There was a pause.

I must not allow him to ponder this, to deliberate on it. He will retreat into the years of denial. I must move him now.

"Where is the child, Nathan?"

"I don't know," Nathan replied.

***

The two men talked late into the night, stopping now and then to refresh their drinks and add wood to the fire. The storm became a cocoon surrounding them. Nathan told Joshua all he knew of the adoption, and the reasons for it.

"I did not want it. Katherine insisted. She told me of your world."

"Not my world," Joshua interrupted, "but I know of her world and of your wife's fears. I am of this world, Nathan, as you are, but I have a special role I play in both worlds. Go on."

"My wife told me she had a sister, Elizabeth, who played an important and dangerous political role in Second World. Katherine said she would be forced by genetic heritage to assume the same role when her sister died or was killed. She did not want this, so she fled and hid herself here. The same fate would eventually befall our child, she said. She convinced me that if we loved our baby, truly loved her, we would let her go. We would make sure she had a secure First World identity and a First World life."

"How was all this accomplished?" Joshua asked.

"Katherine had a close friend, David Sutton, an expatriate like herself. He handled cases like ours. He promised to make sure our baby was placed in a good First World home, with parents who would never know anything about us or about Second World. Katherine trusted him so I trusted him. He took our daughter."

"Where?"

"I don't know."

Nathan leaned back in his chair and relaxed. He had finally told someone. There was a measure of peace in that. He hoped he had not bought this peace at too high a price for his daughter.

Joshua spoke softly:

"Your dear wife had her own reasons for alienation from her world, reasons your daughter does not have."

"How can you be sure?" Nathan said, half asking, half accusing.

"I can't," Joshua replied. "But of this I am sure: In your daughter, necessity has merged with destiny. Her survival, your survival, mine, the Two Worlds—it all depends on her. May I tell you why?"

Nathan glowered at Joshua, but gave a slight nod.

Joshua told him, holding nothing back.

"This must be hard to comprehend," Joshua said at the end of his narrative.

"Not so much as you think," Nathan said. "I was married to a Second Worlder for a long time. As much as she wished to leave her world behind, it was always in her. There was a part of her that missed it, or the idea of it. She did not always speak of Second World with loathing."

"And knowing what you now know, what do you think she would have you do?" Joshua asked.

"It would not matter what she thought," Nathan replied. "This time...this time I would decide."

"And what would you decide?"

"I want my daughter found. I want to know who she is."

"Even if it means remaining separated from her?" Joshua asked.

"Even if it means that."

Katherine chose well, this husband, thought Joshua. *She chose very well.*

8   *The David Sutton Matter*

Exiles from Second World know to hide. They avoid the stage. They sit in the back of the hall, pretending to be uninteresting spectators. They do not yet know they are the main act. When that knowledge comes, will it poison them?

FROM "EXODUS AND EXILE" BY DAVID SUTTON

Borrington watched the Guardian's face drain of color as Joshua stated the terrible fact: Katherine was dead. A tremor passed through Elizabeth. Joshua had spoken as gently as he could; Borrington did not fault the delivery. In any form it would have been what it was: a slayer of hope. Elizabeth had been clinging to the hope of finding her sister and convincing her to return. Joshua's findings changed all that. Now all Elizabeth could do was mourn her sister's loss and turn to a new hope: that her sister's child could be found.

A new hope, thought Borrington, *a new source of pain for Elizabeth. But we are a step closer to finding the Successor.*

Elizabeth and Joshua's images faded from the mirror on the wall opposite Borrington's desk. The mirror was a faracid. It came close to conveying a real presence. That was the faracid's magic. First World teleconferencing and holograms were mere toys by comparison. Still, the faracid only came close. Borrington missed flesh and bone. He missed Elizabeth.

Joshua had provided a new lead in their investigation: David Sutton. Borrington pushed a button on the underside of his desk. A few moments later his office door opened, and a middle-aged woman with bright red hair walked into the room.

Borrington stood and handed her his notes:

"Susan, I need you to get me whatever you have on a David Sutton," he said. "Second World. Might have connections with Second World expats residing in First World. Might be connected with adoptions there, and funeral arrangements. Probably travels frequently between the worlds. Contact Peter Kendal, Joshua's chief of staff, and get them involved. Top priority. Anything you need."

"At once, sir," the woman said. She gave a slight nod and left him.

9 ✦eathers in the Ⱳⁱnd

I can do nothing to stop what is coming. Alexandra is beyond the reach of ordinary people, of First World people. If a powerful hand is not laid upon her, a Second World hand, she will become a monster.

FROM THE DIARY OF ELLEN SUTTON

Stories spread about what had happened at Alexandra's birthday party, and the stories grew in the telling. This was a source of embarrassment for the socially conscious Ward family. Alexandra's father became obsessed with finding something, anything that might explain what had taken place—anything that was not his daughter. Mary sought in vain to calm him.

In time the rumors faded, and it became easier for John to believe that heavy winds, a food fight initiated by young people, panic, the weather, or other unknown but perfectly natural causes accounted for that day's chaos. The Wards settled into this comforting acceptance and things seemed to return to normal.

10   The Puzzle Box

On top of the puzzle box is a picture of what will be formed from the pieces. Life's puzzles are not like this. There are no pictures. Life is a creation made from pieces found along the way. Don't be afraid. Pick them up. Finish the puzzle.

FROM *"UNCERTAIN JOURNEY"* BY *JOSHUA TURNER*

Joshua indicated a high-backed leather chair and Borrington settled into it. Joshua pulled his own chair from behind his desk and sat opposite Borrington. He wanted nothing separating them, no barriers between them, no assertion of anything but mutual respect.

"Your investigations were productive?" Joshua asked hopefully.

"Yes," Borrington replied. "We identified David Sutton. He did indeed grow up in Second World. A bit of a troublemaker it turns out."

"How so?"

"Small things: vandalism, petty theft, other rebellious behavior. He appears to have been influenced by less than ideal friends. He fled to First World just ahead of being arrested for burglary and arson. The last word we have of him, he was in the service of Archibald Edgar Whittle, a First Worlder living in Grand Haven, Michigan."

Joshua scribbled Whittle's name on a legal pad in his lap.

Borrington went on:

"Whittle still lives in Grand Haven. He and his wife run a small shop in the older part of the downtown area. He'll be easy to find. Expatriates tend to live and work in the older parts of most towns. Many run small businesses selling various trinkets. Souvenirs, ornaments, elegant glass works of art, paintings, statuary, that sort of thing. Second Worlders are generally more artistically inclined than First Worlders."

"Is that so?" Joshua said with mock amazement.

Borrington smiled.

"I meant only that exiles from our world can more often be found among your artists than among your engineers and mathematicians. I didn't mean..."

Joshua laughed.

"Comrade," he said, "we are all entitled to our prejudices and preferences. I have mine; you have yours. They need not divide us. I take no offense. I hope you will take none when I say your people sometimes seem a little soft around the edges."

It was Borrington's turn to laugh.

"Well put," he said. "We need not be blind to be fair."

"Indeed," Joshua replied. "So, this Whittle owns a business in the old part of Grand Haven. What about David Sutton? Does he still work there?"

Borrington shrugged. "Don't know. The trail goes cold shortly after Sutton arrives in Grand Haven. It could be he changed his name. We know he was still alive nine years ago, hence the adoption meeting with Katherine and Nathan. But beyond that, nothing."

Joshua leaned back in his chair, closed his eyes, and rubbed his temples.

"So, our next step is to meet with Whittle and see what he can tell us about David Sutton."

"Yes," Borrington said, "and it is a delicate step, one I leave to you."

"Why is that?" Joshua asked. "These are Second World

people conducting Second World business."

"Precisely. Second World people recognize Second World people. It is an awareness particularly acute in exiles. My people making inquiries would be recognized instantly. You and your people must take it from here if our inquiries are to remain discreet."

Joshua considered Borrington's argument.

"I'll take it," Joshua said. "Can I count on you for direct support if needed?"

Borrington chuckled.

"You don't relish mixing it up with a bunch of Second World magicians, do you, my friend?"

"No, I don't" Joshua replied, matching Borrington's joviality. "You're a strange bunch."

Both men laughed. They stood and shook hands. Borrington reached into his robe, withdrew a slip of paper, and handed it to Joshua. "Here's the address of Whittle's shop. I'll have some of my men positioned nearby, but well out of sight. It is a tight-knit community and if we spook them we may not get the information we need."

Joshua took the piece of paper, read the address, and nodded.

"We are close, my friend."

"A step closer, yes," Borrington replied, "but we are following a trail of bread crumbs. The slightest wind could scatter them."

11   The Whittle Connection

Understanding is not enough. One must know why the silence has been broken. One must ask why there is speaking.

FROM "MANUAL OF THE TRUTHSEEKERS" BY ANDRUS MAXWELL

Joshua arrived in Grand Haven, Michigan, three days before his intended contact with Whittle. He learned that Archibald Whittle and his wife made their living selling crafts and baked goods out of Whittles Stopover, a quaint shop on Washington Avenue. Mr. Whittle had been dubbed *Papa* by the locals, a nickname that matched his reported appearance: a bit rotund with rosy cheeks, thick white hair, and a full white beard. The nickname was also a reflection of the esteem in which the man was held throughout the community.

Joshua was told that Whittle was a superior woodworker, the best in Grand Haven, and his wife was a master baker. The locals enthusiastically described Mr. Whittle's products, which included hand-crafted furniture, ornaments, and decorations for every holiday. Mrs. Whittle sold all manner of baked goods: spicy gingerbread cookies, buttery bread, gooey cinnamon rolls. She also made caramel and fudge and a variety of other confections. She prepared her breads and candies from her own quite secret recipes, and cooked in a kitchen at the back of the shop. Joshua was assured the smell wafting from the shop allowed few to pass by without stopping in.

In making his casual inquiries about Whittle, Joshua did

not mention David Sutton, nor did he inquire whether Whittle employed anyone now or in the past. Gathering intelligence carried risks. The asker of questions is soon asked about.

***

A small bell attached to the wall above the door tinkled as Joshua entered the shop.

"Be right there," a man's voice called from the back.

Joshua browsed the shelves. The carvings were enchanting and the aroma of the homemade bread reminded him of how long it had been since his last meal.

"Can I help you?"

"Are you the craftsman?" Joshua said, pointing to a sturdy oak table nearby.

"I am," the man replied, extending his hand. "Archibald Whittle's the name."

"Joshua Turner."

Joshua shook the man's hand.

"Your work is exquisite and the smell of fresh bread reminds me I haven't eaten in a long time."

Whittle smiled. "That's Meg's baking. My wife has some fresh bread cooling on the racks. You interested?"

"Very much."

Archibald walked over to the cooling racks. He retrieved a knife and a loaf of warm cinnamon bread. He sliced off a thick piece and placed a ceramic crock of creamy butter on a table in front of the bakery counter. Joshua took a seat at the table, picked up the knife, slathered a generous layer of butter on the bread, and took a large bite.

"Good, ain't it," Mr. Whittle commented matter-of-factly.

Joshua, his mouth full, nodded enthusiastically.

"My Meg is the best cook in this county, maybe the world."

Joshua swallowed his last bite of bread and wiped his mouth with the paper napkin Whittle handed him.

"No argument there," Joshua said.

"Want more?"

"Not just now. Would you sit with me for a few minutes?"

Joshua indicated the other chair at his table.

"Be happy to, but might have to leave for customers. These old ears sometimes miss the bell; help me listen for it and we can talk. If I have to leave and you want more bread, just help yourself."

Whittle took a seat at the table.

The man's reputation is well earned, thought Joshua. *He could charm a cranky old spinster into a teenage smile in about ten seconds.*

"I'm looking for a friend of mine, David Sutton," Joshua began. "We lost track of each other awhile back. Heard he works for you, or did."

Whittle looked shrewdly at Joshua.

"This David Sutton, he in some kind of trouble?"

Joshua noted two things in Whittle's reply: He had not committed to knowing Sutton and he suspected trouble.

"Don't know of any trouble," Joshua replied casually. "David mentioned a woodworker in New Haven had helped him, given him work when he first arrived here. David was grateful."

"Where you from," Whittle asked.

"Colorado. Denver."

"You're a long way from Denver."

"I'm on vacation. Thought I'd look up an old friend."

"I'll check my records," said Whittle. "Name sounds a bit familiar. Can't be sure. Did he go by Dave or David?"

He's testing me, thought Joshua. *Time for me to show a*

little less interest in David Sutton.

"Dave, when I knew him. Might have changed. Been awhile."

"How long."

"Eight, nine years maybe."

Joshua glanced at his watch.

"Hey, I'm late for an appointment."

"Been here only a couple of days and you've got 'appointments?'"

Whittle was smiling as he said this.

Joshua winked and smiled back.

"Well, maybe a date. The lady gave me reason to hope."

Whittle chuckled.

"How much do I owe you for the bread?" Joshua asked.

"On the house. Just a marketing trick to get you back in here to spend some real money."

Both men stood and shook hands.

"Thanks," Joshua said.

"I'll check my records. Might have something for you; might not. Where are you staying?"

"Johansen's bed and breakfast. I have one of the outside bungalows, number 9."

"I know the place. I'll give you a call if I find something."

***

Joshua slept fitfully. It was cold and the electric baseboard heaters seemed not to be working. He was up at first light. He dressed and was fiddling with one of the heaters when he heard a quiet knock on his door. He opened it and found Whittle standing on the landing. He was bundled in a thick coat and wool cap.

"Let's walk," Whittle said.

"Where to?"

"Nowhere in particular. Just a walk."

Joshua put on his coat and hat and joined Whittle on the landing. Whittle, saying nothing, descended the stairs. Joshua followed. He drew up alongside the older man as they walked north along a dirt road.

Whittle spoke first:

"Ever been to a third world country, like Haiti or Uganda for instance?" Whittle asked.

"I have."

"How about Second World?"

"Not sure I know what you mean," Joshua said.

"With respect, I think you do know what I mean, Joshua Turner, or should I address you by your title, Protector."

Joshua halted and took a step to the side.

Whittle laughed.

"You think we don't know who and what you are?" he asked rhetorically. "I did a little digging after you left, made some calls. This must be very important for you to be here personally."

The two began walking again.

"I don't know what you mean," Joshua said. "Second World, third world, protector. Protector of what? I'm afraid it's all nonsense to me."

"Not a good way to start our relationship, Joshua: You persisting in this charade. I have learned enough about you to trust you. How about throwing a little trust my way."

Could he be one of Aedan's agents? Joshua asked himself. *Could Borrington have missed that? Possible, but not likely. More likely, Whittle is who we think he is. Still, some care is necessary.*

Whittle led them onto a trail that left the road and proceeded into a thick forest.

"I'm the one at risk here," Whittle continued. "A man of

your stature here, with me, alone? I hardly think so. You have protection, probably nearby. I have none."

"What makes you think that?" Joshua inquired warily.

"Because your protection would have come into conflict with mine, if I had any. But I don't need to prove anything to you. You want something from me; I want nothing from you. Beggars can't be choosers, my friend."

"How did you know?" Joshua asked, having made the only decision open to him.

"You are First World," Whittle said, "but not without the taint of Second World. You need to be careful. If I could detect it, others of my kind might also. You ask questions. Others ask questions about you and your questions. We suspect all of you, but I suspect you less than the others."

***

The two men moved deeper into the forest, their exhalations producing puffs of vapor in the chill air. The crunching of their boots on a thin layer of crusted snow announced their coming to the forest creatures ahead.

"David Sutton isn't a long-lost friend, is he?" Whittle said.

"No, but he's important."

"No doubt. You wouldn't be here otherwise. What's his importance?"

"Not sure."

"Allow me to translate," Whittle responded. "You are sure of David's importance but unsure of how much you should tell me. I suggest you tell me whatever you think might make a Second World exile such as my poor old self willing to tell you a damn thing."

Joshua noted Whittle's harsh tone.

I'm going to lose him, he thought.

The thought prompted Joshua to make another decision,

one which felt as inevitable as the decision earlier to admit who he was.

"What I'm about to tell you," Joshua began, "must stay between us, for your safety and mine."

"Again, you underestimate me," Whittle admonished. "Second World expatriates know more than you think we do. You speak of safety? I set that aside the moment I decided to meet with you, walk with you, have this conversation with you. Let us converse as equals, Mr. Turner. I know the risks."

"Do you know of Aedan Shaw?" Joshua asked.

"I do."

Whittle's frank reply startled Joshua. He decided to take the conversation in a new direction:

"I know you and your wife fled Second World fifteen years ago after your only child, Sarah, was murdered. Ennis Croft, one of Aedan's generals, committed this crime."

Whittle's face became a mask of anguish.

"Why do you bring this up?" There was a combination of anger and sadness in Whittle's voice.

"Not needlessly, I hope. I bring up your tragic experience to help you appreciate the seriousness of the situation in Second World and the consequences it will soon have for First World. You fled but you did not escape. The Two Worlds are on a collision course. Aedan, Croft, and others now kill hundreds of innocent men, women, and children. This makes the slaying of your daughter no less tragic, but it does change the political scenery."

"Not my political scenery," Whittle said.

"Precisely my attitude, in the beginning," Joshua said. "I protect human kind in First World. Let Second World magicians solve their own problems. That was what I thought. I think it no longer."

"Perhaps you should," Whittle said.

"No. The separation of our worlds and the system of portals will not stand if we do not unite against Aedan. Mutually assured destruction of the Two Worlds is not a defense of one against the other to him; it is the goal. He thinks to bring this about and rise from the ashes."

"Insane!" Whittle exclaimed.

"Exactly," Joshua replied, "but an end within his grasp if we cannot find a successor to the Guardianship who can block his path."

"Sounds like you are taking me into the political scenery of Second World again. Guardians, successors, the labyrinth of ancient magic and political processes—I'm not interested. That's why I left."

"Believe me, Archibald, I hate it as much as you, but if we turn our backs, our backs will be where Aedan's knife goes in."

Whittle halted and faced Joshua, who had been closely following him along the narrow trail.

"An alarming account," Whittle said, "but a matter far beyond my capacity to influence. Which brings me to the big question: Why are you here? What do I have that you want?"

"It is as I said from the beginning," Joshua replied. "David Sutton. He's the only lead I have to the whereabouts of the successor to the Guardianship."

"And who might that be?"

"I don't know."

"You don't know a lot," Whittle said.

"Then enlighten me, Archibald; how do I find David Sutton?"

"You don't."

"What do you mean?"

"David Sutton is dead."

"How long?" Joshua asked.

"About eight years. His body was found in his office."

"What happened?"

"Autopsy revealed he died of a massive stroke. Took him suddenly they said. No pain."

"He worked in adoptions, right?" Joshua asked.

"That's right."

"Kept records, I'm sure."

"Yes and no. He kept files of his regular adoptions only. He kept no physical records of his 'special ones.'"

"Special ones?" Joshua queried.

"Yeah. Certain Second World and mixed-blood kids. It was his own scheme, like the witness-protection program. Some exiles feared for their children, wanted to hide them, protect them. Some were willing to give them up for adoption to accomplish this. David handled those kinds of cases along with his usual ones."

So this is the end of the trail, Joshua thought. "Did he have a wife, children, anyone who might know something about his adoption cases?"

Archibald gazed up into a tree where a squirrel was chattering.

"There was a wife, Ellen."

"Alive?"

"We got a Christmas card from her."

"Was there a return address on the envelope?" Joshua asked.

"Yes," Whittle said. "I remember Meg telling me not to throw the envelope away. She was going to put the address in her card file."

Joshua smiled.

Not quite a dead end. Not yet.

"Mr. Whittle, this has been a fine walk, but your wife's

card file is more interesting to me now than anything we might encounter out here. Do you mind if we turn back?"

Whittle grinned:

"Lead the way, Mr. Turner."

12   *Questionable Lineage*

Secrets are like water. They flood the empty spaces within and around and between us. They make islands of us, seemingly distant and disconnected. This is an illusion. In truth, the waters, the secrets, bind our islands together. The islands and the waters form a whole that can be discerned only from afar. To the earthbound, the earth is always and everywhere flat. It is revealed as a sphere only when viewed from afar. So it is with all secrets. Stand back. Observe from afar. Secrets want to reveal themselves.

FROM "Manual of the Truthseekers" BY Andrus Maxwell

Joshua was travelling fast and light. He had checked no luggage on the flight, and in less than a half hour after landing was driving a rental car southwest from Bradley International Airport. He could have summoned his New York people to pick him up and take him wherever he wanted to go, by car or private plane. It would have been faster. He had decided not to do this for the same reason he had decided to travel under an alias with papers and credit cards to match. He was getting too close. This lead, David Sutton's widow, might be his last. No one, not even his own people, could know where he was going. Whittle knew—that was unavoidable—but no one else did, not even Borrington.

It was dusk when he arrived at 21 Drake Hill Road, Simsbury, Connecticut. He had been on the ground less than an hour.

He knocked on the door. A few moments later, sooner than he expected, a short, stout woman opened the door and gazed dispassionately at him. Her hair was brown, medium-length. She matched Whittle's description.

"Does the name Whittle mean anything to you?" Joshua asked.

"Sounds familiar," the woman said. "Do you have a first name?"

"Archibald and Meg."

"And your name?" the woman asked.

"Joshua Turner."

"What brings you to this address, Mr. Turner?"

It was the challenge question Archibald had given her. The answer was simple, yet could be known only to Joshua and the Whittles.

"Meg's card file," Joshua said, smiling.

The woman smiled back and extended her hand.

"Ellen Sutton," she announced. "Archibald told me to expect you. Please, come in."

The woman ushered Joshua down a hallway and into a small sitting room on the left. The room was furnished sparsely with a couple of aging leather chairs and a small couch. The furniture was situated around a threadbare Persian rug in front of a small fireplace. Joshua noticed some cupboards at the far end of the room. They needed painting, and one of the doors hung at an odd angle. The room and its furnishings did not match the rest of the house.

Ellen flipped a switch on the wall near the fireplace. There was a short electrical buzz followed by flames pushing up through concrete logs arranged neatly on top of an iron grate.

"Nothing like a winter's day to make one appreciate a hot fire and a warm cup of tea," she said.

Joshua smiled and nodded.

"I was just about to make myself a cup. Would you care

to join me?"

Joshua didn't drink tea. Strong black coffee was his preference, ideally with a finger of Irish whisky. There was something vaguely feminine about tea, though he was aware British generals had consumed it daily while conquering the world.

"That would be fine, Mrs. Sutton."

"Please, call me Ellen. May I call you Joshua?"

"Yes, of course."

"Well, Joshua, make yourself comfortable. I'll be back shortly."

Joshua sat in one of the leather chairs facing the couch. He studied the room. Servant's parlor, he concluded. The room was paneled in dark wood and the windows were hung with heavy woolen drapes. Joshua noticed a few faded oil paintings hanging on the walls. All garage-sale stuff. An antique china cabinet close to his chair held an assortment of mismatched china cups and chipped porcelain statuary.

Ellen bustled into the room a few minutes later. She was carrying a wooden tray holding a plate of sandwiches, two cups, two saucers, a small bowl of sugar cubes, a creamer, and a porcelain tea pot.

She poured the tea.

"Sugar? Cream?"

"Black is fine."

Ellen smiled at his use of a coffee term. She handed the cup and saucer to him.

"You would have preferred coffee?"

"No, no; this is fine."

Joshua lifted the cup to his lips in what he hoped was proper form.

"You would have preferred coffee," Ellen said again, this time as though she were commenting on a fact about the weather.

"This will do just fine," Joshua said. "I appreciate your hospitality."

"You're most welcome. Mr. Whittle explained the situation to me. Unfortunately, I know very little about my late husband's work."

Her preemption of the conversation made Joshua suspicious. She wanted him to know immediately that she knew nothing.

"Are we alone?" Joshua asked.

"For the moment."

Joshua gave her a serious look.

"Will you keep in strictest confidence what we discuss here?"

"Of course. Archibald urged the same when he told me you were coming."

"Good. Thank you. The matter is serious. There are unusual forces contending..."

Ellen raised her hand in a gentle gesture calling for a halt. Joshua waited.

"Before you go on," she said, "I should warn you about my limitations, some not of my choosing, others self-imposed. May I do that?"

"Certainly."

She is hiding something, Joshua thought. *This is not going to be easy.*

"I don't want to become embroiled in Second World affairs. I'm native to First World, as, I understand, are you. David exiled himself from Second World, and he did everything he could to distance us from it. My son, Daniel, was an infant when David passed. I don't want to dredge up the past. I don't want my son to be hurt. My situation here is...comfortable. Please don't ask me to do or say anything that might jeopardize it."

She's trying to put a fence around me, Joshua thought. *There is something here. Something important.*

"I understand," Joshua said. "But there are questions I must ask. Forgive me if I tread on sensitive ground."

Ellen nodded, her gaze steady on him.

"Did your husband ever discuss his adoption cases?"

"Very few," she responded.

"Any details you can recall?"

A pause, slight, almost imperceptible.

"No."

"Did he keep any records?"

"None I know of. David wasn't one to bring his work home. I've gone through all his papers. There were no adoption records."

Joshua looked at the ragged cupboards on the other side of the room as he pondered his next question.

"There was a couple, Katherine and Nathan Grear, who gave a daughter up for adoption nine years ago. I have reason to believe your husband handled the case. Did he ever mention them to you?"

Ellen looked away for a moment, as though distracted by something in the room. She quickly turned back, her gaze steady again on Joshua.

"It's been eight years since my husband's death. I try not to go back to that time. But if I did, I doubt I would remember what my David may or may not have told me about an adoption case."

Not an answer, thought Joshua. *More than not an answer: an explanation where none was called for. Everything she says comes down to a rehearsed, "I don't know," with rehearsed words in between, also rehearsed. What sort of person does this? Someone who knows.*

Joshua decided to move in a different direction.

"You mentioned a son, Daniel."

"Yes, David and I had one child, a fine boy."

Joshua smiled. "Children are our legacy. Did David have any time with Daniel?"

"Yes. He had a wonderful year with him. Daniel is only ten now, and he already looks so much like my David. Do you have any children, Joshua?"

"No. Had a wife once, she was pregnant."

"What happened?"

"She died in a car accident."

"I'm so sorry," Ellen said.

"Time heals all wounds."

"Yes, that is the hope," Ellen said.

"It isn't quite true, is it, that saying," Joshua remarked, his voice soft, distant.

"No, it isn't," Ellen agreed, "but time does bring a measure of peace."

"To some," Joshua added, and then went on: "Nathan Grear is not comforted by time. Time works against him, abrades him. The wound of one loss cannot heal because a loss connected to the first goes on and on."

Joshua studied Ellen's face.

After a long silence, she looked away and said:

"I don't understand."

Her response was not unexpected. She was lying to him. She had lived her life in hiding, the wife of a Second World exile. Joshua considered what course to take. Only a direct one seemed open, so he took it. He would flood her with truth and see what might emerge from the waters.

"Nathan Grear lost his wife, Katherine, to cancer about a year ago. Like you, he was First World and married to a self-exiled Second Worlder. Katherine did not leave Second

World for the usual reasons. She left to avoid an honor to which others would aspire. She knew she would be bound without choice to the role of Guardian had she remained in Second World. For this and other reasons, she fled, married Nathan, gave birth to a daughter, and hid the daughter by giving the child up for secret adoption. This pained them both deeply. They were comforted by a happy marriage. Death withdrew that comfort, bringing to Nathan the daily reminder that somewhere in First World he has a daughter. The man has two voids in him: one left by a wife who died, the other left by an adoption he never wanted but knew was necessary. The first void cannot be filled. He has some hope for filling the second."

Joshua ended his soliloquy.

Ellen stared into the fire. The reflections of the dancing flames played across her face, a face that revealed her retreat from him, her distance from him and these truths.

He broke the silence: "Do the Wards have any children?"

"Yes." Ellen's voice was nearly inaudible.

"I saw a pair of girl's shoes and a pink coat hanging in an alcove near the front door," Joshua said. "Not your son's, of course. Am I right in concluding the Wards have a daughter?"

"Yes," Ellen said, still speaking softly.

"Is she their only child?"

"Yes."

"How old is she?"

Ellen turned to him and asked her own question:

"Why?"

"I just thought it would be fortunate if she were around your son's age. He would have a companion. Neither would be an only child."

Ellen stared at him.

Joshua wondered where to go next.

His thoughts were abruptly interrupted when the door of the sitting room burst open and a young girl dashed into the room. She ignored the two adults as she searched the spaces and corners of the room.

It soon became apparent the child was seeking a hiding place. She chose first the long, heavy drapes. Not satisfied, she dashed across the room and crouched beside the china cabinet. The child looked at him intently. She placed her right forefinger across her lips, signaling him not betray her hiding place.

"Alexandra!" Ellen said disapprovingly, "You can't hide here. Go and play somewhere else."

"Shhhh...," was the child's quick reply. "Please, please...I'll leave in a minute. Just don't tell him I'm here, please, please!"

There was the sound of footsteps in the hallway. A boy around the same age as the girl appeared in the doorway. The boy smiled mischievously. Joshua glanced at the girl's hiding place. She was gone. This surprised him. How had she moved without his noticing?

The boy advanced into the room and took the exact route the girl had taken in finding her hiding place: first to the drapes, then, without hesitation, to the side of the china cabinet. The boy smiled, reached down, and ran his hand through thin air in the space beside the cabinet.

A giggle emitted from the space.

"Found you again. Now it's your turn," the boy said.

"No fair, you were peeking,"

"Was not!"

"Was so!"

Joshua turned to Ellen, then back to the boy. But not just the boy anymore, the girl too. She had reappeared, crouched in exactly the place he had seen empty only a few moments before.

Joshua's mind raced. The children were clearly about the same age. The implications of this and what he had just witnessed were immense.

The children bolted from the room.

Ellen stood.

Joshua stood also.

"I'm sorry, Mr. Turner. I wish I could be more help, but my husband is dead. I do not want to go back to that time. If you will forgive me, I really must get back to my duties."

Joshua was at a loss for how to proceed. What he had just seen answered many of his questions, but he needed time to consider the implications.

"Thank you for your time, Ellen." Joshua used her first name in an effort to keep her close. "Did Archibald tell you the seriousness of this matter? It goes far beyond compassion for Nathan Grear."

"He did. And I have my duties…and promises to keep."

She is bound by a secret, Joshua thought. *And it has nothing to do with her son. It has everything to do with the girl she called Alexandra, the girl who could disappear and reappear in the twinkling of an eye.*

"As do I, Mrs. Sutton. You have told me what I need to know."

Ellen Sutton could not conceal the dismay his words aroused in her.

***

Joshua left Connecticut and returned to his headquarters. His investigation now included three principles: Ellen Sutton, Daniel Sutton, and Alexandra Ward. He put aside Mrs. Sutton for the time being, and turned to the other two.

The Ward girl bore a striking resemblance to Elizabeth,

especially in the eyes and the shape of her face. But a
resemblance to the Guardian, however striking, did not make
her the successor. The age was right, the circumstances
highly suggestive, but still not enough. He had a feeling
Alexandra's parents were not important, but he dared not
make this or any other assumptions. There was more work to
do.

Someone knocked on his office door.

"Come in, come in," Joshua said, not looking up from the
notes he was making.

"It appears the girl is the Wards' natural daughter."

Joshua looked up. It was Peter Kendal, his chief-of-staff.
The dark-haired young man handed Joshua a thick file.
Joshua fanned through it absently, then placed it on his desk.

"What lies beyond the appearance?"

"Well, sir, the Wards moved from Nassau County, New
York, to Simsbury about nine years ago. I found no one in
Nassau who remembered Mary Ward being pregnant, though
it was well known among friends that she wanted children.
In any case, the Wards leave Nassau and soon after show up
in Simsbury with an infant daughter, Alexandra."

"How soon after?"

"That's unclear. There's a gap."

"Birth records?"

Joshua looked intently at his chief-of-staff.

"Absolutely: a pristine certificate of live birth for
Alexandra Ward, naming Mary Ward as her natural mother
and John Ward as her natural father."

"Where was it executed?"

"At a small hospital in St. Albans, Vermont. I went there,
and that's when things got interesting. They had no record of
Mary Ward's admittance. This was explained in part by a
fire that partially destroyed the hospital's administrative

offices."

Joshua raised his eyebrows.

Peter saw the gesture and went on:

"Yes, and the fire was curiously selective. Some hardcopy records did survive, among them the birth certificate. However, no nurse or doctor notes, no clinical records, nothing except the birth certificate. It was signed by a doctor known to have worked at the hospital at that time. Turns out he died a year after the recorded date of the birth. The hospital administrator's signature was indecipherable, but whoever he was, he would not have witnessed the birth or have had direct knowledge of it."

"Electronic files?"

Peter smiled.

"The electronic files were compromised by an unspecified computer virus, again a rather selective one. Most of the computer records were recovered after the cyber attack, but none relating to the birth of Alexandra, except, of course, the certificate of live birth."

Joshua stood:

"So we have from a reputable hospital this perfectly legal, proper, and complete birth certificate for Alexandra Ward. Is it backed up by corresponding county and state records?"

"Yes," Peter replied.

"Of course, it would be. Second World exiles appear to be pretty deeply imbedded in this part of the country. They would not overlook synchronizing the records."

"No, sir, they wouldn't, if that's what happened."

"You have doubts, Peter."

"No, but it is a smoke-fire thing. I see smoke everywhere, but no flames. It is quite frustrating"

"Yes, it is."

Joshua began pacing behind his desk.

"Tell me about the Wards."

"Yes, sir. John Ward is a successful businessman, a venture capital guy with apparently excellent instincts. He has powerful friends, some with links to the White House."

"Any dirt?"

"None I could find. By all accounts the Wards are upstanding citizens, pillars of the community. He rules the roost. She stays pretty much in the background. They donate to the right causes, where people can see their names. His investment company has its hands in many pies, all apparently legit. No FBI package, clean with the SEC. A risk taker—who isn't in that business—but a bit of a self-righteous prig, and that has probably kept him on the right side of the law."

"I saw something about a violent birthday party in your report. What was the significance of that?"

Peter paused before going on.

"Most curious, sir, and maybe our most useful indication of who or what the child may be."

"A birthday party? How so?"

"The party was a year ago, her eighth birthday. A big affair held at the Ward mansion. There were rumors. I dug a little, got the police report, talked casually to some people, and an interesting possibility emerged. Then a certainty. Magic was at work in the violence that occurred, and Alexandra may have had a hand in it."

"Tell me more."

"It seems Alexandra had an argument with her mother or her father. She questioned why Daniel Sutton was not present at the party. When she was told he had not been invited, things got ugly."

"Was the child seen to do anything?"

"No, nothing anyone one could point to with certainty. It was a case of 'when the kid got mad, things turned bad.'"

Joshua smiled. "You made that up."

"No, one of the witnesses standing nearby put it that way. And that pretty well sums it up. Not conclusive, but pretty telling."

"Peter, thank you. You've done excellent work. I know it has hard, doing all this alone, without involving your team or our other assets.

"I understand the need, sir. The vacation cover story held, though I am not known for taking vacations."

"I know, Peter. But I could not have done this alone."

"May I make a comment, sir?"

"Certainly."

"The Wards are both solidly First World."

"I know that."

"The kid is not."

"I know that too."

***

Elizabeth crossed into First World to see the child for herself. She saw the startling resemblance Joshua had described. It was a piece of the mosaic. But no single piece could answer the question. However, the assembled pieces seemed conclusive. Still, she wished for absolute proof. She wished for a single piece to say yes, without doubt, she is your sister's daughter.

There was a knock on her office door.

"Enter."

The door opened and Borrington, wearing a midnight blue robe, stepped into her office.

"Do I bring her here?" Elizabeth asked.

"A tempting option, milady, but one fraught with hazard."

Elizabeth brushed back her hair and waited while the general pondered.

He did not ponder long.

"Moving her would be difficult to conceal, as would maintaining her at Byrnhelen. Aedan would learn of it, and he would then devote all his resources to killing you and controlling her."

"That day will come sooner or later," Elizabeth said.

"Better it be later than sooner. She is a child today, unaware. Let her be raised into her teens in First World. It will broaden her, and it will keep her as far removed as possible from Aedan and his people. Second World exiles have been alerted to Aedan's dangerous intentions. Only Archibald Whittle and his wife know her whereabouts, and we have good reason to trust him. Joshua's people are all First World, deeply vetted, and close to untouchable. I cannot say the same of my people. She is safer where she is."

"Let her stay, and do nothing? That's your plan?"

"Sometimes doing nothing is the boldest thrust of all."

It was Elizabeth's turn to ponder, her eyes steady on Borrington, her Guardian instincts testing his resolve.

"Make the arrangements, General. She stays, but not without...arrangements."

"Of course."

"Assign a contingent of my most trusted guards to be near her."

Borrington frowned.

"You don't approve?"

"I do not wish to alarm you," Borrington replied.

"Alarm me. Speak freely, my friend."

"I want to be where I can watch my men, even those I most trust. I have established a system of checks, watchers watching the watchers, a necessary precaution in the environment Aedan has created. Loyalties are in flux in our world. We cannot trust as we once did. I am sorry to tell you this, but it is a truth that must contribute to a heightened awareness on both our parts."

"What of the child, then?"

"A single trusted Dyrisian should be assigned to watch over her, someone you speak to directly who will report only to you. Dyrisians have strong magical powers and their form of magic is more difficult for Aedan to detect. They are outside our politics, not vulnerable to Aedan's influence."

"That's it: one Dyrisian?"

"And Joshua."

"There was a time you would not have suggested him for anything of this importance."

"That time is long past. He has won my deepest respect. Nearly single-handedly he has brought the successor to us."

"Along with a few questions."

"Yes, and we will continue to watch and listen for other possibilities."

"But you think she is the one, don't you, Andrew; in your heart of hearts you think it."

"I do, and so does Joshua, but we will watch and we will listen, as will Nara and Sigvardr."

Elizabeth stepped around her desk and stood close to him. He made a move to step back. She gripped his arm.

"I could do none of this without you, Andrew," she whispered.

"You could..."

"No, I could not"

She reached up with her other hand and touched his cheek, moved closer, and laid her head on his chest.

"I could not," she said again.

Borrington placed an arm around her waist, tentatively, as though the slightest touch might break her...and annihilate him.

They stood like that for a long time.

13   *Arrival*

Some say I harm the innocents. I do not harm them. I give them new lives, new histories. I defend them from Second World, but I do not close the portal. When the time comes to make their own choice, they can choose to return. Few make this choice.

FROM "EXODUS AND EXILE" BY DAVID SUTTON (COLLECTION OF ESSAYS DISCOVERED AFTER HIS DEATH)

Elizabeth Shaw stood alone at the front door of a mansion in Simsbury, Connecticut. A strong wind scattered the falling snow and numbed her cheeks. It was the twenty-first day of January, early in the afternoon.

Alea, Elizabeth's Dyrisian, had guarded Alexandra and faithfully reported on conditions here for the past six years. Alea's reports had ceased, and she had vanished. Aedan was closing in. It was time to take the child.

Elizabeth raised the heavy Florentine door knocker.

She hesitated.

Now it begins.

She brought the knocker down hard on the brass striker plate.

14   Negotiations

Some stars are binary from formation to death. Alexandra and Daniel must be understood together for either of them to be understood at all.

FROM "CHRONICLE OF THE SUCCESSION" BY MASTER BRADYN ARISTARCHUS

Ellen was surprised anyone would be knocking at the door on a day like this. Overnight a bitter northerly wind had brought heavy snow. The wind continued to blow, sometimes violently, picking up the falling snowflakes and swirling them into a wild, magical dance. It was the kind of day for staying inside by a warm fire while sipping tea and lazily lounging in flannels. It was definitely not a day for anyone to be visiting.

She opened the door a crack and peeked out.

Before her stood a tall, thin woman in her late fifties. The woman's eyes were piercing blue. Wisps of blond hair, so blond it was almost white, extended from beneath the deep cowl of the long emerald-green cloak she wore.

"May I help you?"

The woman's response was inaudible over the howling of the wind.

Ellen opened the door, stood aside, and motioned the woman in. The woman complied swiftly, and Ellen closed the door against the storm.

"May I take your coat?"

"Thank you."

The woman turned and with Ellen's assistance shucked

out of her snow-covered cloak. Ellen hung it on a rack beside the door.

"What brings you out in weather like this?"

"A matter of some importance. My name is Elizabeth Shaw," the woman offered.

"Ellen Sutton. I am the Wards' household manager."

"I thought as much. Thank you for your hospitality. You are as a colleague of mine described you."

Ellen looked quizzically at Elizabeth:

"I'm afraid you have me at a loss. Who is your colleague?"

"Joshua Turner. You might not remember him. It has been six years or so."

Ellen's professional cordiality dissolved instantly.

This again, she thought. *After all this time.*

"I remember him, and I'll tell you what I told him: I cannot help you."

"Cannot or will not?"

"Both. Now, as harsh as the weather may be, I must ask you to leave. You found your way here; you can find your way back."

"It would be better if I stayed and we worked together."

"I must insist."

"And so must I."

"Shall I call the police?"

"That is up to you, Ellen, and I will be gone before they get here. But I will be back. My business is with the Wards. You could help or at least not interfere. That too will be your choice. But the errand I am upon will not wait for either of us."

"You're threatening me!"

"On the contrary. I am offering my assistance in dealing with a threat that is upon us all."

"Your colleague, Joshua, already covered that, years ago as you point out. My position has not changed."

"Your position no longer matters. You have been taken over by circumstances. We all have. Fate and Alexandra's destiny determine our course now."

Ellen's eyes went wide at the mention of the child she had raised along with her son. Her promise to her husband, to the Wards, and to herself bore down silently upon her. The weight of the promise burdened her, but it also strengthened her resolve.

"I have always acted in the best interests of the Wards' daughter."

"She is not their daughter. You know that. They know that. How they come to learn of my knowing it is up to you. I could tell them you betrayed the secret to me."

"I betrayed nothing to you!"

"A matter of opinion, but I will say you did if you force me. And they will believe me, won't they. Who else could have told me?"

"You are an evil woman."

"No, just determined. As are you. Given our shared determination, should we not consider an alliance? This would, I assure you, be in the best interests of Alexandra. The Wards will suffer; this is unavoidable. I fear you will as well, and perhaps your son."

"Why Daniel? I thought this was all about Alexandra."

"Because Daniel has already formed an alliance with her. They each know who and what the other is, not as a fact, but as an intuition and a collection of shared experiences far more powerful than mere facts. While the rest of you pretend not to see this, they live it every day. They have only each other in this world. The Wards have tried to separate them; you know how poorly that has gone."

Ellen nodded.

Elizabeth placed a hand on the woman's shoulder. Ellen winced at the touch but did not pull away.

"You have performed valiantly as guardian of the secret that has hidden Alexandra all these years. We trusted you would, or Joshua would not have left her with you. But during those years, your son's destiny became intertwined with hers. I will try to extricate Daniel, but I fear I will have as little success as the Wards. Too much time has passed; I fear Daniel and Alexandra have become a Gordian knot that can be untied only with a sword."

Ellen was aghast:

"You would kill him?"

"No, but others might seek his life or do even worse to get to Alexandra. Up to now, the secret of her birth has protected her. You and the Wards have protected her. But your protection is no longer enough. I must step in, and I will be no less dedicated in my protection than you have been in yours. If you hinder me, you could reduce or eliminate the protection I offer. I beg you not to do that."

Ellen teetered backward, groping blindly for the chair next to the coat rack. Elizabeth helped her to sit, then knelt on the floor next to the chair.

Ellen clasped her hands together tightly in her lap. She seemed in this way to be keeping the two halves of her from splitting apart. She stared straight ahead, rigid, immobile, distant.

Neither spoke for a long time. The storm grew in intensity, as though it intended something. A scraping sound accompanied a particularly violent gust of wind. Elizabeth looked around Ellen and saw the door had moved inward about four centimeters. She stepped around Ellen; leaned into the door; and secured the deadbolt.

Her action broke the long silence:

"What do you want me to do?"

Ellen sounded like a machine.

Elizabeth delivered her answer with tenderness:

"First, I must meet with Alexandra, talk with her, and with your son. I need to get a feel for the child, for her maturity, for her...readiness. I must also assess your son, in particular the strength of his ties to Alexandra. I will leave him out of what will follow, if I can. Then, when the Wards return, I will meet with them. Simply introduce me. Support me indirectly, as far as you are able, but do not side with me. We did not have this conversation. When I tell them I know of the adoption, they will deny it, at least at first. They will want to know whether you told me, but they will not ask directly, for that would be an admission. When the lies stop, and they will stop, I will tell them how I know of the adoption and why I am here. When they ask, and they will ask, I will tell them you did nothing, said nothing that led to my knowing of the adoption."

"Then what."

"Then comes the hard part."

***

Ellen left Elizabeth in the drawing room off the entry hall while she searched for Alexandra. She found her seated across from Daniel at the long antique servants' table in the kitchen. The two were devouring the crumbled remains of a chocolate cake.

"Hello, children."

Ellen hoped her faux cheerfulness masked her anxiety.

"Oh, Mrs. Sutton, we're not really 'children' anymore," Alexandra said offhandedly. "Daniel and I are fifteen."

"Actually, I'm sixteen," said Daniel, smirking at Alexandra.

Alexandra stuck out her tongue and crossed her eyes, then assumed a regal posture. "Sixteen," she said with mock seriousness. "I had no idea how ancient you were. Perhaps you can instruct me in the ways of the world, being of such advanced years as you are."

Daniel gave Alexandra a gentle shove on the shoulder. She shoved him back, and they both giggled.

Ellen frowned. *The awful woman waits in the drawing room, waits for my children, for Alexandra, whom I hold as dear as my son, and for my son too. What do I do? Flee with them? Hide them? Where would I do that, and how could I be sure I was not doing more harm than good? The woman has great power, I'm sure of that. She would find us. The Wards would find us. What then? Why couldn't we be left in peace!*

Alexandra noticed Ellen's frown and came over to her. She placed her hand on her back.

"You OK?"

"Yes."

Ellen gave Alexandra a small smile:

"Headache."

Ellen walked to the stove and placed the stainless steel teapot over the flame.

"There is someone here to see you, Alexandra."

"Who?"

Alexandra licked chocolate from her fingers.

"Someone you need to talk to. I'll let her introduce herself."

"What does she want to talk about?"

Alexandra picked up another cake.

"I'll let her tell you that."

Alexandra scowled.

"Am I in some kind of trouble?"

Ellen thought about that for a moment:

Yes, my dear, but not in the way you are thinking.

"No," Ellen said. "She just wants to get to know you a little. Now scat. She's in the drawing room. Be a good hostess. Go and meet her and I'll bring some tea."

Alexandra took a last bite of her cake.

"What's she like?"

"Meet her and decide for yourself. Now go!"

Alexandra left.

"Weird, Mom. Really weird," said Daniel.

"Mind your own business, young man. She wants to meet you too."

"Did we win a contest or something?"

"Something like that: won, lost..."

Her voice trailed off.

***

Alexandra found herself strangely apprehensive as she advanced through the hallways leading to the drawing room. She felt something beyond shyness but short of fear. Her feelings contained echoes from somewhere in her past, and there was in these a warning, vague, unclear.

She found the large double doors of the drawing room closed. She reached for one of the door handles but pulled back before touching it. An inexplicable hesitance gripped her for a few long moments. She took a deep breath, grasped the handles on both doors and pushed inward.

A tall woman, hands clasped behind her back, stood facing her. The woman was smiling. Alexandra stared into the woman's deep blue eyes. The woman spoke:

"You must be Alexandra."

The visitor stepped forward and offered her hand.

Alexandra's forebodings vanished. She took the hand and felt a great warmth of spirit emanating from the visitor. A similar warmth poured out of her, without thought, without intention.

"Yes, yes, I am," Alexandra said, as though a little surprised at who she was. "I am so happy you came."

Alexandra's reactions to the woman surprised her, especially the words she had just spoken. They just came out of her.

"I'm your Aunt Elizabeth, Elizabeth Shaw. I am your mother's sister."

Alexandra looked skeptical.

"I didn't think Mom had a sister."

"It's complicated, but your mother does have a sister, and a brother as well."

Might as well get this thing moving in the direction of truth, a little at a time, Elizabeth decided.

"How old are you, my dear?"

"Fifteen on my last birthday, a couple of months ago."

"You are tall," Elizabeth commented, "like I was at your age."

Alexandra considered this. Indeed, she had the woman's height. What else did she have of her? The woman's sapphire blue eyes gazed steadily at her.

I have blue eyes, Alexandra thought.

Her aunt had long, white-blonde hair that fell halfway down her back.

My hair is the same, Alexandra mused, *though I don't have the streaks of gray. But that will come when I'm old, I suppose.*

Alexandra noted the creases at the corners of Elizabeth's eyes and the sides of her mouth.

Will this be me?

The question came into her mind unbidden, followed by a wave of sadness.

"So," Elizabeth said, breaking the silence, "you are probably wondering why I'm here."

"Well, yes."

"There are some things I need to discuss with your mother and father."

"Mrs. Sutton said you came to see me."

"You as well."

"Why?"

"That will come later. First, tell me a little about yourself."

"Well, what would you like to know?" Alexandra asked with a quick smile as she smoothed her skirt.

Elizabeth returned the smile:

"Everything, anything. I'd like to get to know my niece."

"There really isn't much to tell. I live here with my parents, and Mrs. Sutton and her son Daniel. I go to school. The usual stuff for a kid my age, I guess."

"What do you do when you're not in school?"

"Well, most days I do stuff with Daniel."

Elizabeth's serene expression betrayed nothing of the misgivings she felt when she heard the boy's name. School and Daniel. She feared this would be the essence. It made sense, but she still hoped.

"He's my friend, sort of like a brother, but not," Alexandra continued. "His mom works for my parents. She takes care of us. You met her. Daniel and his mom have lived here all my life. Daniel is just a year older than me. He thinks that makes him mister big shot, but I've got news for him. Anyway, school and music lessons and in the summers, we hang out. We have all kinds of adventures together."

Elizabeth walked to a colorfully upholstered loveseat in the corner of the room. She sat and patted the cushion next to her.

"What kind of adventures?" Elizabeth asked after Alexandra had taken a seat next to her.

Alexandra began an account of herself. At first her descriptions were structured in the shy generalities of a child. The old woman listened attentively, asked a question now and then, and in all ways gently but relentlessly encouraged Alexandra to continue, to reveal, to clarify her life. Alexandra obliged with an openness she had never felt with another adult.

"Tell me more about Daniel," Elizabeth said at the opportune moment. "Has he ever had anything exciting happen to him like what happened to you at your eighth birthday party?"

Alexandra tensed.

"You know about that? Nobody knows about that anymore. We don't talk about it."

"You can talk to me about it if you want. I think I would have found the whole thing quite entertaining."

"It was!" Alexandra said, her face betraying a certain delight in the memory of flying food. "But," she added immediately, "at the same time, it was awful. No one knows what really happened; not even the people father hired could figure it out, and it scared so many people, including my parents."

There was a long pause as Alexandra became lost in her feelings about that day. She knew what had happened. She knew why. She knew her part in it. But she had never admitted anything to anyone. Except Daniel. It was their secret and their secret alone, and it was long past, covered over by many other secrets between them.

"So, has Daniel ever had anything exciting happen to him like that?"

Elizabeth lifted her china teacup and watched Alexandra

carefully.

Alexandra dropped her eyes and stared into her own teacup.

"Well," she said finally, "that's...a secret."

"A secret?" Elizabeth asked, putting down her teacup.

"Yes, a secret." Alexandra said firmly. She brought her teacup to her mouth and sipped from it as long as she could. She feared she would say too much, maybe already had.

"There are many kinds of secrets. What kind is yours?"

"The kind you have only with a close friend, someone who understands," Alexandra said.

Elizabeth smiled.

"I see," she said slowly. "A secret between friends is a bond, and such a bond should not be broken."

Alexandra looked at her aunt, but said nothing.

"Would you introduce me to Daniel?" Elizabeth asked. There was no insistence in her tone; it was a question Alexandra could answer either way, yes or no.

Alexandra thought on how none of the adults in her life showed any interest in Daniel. His mother was a marked exception, of course, but Ellen doted over both children. Alexandra's parents treated Daniel with cool politeness; to them he was there and not there, all at the same time. He was not introduced at social gatherings, whether of family or friends, and he took his meals with his mother, and often with Alexandra, who sought out every opportunity to be with them.

Alexandra stood.

"I'll be right back."

She walked out of the room. She returned a few minutes later followed closely by a handsome young man of about her age.

The young man looked distinctly uncomfortable.

"Daniel," Alexandra said with awkward formality, "this is my Aunt Elizabeth. Aunt Elizabeth, this is Daniel."

"How do you do, Daniel," Elizabeth said.

She remained seated. She fixed her eyes on Daniel and held out her hand. He took it, but he did not meet her eyes.

He has the presence. He demurs, pretends a certain shyness, but he conceals power. How much? And of what kind? How would my brother use this boy if he knew of his existence?

She squeezed Daniel's hand a little harder than a friendly handshake allowed, and she pulled him toward her, a slight gesture only he would perceive.

Look at me, boy! Reveal yourself!

As though he had heard her thoughts, he raised his eyes to meet hers and granted her a smile.

"How do you do," he whispered, matching the formality of her greeting and the firmness and pull of her handshake.

A standoff.

There it is, Elizabeth thought, *pride, strength, self-possession.*

She studied Daniel's lean face, straight nose, and thick brown hair. His eyes were gray with tiny flecks of blue. He was tall for his age. The Shaw line? Perhaps. But many have his facial features, not so many the gray eyes. Still, there is something, a possibility.

"Oh, I do quite well, thank you," Elizabeth replied, releasing the boy's hand. "Alexandra was just telling me about your remarkable friendship."

Daniel gave Alexandra a stern glance. She looked down at the hardwood floor just ahead of the toe of her left foot. Elizabeth found her simulated concentration amusing.

They have learned to hide what they cannot explain, she thought. *Because they are different, superior in many ways, they have learned to avoid the stage, to pretend to be uninteresting spectators to all but each other. They do not yet know they are the main act. When that knowledge comes, will it poison them? We shall see.*

"I am so glad she has somebody like you in her life," Elizabeth said.

"Like me?"

There it is again, that false diffidence, thought Elizabeth. *This could grow tiresome.*

"Yes, 'like you,'" she said, hardening her gaze.

"Really, and what am I like?"

Now we are getting somewhere. He listens. No small talk once he is challenged. He edges out of hiding.

"Well," Elizabeth said, "we may discuss that later, in considerable detail, but for now I need only say you seem to be a very kind and caring companion to my niece. She is fortunate to have a friend like you."

Daniel relaxed.

Alexandra desperately wanted to change the subject.

"Aunt Elizabeth, would you like to play a game?" she asked.

"Depends on the game."

"A card game. I got it for my birthday, and it is ever so much fun to play."

Alexandra hurried from the room and moments later reappeared with a small box of cards. She spread the cards across the coffee table in front of the loveseat, detailed the rules with great seriousness, and the three played the game for the next hour and a half.

The card game really meant nothing in itself. It was a means of exploring one another without going too deep too fast. Immersed in the game, they did not hear the drawing room doors swing open.

A man's voice boomed from the doorway:
"And who, may I ask, are you?"

15   The Woman Who Stayed for Dinner

We are fathers, mothers, husbands, wives, children, one to another, taking turns. Life is a circle. Who will break it?

FROM "VESSELS OF DESTINY" BY MASTER MAREK AVALARD

There was a long, awkward silence. John Ward glared at the visitor. Elizabeth looked back at him, steadily, as though he were an artifact in a museum.

It was Mary who finally broke the silence.

"Who are you?" she asked.

"She's Aunt Elizabeth," Alexandra said enthusiastically.

Elizabeth glanced at Alexandra, then looked at Mary.

"My name is Elizabeth Shaw."

Elizabeth studied Mary. She noted her ivory complexion; her straight, slightly upturned nose; and the curious way she held her lips in two tight thin lines. Her petite frame contrasted sharply with her husband's imposing mass.

"I know of no Elizabeth Shaw in my family," Mary said, exchanging a nervous glance with John.

"There is no one related to me by that name," John added too quickly.

"Well," Mary said, "I am at a loss."

There was an uncomfortable silence as John realized who Elizabeth Shaw might be. His shoulders slumped and he looked away.

"I have looked forward to meeting you and your daughter

for a long time," Elizabeth said, glancing at Alexandra and Daniel. "The children and I have enjoyed an informative afternoon. We have become well acquainted."

The thought that had come to John a few moments before now came to Mary.

She knows!

Mary turned abruptly to Daniel, frowned sternly at him, and jerked her head toward the doors of the drawing room. The instruction was unmistakable; Daniel hurried out of the room.

A few moments later, Ellen appeared, standing in the hallway just outside the drawing room.

"Dinner is ready, Mr. Ward. Should I set a place for Ms. Shaw?"

"I would be delighted to join you for dinner," Elizabeth said before John could respond. Her words and demeanor signaled more than acceptance; she was staying for dinner.

"You may set a place for our guest," John said, retaining as much dignity as he was able in the face of Elizabeth's boldness.

Mary turned a practiced smile on Elizabeth.

"Delighted," she said with all the sincerity of a hyena.

Alexandra took Elizabeth's hand and followed Ellen into the hall.

"My dad sounds meaner than he is," Alexandra said, speaking softly. "You just surprised him. Are you really my aunt?"

"I really am, but that will require some explaining."

"Sounds mysterious. Daniel and I sort of live a mystery, if you know what I mean."

"I think I do."

"You'll love dinner," Alexandra continued. "Ellen is the best cook."

"Well, then, I'm sure the meal will be excellent."

Mary and John stayed well back, whispering to one another.

"Who is this woman?" Mary asked her husband.

"I don't know," John replied, "but we have to consider she may be who she says she is: Alexandra's aunt."

Mary was obviously dismayed.

"Then she knows," Mary said.

"Let's not go there yet," John replied. "We have the birth records naming us as natural mother and father. David Sutton is dead. He took great care to make the adoption secret."

"What are we going to do?"

"Stay calm, admit nothing, whoever this woman claims to be. We need to know what she knows. Alexandra is ours and ours alone. We must be strong on that."

"Do you think Ellen...?"

"I don't think anything, Mary; not yet. We have to let this thing play out. Let me handle it."

Mary wrung her hands in agitation.

"For now let's have a polite dinner with this Shaw woman," John continued. "Do not discuss this matter at dinner. Do you understand?"

Mary quickly nodded. John offered her his arm and led her out of the drawing room.

Elizabeth and Alexandra were already seated when John and Mary reached the dining room. John assisted Mary with her chair before seating himself. The hearty aroma of a beef pot roast emanated from the adjoining kitchen. Ellen soon appeared carrying two china plates, each bearing steaming pieces of pot roast mixed with carrots and white onions, a buttery yeast roll, and fluffy whipped potatoes covered with brown gravy. Ellen placed one plate on a gold charger in front of Mary and the other on the charger in front of Elizabeth.

"Thank you, Ellen," Elizabeth said.

Ellen was embarrassed by this acknowledgement. She was not accustomed to being thanked for anything. She glanced at Mary. Mary looked away indifferently.

Ellen returned to the kitchen, and after a few moments re-entered with two more plates of the same food. She placed one in front of John and the other in front of Alexandra. John raised his fork, a sign the meal had commenced.

"Where did you say you were from, Ms. Shaw?" John asked a few minutes later.

"I don't think I did say, Mr. Ward."

John looked at Elizabeth sharply.

"Alexandra, do you have any pets?" Elizabeth asked.

"Yes," Alexandra said, "a parakeet. Domingo is his name. I've trained him."

"So, are you in town just for the day?" Mary interjected.

"Perhaps," Elizabeth replied as she deftly slid her fork under a corner of her mashed potatoes. "How did you train him?"

Mary opened her mouth to answer, then realized the question was not for her. She, like John, was being deliberately ignored. Mary's lips pressed together in a tight line as she glared at Elizabeth.

"Not very well, really," Alexandra said, answering Elizabeth's earlier question about training Domingo. "But Daniel and I are working on it, and Domingo now whistles a certain tune each time I call his name. Well, most of the time he does."

"It can be difficult to train animals," Elizabeth said kindly.

"Yeah, really. I also have a Persian cat. She's impossible

to train."

"Cats can be difficult," Elizabeth agreed. "What is her name?"

Alexandra sensed mounting tension in her parents and hoped her banter about pets might relieve it.

"Hera," Alexandra replied. "She is always trying to get into my bedroom. That's where I keep Domingo. I think that..."

"Hush Alexandra! Finish your dinner," Mary snarled, unable to bear Elizabeth's snub any longer.

Alexandra took a hurried couple of bites of roast beef.

John let out a dramatic sigh, registering something between disgust and exasperation.

Mary picked at her food.

Elizabeth ate heartily.

Everyone finished the meal in silence.

Half an hour later, when the last of the vanilla bean custard with fresh raspberries and cream had been eaten and the dishes cleared away, Elizabeth pushed back her chair and stood. She looked at John, then Mary, then back at John.

"Can we speak privately?" she said.

Mary dropped her crumpled linen napkin onto her plate. She rose slowly from her chair. John glanced at her and also rose.

"Yes, of course," he said. "Please follow me."

John walked toward the dining room doors. Alexandra ran ahead of him and pulled the doors open.

"Would you like to see Domingo now?" she asked Elizabeth. "I'll show you how I can make him whistle."

She took Elizabeth's hand and urged her forward.

Elizabeth looked earnestly at Alexandra but did not budge.

"It's time for me to speak to your mother and father. We

will visit later."

Alexandra stood quite still. A single thought flooded her mind:

This woman is who I will become.

The thought became a feeling, and the feeling became a certainty: Aunt Elizabeth was her future. What that future might hold was not revealed. She looked at Elizabeth. Elizabeth did not look back.

The thought, though not the certainty of feeling, left Alexandra and she turned to her mother:

"I'm not a child, Mother. I know you're going to talk about me. That's why I'm being sent away."

"This will be a private conversation between me, your mother, and this woman," her father interjected, looking directly at Elizabeth and then at his daughter. "And this, young lady, is not the time for you to argue!"

Alexandra hesitated.

"Please do as your father asks," Aunt Elizabeth said, almost in a whisper. "After I have talked with your parents, there will be a place in the conversation for you, a very important place, I assure you."

Alexandra moved aside without further protest.

John found his daughter's response to Elizabeth disconcerting.

She doesn't yield so quickly to me. Why then to this woman?

He looked from his daughter to Elizabeth.

What is going on here?

16   Private Conversation

Silence is golden.

FIRST WORLD APHORISM

John led the way into his office. Elizabeth smiled, noting the contrast between John's office and the drawing room where they had first met. This was a place of business, of mastery. It was furnished with dark, sturdy wooden furniture; a large mahogany desk; and a deep couch upholstered in dark brown leather. Massive book shelves lined three walls of the room. The couch took up about a third of the wall facing the desk. Behind the desk was the room's only window, a large rectangle of light framed on each side by thick mahogany pillars. The curtains were heavy and ornate, with elaborate curving designs in red, orange, black, and gold. The statuary and other accents were of wood, marble, and bronze. The room enclosed echoes of negotiation and confrontation, and of long hours of preparation to do financial battle. The room was a monument to First World.

"Please, have a seat."

John gestured toward one of the high-backed chairs in front of his desk. He occupied the massive overstuffed leather chair behind the desk.

Elizabeth sat on the couch rather than the indicated chair. After a moment of confusion, Mary also seated herself on the couch. John's
eyes narrowed and his jaw tightened.

So it's games you want to play, he thought. *I too can play games.*

John gave his full attention to Elizabeth.

"Enough of this charade. Who are you?"

"I am who I said I was earlier: Alexandra's Aunt."

"Are you suggesting you are a long-lost sister of one of us?"

"I am suggesting no such thing. I am not a blood relation to either of you, just as Alexandra is not."

John's expression hardened and his cheeks flushed.

"She is our daughter," he hissed.

"Adopted daughter, and most fortunate to have come under your care. But now your duties to Alexandra are at an end."

"Absurd," John bellowed. "If it gets no better than this, you're wasting your time and ours. Alexandra is our daughter. We have ample documentation of this, and our "duties," as you call them, are certainly not at an end. Yours, however, are, whatever you fancy they may have been."

Elizabeth was calm.

"I wish it were that easy, Mr. Ward. I truly do. But the situation is what it is, facts are facts. You have some of the facts, as much as you may deny them. I have others. Let us combine our facts and reach a new understanding."

John stared at Elizabeth. He saw neither disdain nor uncertainty in her, only high intention. She was here for a specific purpose and had high confidence in her ability to accomplish it. He was good at judging people in these circumstances, and in engaging them in reaching a conclusion acceptable to all. He sensed that Elizabeth was out of reach of his skills.

No one spoke for a long interval.

Elizabeth stood.

"Alexandra has a destiny to fulfill and she cannot fulfill it here."

"Nonsense," John said. "Have you taken leave of your senses, woman?"

Elizabeth folded her arms.

"Mr. Ward, you spoke earlier of a charade. I think there may be some of that on both sides. Let's end it and get on with the difficult business at hand. I must tell you a story."

Elizabeth spoke for fifteen minutes, not pausing to receive comments or answer questions. She told the Wards of Second World and of her place in it. She told of her sister's rejection of her heritage. She told them of Katherine's marriage to Nathan Grear and of the birth of Alexandra and of David Sutton's handling of the adoption and falsification of records. She told of Katherine's death and her grieving husband's longing to know what became of his daughter. Finally, she told them of her brother Aedan and the ends he sought. She described how these ends would require him to kill her and take control of Alexandra. Alexandra would finally be murdered and the Two Worlds destroyed.

John chuckled dismissively.

"You should seek help, Ms. Shaw. You have convinced me of two things: First, you believe the story you just told us, and second, because you believe it, you are not just a harmless lunatic; you are a danger to our family."

John stood and reached for the phone. He put the receiver to his ear and heard the dial tone.

"Let's hold all calls for the moment," Elizabeth said.

The dial tone disappeared, replaced by an eerie modulating tone. He punched in 9-1-1 and received a recorded message:

"Hang up the phone, Mr. Ward," the message said. It was

Elizabeth's voice he heard on the phone. He looked up at her. She smiled at him. He put down the receiver.

"Thank you, Mr. Ward. A parlor trick. Don't be alarmed. If you wish, I can provide other aids to your understanding. I hope we can get past all this as soon as possible."

"Past all what?"

"The parlor tricks, the demonstrations of magic, mild versions of what your daughter showed you at her eighth birthday."

John sat again in his plush desk chair.

Elizabeth continued:

"I will meet your need for verification as far as I am able and time permits. What would you find most compelling, Second World magic or First World explanation and witnesses?"

"The last would do nicely, Ms. Shaw, since the first is a fabrication of your rich imagination."

"I suspect both will be necessary before we are done, but we can begin with the familiar."

John did not respond. He stared at the oil painting above the couch. It depicted a ship at sea. He gave a little cough. Mary crossed her legs and leaned slightly forward. She concentrated on the intricate designs in the throw rug in front of the couch. As if by some secret signal between them, they looked up at one another and then turned to Elizabeth.

"Let's begin with your house manager and nanny, Ellen."

John became livid.

"I knew it! She put you up to this, didn't she?"

"She most certainly did not. She has kept your secret and her own with great loyalty, both to you and Alexandra."

"She told you of the adoption though. Had to. She did that."

"You are quite wrong, I assure you. A colleague of mine

approached her some six years ago, laid out the story I have told you, and sought her cooperation. She denied all and refused further contact. She tried to lie to me as well, but I did what I have done for you: I told her a story. She already knew the truth of much of it, an advantage she had over you. Do not fault her, Mr. Ward. She is loyal to you and Alexandra. I challenged her loyalty. She withstood the challenge."

"Not as loyal as I require," John said. "If what you say is true, she experienced an unforgiveable lapse in loyalty: She did not tell us of the visit of your colleague. What did you say his name was?"

"Joshua Turner."

"The man who runs the Eastern Mountain Climbing School?"

"The same, who, among others, has been guarding Alexandra these past years."

"So, I have this 'trusted' nanny who has known all you are telling me...

"Not all, Mr. Ward, but some. To understand her, you must look at yourself. I come here with a seemingly preposterous story. You want to have me arrested..."

"Not arrested, just taken into custody for psychiatric observation."

"A difference that makes no difference."

"Very well, go on."

"Your dear nanny is First World, like you. She has no magic to demonstrate, nothing to convince you of a world you have never conceived. You would not have listened. I don't think you listen now, but you will before we are done. Don't fault the woman who brought you the daughter you love as your own. Fault me as the one who must take her from you."

"You may try. You will not succeed."

John's tone carried menace.

"I understand your feelings, sir. I would think less of you if you did not have them. But affections, yours or mine or your wife's do not matter at this stage. A child's life is at stake; indeed, far more than that. I hope to make her transition as painless as possible."

"Now a threat?"

"Not a threat, a hope. Don't read into what I say."

"OK. I'll play along for awhile. Why should she go with you?"

"Because she is a sorceress. Without Second World training and supervision, her powers will grow in ways harmful to you, others around her, and herself. The outcome will be something no loving parents would want for their child."

The mood instantly changed.

"Well, is that all," John said snidely. "In that case, I can quit my job and have Alexandra conjure up the money it takes to support this household, the servants who run it, Alexandra's private education, and all the rest of it."

"You're not listening, John."

She used his first name deliberately, hoping to establish the next stage of rapport.

John swiveled his chair toward the window, turning his back to Elizabeth and Mary.

"Do tell us more, Ms. Shaw. Tell us how to raise a 'sorceress.' Or is it more proper to call her a 'witch.'"

"Call her a witch if you like," Elizabeth replied, "but to be accurate, you will have to shed the common notions of a witch. Alexandra is not a wicked witch. *Witch* is merely a label, one that means many things to many people. It will do for the moment."

John turned back to her.

"Well, that's a relief. I was beginning to think she might be a bad witch. Now that I know she is a good witch, I won't have to confiscate her broom."

Elizabeth walked up to the front of the desk. She folded her arms.

"This may seem to you the appropriate time and place to exercise your charming wit, Mr. Ward, but I assure you I am not here to provide entertainment. I have a deep concern for Alexandra's welfare, and so, I submit, should you. Alexandra has great gifts, but unbridled they can become a curse, on her and everyone close to her."

"See here, Ms. Shaw, we love Alexandra. She would never hurt anyone and we would never hurt her."

"You hurt her right now with your unbelief, your denial of the obvious."

John stared defiantly at Elizabeth. She was not the least intimidated.

"Your daughter knows she is different, but she does not know the extent of her difference.

"This is absurd!" John roared.

"Not so," Elizabeth interjected sharply.

She was not heard. She was talking into a whirlwind.

"Listen to me, John!" she commanded as her hand moved in an odd pattern. The pattern silenced the man.

"I know Alexandra in ways you are incapable of knowing her."

"Why should we believe this drivel?" John said.

"Because I live your daughter's life. I too am a witch, as was Alexandra's mother before her, and it is time for your daughter to know who and what she is and where she came from. Her safety requires it. Her development as a human being requires it."

Elizabeth returned to the couch and seated herself.

Mary shook her head.

"I bring a message you cannot bear," Elizabeth continued. "I understand how difficult this must be for you. What you loved or feared as children, and left comfortably behind as adults, is real. A world of witchcraft and wizardry is real, and nearer than you think, if you think of it at all. Much of what you have walled off in fairytales, fantasies, and your dreams is real. You could have finished out your lives without ever confronting this. You would have been content and you would have grown old and you would have died...untroubled by your ignorance. But you adopted a daughter, a very special girl born to a powerful sorceress. The gifts and powers she was born with are just beginning to be unleashed. This is a fact, and you must face it."

This time there was no interruption. Elizabeth had their attention, if not their belief.

Belief is more difficult, Elizabeth thought. *It makes things easier, but it is not essential here. I will do what must be done whether these people believe it or not.*

Elizabeth stared at the floor. She had withheld the most important part of her message, and she found herself strangely uncertain how to go on.

These are people of First World. To them, their world is the only world. It is an unquestioned certainty to them. How do I open a crack in that certainty? How do I lead them to accept that their fantasies are reality, just in a different place and a different way? It will be like asking them to believe up is down and down is up.

But there could be no turning back. War was imminent. Alexandra was the probable successor. Daniel was an unknown, a potentially destructive wildcard that had to be eliminated one way or another, and John and Mary would soon be without a daughter.

Elizabeth broke the silence with a long, weary sigh.

"There is more," she said.

17   The Unexpected Wizard

Was the blood of Alexandra's father a weakness or a strength in her genetic endowment? Would she be a bridge uniting the Two Worlds, or a chain binding the destruction of one world to the destruction of the other? We did not know the answers to these questions. What we were doing had not been tried before. We only knew the attempt was necessary.

ELIZABETH SHAW FROM "COMMENTARIES ON GOVERNANCE" BY MASTER BRADYN ARISTARCHUS

Elizabeth sat quite still, her gaze shifting from Mary to John until finally she said again, "There is more."

"Yes. Go on then." The bravado in John's voice was false.

"Daniel," Elizabeth said. "He is like Alexandra, gifted in her way. I saw it in the memories of your daughter. There is other evidence. I'm afraid there is no doubt. I do not reach this conclusion lightly, and I do not like it. You are right to see Daniel as a problem."

This is too much, John thought, *too much!*

He stood abruptly, his face twisted in an angry scowl as he leaned forward and planted his large fists on the polished surface of his desk.

"I told you Mary!" he bellowed. "From the beginning, I knew it. That boy has made her...this, this, whatever she is!"

Hmmm...their animas for Daniel lets them begin to believe in the special nature of their daughter. This might be useful.

"No," Elizabeth corrected calmly, "you misunderstand.

Wizardry and witchcraft are not infectious diseases. You cannot 'catch' them like a cold or be driven into them by the influence of another. Neither can they be learned. Alexandra and Daniel's gifts are written into their genetic code, and to whom much is given, from whom much is required."

"Poppycock!" roared John. "This boy...this...boy caused this. I want him gone! He is never to set foot in this house again! Mrs. Sutton and her son shall leave, NOW, TONIGHT!"

As though his words had been a command, the double doors of the office swung inward, and Alexandra entered. She held her pet parakeet in her right hand. She glared at her father as a memory of her eighth birthday party formed in her mind. She was there, in the moments just before the horror began, just before her anger brought magical destruction to everything around her.

Do not do this, Alexandra.

The inner voice was stern. It was Elizabeth. Alexandra turned to the woman, and the inner voice spoke again:

Do not do this. We are in a process. Flow with it, like a river, but stay within the banks. I am with you.

Alexandra surmounted her dangerous emotions, and observed them as one might observe the wake of a ship from the vessel's stern rail. Elizabeth was her ally: An adult who understood had found her at last.

"I heard," Alexandra said calmly. "All of it. If Daniel goes, I go, Father."

"Ignore this woman's rubbish," growled her father. "She lies!"

Alexandra lowered her head and went on, almost in a whisper:

"I'm adopted? Why didn't you tell me? I have powers like my real mother? I knew there was something strange about me. All this time, whenever I wanted something or was very upset, things would happen."

Mary extended her arms and took a step toward Alexandra. Alexandra raised her hand in a twisting gesture, like Elizabeth had a few moments earlier: less elegant, more awkward, but just as effective.

Mary halted as though she had come up against a physical barrier.

Alexandra turned to Elizabeth.

"Who is my mother?"

"Your mother is Katherine Shaw. She was a great woman and sorceress. You look very much like her."

"What do you mean, *she was*?"

"Your mother is dead."

A lump formed in Alexandra's throat.

"What about my father?" she asked.

"He's alive. His name is Nathan Grear."

"Can I meet him?"

"Not yet, but eventually."

"My powers...can I change?"

It was more a plea than a question.

"That's enough!" John said menacingly. His eyes radiated fury.

"You come into my home, speak dangerous foolishness, and make my daughter out to be a freak. Enough of this. Get out!"

Elizabeth stood and calmly fixed her gaze on John. The blue of her eyes pulsed into greater brilliance, as though powering up from an energy source deep within her. She fixed him in place, like a beetle mounted on velvet in a museum case. He could not speak; he could not move a muscle.

"Alexandra must take her leave of you, of this house, and

of this world; she must come away with me into another world. Only there can she grow into who she is. Only there can her humanity be preserved. She must be trained. She must fulfill her destiny."

Mary hastened to her daughter's side, put her arm around Alexandra's shoulders, and looked defiantly at Elizabeth.

"Alexandra's our daughter by law. You have no right to her. She can stop doing...whatever it is she is doing. Like a bad habit, it can be broken."

"Not without breaking her," Elizabeth replied.

Softening a little, Mary said, "We can help her turn away from this. She is our daughter, a member of our family. You're just...you're nobody to her."

"No," Elizabeth said, "that is not quite right. I am someone of great importance to her, but I do not expect you to understand."

Mary tightened her grip on Alexandra.

Elizabeth went on:

"I will take her to my home and there I will teach and guide her so she can use her powers for good, and not be overwhelmed by them. If you could fully understand the forces at work here, you would want this for her."

"Enough," John thundered. "Alexandra is ours and she will be going nowhere with you."

"Ouch!" Alexandra exclaimed as she abruptly dropped her parakeet and pulled away from her mother.

The blue and green bird fluttered his wings and settled to the floor.

"He bit me," Alexandra said, sucking her thumb. "He never does that!"

Elizabeth smiled enigmatically.

It is time for some visual aids, she thought. *Where seriousness fails, farce may prevail.*

The parakeet began preening himself, quite unaware Hera, the cat, who was a surpassing opportunist. Hera had been assessing her opportunities, and had decided it could not get better than this. She dashed silently through the open office doors.

Alexandra reached down for Domingo as Hera catapulted into the air.

In a single sweeping gesture, Elizabeth withdrew her wand and leveled it at the hurtling cat.

"Mutandis!"

The two animals collided in a golden glow. Where before there had been a cat, now there was a bird; where before there had been a bird, now there was a cat.

Hera and Domingo did ridiculous imitations of each other in the ensuing comedic footrace. Hera's new bird legs moved in wild oscillations that produced little forward motion. Domingo's new cat legs interacted as though each had a mind of its own. He stumbled, fell, pushed himself up, walked sideways, got himself straightened out and bore down on Hera.

Elizabeth casually tracked the bedlam with her wand.

"Mutandis!"

Hera and Domingo were restored instantly to their own bodies. Alexandra scooped up Domingo, while Hera fled.

"Thank you," Alexandra said casually, as she stroked Domingo's head.

"You're welcome," replied Elizabeth just as casually.

John and Mary stared at Elizabeth.

"Well, then," Elizabeth said as though nothing unusual had taken place, "I will leave you to consider all you have heard and seen, and I will return tomorrow to make arrangements for Alexandra's departure. I trust you will place her welfare above all other considerations. I will not be taking her *from* you; I will be taking her *for* you, and for her."

Elizabeth smiled cordially at John and Mary, winked at Alexandra, flicked her wand, and vanished.

18   Banishment

Desperation finds openings, makes a path for escaping the inescapable, for conquering the unconquerable.

FROM "EXODUS AND EXILE" BY DAVID SUTTON

"You should have told me," Alexandra said to no one in particular.

"We didn't know about that awful woman until today," Mary said.

"That's not what I meant. You should have told me I was adopted. And Elizabeth doesn't seem awful to me. She is like me, like Daniel. We aren't awful."

"Dear child, I didn't mean..."

"You never mean anything, mother; you just smooth things over."

"Don't you speak to your mother that way," John ordered.

"My mother? My mother is dead. And my father is...somewhere, part of your big secret."

"Not just ours, young lady, and not because we don't love you," John said. "It was part of the arrangement."

"Exactly. My life, it turns out, is one big 'arrangement.' I just think it would have been nice for me to be in on the 'arrangement,' it being my life and all."

"You don't understand," John said, taking on a more conciliatory tone. "It was for your own good. Mr. Sutton insisted."

"And you insisted, Father. I know you. Nothing is done

without your insistence. You would not want people to know you couldn't have children of your own..."

"That is quite enough, Alexandra!"

"No, Father, it is not nearly enough. Does Daniel know?"

"He knows nothing, and that is the way it will stay. You are to tell him nothing. Do you understand? Nothing."

An enigmatic smile smoothed across Alexandra's face.

"He already knows."

"How?"

"You wouldn't understand."

"I think I understand perfectly. This magical thinking has to stop, Alexandra. You are too old for it. The Shaw woman is a fraud, misleading you, seeking to mislead all of us to take you from us. For all I know she is in the employ of this Nathan Grear."

"The Nathan Grear who is my *real* father?" Alexandra asked in a tone dripping with irony.

"I am your father," John roared. "Everything we did was for your good. Even the woman who just did her disappearing act said she wanted the arrangement. It was not a lie, not a secret; it was something...not disclosed."

"Fancy words; same thing. It was a secret you kept from me."

"Call it what you will, young lady, but our intentions were noble.

Mary stood slowly, as though awakening from sleep.

"Can we be done with this?" she asked wearily.

"Yes," John replied without hesitation. "We will take this up again in the morning. Mary, see Alexandra to her room and then send Mrs. Sutton and Daniel to me. Get them out of bed if necessary. And Alexandra, you are to remain in your room. Is that clear?"

Mary stared at her husband.

"Don't do this, Father," Alexandra said. "Don't punish others for mistakes you've made."

"Mary! Go! Bring the Suttons to me."

Alexandra faced her mother:

"This is so wrong. You know it is!"

For a fleeting moment, Mary's expression was a reflection of her daughter's pain. The moment past and she donned the bland, lifeless mask she hid behind on occasions like this.

"We must do as your father says." Mary's voice was as empty as her expression.

Alexandra turned back to her father.

"If you do this, I will go with them," she said.

"You're not going anywhere," John snarled, "except to your room. You don't decide how things will be; I do."

Alexandra clinched her fists and stomped out of the office. She bounded up the stairs to the second floor of the mansion, ran into her bedroom, slammed the door as hard as she could, and began pacing back and forth at the foot of her bed.

"How can they do this?" she asked out loud. "I hate them!"

She held her arms tight against her sides and began to sway back and forth like a wooden puppet dangling from the hands of a drunken puppeteer. She walked to the head of her bed and gripped the thick wooden bedpost. She pulled, pushed, tore at it side-to-side, forward-and-back.

With a resounding crack, the thick bedpost broke off at its base. Alexandra staggered backward, regained her balance, and peered in wonder at the stout piece of wood in her hand. She flung it to the floor as a wave of sadness displaced her anger. Tears welled up in her eyes. She threw herself onto her bed and wept. Minutes passed and

Alexandra's sobs faded into soft murmurs. She listened. At first there was only silence. Then she heard voices sounding distraught and angry chords.

"Can't I just say goodbye?" demanded one of the voices. It was Daniel.

Her father's voice thundered in reply:

"You have caused enough trouble! No more. Go!"

Alexandra pushed herself up from the bed, ran to her door, and opened it. She peered to her left, down the long corridor that led to the head of the stairs overlooking the entry hall. Her father, Ellen, and Daniel stood there. Ellen and Daniel were carrying luggage.

"I will send the rest later," John said, then led them down the stairs.

Alexandra dashed after them.

The corridor had never seemed so long. She arrived at the railing overlooking the entrance hall and saw her father standing stiffly at the front door, holding it open. Ellen was just outside the door, standing in the blowing snow. Daniel was dragging a large trunk over the threshold. Snow was blowing into the entry hall.

"No!" Alexandra exclaimed.

Daniel looked up at his lifelong friend. His face was streaked with tears. He halted and stood upright.

"Goodbye, Alexandra."

Daniel paused and then added, "I will not forget."

"Keep moving," John said, advancing menacingly toward Daniel. Daniel glared at Alexandra's father and made a subtle gesture.

John halted, knowing what to fear.

Daniel looked up once more at Alexandra, gave a little wave, and dragged the trunk out into the night. John stepped forward, slammed the door closed, and turned the dead bolt.

Alexandra began a strange keening. The sound rose up and became a primordial howl, like a wolf calling into the night. She seemed to fly down the stairs, hurtled herself at her father, and pummeled his chest with her fists. Garbled words poured out between uncontrollable sobs.

John pulled her close and encircled her with his strong arms. Alexandra slowly ceased to struggle.

John felt stirrings of compassion.

"There, there, my dear. Calm yourself. Daniel will be fine, and so will you. Your mother and I have been putting off this day because we love you. But this nonsense with Elizabeth was too much. She is a dangerous trickster. But even she saw the problem with Daniel; even she saw the harm in your relationship. You heard her. It had to end. We are doing this for your own good."

Alexandra hurled the parental refrain back at him.

"*For my own good! For my own good!* You think you are better than everyone. Only because I'm your daughter do you think the same of me. You don't know me and you don't know Daniel. And you aren't my father."

It was the most hurtful thing she could think to say, and she relished its effect on him.

If Daniel goes, I go, she reminded herself.

Daniel had gone.

Now it was her turn.

Alexandra calculated the distance, took a last look at her father, and sprinted for the front door. In a single fluid motion, she turned the lock, took hold of the brass handle, and jerked the door open. A gust of blowing snow billowed into the entrance hall. Alexandra heard a choked cry and looked back. Her mother was looking down on her from the upper landing, her arms outstretched in an awkward gesture that was both pleading and grasping.

Her father lunged at her.

Alexandra darted through the doorway, ran down the snow-covered driveway, and spied the taillights of a car disappearing into the bitter January storm. She looked back. She could not see her father through the blowing snow, but she could hear his footfalls. He was running toward her. Suddenly, out of nowhere, a gloved hand roughly grasped her shoulder. It was Henry Lusk, the Wards' butler.

"I have her!"

Before John could answer, Alexandra jerked free and ran through the line of trees south of the mansion. She raced through the forest undergrowth. The storm and the night obscured all in her path, rendering objects in vague, semi-opaque lights and darks, nothing clear, nothing distinct. Thin branches of sapling pines whipped across her body. She stumbled forward over a fallen oak tree, regained her footing, and continued her flight. Thirty meters later her shoulder collided with the rough bark of an Eastern White Pine and she nearly fell. She could hear the crashing sounds of her pursuers.

"Alexandra, stop. Come back!"

It was her father's voice, barely audible over the wind. Alexandra lurched to her left, away from the sound. She knew she would probably not find Daniel, but at this moment she did not care.

If he goes, I go.

Alexandra heard the two men yelling back and forth. Their voices became increasingly distant until finally she heard nothing but her uneven footfalls and increasingly heavy breathing.

She ran for a long time, turning this way and that to confuse her pursuers. The icy air began attacking her lungs. Exhaustion overtook her as well: a primordial tiredness of muscle, limb, and lung.

A fallen sycamore blocked her path on a short descent into a gully. She saw it too late, tripped, stumbled, and fell headlong into the ice-hardened earth. A jolt of pain shot through her right knee. She saw her jeans had been ripped and her thigh just above the knee lacerated by a jagged branch. Something black in the night seeped through the fabric and became a broadening pattern. She was bleeding heavily. She rolled over in the snow and curled up in pain. The wet snow began seeping through her clothing. She pulled her knee against her chest and rocked back and forth in time with the throbbing pain.

She began chastising herself:

Chasing after a distant car in the middle of the night! Probably wasn't even them. Definitely not one of my smarter moves!

Alexandra struggled to her feet and took a few trial steps on her injured leg. She limped from the pain, but she could walk, and she knew with sudden clarity she could not stay where she was, exposed to the bitter cold. She moved forward with awkward steps, taking the direction she thought would lead to the nearest road.

A half hour, maybe an hour went by. Maybe. She was losing her sense of time. No road appeared. The night and the snow and the cold became her universe. Mild shivering was replaced by violent shaking. Still she pressed on, feeling as though she was moving in slow motion. Soon after the shaking stopped she felt a mild euphoria. She no longer felt cold.

I am just so tired, she thought. *I need to go home. Maybe in the morning Father will change his mind. Daniel and Ellen will come back. I know mother...mother...which way is home? It's hard to think...hard to picture things.*

Alexandra stopped. The wind gusted intermittently. Snow and tiny crystals of ice danced before her tired eyes.

So beautiful, she thought. *I will follow the footprints in the snow...everyone needs footprints to follow. Footprints...people make footprints...*

Alexandra reversed her course and began following the footprints she had made in coming. In ten steps, her old footprints were mere depressions, filled in with the blowing snow. In fifteen steps the footprints were gone: There was only trackless snow.

So beautiful, so smooth...the snow, she mused.

Alexandra sank down onto the smooth snow and leaned against the trunk of an ancient eastern white pine. Leafless scrub oaks surrounded her, guarded her. Panic had faded, replaced by a peaceful sleepiness.

I feel warm...tired. Maybe warm. Maybe a little warm. I will just rest here for awhile. Maybe sleep. I could crawl under the bushes, curl up there. Just sleep a little. Warm...

Alexandra did not know her body temperature had dropped below ninety degrees Fahrenheit.

Alexandra did not know she was dying.

19   *Desperation*

Not all efforts are inspired. Some are just grunting after what has already been lost.

FROM "UNCERTAIN JOURNEY" BY JOSHUA TURNER

I lost her, Mr. Ward. She just pulled away."
John ran past Henry.

"Follow me. Now!"

The two men plunged into the dark woods.

The moon gave some light, but not enough to penetrate the thick curtain of falling snow. Anything beyond a few meters was invisible.

John called out to Alexandra again and again. The only response he received was the sighing of the wind in the trees.

Henry had fallen behind. His labored breathing became louder as he caught up. John waited. The butler doubled over and struggled to catch his breath when he arrived.

"Sir,...we should...go back...call...the police," he said between ragged breaths.

John seemed not to hear. He set off again, and Henry labored to follow.

Intense cold hung over the woods, wove itself through the leaves and branches and needles of pine. It was a silent menace that began to penetrate John's awareness. The dense undergrowth slowed his pace. The cold reached into him. He flexed his fingers, slapped his hands together, and was alarmed at how little sensation he felt.

This will kill her.

The thought stopped him. He listened. He strained to hear his daughter's voice or the sounds of her flight. If he could just hear her, he could touch her. If he could touch her, he could save her.

An icy wind, deadly partner to the cold, penetrated his thin shirt and stung his face. He continued on, veering left. A fallen limb caught his foot. He fell, stood up, took three more steps, and fell again.

This is insanity, he thought, pushing himself up from a low snow bank. *I don't even know where I'm going. I must get help.*

Henry caught up again.

"We must go, sir; g-g-go back, call the p-p-police," Henry said, his teeth chattering.

John nodded his assent.

"Look!" Henry exclaimed.

A globe of light flickered beyond the swaying tree limbs. John began to jog toward it, his butler once again in labored pursuit. Soon they broke out of the woods and halted under a streetlamp. It illuminated a wide depression in the virgin snow, a road. Nothing could be seen in either direction. The falling snow formed a halo around the streetlamp and made Henry's silver hair, now heavily flaked with snow, appear white.

John collapsed onto his knees and covered his face with his hands. Henry watched helplessly as his employer's body began to jerk with uncontrollable sobs.

"Mr. Ward," Henry said, touching John's shoulder, "We must g-g-go back."

Henry helped John to stand.

The men walked together along the road. Henry was the first to see the street sign. He stepped up to it and swept it clear of snow. "Jade Street," it said. They knew where they were, and they jogged toward home as fast as their remaining strength allowed.

20   The Purloined Parchment

Let go. You cannot un-ring the bell. What harm you have done, what good you have done cannot be un-done. Move on. Let the sound of your bell merge with the sounds of countless other bells that cannot be un-rung across the world. Listen. Hear the symphony. Play your part in it. Laugh when you laugh; weep when you weep. Play on.

FROM "PATHS TO SAINTHOOD" BY DOM ANDRÉ DU BOURGAY

Candra described what had happened at the Ward mansion.

"You had means for finding her the Wards didn't have," Elizabeth fumed. "Why did you not use them?"

"My powers were useless in the storm's molecular chaos, but I didn't stop there. I searched on foot to no avail. Visibility was nearly zero, and the wind-driven snow obliterated all evidence of the course Alexandra took. I returned to see if we might do something more effective together."

Elizabeth shook her head and chastised herself:

I'm sure Candra did her best. I should have assigned this to Borrington. But would that have made a difference? Probably not.

Elizabeth stood.

"With me, Candra."

Elizabeth murmured through gritted teeth the incantation that took them instantly from Byrnhelen to the forest hiding Alexandra. It was as Candra had reported. Wind, snow, and cold swirled in random chaos around them. The storm's violent combination of primal earth forces formed a static through which no psychic communication was possible.

Alexandra lies dying, perhaps within a hundred meters of me, and I can do nothing to save her, Elizabeth lamented.

She saw the flashing red and blue lights of emergency vehicles in front of the Ward mansion. Men moved like ghosts among the lights, their features obscured by the blowing snow.

Maybe they have some First World technical magic that can work here, Elizabeth thought. *I can do no more. I must go back, put Borrington on this.*

Moments later she and her assistant were back in her office at Byrnhelen. She placed a hand on Candra's shoulder and spoke kindly to her:

"Assemble the Dyrisians, counsel with them, and report back to me. I will contact General Borrington."

Candra nodded stoically and departed.

Elizabeth sat behind her desk. She dipped the tip of her feather pen into the silver ink cup, shook off the clinging bead of black ink, and scratched out her letter to Borrington. Her expression was grim. She wrote with urgency, the feather twitching and twisting as she scratched out her message. A thick candle cast erratic shadows on the parchment as Elizabeth's hand moved back and forth over it.

> My Dearest Andrew:
>
> There is little doubt Alexandra Ward is the heir. After all these years of observing her, I have managed to contact her and lose her, all in a day. She has fled into the forest south of her home. A winter storm rages there, and it will surely kill her if we do not take swift action. My foolish negligence has placed her in peril. I should have involved

you earlier, made more extensive preparations for this or any eventuality. I am powerless against the storm; my thoughts cannot penetrate it. I have considered Nara, but there is no time, and no guarantee she would be willing to manipulate conditions. So, as always, I turn to you. Find her. Save her. And bring her to us.

Yours,

Elizabeth

Elizabeth rolled up the parchment, opened the wide center drawer of her desk, and took out a short black ribbon. After tying the ribbon tightly around the letter, she picked up her feather pen, dipped it twice in the ink cup, and scrawled "A. Borrington" in large letters on the side of the tube. She summoned the elf, Gidram Hinbanterfeld, and thrust the rolled parchment into his hand.

"Send it," she ordered.

Gidram nodded, crossed the room, and took up a formal stance in front of the empty fireplace. He thrust his arms forward in a rolling motion and the fireplace filled with amethyst colored flames. Gidram threw the scroll into the conflagration. There was a flash of white within the blaze just before the fire winked out.

"It is done mistress," Gidram said, bowing deeply.

A man hiding on the roof above Elizabeth's office heard Gidram's words. He rose, placed a black and red net over the chimney, and captured the rising ashes of Elizabeth's letter. He twisted the net, tapped the ashes with the tip of his wand, and hissed, "Seravillo!" The ashes stirred, coalesced, and knitted themselves together to form the scroll Gidram had sent into the flames.

The man unrolled the scroll.

"Hmmmm, this is a fine thing," he whispered to himself.

"No, General Borrington, you will not be the hero today. My master has a quite different plan."

The man rolled up the scroll and tucked it into a pocket inside his gray cloak. Then, with a barely perceptible gesture of his left hand, he was gone.

21   The Search

Human eyes complain, never satisfied with the light as it is. The eyes of the owls are wiser than human eyes. Owl eyes open at dusk and close at dawn. They do not complain.

FROM "ANIMAL TEACHERS" BY MASTER GREGORY TRAVITS

The police arrived minutes after they were called. Two officers in separate blue-and-white patrol cars were first. They made a perfunctory effort to stamp the snow off their black leather boots before entering the home. John escorted them into his office.

"She ran away," John said. "My butler got hold of her but she broke loose and ran into the trees. We chased her but she was too far ahead and we couldn't see."

"Description?" asked one of the officers.

John gave a description: height, weight, hair color, clothing. He hated talking of his daughter as a collection of descriptors.

"How long ago?"

John calculated and gave an estimate.

"My wife witnessed the whole thing," he added. "She might know the time better."

"Not necessary," said the officer. He leaned his head into the radio microphone at his shoulder and broadcast the basic facts of Alexandra's disappearance. He spoke in terse coded sentences and received squawked replies, just as terse. His broadcast complete, the officer left the office.

The other officer listened patiently as John rambled on

about what had led to Alexandra's running away and how this had never happened before and how something had to be done and done now. The officer nodded, listened politely, made notes, and asked a few questions.

John felt mounting panic.

"Are you just going to stand there and make notes? Do something! Do something now!" he demanded.

The officer looked up from his notebook and gazed steadily into John's eyes.

"We are doing something, Mr. Ward. You can be assured of that. Please, why don't you take a seat. I know how hard this must be for you."

"I will not sit. Don't tell me what to do in my own home. You should be out there searching, not standing there telling me what to do."

As though on cue, the white double doors of the office swung open, and another officer walked into the room. He was tall and lean. He appeared to be in his late forties with gray, almost white hair cropped short, military fashion. He had the face of an outdoorsman: lined and ruddy, and he wore a heavy, thigh-length Gore-Tex parka, which he removed as soon as he entered the room. His uniform combined navy blue pants with a gray shirt, both neatly pressed. On his collars were bright gold lieutenant bars. The lieutenant motioned the other officer out of the room with a sideways movement of his head. Then he addressed John:

"I am pleased to meet you, Mr. Ward. I am Lieutenant Tanner, Stanley Tanner, watch commander and now incident commander until we find your daughter. Please know I share most deeply your concern for your daughter. The weather makes the situation serious and quite difficult. I would like to use this office as a command post. Do you have any objection?"

John knew businessmen and politicians who had considerable presence, but Tanner was different. The man seemed to fill the room. He exuded command presence. John would have bristled at this under other circumstances, but in the present situation he was relieved. This was a man who got things done, and more than anything else, John wanted things to get done.

"Certainly, lieutenant. The office is yours."

"Thank you, sir. Please look out the window. I want you to get a sense of how seriously we are taking this matter."

John moved to the window.

The scene was surreal. Police, fire, and search and rescue vehicles clogged the driveway and were parked along the street. Other vehicles were arriving, their red and blue lights blinking, tapping out a visual code of urgency. The snow dulled the sound of the men and equipment gathering in front of John's house. Other things quieted the usual noise associated with staging emergency assets: the time of night, the severity of the storm, the cold, the operational necessity to listen for the faint cries of a young girl in desperate need. Men stood in small groups and a few, carrying things in their hands, moved between groups. More were arriving. Four men were huddled together near where Alexandra had entered the forest. Beside two of them sat German Shepherds on leash. Beside the third sat a Belgian Malinois. The fourth man was taking what appeared to be an article of clothing from dog to dog. The dogs, each in turn, nuzzled the article.

John turned back to the lieutenant as other officers, carrying metal briefcases and cardboard boxes, entered the office and began removing papers and other items from John's desk and setting them on a nearby bookshelf. John allowed the lieutenant to lead him into the hall outside his office. Tanner looked at John with genuine concern.

"Thank you for your cooperation, Mr. Ward. We will take it from here," he said. "Your wife supplied us with some of your daughter's clothing and told us something of what led up to this. K-9 units are joining the search. A grid search is already underway, but it was organized on the fly. I will fix that in a moment. We will do all we can to find your daughter."

John heard the reassurance but was not entirely comforted by it. He was accustomed to being in control: of himself, of others, of deals and negotiations, of the many pathways to money. Now, under the gaze of this man he felt utterly powerless. It all rested now with this stranger, this civil servant, this man whom he had neither vetted, nor chosen.

"How can I help?" John asked.

"You can help by working with your wife on making a list of all your daughter's friends, family, teachers, and acquaintances—anyone she might have contacted or who might know where she would go. Call them all. I will assign some people to assist you. Also, search your house thoroughly. I will have someone with experience in these things accompany you. Young people who appear to have run away are often found hiding in or near the home. But in this case—at night, snow falling, temperatures dropping— we are making no assumptions. We must do everything at once, not one thing after another. Do you understand?"

"Yes."

"One more thing. As I'm sure you're aware, in cases like this we must look at all the possibilities."

John nodded, not sure where this was going.

"Some of my people will be asking questions that do not bear on the search but on what led up to your daughter's running away. We must ask these questions. It is both routine and necessary."

"See here!" John said. "You don't suspect me or members of this household..."

Tanner held up a hand.

"I suspect nothing, Mr. Ward, but I have to look at everything. None of this will in the least diminish our search efforts. I simply wanted to prepare you. Nothing we have heard or seen so far indicates foul play, but we must make reasonable inquiries. Surely you understand?"

John folded his arms and stared at the floor.

"Mr. Ward?" Tanner pressed.

"I understand," John replied. "Do what you have to do."

The lieutenant nodded and re-entered John's office, closing the doors behind him.

John felt a gentle hand on his shoulder. He turned and looked into the face of the young officer whom he had chastised earlier for doing "nothing."

"Let's get to work," the officer said gently, as though the earlier unpleasantness had never occurred. John nodded. "Your wife is waiting in the kitchen with some of your neighbors. Bring your cell phone. We have some calls to make."

John remembered something, a pixel out of the larger image of the man, Tanner. When the lieutenant had stretched his arm down to lay his coat on the couch, his shirt sleeve had pulled up and a tattoo had been revealed, just above the wrist. It was the eagle, ball, and anchor of the United States Marine Corps. Below it was the motto: *Semper Fi.*

A bird, surrounded by air, knows not air; a fish, surrounded by water, knows not water; essence surrounded by essence knows not itself.

NARA

Thoughts of John and Mary, of home, and of all else she had known crept into Alexandra's consciousness. She lay on her side, felt the snow against her cheek, and marveled at how warm she had become.

"I love you," she whispered into the wet snow touching her lips. She thought of all the people she had known. John and Mary had been so good to her, father and mother, but not wholly that. She thought of her birth parents, tried to imagine their faces. A wave of sadness passed over her.

I cannot see their faces. I never knew them. I want to know them.

She thought of Daniel, Ellen, and Elizabeth. They were neatly lined up in her mind. She imagined Elizabeth was speaking to her, but she could not make out the words. She willingly descended into the frozen slumber that beckoned her and let her thoughts drift away. When all but the last few drops of her life force had drained from her, two arms reached through the veil of the surrounding dark and lifted her up.

***

Alexandra struggled to awaken, but she was trapped. A dream held her. She was in a dark forest. She heard the howling of wolves or dogs and the shouting of men. She tried again to move, but was confined by a tangle of images: people she knew, people she did not know, events past, delights, horrors. Gentle hands reached through the tangle and caressed her. Alexandra willed her body to move, but her muscles were not her own. Her eyelids fluttered as she tried to open them.

"I think she's awake,"

It was a girl's voice, friendly. Alexandra tried to see who it was, but her eyes would not focus.

"Hello. Can you hear me?"

This was another voice, soft and very close, a boy's voice:

"My name is Euwen."

Alexandra managed a whisper, "Wherese am shy?"

"You're safe," Euwen said, translating Alexandra's slurred question.

Alexandra tried vainly to respond, but her dream rose up and led her back into the darkness from whence she had come.

23   Moving On

The police and the search-and-rescue team worked unceasingly through the night. Early in the search, the dogs followed with determination a circuitous route to a fallen sycamore deep in the forest. They alerted on dried blood there. They continued on, ranging back and forth until they reached a stand of scrub oak next to an eastern white pine. There the trail ended. The handlers urged the dogs on, but the animals always returned to the sycamore, resolute in their findings. Alexandra had come here leaving a powerful scent trail; she had left leaving none.

Skeptics doubted the dogs. The three K-9 officers could not explain why the dogs could find no scent leading away from the place, but they were unified in their conviction that Alexandra had come here from the house. The handlers were experienced, and the dogs well trained. The three K-9 teams had proved themselves in many prior searches. The results of this search were a mystery.

The snow had erased all footprints, and no artifact belonging to the lost child was found. A rough stone archway, high and wide enough for a man to pass through, stood near the sycamore. There were no signs that a fence or wall had ever been linked to the archway. The archway was examined for clues. None were found.

By morning, hope of finding Alexandra alive had

declined sharply. Temperatures overnight had dropped to thirty below, and the forest offered no cover, no place to curl up, conserve body heat, and survive. Dressed as she had been, the girl had no chance, although no one mentioned this to the Wards.

The forest search continued throughout the following day, but by the end of that day, it had become, for the professionals, a search for a body, not for Alexandra. Serious questions arose: Why no body? Why no word of Alexandra appearing elsewhere? It was these questions, more than hope of finding the child, that drove the search through the next night.

The media was an additional presence by now, driving its own narrative of what might have happened. The family's and the searchers' grasp on hope was further weakened when extensive media coverage produced no leads. It was not for want of publicity, commitment, and sound leadership that Alexandra was not found; it was because she was simply not there.

John had an arm around Mary when Tanner approached them at the end of the second day. He looked tired.

"I am shutting down the command post," he said.

"You're not giving up!" Mary exclaimed.

"No, absolutely not. In fact, we are expanding our operations. But for that we require the command, control, and communications capabilities at our headquarters. We will manage the search from there."

Tanner paused. He looked thoughtfully at the Wards.

"Not all of this is bad news," he said. "We did not find Alexandra. Two days and two nights we have been at it. If your daughter were anywhere nearby, we would have found her. I wish we had. But we also did not find her body. That's a good thing. I've added investigative resources to our search for her. You continue your efforts to reach anyone you know who might have information. Together I am confident we will come up with something."

The Wards stared blankly at him.

Lieutenant Stanly Tanner then did the unexpected. He walked up to the Wards, placed his arms around both of them and held them close.

"Bless you," he whispered. "I won't give up on this. Don't you give up. You hear me? Don't give up, and neither will I."

Tanner stepped back.

"Don't give up," he said again. It was almost a command. "Here is my card. I have written my direct line on it. Please don't give the number to anyone. Call me if you learn anything, anything at all. Small pieces of information can add up. You will do this?"

"Yes, yes of course, Lieutenant. Thank you," John replied, his voice choked with emotion.

Tanner stepped back in a way that seemed oddly formal.

"Always faithful," he said, and John remembered the tattoo on Tanner's wrist. The search would go on; Alexandra would not be abandoned.

24 *Awakening*

I, Chuang Tzu, once dreamt I was a butterfly. Then I awoke and was Chuang Tzu again. Now I do not know the truth of it: Am I Chuang Tzu who dreamt he was a butterfly or am I a butterfly who dreams he is Chuang Tzu.

CHUANG TZU, FIRST WORLD PHILOSOPHER

Alexandra slept.

For two full days she slept.

In the late afternoon of the third day, she disentangled from her dream and awoke. She sat up in a bed and room she did not recognize. Memories began to take shape in her sleepy consciousness.

I went after Daniel. I ran and ran until I couldn't run any more. I hurt my knee. I was very cold. I lay down in the snow and then I was warm. It all stops there. I was warm. Why does it stop there?

Someone had dressed her in a white cotton nightgown. She felt a twinge of embarrassment.

"Hello, is anyone here?" she asked, pushing back the covers.

No one answered.

She took in the peacefulness of her surroundings. She felt like she was sitting on a cloud, so large and soft was her bed.

Someone named Euwen lives here, she thought, *or maybe I just dreamed that.*

She slid sideways and stood on the cool tiled floor. After a few steps she realized there was no pain in her right knee, the one she had injured. She pulled up her nightgown. There was no laceration, no scar, no evidence of injury.

Maybe I'm still dreaming.

But the bed was real, the cool tiles under her feet were real, the fire burning in the white fireplace in the far corner of the room was real, and it was giving off comforting warmth. Afternoon sunlight streamed through sheer white curtains. On the walls and the mantel of the fireplace were pictures of wildflowers and colorful landscapes. Facing the fireplace was an overstuffed damask armchair with a footstool. This was definitely not a dream.

On the other side of the room, beneath the curtained windows, was a white and yellow dressing table. On it rested a dark mahogany box. On its lid was etched a large ornate flower whose diamond stamen sparkled in the sunlight. Alexandra slid her fingers over the lacquered surface of the box, while her eyes took in the many strange dancing figures chiseled into its dark surface. There were twirling elves and galloping centaurs, dancing trolls, and many other strange creatures. The box reminded her of the music boxes at her grandmother's house. Those music boxes had heavy lids and concealed dancing figures that moved rhythmically to enchanting melodies.

Alexandra's attention turned to the rest of the room. It was spacious and simply decorated. She saw a door about ten meters to the left of the fireplace. She padded across the tile floor, opened the door, and peeked into a dim hallway. She counted six closed doors identical to hers, three on each side of the hallway.

Alexandra stepped cautiously into the hall. She closed her door and walked across the hall to the door opposite. Her bare feet made no sound. She placed her hand on the doorknob and was about to turn it when she heard a faint scratching at the end of the hallway, to her right. She pressed her back against the door and stilled her breathing. The scratching sound stopped and the hallway was silent.

This is stupid. I need to find out where I am.

With newfound boldness, Alexandra walked past the other doors and into the light at the end of the hallway. She descended a stairway that twisted down into another hallway, also with closed doors on either side. She followed this hallway to a large staircase that led down to a spacious hall. She stopped at the top of the staircase and leaned over the heavy iron railing.

This place is big enough to be a castle, she thought.

Two men stood directly beneath her in the doorway of a room adjoining the hall. They differed significantly in age and appearance. The older man was unusually tall and thin, with a gray, close-cropped beard and shoulder-length hair. He wore a long brown robe. The younger man wore a tunic over tight-fitting trousers. He was a bit taller than Alexandra and about her age.

Weird, she thought. *They look like actors in a medieval play. What is this place.*

The men spoke in low voices, but Alexandra could make out most of what they were saying. She made her breathing shallow and listened intently.

"Care for her," the man said. "The rest will fall into place."

"I understand, Sire," the youth replied, bowing his head.

The man backed out of sight into the adjoining room while the youth walked slowly into the hall. He approached the staircase below Alexandra, mounted the first step, and looked up. His gaze met Alexandra's.

"You're up," the youth said, smiling as he hastened up the stairs.

Alexandra saw he was handsome, with wavy black hair and green eyes. She became very aware her only garment was a thin cotton nightgown.

"Who are you?" she asked, "and where am I?"

"I'm Euwen McConnelly," the young man replied, "and you are a guest at my family's estate."

"I don't know you," Alexandra said.

Euwen stepped forward and extended his hand.

Alexandra hesitated, then took it, firmly. Euwen smiled at her without guile or flirtation. Alexandra relaxed. She was here, alive and in a warm place. The young man seemed friendly enough.

"Are you all right?" Euwen asked.

"I'm fine."

"And what is your name?"

"Alexandra, Alexandra Ward."

"I'm sure you have many questions, Alexandra Ward. Let's get something to eat and I'll answer as many as I can."

Euwen led her down the stairs, across the spacious hall, along a lengthy hallway, and finally into a large, unoccupied dining room. Euwen guided her to a table in a corner and pulled out a chair. She sat and he took a seat next to her.

So formal, so polite. I could get used to this, thought Alexandra with a smile.

A door opened and a creature of surpassing feminine beauty drifted into the room. The creature appeared human, but with facial features more refined and delicate than any human's. The creature wore a long diaphanous gown that swayed and shifted as she floated across the room. The creature radiated light, white with a hint of gold. Her long blond hair was pulled back into an elegant twist that shimmered as though reflecting sunlight. She hovered about a half meter above the floor.

Alexandra stared.

"Miss Ward and I would like some dinner," Euwen said.

The creature nodded and without uttering a word glided from the room.

"She is quite beautiful," Alexandra said. "But she didn't ask what we wanted. Do we get no choice?"

"She is Dyrisian, Anneliese of Wilacross. She will deliver your heart's desire," Euwen said with a hint of playfulness.

"You're teasing," Alexandra said.

"I guess I am, just a little. You must wonder about all this."

"Yes. It all seems so real, but everything is so old fashioned. Like your clothes, no offense. I can't help thinking I'm in a dream."

Euwen smiled and folded his arms.

"How do you think you got into this 'dream'?"

"I died, or thought I did, in the snow. It was so cold, and then it was warm, and I woke up here, or maybe I didn't wake up. Maybe I'll never wake up. Am I dead?"

"You don't need to worry about waking up. You've already done that. And you're not dead. You did come close to death. This is no dream, but you are in a very different place from the one where I found you. You are far from home in another world, very different from your own. You don't believe a word of this, do you?"

"Of course not," said Alexandra with a laugh. "So, really, where are we? I should call my parents. They must be worried, very worried. Did you say I have been asleep for two days?"

"Two days, yes, but calling your parents is a problem."

"You don't have a phone?"

"It's complicated," Euwen responded.

"Having a phone isn't complicated. Everybody has a

phone."

"Not everybody. Not here."

"Whatever. Am I free to go?"

"Yes, of course. But come, let me show you something."

Euwen led her out of the dining room to a tall window set in a thick stone wall. Alexandra looked down upon a darkening landscape that was completely unfamiliar. She was at least five stories above ground. She was definitely no longer in Simsbury or Connecticut or anywhere else she had ever been before. She touched the stone wall. It was cold. She ran her hand over its roughness. She slapped it.

Real, not a dream, she thought. *But it might as well be, for all the sense this is making.*

She and Euwen returned to the dining room, where a sumptuous feast had been laid out on their table. There were fresh strawberries; peaches; chunks of pineapple; bananas; a large assortment of warm dinner rolls; a variety of freshly grilled meats; mashed potatoes and brown gravy, rice, pasta, and a selection of hot drinks in ornate pewter goblets.

Euwen made a sweeping gesture over the food. "As I promised, your heart's desire or in this case your stomach's."

25 Questions and Confusion

Belief precedes knowing. Most in First World no longer believe in us. Thus we can walk among them unseen, unheard, unknown. This keeps the peace. It is a good arrangement. I step in when extraordinary arrangements must be made.

FROM "EXODUS AND EXILE" BY DAVID SUTTON

You're in Second World," Euwen said matter-of-factly. They had finished the main meal and were waiting for dessert.

"That makes things perfectly clear," Alexandra replied.

"You're being facetious."

"How perceptive of you."

Neither spoke for a minute or two.

"Let's try again," Euwen ventured.

"OK."

"You're on Earth."

"Uh huh. So, where on Earth am I? Get it? 'Where on Earth?' Forget it."

"You're in Second World," Euwen said, not in the least comprehending her effort at humor.

Alexandra glared at him.

Euwen laughed.

Alexandra softened her look just a little, and decided to listen with more seriousness.

"You were born and raised in First World," Euwen continued. "First World culture emphasizes technology. You came, or rather I brought you, to Second World. We favor magic over technology here."

Alexandra abandoned her effort to be serious.

"Excellent. I'm in a magical world. Please show me to the magic wardrobe and I'll find my own way home."

"It's not that easy.

"Why? This is a magical world. Do some magic. Walk me through a wall or something."

"I won't do anything like that right now and you can't go through the portal on your own, not yet anyway."

"Port hole, like on a ship? I wouldn't fit."

Euwen chuckled. He didn't know if this was more sarcasm or just misunderstanding.

"No, P-O-R-T-A-L," he said, "like a gateway or an entrance or exit. That's how you got here and that's the only way you can get back."

"Why can't I go through this P-O-R-T-A-L (she imitated his tone and cadence) on my own? Or do you have to beam me up?"

Euwen looked at her quizzically. "I don't understand."

"You know, *Star Trek*. Don't you have television here?"

"No. Nor do we have trains, planes, cars, or telephones. I told you, we prefer magical means to your hardware."

"No cell phones? No texting?"

"Nope."

"This is worse than I thought."

"We think it's better," Euwen said.

Euwen decided portals were a safe topic, so he went into considerable detail about them.

"Sounds like technology to me," Alexandra said after hearing his description.

"I didn't say we don't have devices and machines. They're just not as important to us as they are to you. We don't rely on them as you do. Anyway, portals aren't machines; they're magical frameworks."

Alexandra raised an eyebrow and smirked.

"Trust me," Euwen insisted, rather gruffly. "You're a smart girl. You'll pick up what you need to know as you go along."

"Ooookaaay," she replied.

Euwen gave her a hard look.

"You shouldn't go back to your world until you understand," he said.

"Understand what."

"Understand this isn't a joke. Understand about the Two Worlds."

"Where am I really?" Alexandra asked, her tone turning quite serious. "And don't tell me I'm on Earth or in Second World or any of that."

Euwen pondered what to say.

"Where you are now, sort of, is the same as where you were before except for the man-made things. You said not to call it what it is, so I won't."

"Okay, call it whatever you want. Where am I?"

"Second World."

Alexandra glared.

"So, are we anywhere near Simsbury in this second world?"

"No, your home town exists only in First World. It does not exist in Second World, though the place on Earth where it does exist is in both worlds."

"Oh, well, why didn't you say that to begin with? It all makes perfect sense now."

"Really? You understand?"

Her smirk told him she didn't understand and didn't believe a word he was saying. He decided there was no point in going on.

Alexandra did not make the same decision.

"I think I understand," she continued, "and by the way, Euwen, I am Snow White and I have my Seven Dwarves waiting outside to take me home in my pumpkin chariot which the Wizard of Oz gave to my sister, Cinderella, and for which she, being a money-grubber, is making me pay rent. There is probably a fairy prince in there somewhere, but I can't find him. In any case, I must be hurrying along, don't ya know."

Alexandra gave Euwen an exaggerated smile.

Euwen just stared at her.

"I want to go home," she repeated, serious again, "and I want to go home now. Are you going to help me or not?"

Euwen decided to take another tack:

"Alexandra, you need to know who you are."

With sudden clarity she knew he was right. She was long past thinking of herself as just another teenager. Nothing made sense within that thinking. Her childhood was checkered with strange experiences that placed her outside the bounds of normal. Aunt Elizabeth had confirmed this, much to her parents' dismay, and had insisted Alexandra come away with her to an unknown place to fulfill an unknown destiny.

Is this the place? Is this the destiny? She asked herself.

If it was, Euwen's fantastic explanations would not be so fantastic.

"My aunt said I was a witch."

"Your aunt?"

"Yes, my Aunt Elizabeth, Elizabeth Shaw."

Euwen blinked and the muscles of his neck tightened. It was a small reaction, but Alexandra noticed it.

"Is she behind all this?" Alexandra asked.

"No," Euwen replied flatly, "unless she had something to

do with your becoming lost in the storm. I found you quite by accident."

"Can you see how this looks to me?" Alexandra continued with a trace of cynicism. "My aunt said she was going to take me away with her. She didn't say where. My parents were not at all happy with that. Before it could happen, I got lost in the storm. Then you found me 'by accident.' Help me with this, Euwen."

Euwen's expression became thoughtful.

"I understand," he said. "You're suspicious. I'd be suspicious too. But I can only tell you what I know. I'm a bit of a storm-chaser. My father doesn't approve, especially when I go into First World. Your storm was especially severe. Very interesting. My being in it was no accident. Finding you was. I don't know what else to say."

"You know Elizabeth Shaw. I saw it in your face," Alexandra accused.

"I do know her. Everyone in Second World knows her. She is the Guardian."

"Guardian? Guardian of what?"

"Of the Two Worlds. I'll let her explain the rest."

"Is she here?"

"No, but she would certainly expect me to tell her *you* are. I will send a message to your aunt. She will be much relieved to learn you're well. There are things going on here I don't understand. I found a dying girl, saved her, and am rewarded with her suspicions. I don't wish to suffer the Guardian's suspicions on top of yours."

In a rush, Alexandra saw her ingratitude and felt ashamed.

"I'm sorry," she said. "Thank you for all you've done."

Euwen nodded.

***

They finished desert and relaxed and content. Both were recovered from the earlier unhappiness, and their conversation was cordial.

"You should sleep now," Euwen said finally. "I expect someone will arrive in the morning to take you to your aunt."

"Will you be going with me?"

"If you wish and the Guardian permits."

Alexandra studied Euwen's face.

"I do wish it."

"I will convey your wish in my message."

***

The next morning Alexandra found an assortment of warm clothing in the closet and dressed for the outdoors. It was winter here, as it had been in Simsbury. But all similarities ended there.

I'm not in Simsbury anymore, she thought with amusement.

She found Euwen waiting in the entrance hall. She stood next to him. He wore a heavy coat, one closely resembling the one she had chosen. Two loud thuds came from the broad oak-paneled front doors. A short pause was followed by another two thuds.

Euwen hastened across the room, slid back the heavy iron bar that secured the doors, and pulled them open. The hinges groaned as the doors swung wide.

Sunlight spilled across the entrance hall, momentarily blinding Alexandra. She squinted at a featureless, backlit shape.

It was not Aunt Elizabeth: much too short and much too plump.

The creature resembled nothing Alexandra had ever seen.

26 *Repentance*

Do not be tardy to forgive. Forgive while the transgression is hot; this is how we advance. When the transgression has cooled and we are ready, it is too late. This is how we fall back.

FROM *"PATHS TO SAINTHOOD"* BY DOM ANDRÉ DU BOURGAY

John checked his watch. It was 7 a.m.

The searchers, the make-shift command post in his office, and Lieutenant Tanner were gone. Gone too were the reporters, cameramen, and the media trucks. The quiet of the neighborhood had been restored, and the halls of the Ward mansion were silent.

John re-examined the list of addresses and phone numbers he had compiled. He took a deep breath, picked up the phone, and began again. Three hours later he scratched the last name off his list, wadded up the paper, and threw it across the room. He stood, walked to the kitchen window and opened it. Cold air drifted across his face and arms. The cold reminded him of Alexandra and filled him with renewed dread.

"God, where is she?" he murmured.

He felt fatigue tightening its grip on him as he placed his hands on the window sill and leaned his forehead against the cold metal screen. He recalled Tanner's assurance: The search would continue indefinitely. But that would be elsewhere, not here. Tanner's assurance brought little comfort.

A certain unreturned call nagged at him. It had been to

Ellen's sister and had been scratched from the list because many messages had been left and no response received. He picked up the crumpled list, found the name, and punched in the number. There was a pause and then ringing. One ring...two...three... He clicked the ball point pen in his hand: click in, click out, click in...

Someone picked up on the fourth ring.

"Hello," a female voice said.

John leaned forward, alert. "Yes, hello. Is this Mrs. Murphy?"

"Yes. Who's calling?"

"Mrs. Murphy," John said, avoiding her question, "I am looking for Mrs. Ellen Sutton. She gave me your name as someone who, ah, would know how to reach her. Can you help me?"

"I'm sorry. Who did you say you are?"

John braced himself.

"My name is John Ward."

There was a long silence.

"Mrs. Murphy?"

"Mr. Ward, I don't think my sister would welcome a call from you."

"And she has good cause," John said, almost in a whisper.

"More than good cause! This conversation is over, sir. Please do not call again."

"Wait, please wait. This is about my daughter. She's missing. Ellen would want to know."

Another long silence.

A minute went by.

"Mrs. Murphy?"

"I'm still here. Tell me what happened."

"Alexandra ran after Ellen and her son when they left."

"The boy has a name, and by all accounts they didn't 'leave'; you cast them out."

"Yes, Mrs. Murphy, and I regret that; I truly do. Now my daughter is missing or dead. The police searched, they are still searching. It has been two days and three nights. There is no sign of her. Maybe she found Ellen and Daniel. Maybe she knew where they went. I was wrong, terribly wrong."

"Indeed you were," Mrs. Murphy snapped, "but Ellen would want to know about Alexandra. I will call her and ask if she wants to speak to you."

Mrs. Murphy hung up abruptly.

Her return call came a couple of minutes later.

"Hello?"

"She does not answer and her voicemail is full," replied Mrs. Murphy. I will give you her phone number and address if you promise to leave them alone if they ask you to. Do I have your word?"

"Yes, of course. Thank you very much."

"Are you ready? Do you have pen and paper?"

"Yes, go ahead."

John took down the information and read it back.

"Correct," Mrs. Murphy said curtly, and then the line went dead.

John dialed the number. The phone rang maddeningly over and over. John let it go on ringing past any expectation it would be answered, imagining the accumulation of rings might somehow soften Ellen's heart. Finally, he pressed the off button.

He tried several more times, but got no answer, just the incessant ringing.

It was time to act.

"Henry!" he called out.

The butler appeared immediately.

"Have Layton bring the car around."

Henry hastened to find the chauffer. John took a wool coat from the hall closet. It was long and thick, a winter coat.

I could have put this over her, warmed her, saved her.

He put on the coat and checked his watch again. Eleven o'clock. He walked to the waiting car.

"Take us to this address," John said.

The chauffeur, Layton Hunt, looked down at the small piece of paper John handed him. He punched the address into the car's GPS and accelerated down the driveway. The route took about thirty minutes, ending along a narrow winding road that ended in a cul-de-sac.

"There," John said. "Pull over."

Layton angled the car into the curb and John got out. The mailbox displayed the numbers he had been given. He walked along the cobblestone path leading to the front door. Snow-covered holly bushes, overgrown and misshapen, lined the path. The property looked neglected. He knocked on the door.

He heard footsteps, a safety chain being attached, a lock being twisted open. The door opened a crack, and Ellen peered out at him. Her eyes narrowed and she pushed the door closed.

"Mrs. Sutton, please, I need your help," John said. "It's Alexandra."

The door opened again.

"What about Alexandra?" Ellen asked.

"May I come in?"

Ellen hesitated, her expression hard.

"Please," John said, "for Alexandra's sake."

Ellen removed the chain and opened the door. John stepped into a sparsely furnished living room. Ellen led him into a dinette that adjoined a small kitchen. She gestured for him to sit at the dinette table and seated herself opposite him.

John glanced at the wall behind her. A faded photograph in a cracked wooden frame hung there, not quite level. In the photograph a younger Ellen Sutton held an infant. She seemed to be presenting the child to the unknown photographer. Next to Ellen stood a smiling young man. John recognized David Sutton, Ellen's husband, now long dead from a stroke. This was the man who had brought Alexandra into his childless marriage, who had been so careful to arrange for it to appear she was theirs alone, so careful to erase all evidence of her true lineage.

Not careful enough, he thought.

He regretted the thought immediately.

This is no one's fault but mine.

"What has happened?"

Ellen's soft voice startled him.

"Alexandra's gone," he said.

"What do you mean?"

"She chased after you. We tried to catch her. Henry and I searched for her. It was snowing and so cold. She did not want to be found."

John considered what he had just said:

She did not want to be found.

"The police came. They searched for days; we all did. It was so cold. The police say not to give up hope. It is a sad day when the best that can be said is we didn't find her."

John stopped speaking. He looked again at the picture on the wall. He couldn't look at Ellen.

She turned to look at the picture with him, just for a moment, then faced him again. He was a man she had never seen before. Grief had transformed him. His shoulders jerked spasmodically, small, suppressed movements. His face was distorted, a caricature of the former John Ward.

"How can I help?" she said.

"Come back." he said in a choked whisper. "Help us. Come back to us."

Ellen gave John a long, hard look.

He did not see it. His eyes remained on the photograph. It was his refuge from her face, from the hatred he feared he would see there.

"Of course," she said. "Let's have no more of this. We will find her."

John looked at her. What he saw was a woman giving no place for her fears or resentments, or for John's grief. She was all the dedicated nanny, ready to return to work. Alexandra was the work, not him, not even her own son at this moment. It was Alexandra, her other child, who needed her now.

John considered how this woman had raised Daniel and Alexandra together, making no distinction of affection between them. She had loved them both, nurtured them both, while he had rejected her fatherless son, and in the end had banished them both.

Ellen has a place in her I do not have, he thought. *Now my daughter is lost, probably dead because of me, because of the place I don't have in me.*

Daniel entered the room and glared at the man seated at the table. Ellen saw Daniel's look and recognized immediately the danger John was in.

"Daniel! No. You will do nothing." Ellen said. "That is how we got here! It is time to think of Alexandra! Pack your things. Now!"

Daniel moved left and right, like an angry lion, but he did not advance. He looked from the man at the table to his mother, yielded to her, and left the room.

John called Layton in to help with the packing. When

John moved forward to join in, Ellen signaled him back, made a subtle gesture toward her son, and shook her head.

John understood and backed away.

I have been blind, he thought. *All these years, how could I not have seen: it is both of them. Maybe my daughter is out there, somewhere, preserved by her special powers. Maybe what I have fought so hard against can save her.*

Layton navigated them over the icy roads leading back to the mansion.

No one spoke.

27   Byrnhelen

Hone your vicarious awareness. Observe without opinion. Do not touch. Do not disturb the flow. Problems solve themselves when they are fully known. Touching kills knowing.

NARA

The creature nodded politely and announced in a croaky voice: "I am Gidram Hinbanterfeld, servant to the Guardian. I will escort you to Byrnhelen."

Alexandra stared. She had seen dwarfs. This creature, while short, looked nothing like a dwarf or a midget or a short human of any sort. His head was oddly shaped, his ears large and pointy, his skin coarse, and his complexion distinctly green. He appeared human in many ways, like the Dyrisian, but in as many other ways, he did not.

Gidram noted her amazement. "I am an elf," he said. "Your aunt said that you had never visited Second World before, and that my appearance might, ahhh, hmmm, surprise you. You need not be afraid."

"Forgive me for staring," Alexandra said."

"Shall we go," Euwen interjected, speaking to the elf. He handed Gidram a heavy traveling quilt. He gave Alexandra a thick fur cap and a brightly colored scarf.

"Yes, at once, sir," Gidram said.

Alexandra and Euwen followed the elf. Once outside, Euwen pulled the heavy doors closed and tapped an odd cadence on the door frame. The interior metal bar slid into place and the plungers clacked into their slots.

Crystalline frost lay over the expansive lawns. Ice arrows dangled from the barren limbs of deciduous trees and from the rails of the low fence surrounding the garden. The needles of the evergreens, fir, pine and juniper, were encased in tubes of clear ice. The sky was blue and cloudless, and the sun was bright.

The garden was undergoing a transformation: Frost and ice were turning from solid, to liquid, to vapor, misty columns rising into the cold air. The columns of vapor were merging into a transparent fog as they made their way to the carriage.

Gidram opened the carriage door and pulled down the hinged passenger step. He turned to Alexandra and saw she was walking toward the animals harnessed to the traces.

Alexandra marveled at yet another wonder in this world. She loved horses, and the animals harnessed to the carriage had the general appearance of horses. But the feathery wings folded neatly at their sides indicated an altogether different species. One of the animals turned its head and looked at her.

Gidram smiled. "They are Pegasus, actually 'pegases', since there are two of them, though some of my friends insist on 'pegasuses', which I think is silly. Yes, yes, quite silly." Gidram paused as though he had lost his train of thought.

"Anyway," he continued, "they're winged horses common in Second World. The name we use for them comes from the Greek legends of your world. Or is it the other way around. There's debate about that among elves. Yes, hmmm, well, anyway they can fly but we won't fly today. No need to worry. The one looking at you is Eudora."

Eudora, having heard her name, swung her head back and forth and whinnied. "Yes, Eudora, I am introducing you," Gidram said, chuckling as he stroked her flank.

Talkative fellow, this elf, thought Alexandra.

"Why can't we fly today?" Alexandra asked.

"They can't fly while pulling a carriage. It is most inconvenient, but we all have our limitations."

"Can I touch her?" Alexandra asked in an exaggerated whisper.

"Absolutely, but a proper introduction is required. You must say in your mind that you would like to touch her. Look into her eyes and inform her of this. That will work quite nicely."

"She can understand me?" Alexandra asked.

"Oh, yes. Oh, my goodness, yes. They are quite clever creatures."

Alexandra went through the mental introduction ritual with Eudora and reached out her hand. Eudora whinnied and pulled her head through a sweeping half circle before bringing her nose down and nuzzling Alexandra's hand. The animal's nose was warm and soft.

Softer than satin, thought Alexandra.

She moved her hand along the side of Eudora's head and under her jaw. The Pegasus remained relaxed and perfectly still.

"Euwen, come feel her," Alexandra said.

"That's all right. You go ahead."

"You've got to feel this," Alexandra urged. She walked over to Euwen, took his hand, and pulled him gently forward. He yielded, reluctantly, but as he drew near, Eudora pulled back, leaning against the other Pegasus. Both animals showed signs of distress.

"It's okay girl. He just wants to pet you."

But Eudora was having none of Euwen.

"Do the introduction," Alexandra said.

Euwen stood for a moment in silence, staring at Eudora and looking quite uncomfortable. He lifted his hand. Eudora lurched backward, nostrils flaring, eyes wide. The traces rattled and the carriage shuddered as it bumped backward.

Gidram quickly intervened. He took a firm grip on Eudora's bridle and motioned Euwen and Alexandra away. He spoke to the animal in soothing tones.

"She knows we're going home; probably just a little excited," Gidram said. He kept to himself what his elfin connection with Eudora had revealed:

This young man is not what he seems.

But Gidram's instructions had been clear: Bring them both.

Euwen assisted Alexandra into the carriage and climbed in behind her. Gidram placed the thick traveling quilt over them both, folded up the passenger step, and closed the carriage door. He mounted the driver's bench and murmured an elfin command to the animals.

The carriage lurched forward with a force Alexandra had not expected. Though the creatures had not unfurled their wings, they and the carriage seemed to be flying over the road. The resulting blast of cold air took Alexandra's breath away. She pulled down the flaps of her cap and made another wrap of the scarf around her face and neck.

The speed and the cold were exhilarating. Evergreen trees flashed past on both sides. The hoof beats of the animals combined almost musically with the uneven sounds of the carriage wheels. She felt Euwen pressed against her in the narrow seat. She reveled in the mix of sensations she was experiencing.

The McConnelly estate lay far behind when they emerged from the shade of the forest and descended to the valley floor. Soon they reached the valley's main road. Gidram steered to the right onto this road, and headed toward a distant village.

This is all so different, she thought, *all so old-fashioned, so fairytale. I keep expecting a knight in shining armor to appear.*

As their carriage passed through the village, Alexandra saw children playing in the snow in front yards, on pathways, and in fields. She saw women peering out of windows and doorways as the carriage passed. Some of them waved at Gidram, and he waved back with great enthusiasm.

The village looked centuries old. The streets were of cobblestone, which set up a pleasant vibration within the carriage. The buildings were quaint and medieval. Narrow winding streets led off from the main road. Flower boxes, empty now because of the season, hung beneath every verandah, and lace curtains covered the windows. The roofs were made of red tile, and the buildings were constructed of smooth adobe bricks supported by large, colorful wood beams.

Here and there, Alexandra saw murals painted on the sides of buildings. They illustrated in great detail the kind of wares being sold within. And the figures in the murals moved! Some even waved at the passing carriage. Alexandra giggled and found herself waving back. Odd yet so familiar she thought again as they left the village behind.

They continued on many kilometers through the rural countryside before coming to the next village. It had the same friendly atmosphere as the first, though it was smaller and they were soon past it.

Gidram glanced back at Alexandra. He could see joy in her countenance. This pleased him. "Ah, yes, it's a beautiful world, Second World," he yelled over the noise of pounding hooves and rolling wheels. "You will truly enjoy it here, Miss, of that I am quite sure. Now, look there!"

Alexandra looked left and right but saw nothing unusual.

"No. Look up."

He pointed to a mountain on their right. It was still distant and rose up some 1,500 meters above the valley floor.

"That," Gidram said, pointing at the forested summit, "is Byrnhelen."

He spoke the name of the place with reverence, turned away, and said no more.

The mountain loomed up slowly, blocking much of the sky as the carriage drew near. Gidram turned off the main road and headed toward the trees at the foot of the mountain. The route became steeper as they entered the forest and soon turned into a series of switchbacks. Deep snow lay on either side of the road. Back and forth, up and up the serpentine road they climbed, rising higher and higher up the face of Byrnhelen's mountain.

After about two hours, Gidram turned through the final switchback. Before them was a wide snow-covered meadow. A meandering stream cut through it. Beyond the stream was a massive stone wall, thirty meters high and three meters thick. Gidram took them over the stream on a narrow wood bridge and halted at an immense gate in the wall. The gate was constructed of stanchions and cross members as large as those used in the construction of great bridges.

What is waiting for me beyond these gates? Alexandra asked herself. *Why am I here?*

As though her thought was a trigger, the two panels of the gate swung ponderously inward. Gidram took the carriage through the opening and halted when he was clear of the gate panels. He looked back and scanned the trackless snow as the gate closed. Satisfied that no one had followed, he took the carriage into a new stand of tall pines, through a long turn to the left, and out onto a vast grassland plane, also blanketed in fresh snow.

Byrnhelen castle rose majestically before them. The large rough hewn stones at the base of the castle gave way to walls of smooth white stone capped by gray angled roof tops. Intricately carved marble statues depicting men and women in various dress stood in watchful wake of those entering Byrnhelen's grounds. She counted at least fifty large arched windows located in neat rows across the side of the main structure and tried to imagine the grandeur within the castle walls.

Alexandra felt a surge of emotion, a comingling of joy and surprise.

I know this place!

"This is Byrnhelen," Gidram said, looking back at her and smiling.

"Wow!"

The human being is most impressionable in its first year of life. David Sutton was with Daniel during that year. He made the essential Second World impressions before his death. Ellen, his wife, raised the boy after that. She made the essential First World impressions. The genes combined. The nurture combined. The hybrid that grew out of this combination altered the course of the succession.

FROM "CHRONICLE OF THE SUCCESSION" BY MASTER BRADYN ARISTARCHUS

I'm not going to sit around and do nothing!" Daniel said angrily.

"I understand," soothed his mother, "but there is nothing either of us can do except help with the calls and wait and pray. Have you called all her friends?"

"Yes, and I keep calling. They don't know anything, and I'm doing nothing!"

Ellen pulled Daniel into a hug. They stood together in silence.

"I have the powers you know about," he said, "like Alexandra. I just don't know what to do with them, how to help her now."

"Helplessness in the face of a loved one's need is the worst kind of helplessness."

"Yes. We both just wanted to be like everybody else. We wanted to be normal, to fit in. We had to practice being normal. But when it was just her and me, we could be ourselves. We could work on the special things we could do.

You know, people don't like people who are different."

Ellen smiled.

"Not all people. Your father was very different. I loved him for it and for so many other things."

"I wish I had known him. Mr. Ward hates me."

"He doesn't hate you. He...fears you. He thinks you are the cause of Alexandra's being...different. Think of what he is going through now."

"It's hard not to hate him back."

"The two of you are chewing on the same piece of leather."

"What does that mean?"

"It means you are connected by your fears and hatred. Consider this, son: It is no accident I am here. It is no accident you are here. It is no accident Alexandra is the adopted child of the Wards. It is no accident I raised you both."

"You knew she was adopted?"

"Of course. Your father arranged it. Secrecy was required on all sides. Alexandra is wrong to blame her father for that, or for you to blame me."

"I don't blame you."

"Not even just a little?"

"Nope. Really, I don't. I blame Mr. Ward."

"Same, piece of leather, son."

Like all children, Daniel did not have a clear view of his parents. His father had died before he was born. His mother, the woman standing before him, had always been there, a trusted constant, with no separate life of her own, until this moment. This filled him with disquiet, and something like regret, a child's regret for having lost something important that can never be retrieved.

A poisonous distillation of grief, anger, and loss washed

over him, and silence set in again between the mother and her son.

Ellen broke the silence:

"So, now we talk."

Daniel looked at his mother. His cheeks were wet.

"We didn't think you or anyone would understand. We didn't understand. I still don't; I just live it, try to fit in, keep my secrets."

"It must have been hard. Perhaps I should have pressed you," his mother said.

"No, it was OK, Mom. Alexandra and I helped each other. And you were always kind and understanding. All kids have problems."

A startling thought came to Ellen.

The police and their dogs and their hundreds of searchers couldn't find Alexandra. Now my son wants to try, and I am telling him he's powerless. I have picked up the hopelessness of this place. I must fight it!

"Daniel!" Ellen said, grabbing his shoulders. "Remember how you and Alexandra played hide-and-seek? Remember how you always found her right away but she could never find you?"

Daniel beamed with understanding.

"Yes! She could not turn off her light."

Daniel hesitated.

"Talk to me, son. Now is not the time to hold back. Alexandra needs us."

"Well, she gives off a kind of light when she's excited, like a halo around her body. Sort of like that. Anyway, she would leave traces of light when she ran away to hide. I could stay calm, so I left no trace; I could find her, but she could never find me. So maybe she left traces this time! Dogs, police, no one, not even Elizabeth, because she doesn't know Alexandra's light, would be able to find the traces. Maybe they're still there! Maybe I could find them."

"Maybe you could," Ellen said, "but not if you keep standing around and talking to this old woman."

"You're not old, Mother."

"Go," she replied with a smile.

29 Capture

Find yourself. Then lose yourself. Then find yourself.
This is the great way, the pathless path, the roofless joy
and the bottomless sorrow.

FROM "UNCERTAIN JOURNEY" BY JOSHUA TURNER

Alexandra's father had been very clear about where his daughter had disappeared. Daniel stood on the spot. It was at the end of the Wards' long driveway. He saw nothing, no trace of her.

He looked back at his mother. She was standing just outside the ornate archway that framed the front door. Her hands were clasped in front of her and she was smiling at him. Locks of thinning dark brown hair framed her face. She wore a simple cotton dress with pastel orange and blue flowers. The absence of her black-and-white uniform reminded Daniel of his uncertain future, and hers. He felt an urge to run to her, hug her, thank her for everything. He wanted to tell her how sorry he was for the mean and thoughtless things he had done and for the countless things he had not done but should have.

Instead, he simply lifted his hand and waved.

Ellen waved back and watched as Daniel hitched up his daypack, fastened the hip belt, and walked from the driveway into the forest. She did not move, though it was cold and she was beginning to shiver. She folded her arms tightly across her chest and stared at the empty space where her son had stood. She felt the necessity of standing, waiting, worrying: what mothers do. Her whole life as a mother passed before her and resolved into a peaceful understanding: Alexandra was gone, maybe dead, and her son was separating from her, taking on his own duties. Her standing in the cold was no longer necessary. She turned, stepped through the front door, and closed it behind her.

***

Daniel studied the trampled snow and crushed juniper bushes over which the teams of searchers had passed. They had been thorough. No patch of ground was unmarked by their passage.

But he was not there to repeat the search performed earlier; he was there to play their old game of hide-and-seek, the one where she trailed her unique glow of excitement. Anger and fear were forms of excitement. Daniel was counting on Alexandra having experienced both.

He sank cross-legged onto the forest floor. He sat upright, his hands resting loosely on his thighs. He closed his eyes and imagined Alexandra running ahead of him in the dark, glancing over her shoulder, weaving around trees, stumbling over bushes and fallen timber. He pictured the aura that trailed behind. He penetrated its molecules, felt it surround him. He examined it, classified its exact place in the color spectrum.

He opened his eyes. He calibrated his seeing, and the forest became a pointillist tapestry of light. He easily filtered out the lingering auras of the searchers, and tracked only Alexandra's. It was there: a thin layer of fog, hovering, vague, the gold of it faded almost entirely to gray. It was a remnant only, dispersed by the passage of time and almost invisible. But it was clear to his eyes, and it was enough.

Daniel pushed himself up and began following Alexandra's trail. As he proceeded, the thin fog close to the ground began to collect into distinct patches. Her path had been circuitous. He followed her as he had when they were children.

His heart pounded. He plowed through the underbrush, making a nearly straight line of Alexandra's meandering path as he sought for the end of it, where there might be some evidence of her, where there might be some clue the others had missed. He blocked out the possibility that the evidence might be her lifeless body.

Daniel stopped, backed up two or three paces, and examined a tree he had just passed. He lifted a tiny piece of cloth from the broken point of a branch that stretched, shoulder-high, into the path Alexandra had taken. The piece of cloth was no bigger than the flat of his thumb, but it was the same color as the shirt Alexandra had been wearing when he had last seen her.

He caressed the tiny scrap of material. The trail of light was still the best evidence of Alexandra's course, but this piece of cloth was physical, a talisman that made Alexandra seem almost present. He placed the tiny piece of cloth in his shirt pocket.

He ran on for perhaps another thirty minutes before he made a sharp turn to the right and halted. Alexandra's trail had coalesced into a transparent cloud enclosed within a hollow formed by a dense stand of scrub oak. An eastern white pine stood nearby. A rough stone archway, high and wide enough for a man to pass through, was partially concealed by the scrub oak. It was evident the searchers and their dogs had been here and had found what he found:

Nothing.

This is wrong, all wrong, thought Daniel.

When he found her hiding place; he found her. That was how it had always worked.

Daniel searched for new evidence, a route Alexandra

might have taken away from the place. He walked around in expanding circles, searching for a sign, a clue, anything.

He found nothing.

All signs of her stopped here and went nowhere else.

Not possible, Daniel thought.

He returned to the misty hollow in the scrub oak. He turned his back to it and studied the ground.

There!

He had missed it earlier because it was nearly invisible, no more than a wispy mist leading away from the hide. The mist had fragments of Alexandra's aura, but they were mixed with foreign fragments that were not hers.

He followed the trail of mist to where it ended some eighty meters from the hide.

He turned back as he guessed Alexandra had done.

"Hello?"

Daniel froze. The voice was distant and came from the direction of the hide.

"Hello!" Daniel yelled back.

"Daniel?"

It was her voice; Daniel was sure of it.

"Alexandra, it's me!"

He did not wait for a reply. He ran toward the sound, dodging around trees, plunging through willows, and fighting his way through scrub oak. He broke into the open some twenty meters from the hide.

She was not there.

But something else was.

A dense green fog slithered through the archway near the fallen sycamore.

Daniel stumbled backward.

Too late.

The fog transformed into a wave of white light. It rushed

over him, consumed him, and then collapsed upon itself like a dying star.

30   The Welcoming

The children of Byrnhelen must reach higher to survive.
They are past being average. They must rise or die.

FROM "THE CHILDREN OF BYRNHELEN" BY MASTER MAREK AVALARD

Alexandra had seen castles while travelling with her parents through England, Scotland, France, and Austria. None matched Byrnhelen. Its architecture and the manner of its construction made the castle seem an extension of the summit of the mountain. She wondered how deep into the mountain these buildings penetrated.

"Shall we go in, Miss?" Gidram said.

A team of elves took charge of the carriage as Gidram led Alexandra and Euwen forward on foot. He opened the intricately carved doors of the main entrance, stepped aside, and beckoned for them to pass.

"I shall inform your aunt that you are here," he said.

Elizabeth Shaw soon appeared out of a hallway on the right. She moved with controlled grace, straight and tall, in a flowing gown of red and black. Her eyes were bright, and focused intently on Alexandra.

"Alexandra," she said, enveloping the girl in her arms. "You're safe and well, my dear; safe and well. I've been so worried. I'm so glad you're here."

Elizabeth stepped back, turned to Euwen, and with formal dignity announced: "I am Elizabeth Shaw. You must be Euwen McConnelly. Thank you for your letter. It came as a great relief, more than you could know. Thank you for returning Alexandra to me."

She did not offer him her hand.

"It was nothing, really," he said. "I just happened along."

"Happened along?"

Euwen glanced from Elizabeth to Alexandra. Alexandra gave him an impish smile.

He looked back at the Guardian.

"Well, sort of happened along."

Elizabeth tilted her head slightly and raised her eyebrows.

"He likes storms," Alexandra interjected. "The one in Simsbury was—what did you call it, Euwen?—oh yes, 'interesting'."

Euwen wasn't sure whether Alexandra's explanation helped or hurt him in the eyes of the Guardian.

Elizabeth made no reply. She turned her attention back to Alexandra.

"We must send a message to your parents. They have suffered much since your disappearance, and I've been helpless to comfort them."

Alexandra was surprised. Euwen had made such communication sound problematic, if not impossible.

Elizabeth turned to Euwen, "I will have Gidram show you to the library if you care to stay for dinner. You must. I insist."

Gidram appeared, seemingly out of nowhere, and escorted Euwen out of the room. Elizabeth led Alexandra down the hallway from which she had come.

Alexandra marveled at how large the rooms were, how high the ceilings. Euwen's estate was vast, but it did not compare. The hallway led them past many rooms, some with their doors standing open. There were parlors, meeting rooms, library sitting rooms, an art gallery, and other exquisitely decorated spaces. The rooms had large windows.

Sunlight streamed through pastel colored sheers, bathing the interiors with a warm glow.

Elizabeth led Alexandra into a small conference room.

"Please, make yourself comfortable," she said, gesturing to a thick-padded chair at the end of the conference table. Alexandra seated herself. Elizabeth sat in a chair next to her and lifted a piece of cream-colored parchment from a nearby stack. She pulled a feather pen from its ink cup beside the stack, pressed the parchment flat, and paused.

"I'm going to write to your parents and tell them you are safe and well and with me. Do you have any special message for them?"

Alexandra thought for a few moments.

"You and Euwen know more about what's happened to me than I do. Just tell them I'm OK and I love them."

The only sound in the room for the next three minutes was the scratching of Elizabeth's pen against parchment. When she was done, she picked up the letter and read it aloud.

"I can't think of anything else," Alexandra said when Elizabeth finished. It did not occur to Alexandra that she had not seen the contents of the letter.

Elizabeth signed the letter, rolled it into a tight scroll, tied it with a ribbon, and walked to the empty fireplace on the far side of the room. She pointed her wand at the fireplace.

"Firecipent!" she commanded.

Brilliant amethyst flames erupted, and Elizabeth spoke into them: "Mary and John Ward, twenty-one Drake Hill Road, Simsbury, Connecticut." She casually threw the scroll into the flames. There was a flash of white, and the fire extinguished itself.

Alexandra's eyes were wide.

"That is really cool!" she exclaimed. "Way better than a

text message."

Elizabeth smiled.

"Let's introduce you to the other apprentices. They have returned for a special event."

"Apprentices? You have a school here?" Alexandra asked, joining Elizabeth in the hallway.

"If by school you mean desks, textbooks, and teachers droning on in stuffy classrooms, then I must disappoint you. Our apprentices do little work in classrooms. They work primarily in real materials; they solve real problems, learning as they go."

"No teachers?" Alexandra asked incredulously.

"Not in the sense to which you are accustomed in First World."

"So we just read books."

"Reading is required," Elizabeth said, "but reading is not how you will spend most of your time."

Alexandra looked bewildered.

Elizabeth smiled and went on:

"You will be assigned to a group of five or six first-year apprentices. Most are about your age. Our intention is that you stay together throughout first-level training, but that depends on attrition and occasional new arrivals. You are a new arrival."

"How long is this first-level training?"

"Six years."

"Wow! That's a long time, Aunt Elizabeth."

"It may seem so to you now, but it is not, for example, as long as the training of medical doctors in First World. You will go on to other levels after the first, but that will be specialized training, and not as intensive."

"Six years," Alexandra repeated. "I don't know. What happens during the year? What do we do?"

"During each year, you will complete eight five-week master courses, with a one-week break between each master course and a five week break before the next year begins."

"That's too much going to school."

"It isn't at all like school."

"Sounds like it to me."

"I understand. This will be quite different. In each of the year's five master courses you will be apprenticed to a master who is an active practitioner of the discipline of that master course. You will be guided by this master, but you will be responsible for your own learning."

"You're right," Alexandra said. "This doesn't sound like any school I've ever been to."

"Think of it this way: Byrnhelen is the hub of a wheel. The hub turns very slowly. The spokes, my apprentices, go out from the hub to the rim of the wheel. The rim turns very rapidly, and one can lose one's hold. That is the danger. But knowledge is always dangerous. On the rim of the wheel, on the edge of all things known—that is where our masters open the minds of their apprentices. Clinging to the rim, to the very edge of the known—that is where you will learn. That is where you will develop and discipline the powers you have found so disturbing in your past. That is where you will learn your purpose. No First World school could teach you this."

I'm here only because my real mother is from here, thought Alexandra. *But she's dead. My real father is not from here. He's alive and somewhere in the other world or dimension or whatever I came from. I don't really belong in either place.*

Alexandra felt a surge of longing for home, John and Mary, her school, Ellen, Daniel, her own bedroom and the gardens beneath it. The familiar things and people called out to her.

It seemed she had been given no choice in any of what was happening. She pondered this and came to a strange conclusion: Even if she had been given a choice, she would have taken no different path.

She was bound for the rim of the wheel.

Mary's Stand

You are the message; deliver it.

ELIZABETH SHAW FROM "COMMENTARIES ON GOVERNANCE" BY
MASTER BRADYN ARISTARCHUS

John mounted the stairs two at a time. "Mary!" he shouted. "They found her. She's safe. Alexandra's safe."

He arrived at Alexandra's bedroom door just as it opened. Mary stood there, her face a mask of fatigue and anguish. She wore the same nightgown she had been wearing for several days now. Her hair was askew, her eyes wild and glassy.

"What makes you so sure?"

She spoke without feeling. She feared hope. Hope had been so painful these last days. Yet a tiny flame of hope, like the flame of a dying candle, burned unseen, unexpressed within her. She hid it from others, but she could not hide it from herself.

"A message from the Shaw woman. It just came. She says Alexandra has been found and is safe and with her."

Mary stared at him.

"I was sitting at my desk. I closed my eyes for just a moment. I guess I fell asleep. Something tapped me on the shoulder."

John held out a loosely-rolled piece of parchment.

Mary stared at it, her expression still blank.

"It was just floating there in midair. It gave me another rather nasty jab, hitting me in the forehead, before I realized I wasn't dreaming. I grabbed it and, well, see for yourself!"

John handed the curled parchment to his wife. She pressed it open and read:

> Dear John and Mary,
>
> Alexandra is safe and well.
>
> I assure you I had nothing to do with her disappearance. Nor can I claim any credit for saving her life. It was a young man with whom I was not previously acquainted who found her and eventually brought her to me at Byrnhelen, a place unknown in your world and unreachable.
>
> I know how hard this must be for you. But Alexandra is perfectly healthy. She misses you, but she has vital work to do, as I told you during my visit. She has chosen to remain here and do this work.
>
> She will write to you soon, but it will be some time before arrangements can be made for you to see her. This cannot be helped. I know this letter is a poor substitute for her return to you, but it will have to do.
>
> She asked me to tell you she loves you.
>
> Sincerely,
>
> Elizabeth Shaw

Mary looked up at her husband.

"She's alive?"

Her question was nearly inaudible.

"Yes, and I will find this Shaw woman and bring Alexandra back. I promise you. Mark my words."

Mary did mark his words, and she found them hollow. She found herself hollow. She looked hard at her husband, as though she was looking at a stranger. The right side of her mouth twitched. She felt a profound shift in herself.

"We will do exactly nothing, John. Alexandra will be gone for a long time."

"Nonsense!" he shouted back in the old way, harsh, dismissive.

"Stop!" Mary shoved the parchment against his chest. "Now, you read it! Read it again."

She glared at him.

John heard sadness in her voice. He took the parchment, read it again, then looked up at his wife.

"We are very influential people, Mary. This is just a letter."

Mary saw her husband more clearly than she had ever seen him before. She saw the façade, the pretense they had shared for so many years. She had seen it fade away in the denouement of this crisis. Now it was back.

Influence, she thought, rolling the word over in her mind and seeing it dissolve into nothingness. *What is influence?*

Her husband's influence worked well in their world. But this message had not come from their world. She and her husband were, at best, between worlds, and a façade would not do. It would not take them to Alexandra, wherever she might be at this moment, nor would it bring her back. Something more than influence was required.

She smiled at John, and shook her head. It was a slight movement that somehow settled the matter.

"You don't understand, you really don't," she said with maternal tenderness.

John did not like her new tone. It lacked a certain respect. Her usual deference, to which he'd become quite accustomed, was missing.

"I will put our lawyer on this immediately," he growled, "and I will alert Senator Millhouse."

"And what will you tell them?" Mary responded, her tone still irritatingly calm. "Will you tell them your daughter's a witch? That she could not be found because she was taken to another world by her aunt, who is also a witch? The letter does not say it in so many words, but this Byrnhelen is not around the block. It is in another world. Does your influence stretch into that other world? And even if it did, could you guarantee me, absolutely guarantee me your efforts would not be to our daughter's detriment? And tell me how you will explain all this to your oh-so-influential friends?"

"They're your friends too."

"No, John, they're not."

John could think of nothing more to say.

His wife went on:

"No, John, you will not embarrass yourself and me by trying to explain this to the lawyer or Millhouse. You will not call a press conference or convene a meeting of powerful colleagues or write a letter to the editor. You will not do any of these things because you will not be believed. Worse, you will be suspected, and you could bring the whole world, this world, crashing down on both of us. And in the process, you would very likely do our daughter no good whatsoever. You are so fond of thinking outside the box, John; do a little of that now."

"I will do whatever's necessary," he stammered.

"You will do exactly nothing," Mary said again, her voice now tinged with years of pent-up anger. "This is something you cannot buy, threaten, or manipulate your way out of. Our Alexandra is gone, and there is nothing we can do about it. We are helpless. *You* are helpless, and maybe Alexandra is better off for that."

John took a deep breath, and something deep within him broke.

***

Ellen heard Mary's voice and walked from the kitchen to the foot of the stairs.

"Is there news, Mrs. Ward?"

Mary looked down at Ellen.

"Yes," Mary replied.

Ellen's eyes went wide. She covered her mouth with her right hand.

John stepped around his wife and descended the stairs. He stood before Ellen and spoke softly:

"Alexandra has been found. She is well. She is safe."

Ellen stared at him.

"You're certain?"

"We have it in a letter from Elizabeth Shaw. She's says Alexandra is with her."

"I would trust that. Daniel will want to know." she said.

"Of course. Where is he?" John asked.

There was genuine concern in his question.

"He left a few hours ago to search for Alexandra. He promised me he would be home for dinner. He has always been good about that. I'm concerned."

The usual time for dinner came and passed with no sign of Daniel. John and Mary talked quietly at the dining room table. Mary had insisted dinner be delayed until Daniel's return. After a half hour, Ellen, without seeking permission, placed food in front of John and Mary. She was about to leave when Mary reached up and touched her arm.

"Please bring a plate for yourself and join us."

Ellen glanced at John.

"Get some food and sit here," Mary added, gesturing toward the chair next to hers.

Ellen went to the kitchen, filled a plate, and returned.

The three of them ate in silence.

After dinner, Ellen took a seat on the sofa beneath the living room window. She sat at an angle that permitted her to see the grounds in front of the house. She stared into the forest bordering the driveway. She willed for Daniel to reappear there as she prayed for his safe return.

John sat in a chair across the room. He looked through the same window. They did not speak. After midnight he left.

Ellen continued to watch the forest at the edge of the driveway.

Daniel did not appear.

She kept watch until, unseen by her, a soft red line painted the eastern horizon. The line widened, slowly, like a curtain being lifted at the edge of the world. Her eyelids grew heavy and she rested her head on the back of the couch. As the red curtain rose, her thoughts merged and blurred and became nothing at all.

Hostages will come to love you for simply not killing them. This love will be sealed by their secret shame for being glad you killed another—a friend, a brother, a mother—instead of them. Your smallest favors will add to the sealant of shame, binding them ever closer to you. This is how we recruit. This is how we command loyalty.

From "Essays on Supremacy" by Aedan Shaw

Daniel's nightmare was fresh and unconcluded.

He had been running through the snow. Alexandra's voice had called to him again and again from someplace just out of reach. A flash of light had blinded him, and unseen hands had pushed, pulled, and pummeled him. He had tried to fight back, but the dream separated him from his body, and his body had no will of its own.

Daniel rolled onto his side. He was lying on a cold stone floor. The hardness of it brought him fully awake. The darkness surrounding him was complete. It seemed to be probing for entry into his body, an evil blackness seeking to drain his life force.

He remembered Mr. Ward knocking on the front door and telling his mother about Alexandra's disappearance. He remembered going back to the Wards' home. He remembered searching for Alexandra in the forest and finding pieces of her clothing.

He sat up. The movement caused pain. He ran his hands over his legs, chest, torso, and arms, searching for lacerations or evidence of broken bones. He found himself seemingly whole, without serious injury, but he felt as though he had been caught up in a tornado.

"Hello," Daniel whispered into the dark. "Can anyone hear me?"

No answer. No sound at all, except his own breathing.

Daniel rolled onto his knees, pressed his palms against the rough stone floor, pulled his right foot under him, and stood. He put his arms out in front of him, like a blind man, and edged forward, one short step after another. He tentatively lengthened his stride when he encountered no obstacles.

This was his undoing. With his right foot planted on the stone floor, he took a long step forward with his left and fell forward into airy darkness. His hip collided with something solid, momentarily arresting his fall. He twisted his body to the left and dug his fingers into what felt like course, nearly vertical rock. Dirt and debris dug into his hands, lodged under his fingernails, and scoured his arms and knees as he continued his rough descent, slipping haltingly from one tenuous hold to another, unable to stop his slide downward.

I must not die! Alexandra needs me!

The thought of Alexandra's necessity renewed his determination. He felt the tendrils of a protruding root, took desperate hold, and scrambled blindly for a foothold. Rocks broke away after giving only momentary support, but this was enough. He pulled himself upward, hand-over-hand. The root held. It finally curled into the wall. He held it with one hand and reached up with the other. He found a ledge and gripped the edge of it, took a deep breath, let go of the root, and scrambled frantically onto the ledge. He collapsed into a deep alcove for which the ledge served as a floor and lay exhausted, his heart pounding, his breaths coming fitfully as he coughed up dirt he had inhaled.

He heard footsteps coming from somewhere above. The footsteps stopped and Daniel heard the scraping of a key within a lock and the clanking of a heavy deadbolt being drawn back. He leaned carefully out of the alcove and peered intently into the blackness above. The rusty hinges of a door groaned as a narrow shaft of light spilled across the top of the pit into which he'd fallen.

The faint light gave Daniel a limited view of his surroundings. He could see the opposite wall of the circular pit. The walls were vertical, or nearly so, and the masonry was quite rough. Large stones jutted out from the walls. They were what had saved him from falling into the blackness below.

The footsteps above drew nearer.

"Hello!" Daniel yelled. "I'm down here!"

The footsteps stopped abruptly.

"Help me, please," Daniel pleaded.

The tempo of the footsteps increased.

A movement on the opposite wall of the pit caught Daniel's attention. A face appeared there, bathed in a soft glow. It was a girl, a very pretty girl. She laid a finger over her lips and shook her head from side to side, urgently signaling quiet.

The footsteps halted just above him at that very moment, and the face disappeared. Daniel felt an electric shock pass through his body as a sphere of yellow light enclosed him. He felt himself lifted steadily upward out of the pit and sideways over the stone floor of the chamber. A cloaked man stood before him, holding something that looked like a stick or an orchestra conductor's baton. A thin beam of light from the end of it was connected to the sphere. The man twitched his hand, and Daniel lurched backward, crashed into the wall near the pit, and fell to the floor.

"Get up!" the man ordered.

Daniel groaned.

"I said, get up!"

The man's hand twitched again. Daniel felt himself yanked upright and suspended like a rag doll a few centimeters above the floor. A moment later he was released. He landed hard but retained his footing.

"Out!" the man commanded, pointing to the cell's open door.

Daniel limped toward the light. The stranger followed close behind. Daniel stepped over the threshold of the cell door and squinted into the light coming from torches that lined both sides of the hallway. He hesitated. The stranger gave him a harsh jab, indicating left, and Daniel proceeded in that direction.

The corridor snaked steadily onward, twisting and turning in uneven windings as it passed other corridors appearing on the left and right. The walls along the serpentine passageway seemed to move as though they were alive, and Daniel began to feel vaguely claustrophobic. The two of them passed other men in hooded cloaks, all heading in the opposite direction. Daniel and his captor rounded an unusually tight curve where the corridor was blocked by a large wooden door. The hooded man gestured toward a large iron ring in the center of the door. Daniel grasped the ring, and pulled the door open.

"In!" the man ordered as he gave Daniel a shove.

Daniel stumbled into an enormous circular room. The room's expansiveness was in sharp contrast with the narrow corridor. The massive stone walls supported a high cathedral dome. Hundreds of flaming torches were set into closely-spaced brackets that lined the walls. The room seemed aflame with light.

A group of hooded figures conversed in hushed tones

with a tall, thin man who stood in their midst. The man had a short-cropped gray beard. His matching gray hair fell to his shoulders. His features were aquiline: a jutting jaw that ended in a pointed chin and a nose that was narrow but prominent. His eyes were black and set deep in his skull. He wore a long black tunic. The pointed toes of his boots protruded from beneath its hem. The behavior of those around him signaled his authority over them.

Daniel's arrival brought their conversation to an end. The hooded men stepped away from their leader, making room for Daniel to approach. The silence was oppressive. Daniel felt the intense gaze of unseen eyes.

"I see you've brought our young visitor, General Croft."

"Yes, Master Aedan."

Croft prodded Daniel closer to the center of the room, bowed deeply, and backed away. He shuddered at the thought of Aedan's wrath had Daniel fallen to his death in the pit. By what powers had the boy cast off the spell that should have kept him comatose? The lad bore watching.

"Where am I?" Daniel asked Aedan.

"You are standing before me in a chamber of my castle."

Not a very useful answer, Daniel thought. *He toys with me.*

"Is Alexandra here?"

Ah, he goes right to the girl. I take him from his world, imprison him in a windowless cell, and still his concern is for her. Excellent. He already plays his part in my little drama.

"I might know something of her," Aedan said.

Daniel studied the cruel black eyes that dominated the man's face. He looked there for some clue to his fate and that of Alexandra. He saw only menace.

"Forgive me," Aedan said in mocking apology, "I did not

introduce myself. I am Aedan, master of Durnakk."

Daniel felt anger and fear alternating dangerously within him. Neither could exist fully in the presence of the other, and Daniel knew he tended toward anger. He searched for something in between.

"Can I take her home?"

Aedan paused, his black eyes reflecting the flickering torch light.

"Home? Such a quaint conception. You should be more concerned about staying alive here, right where you stand. Home is where the heart is, and your heart is here. You should be thankful it is still beating."

"Why am I here?" Daniel asked, speaking less boldly than before.

"I ask the questions, warlock."

Warlock? Why does he call me that?

Daniel sensed he was in great danger. He kept his silence.

"You are probably wondering what use I have for you," Aedan said, gesturing oddly. "You are a minor player in my drama. I waver on whether to keep you in the drama at all. Your part is small, but it might prove useful. When the time comes—if it comes—I will give you your script and you will speak your lines."

Daniel's anger overrode his fear. "I won't be in your drama," he yelled defiantly. A sharp blow to the side of his head sent him sprawling across the floor. He lay still for a moment, face down, stunned. When he regained a measure of his senses, he rolled onto his back and stared up at General Croft. Croft's black hood had pulled back, exposing his shaved head, dark brown eyes, and thick lips. A long, ugly scar cut across his right temple and down his cheek.

"Watch your tongue, lad, or I will cut it out!" he roared. Daniel sat up slowly, bringing his hand up to wipe away blood flowing from his bottom lip. Aedan came forward and stood over him.

"You should keep this in mind, my young friend: Your part in the drama can be played by a dead actor, if necessary. You would certainly be less troublesome all scented down and lying in a coffin. Perhaps it is time for you to go. I have grown bored with our little chat."

Aedan brought his right hand forward and curled his fingers upward. Daniel felt his body lifting off the stone floor, though Aedan had not touched him. Aedan raised his arm higher and Daniel's body rose further, his feet soon dangling centimeters above the floor. Aedan swiveled his hand and squeezed his fingers inward, slowly, as though he was squeezing an invisible ball.

Daniel felt a tightening around his throat. He began coughing. His coughing quickly turned to desperate gasps for air. He began to flail in midair. Then his gasps ceased. No air could pass. His flailing continued for a few seconds and then subsided. His arms and legs hung by his sides, limp and lifeless; his head lolled backward.

Aedan brought his arm slowly closer to his own body, and Daniel's body floated forward until his upturned face was centimeters from Aedan's. Aedan smiled as he watched the color drain from Daniel's face. Then he opened his hand.

Daniel's limp body dropped onto the stone floor.

33   Hello and Goodbye

*Byrnhelen is a dewy reed brushing against the bare legs
of the apprentices. It deposits moisture on them. The sun
heats the moisture. The wind evaporates it. Rain, snow,
seas, and storms combine with it and take away its
name. Where then is Byrnhelen?*

FROM "THE CHILDREN OF BYRNHELEN" BY MASTER MAREK AVALARD

Elizabeth sat at the center of the elevated head table.
Master Marek Avalard and Master Bradyn Aristarchus
sat to her right. Master Albumter Drouse was on her left.
Before them, Alexandra, Euwen, and thirty-five apprentices
sat at tables arranged neatly around the dining hall of
Byrnhelen.

The apprentices were engaged in boisterous conversation.
Laughter was frequent and joyous. Elizabeth began tapping
her fork against her crystal goblet. Others joined in and the
room filled with the cacophony of ringing crystal. Elizabeth
stood. She raised her goblet and the hall fell silent.

"Welcome back apprentices of Byrnhelen!"

Her words triggered cheers and the stamping of feet, first
in random juxtaposition, then in unison. The clacking and
clanging of crystal goblets began again.

It was a symphony of enthusiasm, and Elizabeth was
conductor.

"You have all completed another small step in the work.
You were taught and tested all over the world by the finest
masters. You adapted. You improvised. You overcame.
Those who did not are not with us tonight and will not be

with us again. They have returned to their homes, to lives you may one day wish had been yours."

Some of the apprentices heard the warning. These looked down at their plates or furtively at one another, wondering if others had heard, wondering at the meaning. Most did not hear or did not want to hear.

"Alexandra Ward, would you please stand."

Alexandra was seated at a forward table with Euwen and four apprentices. She stood and turned to face the young men and women behind her.

"Alexandra is now, like all of you, an apprentice of Byrnhelen. Her late start with us was unavoidable. She will need your support in catching up. I trust she will have it."

Elizabeth looked steadily from one face to another until she saw the affirmative nodding she was seeking.

"She needs you, but in ways that will in time become clear, you need her even more."

Elizabeth's voice had deepened, and she at last had their full attention. This was *not* just another apprentice. All eyes were on Alexandra. A boy at one of the middle tables stood, then a girl across from him. Then others at other tables stood. The only sound was the shuffling of chairs as every apprentice in the hall stood.

"Thank you," Elizabeth said.

She took her seat and the apprentices, including Alexandra, took theirs. The symphony of enthusiasm began again, more subdued now. New conversations were begun; old ones renewed. Laughter returned. A few of the apprentices, the more thoughtful ones, stared at Alexandra, whose back was to them, and they wondered. The Guardian had spoken, but there was much to fill in between her words. Second Worlders, particularly the young, loved enigmas; now they had a living, breathing one in their midst.

Euwen, who was seated next to Alexandra, leaned in close and whispered: "I think she forgot how embarrassing it is to be the new kid."

Alexandra smiled: "I'm glad you're here. At least I know someone. I miss my friend."

"Friend? Did you have only one in your world?"

"No, but I miss Daniel the most. We were raised together."

"You make it sound like you were an orphan."

"No, nothing like that. Daniel's mom was my nanny."

She smiled, remembering.

"Daniel is only a year older than me but he liked to make it sound like he was born a lot before me so he could play the big brother role."

"Is he coming here?"

Alexandra pondered Euwen's question.

Elizabeth had spoken of Daniel in two ways, each seeming to contradict the other: Daniel was a wizard, or something like that, but he was an obstacle, a threat of some sort to Elizabeth.

"I hope he can come here," Alexandra said. "I have to talk to Elizabeth about it."

Euwen looked away, considering what he should say next. He finally decided to say nothing. The matter was working itself out in Alexandra. She needed no coaching from him.

Sixteen Dyrisians swept into the room. They carried golden trays of food. Two Dyrisians approached each of the six apprentice tables. Four of them glided across the floor to the long staff table.

Alexandra noticed how they worked in pairs. The trays they carried were large, imperfect semi-circles. When the Dyrisian couples arrived at each table, they interlocked their two trays to form a single seamless circular platter bearing an abundance of food. The united trays were deposited on a low wooden platform that hovered over the center of each table. The platforms floated in the direction of whatever hand was extended. Alexandra found it all quite bizarre. She wondered most about the joining of the trays: Why two trays made into one platter? Was this symbolic or simply necessary for reasons not apparent to her? These questions did not occupy her for long; there was delicious food to eat and she was ready to eat it. It appeared the culinary theme was Chinese. There was a steaming mountain of white rice in the center of each platter. This was surrounded by piping-hot dishes that included Orange Chicken, Teriyaki Chicken, Happy Family, Kung-pao Beef, Firecracker Chicken, Sweet and Sour Shrimp, Sesame Chicken, Hungarian Beef, and many other dishes Alexandra did not recognize. Some of the offerings were covered with sauces that made identification impossible; others were entirely new to her. There were several varieties of egg and spring rolls, arranged around covered soup tureens. The smells were intoxicating.

The familiar food reminded Alexandra of how the things of this world intermingled with those of her world. Chinese food here, at Byrnhelen in Second World, was clear evidence of this intermingling.

"I love Chinese food," said the brown-haired girl on Alexandra's left. "Every meal we have together during the year is from a different country in the other world. I think they do this so everyone can get a taste of home."

"Home?" asked Alexandra. "Is everyone here from where I came from?"

"Oh, no. Most are born in Second World, but First World is in a sense home to us all, if you know what I mean."

Alexandra didn't bother to tell her she didn't know at all

what she meant.

"My name's Rebecca," said the girl, "but everyone calls me Becca. This is my first year studying at Byrnhelen as well. The great thing is you don't have to eat Chinese food if you don't want to. Watch this."

Becca gestured to a Dyrisian standing nearby. The Dyrisian floated to her side.

"Please bring us some jagerschnitzel."

"Of course, Miss," the Dyrisian said. The creature raised her arms waist-high and moved her hands in three slow circles. A steaming platter of jagerschnitzel appeared between her hands. She gripped the handles of the platter and held it out to Becca.

"Thank you," Becca said, winking at Alexandra as she dished thin slices of meat smothered in mushroom gravy onto her plate.

"Would you like to try some?" Becca offered.

Alexandra nodded eagerly and Becca dished a few slices of meat onto Alexandra's plate.

"I've been to three farewell dinners this year. Do you want to see something else that's neat?"

Alexandra nodded. Becca reached out and with an exaggerated flourish, raised her empty goblet. She brought the goblet to her mouth and whispered into it.

"Gluehwein."

Steam began drifting up from within the goblet. Becca laughed at Alexandra's puzzled expression as the goblet filled with a dark purple liquid.

"Gluehwein is a hot, spicy cider we drink back home during the winter. Easy to get here too, if you know how."

"Cool," said Alexandra. "Where is home for you?

"My family and I live in First World, in Germany."

"I thought I heard a sort-of accent," Alexandra said. "My

family lives in First World too. I'm from America. How did you do that with the goblet?"

"By being extraordinarily gifted and amazing," Becca said playfully.

Both girls laughed.

"Really, how does it work?"

"Well, these are magic goblets. All you have to do is tell the goblet whatever it is you want to drink, and the drink will appear. And if you decide two sips into the glass that you want something else, all you do is name what it is you want and the new drink replaces the old one. You also can do something really disgusting."

"What?"

"Well, you can mix your drinks. For instance, you could tell the goblet you would like a mix of whatever kind of liquids you want and that is what you get. What makes it disgusting is that sometimes the boys will take a goblet and say all kinds of disgusting things: things like toad blood, worm slime, or goblin drool and then they will dare each other to drink it. You should hear some of the concoctions they come up with. At Halloween there was this one boy named Luke Patterson, who is a couple of years older than us, and he was dared to drink a mixture of bat's blood, pumpkin juice, ghoul slime, and toad spawn and he actually did it. Of course he did end up sick as a dog and had to go to the healer. Can you believe it?"

Alexandra laughed and shook her head.

"Of course you can make some of the best mixed drinks too. My favorite is when I ask the goblet for a mixture of carbonated pineapple, orange, strawberry, and mango juices. It's great! Actually I think I'll have that right now."

Becca gave the order to her goblet. It stopped steaming and filled itself with a light pink mixture that fizzed.

Alexandra turned to Euwen. "Did you see that?"

"I've seen goblets like that before."

"Oh, I forgot you've lived here all your life, so stuff like that is old news to you," Alexandra said with a touch of irony.

Euwen's disinterest made her long for Daniel to be here to share all these new things. She wondered where he was and what he might be doing. Hunger again took precedence over her ruminations. She dished small amounts of the various food offerings onto her plate and ate heartily.

Everyone completed the main course and the Dyrisians drifted to their assigned tables and positioned themselves directly in front of the now-empty golden platters. In one fluid movement, all the Dyrisians brought up their fists, opened them palm-up and paused. In the palm of each Dyrisian was a sparkling mound of golden dust. The Dyrisians blew the dust over the platters. The dust swirled in graceful patterns as it settled onto the platters. The moment the dust touched each platter, the remnants of the main course were replaced by a sumptuous Chinese dessert buffet. Small sugar-coated doughnuts occupied the center of the platters. The doughnuts were surrounded by bowls of various types of pudding. Another large bowl held a selection of fresh fruit and cookies. Various types of cakes, a couple large bowls with different flavors of ice cream, and many other types of desserts filled the platters.

Apparently this trick of replacement, which amazed Alexandra, was not new to the other apprentices. They continued chatting with their neighbors while they carefully chose the desert they wanted. Alexandra was pleased to see Euwen's expression showed some surprise. Again she wished for Daniel's presence to witness these wonders with her.

Alexandra enjoyed conversations with the other apprentices at her table: Katrina Thomas, Rondegal Demperton, and Jonathon Eaton. But it was Becca with whom she bonded.

The apprentices moved to the entrance hall after dinner, said their goodbyes, and left by the front doors. Some rode away on bicycles, others departed in horse-drawn buggies, and a few were simply there one moment and gone the next. Becca, after giving Alexandra a long hug, departed in this manner.

Alexandra shook her head and smiled.

What a place, she thought.

Euwen was standing with Alexandra just outside the front doors. He watched the last apprentice disappear into the night, heading for home. He thought of his home.

"It's time I say goodbye."

Alexandra turned to him.

"Thank you for bringing me here, and for staying. You made it easier."

She could not see Euwen's face clearly in the fading light. They had journeyed here together and he had stayed, if only for awhile. Hearing him announce his departure made her feel very much alone.

"If it's all right with you, I'll visit during your next break," Euwen said.

Alexandra calculated the interval.

"That's six weeks from now!" she said, making no effort to conceal her disappointment.

"Yes it is," Euwen said.

Then, like Becca, he simply disappeared.

34   Imprisonment

*There are no evil objects. A violin may be of poor
quality, but a master violinist can make it sing. When
the music fails, look to the violinist, not the violin. The
evil is in us, not in the wand we wield.*

FROM "THE WAND AND THE WAY" BY MATHIAS WILAMSFELD

General Croft's men carried Daniel back to his cell and
laid him on the cold stone floor. Daniel groaned and
rolled onto his side. Croft kicked him in the ribs, then placed
his boot on the boy's back and flattened him. Daniel had not
the strength to resist. Croft knelt at Daniel's head, gripped
his hair, and pulled upward.

"Hear this, young wizard," he hissed. "You know of the
pit by painful experience. Do not repeat your adventures
there. I will leave you some light, enough to keep you from
your earlier misfortune. Consider it my gift. Can't have you
killing yourself, can we. Aedan would not like that. You are
his honored guest."

Croft nodded and one of his men placed a small candle
lantern and a two-liter waterskin on the floor between Daniel
and the pit. Croft waved his men out of the cell. He followed
and closed the door. He peered through the view port as he
locked the door. The opening was not wide enough to
require bars or to give him a view of the entire cell, but he
could see the faint flickering of candlelight against the far
wall. He could not see Daniel.

*The killing will come later, my young whelp. And when it
does, you will beg for it to come.*

35 Conspiracy

I do not want them to love me. I want them to fear me. Lovers are erratic. Cowards move in quite predictable ways.

FROM "ESSAYS ON SUPREMACY" BY AEDAN SHAW

Euwen stood in the shadows and surveyed the large room he had just entered. The deep cowl of his traveling cloak was pulled over his head, keeping his face hidden. He saw Aedan standing alone near the center of the room.

"Come to me," Aedan said. His voice was black velvet.

Euwen stepped from the shadows, bowed low, and met Aedan at the center of the dimly-lit hall.

"What have you to report?"

Euwen swallowed nervously.

"I have gained her trust," he replied. "I'll see her again in a few weeks."

"Why a few weeks? I should think more time with her now, while your good deed is fresh, would have strengthened the bond?"

There was a hint of disapproval in the Aedan's voice.

"It did not seem prudent. The girl trusts me; the Guardian does not. She suspects something, but she's not yet confident in her suspicions. I feared I might give myself away."

"My sister's powers of discernment are strong," Aedan agreed. He clasped his hands behind his back and graced Euwen with a smile that was no more than a momentary twitch of his lips. "You are wise not to underestimate her. But her powers will not be strong enough in the end, and there will be an end to this—the one I desire, not the one she plans."

Euwen nodded. There was no message for him in the last statement. It was a matter between brother and sister, between Aedan and Elizabeth. His part was with the girl, Alexandra.

"Go again," Aedan said, "when you deem the time right. Draw closer to Alexandra. The appearance must be altruistic concern, not romantic pursuit. Let the hunger grow from the other side. The finest seductions appear first in the seduced, not in the seducer. Attend carefully to this subtlety."

Euwen shifted uneasily.

Aedan sensed his unease.

"You disagree?"

"No, sire."

There was a moment of silence between them.

Aedan eyes narrowed.

"Perhaps you doubt our cause. Shall I arrange for another to take your place?"

Euwen knew he was ideal for the part he was playing. It would be nearly impossible to introduce another in his place this late in the game. He knew Aedan knew this. Aedan's question was not a sincere offer of release from a difficult duty. It was no offer at all; it was a threat.

"No, sire," Euwen replied, putting steel into his voice. "I do not doubt our cause. I will do as you have ordered. I merely consider the complexities, the subtleties, as you have said. I must accomplish this under your sister's watchful eye, and Alexandra is no fool. I merely consider these things; I do not falter."

Aedan favored him with a thin facsimile of a smile.

"If you do your part, I will succeed even if my sister tries to intervene. The girl is young, impressionable. I am confident of your skills. You will succeed."

There it was again, the threat concealed within an affirmation.

Succeed or die.

"She keeps asking about Daniel," Euwen said, hoping to return Aedan's attention to their mutual plot. "She works to persuade your sister to bring him to Byrnhelen. This may be a problem."

"I think not. The young man is securely and quite secretly confined," Aedan replied. "No one will find him. He will never see Byrnhelen or his dear Alexandra.

Aedan's smile became genuine as he pictured the climax of his drama. "The girl's concern for Daniel will grow," he continued. "This will also work in my favor. You must encourage the girl to have concern for him, even to seek him. Their bond is strong, forged over their entire young lives. It will combine with the bond you form with her. The clash of emotions will weaken her. You will weaken her. I will then shape her to my purpose. The possibilities delight me."

Euwen said nothing.

"You may go," Aedan said with sudden coolness.

Euwen bowed, took a few steps backward, turned, and disappeared into the shadows from whence he had come.

36   Challenge and Choice

There are no masters. There are only beginners.
Beginners many times over. Now here, now there.
Riding the wind in one moment, trudging through mud
in the next. The great hearts do not achieve anything;
they only begin again.

FROM *"VESSELS OF DESTINY"* BY MASTER MAREK AVALARD

Alexandra lay in a cold sweat, her heart racing, the bed's satin top sheet bunched around her feet, the bottom sheet saturated. Her feather comforter lay in a clump on the floor next to the bed.

The nightmare had been vivid and Alexandra required a few moments to be sure it had been only a dream. That it had been frightening was not unusual: Nightmares are nightmares, she reminded herself. It was the urgency she felt now that she was awake and fully aware that was unusual. Something must be done; the dream was important.

It had begun pleasantly enough. She was playing hide-and-seek with Daniel among the trees and shrubs on her family's estate. Something bad happened, something terrifying, and joyful running turned into desperate pursuit. Daniel became a fleeting movement, a wraith barely visible ahead of her, calling out, pleading. She ran after him in maddening slow-motion. He remained elusive, always just out of reach, sliding under bushes and trees, popping out of the ground further ahead. His movements were not his own: He was a puppet scurrying (or being dragged) up, down, left, right. And then he was gone, and Alexandra was alone in a place she did not recognize.

The images faded too fast; Alexandra could capture only a few. And then, like Daniel, they were gone.

Alexandra looked around her room. The golden light of early morning illuminated the forest green walls. There was a white brick fireplace across from her bed and a desk in the corner. Paintings of idyllic landscapes hung on the walls. White sheers covered glass double doors that opened onto a small balcony. Partially opened doors on the other side of the room revealed a small bathroom and a closet.

Alexandra walked to the bathroom. She looked in the mirror. The face looking back at her showed no signs of the distress she had felt moments before. Her urgency about the dream had dissolved. She was hungry.

She dressed and made her way to the dining hall. Three apprentices occupied one of the tables. She had just pulled out a chair at their table when a Dyrisian approached. Alexandra looked at the Dyrisian's long golden braid and petite figure and marveled once again at the beauty of these creatures.

"Your aunt wishes you to join her for breakfast," the Dyrisian said, "I will show you the way."

It was a command given in soft tones and gentle words, but a command nonetheless.

"I'm sorry," Alexandra said to the others. They nodded impassively and continued to eat.

Alexandra followed the Dyrisian out of the room, around a corner, and into a corridor she had not visited before. The Dyrisian led her along the corridor to a large oak door. The creature opened the door, walked through it into a tiny room, and beckoned Alexandra to follow. The room was no larger than a closet. In it was a collection of old brooms; a shelf on which sat an array of half-used candles; and a pile of boxes of various sizes, shapes, and colors. The Dyrisian reached around Alexandra and pushed the door closed. She left the flat of her palm on the door and said rather ceremoniously, "Alterraina." The door opened. Beyond it was a spacious office or library, not the empty corridor they had just left. Her aunt was there, seated at a large mahogany desk. The desk was on the right side of the room. On the other side was a massive stone fireplace.

Alexandra, quite bewildered, entered the room. The Dyrisian bowed to Elizabeth and vanished.

"Welcome," Elizabeth said, rising from behind her desk.

"What happened?" Alexandra asked while turning in a slow circle to take in her surroundings.

"A device installed to make the location of my office less...obvious. But more on that later, my dear. Please, join me."

Alexandra followed Elizabeth to a circular table laid out with a variety of inviting breakfast foods.

"You should be able to find something to your liking," Elizabeth said, picking up a cheese Danish and dishing out some fresh fruit for herself. Alexandra did the same and sat beside her aunt at the table. The two ate in silence for a short while.

"Orange juice," Elizabeth said to her crystal goblet. It complied by filling itself with the requested beverage. Elizabeth held the goblet delicately and looked at Alexandra.

"After breakfast, we will journey to Wilamsfeld to purchase the clothing and supplies you need. You need to know a few things before we go, so Please listen carefully."

Alexandra glanced up from her plate, nodded, and continued to eat.

"You have missed four of the eight master courses that make up the curriculum of a first-year apprentice. Each of these courses is normally five weeks long. You will complete the remaining four courses with the other apprentices in the normal way and in the normal time. However, when the others go home for their week-long break between each course, you will not go home. You will remain here, with me and certain other, ah, teachers. You will have to make up in four weeks the courses that normally require twenty."

"How will I do that?" Alexandra asked incredulously. She had stopped eating and was giving Elizabeth her undivided attention.

"With great difficulty, my dear," Elizabeth responded, coldly, "and it is unlikely you will succeed. It is unfair of me to ask you to try. You must choose for yourself."

To capture the bird, one must open the cage, Elizabeth thought.

With exaggerated precision, Alexandra laid her fork on the edge of her plate. A barely perceptible smile formed at the corners of her mouth, a secret smile, more concealing than revealing. She picked up her goblet and sipped from it. She set it down and held the stem between her fingers. She studied the clarity of the glass, twisted the stem through a half turn counterclockwise, and gazed steadily at Elizabeth:

"When do we begin?"

37   Call to Action

People who long for solitude find themselves surrounded by crowds. People who long for the company of others find themselves alone. It is the longing that curses us. Embrace what you have, but not too tightly. It will soon depart.

FROM "CONSTANCY AND CHAOS" BY MASTER FARID SAHURA

Daniel lay face-down on the floor of his cell, his head turned to the side, his cheek resting on the cold stone. He stared at the candle lantern a meter in front of him. Beyond it was the pit. His head hurt, other places hurt. He did not want to move. He did not want to think, to consider his situation. He just wanted to stare at the flickering candle flame within its small metal enclosure.

Thoughts intruded. He thought of the father he had never known. He tried to conjure his appearance. His conjuring was interrupted by an image of his mother, Ellen. She seemed to be speaking to him, but he could not hear her. John and Mary Ward were there, in the background, the material pillars that supported his life and his mother's. But they were more than that. From them arose Alexandra, his sister in all but blood and the only person who shared his strangeness, who understood.

It was because of her that he and his mother had remained with the Wards. John and Mary would have sent them away years ago had they thought Alexandra would stand for it. She had demonstrated rather forcefully that she would not. This and other forces made them, all of them, an unlikely family. His mother was not merely a maid, nanny, and cook, and he was not merely the son of a household servant.

He knew this. Alexandra knew it. They all knew it.

But none of this mattered now. It was all finished. Alexandra was gone, disappeared without a trace. He was confined in this unknown place by means and for reasons he could not fathom. He no longer knew himself or his life or anyone's life. He was not dead but he might as well be.

Daniel's thoughts punished him. They accused him of being the reason Alexandra had fled into the storm, maybe the reason she had died or, little better, was confined as he was, in this terrible limbo. He was of no use to Alexandra or himself or anyone else.

This last thought dragged Daniel out of his reverie.

He sat up.

Helpless prisoner? If I stay that, I have no chance at all, Alexandra has no chance at all. By thinking of her as dead, I may be condemning her to death. The man who calls himself Aedan said he had "some knowledge" of her. Was that merely a taunt? Does he know something? Simply enduring, simply waiting to die is not an option.

I must survive.

I must escape.

Nothing is ready to be until it is. There are no preparations. All things in heaven and earth are continually becoming. Beginnings and endings are illusions, some comforting, some terrifying. The wise man smiles. The wise woman lifts her arms. The creator is pleased.

FROM "HISTORY OF THE EXODUS" BY ANDRONIUS CALEDON

Alexandra had accepted the challenge:
She would get no breaks between courses; she would make up in four weeks the courses that normally required twenty. Only in this way could she catch up to the other apprentices.

"You're sure?" Elizabeth asked again.

Alexandra gazed steadily at her aunt and replied with steely conviction:

"I'm sure."

Elizabeth felt a partial lifting of her burden of doubt. An important milestone had been passed.

This one does not need the gold star, the blue ribbon, the winner's medallion. She needs raw challenge to match her raw audacity. I must supply her with opportunities to be defeated over and over again by greater and greater foes.

Elizabeth was surprised by the clarity with which she saw this need in Alexandra. Elizabeth had devoted her life to gifted children, but she had never encountered one so prepared. In many ways, Alexandra was a typical fifteen-year-old girl. But in moments of challenge, like the one that had just past, she was far from typical. In those moments, she became ancient, a force of nature possessed of the grinding patience of a glacier on the one hand and the unpredictable impulsiveness of a lightning strike on the other. This reminded her of brother, Aedan. The reminder was unsettling.

It is a dangerous game I play with her.

"There is one more thing," Alexandra said.

"What is that?"

"I want Daniel here, with me. He will want to come. His mother will approve. You can make it so."

Alexandra glared at her aunt. Back was the fifteen-year-old girl, wanting what she wanted when she wanted it, needy, reaching back for an old attachment, a "best friend."

Elizabeth suppressed a smile.

Alexandra's gaze remained steady.

Elizabeth let her smile show. The smile conveyed understanding, but without warmth. It said that she had heard but not that she had yielded. What it did not say was that she knew things Alexandra did not know and had no intention of revealing them to her. Not yet. Perhaps not ever.

"For this we need a contract," Elizabeth responded finally. "In it you will give your solemn promise of obedience to my instructions and the requirements of your accelerated training, regardless of the real or imagined needs of your relationship with Daniel. Only then will I consider his presence here."

"Yes, of course," Alexandra said.

"You agree too easily. This is a hard thing I propose."

"I promise. I will do everything you ask."

"We shall see. I'll have the contract drawn up, and both of us will sign it. If you breach your promise, Daniel will be gone, and you will continue here, undeterred, and all this will be according to your sacred promise. Is that clear?"

"Yes, yes. I promise," replied Alexandra, beaming.

"There is a problem," Elizabeth said, her voice low.

Alexandra's smile vanished.

"I don't know your friend's whereabouts. There are conflicting reports. I am sorting them out. The arrangements may take time. Do you accept this?"

Alexandra hesitated.

"Do you? I must know."

"Yes," Alexandra replied.

"This too shall be written into our contract."

Alexandra nodded.

Elizabeth looked away from her niece.

How am I going to manage this? she asked herself.

First Worlders are incapable of comprehending our exodus. It began in the early Middle Ages. People of that time and many centuries after allowed only what they knew, and they knew very little. Stepping from darkness into light was a reversal of spiritual fortunes to them, the acceptance of an invitation from the devil. It did not occur to them that the devil resided in their inquisitions and their trials and their burnings, not in the mysteries of magic. Some call that time the Dark Ages. This is wrong. It was the Gray Ages. It was the beginning of the end of magic in First World and the flowering of it in Second World.

FROM "HISTORY OF THE TWO WORLDS" BY MASTER BRADYN ARISTARCHUS

An outing to Wilamsfeld would be just the thing. Certain supplies were needed, but more important, Alexandra needed to be seen by the locals and introduced to Mathias.

Elizabeth called for Gidram to bring the carriage, and she and Alexandra took their seats. Eudora, the Pegasus harnessed to the carriage, looked back at Alexandra and whinnied.

"She recognizes you," Elizabeth said.

Alexandra smiled. Four hours later, Gidram pulled up to the stone gates of Wilamsfeld.

"Shall I wait here, Madam?"

"Yes. I'll send you our packages."

Alexandra marveled at the sights, sounds, and smells of the quaint village. People were walking to and fro, greeting one another and conversing. The cobblestone streets were narrow and winding. The smell of hot bread and doughnuts was in the air, making Alexandra hungry for the warm, sugary pastries. There were many shops, each displaying a large assortment of goods. The exterior walls of the shops were adorned with large murals. The murals appeared quite three-dimensional, and objects in them moved, arranging themselves invitingly according to the offerings of nearby shops.

Holograms, she thought. *Just like at home.*

Soon they came to a mural where the characters were especially lively. Men and women in the mural danced gaily around wicker picnic baskets on colorful blankets. The baskets contained an assortment of food, napkins, plates, bowls, flatware and other items offered within the shop.

Alexandra found the scene captivating. She approached to take a closer look. She touched the mural with her right hand. One of the dancers, a plump little fellow with pudgy fingers, grabbed her hand and held it fast. Alexandra tried to pull away, but the little man was strong. She planted her left foot against the wall and pushed back. The mischief-maker suddenly released his grip and Alexandra staggered backward fell into a deep snow bank bordering the sidewalk. She struggled to rise, slipped, rolled over, and came up covered in powdery snow from head to toe. She maintained as much dignity as she could muster, brushed herself off, and rushed at the figure in the mural. The mischief-maker retreated and went on dancing with the others as though nothing had happened.

A cheer went up behind her. She turned and found a small crowd had gathered. People were smiling and laughing good naturedly, as were the figures in the mural behind her. Alexandra turned in a semicircle and with mock seriousness bowed repeatedly to the crowd.

"Good show, girl," said a wizened old man, smiling.

"Don't let those good-for-nothings get you down," said a portly woman next to him.

"You showed 'em," said another.

Some touched her, some nodded approvingly, others looked on with something like awe. This surprised her. She had done nothing remarkable. If anything, she had made a fool of herself. But the looks, the gestures, the demeanor of the crowd did not reflect this. They saw something else, and Alexandra had no idea what it might be.

She caught sight of her aunt. The Guardian was standing across the street, expressionless and apart from the crowd. Alexandra joined her.

"Did you enjoy yourself?" Elizabeth inquired as the two walked on.

Alexandra looked back at the dispersing crowd. Several people waved, and she waved back.

"Yes, I did. They were so nice."

"Yes, they were," Elizabeth said, seeming vaguely displeased, "and you enjoyed it a bit too much. Adulation, especially that which is unearned, can be toxic. Consider that. Consider also that it is not you who captivates them; it is something about you that you have yet to discover. The things *about* you—rank, titles, even your lineage—are not you. Keep that in mind."

Well, she managed to spoil the moment with nonsense, like she does most things, thought Alexandra with more than a tinge of resentment.

The mood lightened as Alexandra and Elizabeth spent the next few hours wandering up and down the narrow village streets. Elizabeth was engrossed in a list she carried, and ticked off items as they were purchased in various shops. Alexandra found the shops quaint and the shopkeepers jovial and friendly. But behind their joviality, she detected a certain tension, something between awe and curiosity. She wondered what made her presence so fascinating to these people.

Maybe it's just that I'm with the Guardian. I certainly won't ask Miss Grouchy-pants Elizabeth about it. She has already had her say.

After each collection of purchases, Elizabeth tapped the packaged items with her wand and they instantly disappeared. Alexandra decided the packages were on their way to Gidram.

"Wilamsfeld is our last stop," Elizabeth said as she turned right and began walking down one of the narrow side streets.

"Wilamsfeld? I thought we were in Wilamsfeld," Alexandra said.

"We are in the village of Wilamsfeld. I'm talking about the shop."

Alexandra thought for a moment:

"Why does the shop have the same name as the village?"

"It doesn't. The village has the same name as the shop."

Alexandra rolled her eyes.

Elizabeth did not see this and continued with great seriousness:

"This village and Byrnhelen were established at about the same time. The village was named Hinker-Stanwavitz, after some long-forgotten worthy who played some long-forgotten role in its founding."

Alexandra burst into laughter.

Her aunt gazed at her, perplexed, but kept walking.

"Say it again," said Alexandra, her mirth barely concealed.

"Say what again?"

"The village."

"Hinker-Stanwavitz?"

Alexandra went into another paroxysm of laughter.

The contagion of laughter touched Elizabeth but did not collapse her dignified reserve. She allowed herself a chuckle or two.

"I can see why they would want to change the name," Alexandra said when she was again able to speak.

"Indeed, but it was not so much a change as an evolution in common reference."

"Sounds like a change to me."

"Well, yes. Anyway, a particularly talented wizard lived in the village. His name was Theodorus Wilamsfeld. Theodorus was a wand maker, a very special wand maker."

"Hinker-Stanwavitz wands, right?" Alexandra said impishly.

"Alexandra, stop! Listen to my story."

"OK, I'm listening."

"Well, most wand makers create an inventory of wands. Buyers select from that inventory. This was not Theodorus's way. Like a tailor who measures the customer head-to-toe, fashions the garment, and fits it to the buyer, Theodorus measured and fitted each of his wands to the buyer. The buyer came first. The wand came after. He kept no inventory. By a secret process of magical tests, Theodorus determined the match of wood and magical core that was ideal for each customer. And he charged a high price, a very high price. Few could pay it. Some he would not sell to at any price."

"Just because a guy sells expensive wands, they name a town after him?"

Elizabeth went on, ignoring the interruption:

"These wands were more than finely made and expensive. They gave the owner full access to his or her magical powers. Most wands give only partial access. Word spread of this and buyers came from far and wide, asking directions to Wilamsfeld, not Hinker-Stanwavitz. By the time of Theodorus's death, Hinker-Stanwavitz, always irritatingly difficult to pronounce, had been replaced by Wilamsfeld as the name of the village."

"That's a long story," Alexandra said.

"Yes, I suppose it is, but we enjoyed it, didn't we."

"I did, I really did. You made me laugh, and that felt good. You're different out here, Aunt Elizabeth. You're different from the way you are at Byrnhelen. I like it."

"Don't get too accustomed to the difference. I have a role to play, and so do you. Rare will be the time and place where you can laugh. Rarer still will be the people you can laugh with. Yours must be a cautious existence."

"But not now, OK, Aunt Elizabeth?"

"Yes, not now."

The two walked together in silence for a minute or so before Elizabeth continued.

"The secret of Wilamsfeld's special wands did not die with him. He passed the secret on to his apprentice, his young nephew, who inherited the business. And so it continued in an unbroken line to this day."

Alexandra felt a twinge of excitement that soon combined with vague foreboding.

This is not just a history lesson, she thought.

"How long has this been going on?"

"More than a thousand years," Elizabeth replied.

Everything around here seems to have started more than a thousand years ago, Alexandra thought. *And nothing much has changed. The whole place seems trapped in the Middle Ages.*

"Why is everything here so old-fashioned?" Alexandra

asked.

"We cling to the forms and traditions of the Middle Ages because that's when the Exodus began."

"What exodus?"

The question reminded Elizabeth how wide was the gulf between their two worlds, how different their histories. The sacred incantation arose in her:

Andronius Caledon, Protector of All Magical Beings, Master of the Dimensions, and Creator of Second World.

"Andronius Caledon," Elizabeth murmured.

"Who is he?"

"The man who discovered the dimensions. He mastered passage between them and gave them their names: First World for the dimension you came from, Second World for where you are now."

"You're saying this exodus happened during the Middle Ages," Alexandra observed, "but the only one I know about was the Israelites fleeing Egypt. They call that the Exodus and it happened way before. I never heard of what's-his-name and the exodus you're talking about."

Elizabeth frowned at Alexandra.

"You speak too lightly of what is sacred."

"Sorry. It's just I never heard of any of this."

"Nor have your First-World kin," Elizabeth said, "except as myth. Andronius saw to it in his time; I and others see to it in ours. Myth is what keeps us safe."

"Safe from what?"

"Safe from First Worlders," Elizabeth responded.

"I'm a First Worlder."

"Not quite or you wouldn't be here. Andronius made the Exodus possible. Most witches and warlocks joined the Exodus, but some could not bear to leave. Ninety thousand were executed for witchcraft from AD 1500 to 1660 alone."

"But all that has changed," Alexandra said. "There are no witch trials. No one is burned at the stake anymore."

Elizabeth smiled wanly.

"Yes, progress has been made, but not as much as you might think. The most recent witch trials were held in the United Kingdom as recently as 1944 under the Witchcraft Act of 1735. That's only seventy years ago. The law was repealed in 1951 and replaced by the Fraudulent Mediums Act. In 2008, that law too was repealed."

"So, everything's okay now, right?" Alexandra offered hopefully.

"Not quite. First World fear of magical powers has simply moved away from belief in witches, wizards, and warlocks as evil servants of the devil to disbelief in their existence at all."

Elizabeth chuckled ruefully before going on:

"People like me—and you—were either burned at the stake for being witches or in modern times prosecuted for not being witches but pretending to be. Now, the best you and I can hope for in First World is to be ignored as fools and charlatans. The wisest course for us in that world is to hide our powers and pretend to be what we are not."

"Wait, I know kids who think they're witches and warlocks, and there are people who worship the devil and stuff like that. No one seems to bother them much."

"None of them are Second Worlders," said Elizabeth. "They are pretenders. They are tolerated—when they are tolerated—because they are known to be pretenders. They are not our people."

"What about magicians. They're very popular in First World."

"And why do you think that is?" Elizabeth asked.

Alexandra pondered for a moment.

"Because they're fun. People are surprised by what they do and they laugh and they pay lots of money to see their tricks."

"And if they were not merely tricks?" Elizabeth asked. "What if it were thought they could in an instant teleport a real elephant from Africa to a casino in Las Vegas? What then? Not so fun, not so entertaining, not so funny. There is an order to things people depend on. Violate that order and you will be punished."

Alexandra became serious as she considered the truth Elizabeth had spoken.

"What about miracles? People love miracles, even if they've never seen one," Alexandra offered.

"Ah," said Elizabeth, smiling broadly, "miracles do please, as long as they are the right brand. Miracles occur frequently at the leading edge of First World technology. First Worlders love such 'miracles.' Many also love religious miracles, as long as they have the appearance of acts of God. But you show me a man or woman who can speak the words of a spell or make a hand gesture that instantaneously moves a real elephant from Africa to Las Vegas, and I will show you someone soon to be arrested."

Alexandra looked shocked.

"Couldn't we use our powers for good and be accepted?"

"That's been tried. Andronius rescued us from that failed effort more than a thousand years ago."

"So it's hopeless."

"I didn't say that."

40   *The Wandmaker*

Cavort with angels and learn their ways. Yet be not one of them. There is time enough to be of that kind. Now is for human beings. Now is for triumph and tragedy, joy and pain, courage and cowardice, heroes and common men. We think to be angels, while they wish to be us.

FROM "PATHS TO SAINTHOOD" BY DOM ANDRÉ DU BOURGAY

The word *Wilamsfeld* was carved into the weathered gray wood of the sign above the door. Neither the carving nor the sign nor the building it labeled had been painted in many years.

Alexandra peered at the display shelf behind the dirty front window. The items on it were neatly arranged, more in the manner of a museum than a place of business. Included were small toys and replicas of larger things. There were some dolls and a few statues. Here and there nondescript wands rested in open boxes that bore the Wilamsfeld imprint. Dust lay over all these items. The dust seemed part of the display, a statement about time and patience and the laying down of things in layers, one upon another.

Alexandra saw no tags announcing names, purposes, or prices. It was as though the proprietor had given up trying to sell the things on the shelf. They were just orderly bric-a-brac: forgotten, uninteresting, and sad.

Reflected daylight was all that illuminated the display and the interior beyond it. Nothing moved within the shop. Elizabeth opened the shop door and beckoned for her to follow. A small bell above the door tinkled to announce their arrival.

"I'll be with you in just a moment."

The man speaking to them was hidden by a wide grey curtain behind the front counter. The curtain moved here and there but no one appeared.

Alexandra examined the interior of the shop. It was small, no larger than the sitting room in her parents' home. The wood floor was worn and unfinished. A threadbare rug covered three-quarters of it. Several low shelves were built into the pale ochre walls on the left side of the room. Strange artifacts were arranged along these shelves. There was no dust on them. A small fire burned in a red-brick fireplace to her right.

"Elizabeth!"

Alexandra turned to see an elderly man emerge from behind the curtain. He appeared as ancient as the shop, his white hair sparse and thin, his face deeply lined. His eyes were clear, the irises almost golden. He appeared quite robust and handsome despite his age.

"My dear Elizabeth, how good it is to see you again."

He walked from behind the counter and extended his hand.

"Hello, Mathias," Elizabeth said, clasping his hand in both of hers.

"I've been expecting you," Mathias replied.

"I'm sorry. I've been quite busy since we last talked. I should have kept you informed."

"I meant no complaint," Mathias said, turning serious. "Is this the one?"

He nodded toward Alexandra.

"That is my hope," Elizabeth said.

"It needs to be more than a hope for my work to matter."

"It is more than that, and there is no time."

"Very well," Mathias said. "When shall I come?"

"Tomorrow at 10:00 would be ideal. Does that give you time?"

"Yes. I've taken all but the final steps, as we discussed. I can take her critical measurements tomorrow."

Hello, it's me, Alexandra thought, *the person you're talking about measuring. I'm right here. Hello.*

Mathias turned to Alexandra as though he had read her thoughts.

"I am Mathias Wilamsfeld," he said, not waiting for Elizabeth to make the belated introduction, "and you are Alexandra Ward."

His use of her full name surprised and somehow delighted her.

"How do you do, sir," Alexandra responded demurely.

Wilamsfeld bowed with exaggerated formality.

"I do quite well, young lady."

He turned to Elizabeth.

"You left something out of your description of your niece. You described her formidable talents, but you omitted…"

Elizabeth laughed. "That will be quite enough, Mathias. For all your wisdom, you can be so easily distracted."

"Easily and quite willingly," Wilamsfeld admitted."

Alexandra blushed.

"At Byrnhelen tomorrow, Mathias," Elizabeth said, returning them to the business of the wand.

"Excellent," Mathias said. "Now, I hope you ladies will join me for some refreshments."

Alexandra intervened when she sensed Elizabeth was about to decline:

"Oh, that would be very nice, Mr. Wilamsfeld."

"Yes," Elizabeth added, giving Alexandra a warning

glance, "very kind of you, Mathias, but we can only stay a short while."

She seizes control by impulsive words and actions, thought Elizabeth. *That will require some...refinement.*

"Excellent! Very nice," Mathias said. "Darien, bring some tea for our guests, and lock the door. We are closed for the day."

A thin, dark-haired young man appeared from behind the curtain. He locked the front door and without speaking disappeared again behind the curtain.

"So, Elizabeth, tell me where things stand."

"Alexandra is beginning her apprenticeship. It will be quite demanding. Your wand will be a great help."

"This I knew. I will endeavor to make it my best work."

He smiled warmly at Alexandra.

Alexandra decided she definitely liked Mathias, and she could see Elizabeth liked him too, in spite of (or maybe because of) the playful way he chipped at her rigid decorum. He was a flirt, clearly, but one of surpassing skill. There was no threat in him.

The dark-haired young man appeared again. He placed a wide silver tray with a porcelain tea set on the small table in front of the sofa. The tray held a large plate of sandwiches, tiny cakes, and tarts. The young man left, again without having uttered a word.

"That is Darien, my nephew. He's painfully shy and quite uncomfortable with introductions. Please don't be offended. He's my apprentice and very good at what he does. One day in the not-too-distant future he will take my place."

Elizabeth poured tea for all of them while Alexandra sampled two or three of the pastries.

"These are delicious," she said with enthusiasm.

"Thank you, my dear," Mathias responded. "Please help

yourself, Elizabeth. They are excellent. I have it on good authority: one Alexandra Ward, esteemed niece of the Guardian. She says so."

Elizabeth was unsuccessful in suppressing a smile.

Mathias returned his attention to Alexandra, and the two were soon engaged in animated conversation. Elizabeth listened carefully: Alexandra was being quite open. Mathias was being genuine, but he was also subtly guiding the conversation, learning about Alexandra, assessing her strengths...and her weaknesses.

The wand maker was at work.

41   Tangled Webs

A foolish elf thinks he can know without asking. A wise elf asks without knowing. The first learns nothing and stays a fool. The second learns the next question.

FROM "ELVIN NONSENSE" BY YODLESTAN PLUMKERFELTER

Elizabeth went immediately to her office after returning from Wilamsfeld. She walked to the wall behind her desk and stood before a large gilded mirror. She pressed her right index finger against the lower left corner of the glass and the mirror glowed bright green. She pulled her hand away as the image of a man with white hair and amber eyes filled the mirror.

It was Borrington.

"Alexandra has agreed," Elizabeth said, "a bit too easily perhaps, thinking Daniel will join her."

"Why would she think that?" Borrington asked.

"I promised it."

"I thought…"

"I know, I know. But it was the only way."

Borrington smiled:

"The young man plays a larger part than you thought," he said.

Elizabeth pursed her lips and nodded. She remembered how she had originally decided Daniel's presence at Byrnhelen would be a distraction, indeed a needless hardship for Alexandra. She remembered being confident the aura of Byrnhelen and the challenges of the apprenticeship would dull Alexandra's longings for the past, including her desire for the companionship of her friend.

"What changed?" Borrington asked.

"My last two days with her. I grossly underestimated the filial bond between them. The young man's continued absence would be more distracting than his presence. It is imperative you find Daniel and bring him to Byrnhelen."

"You're sure of this?"

"I am. Contact Ellen Sutton, Daniel's mother. I think she can be convinced to allow her son to be enrolled in the apprentice program with Alexandra. Bring him to Byrnhelen.

"I can do this."

"You sound hesitant, Andrew."

"Not hesitant, Guardian. Thoughtful. Is there anything else I need to know?"

Elizabeth paused, considering how much to tell her trusted general. She had her own purposes for bringing Daniel to Byrnhelen. One of them was the exploration of linking Daniel's powers in parallel with Alexandra's. This had never been attempted, as far as she knew, but the unique relationship between the two might make it possible.

Very risky, she thought, *and highly unpredictable. This is not the time to broach this to Andrew. He will have objections. I am not ready to hear them.*

"There is another reason, Andrew. Alexandra's relationship with Daniel is well established; I can't change that. However, I can use Daniel to prevent the hatching of a romance between her and Euwen McConnelly."

"You have reason to believe there is a romance?" Borrington asked incredulously.

Elizabeth smiled.

Sometimes men can be so dense about these matters.

"Andrew! The girl has been plucked from First World; separated from the only parents she has ever known; and torn apart from Daniel, her lifelong friend and kindred spirit. I am amazed at how well she is adapting, but it would be naïve to ignore her vulnerability. She is young and beautiful. Euwen is a threat to her concentration, if nothing else. And I know nothing of him or his family. He appears out of nowhere. I want you to make discreet inquiries about him and find Daniel."

"May I speak freely, Guardian?"

"Certainly, always. What is it?"

"You weave a tangled web, Elizabeth. It may not hold together as you plan. Daniel and Alexandra were raised as brother and sister, but they are not that, neither by blood nor adoption. The day will come when they look at each other with mature eyes. We cannot guess what their feelings might be then. Euwen is a similar problem, as you say, but you cannot predict which relationship will need neutralizing or who will be effective in neutralizing it."

Maybe I am the dense one, thought Elizabeth. *Andrew sees in multiple dimensions and makes no assumptions.*

"What are you suggesting?" she asked.

Borrington pondered, his arms folded, his eyes cast downward. He stroked his chin. Finally he spoke:

"I am suggesting I do as you've asked, up to a point. I contact Daniel's mother and inquire of her wishes. I ask her to keep our conversation to herself. I do not bring Daniel here. Not yet. I buy time to consider the ramifications. We watch. We watch Alexandra and we watch Daniel. And we watch Euwen. If we see nothing to change your mind, I bring Daniel here. In the meantime, I continue my investigation of Euwen."

Elizabeth nodded slowly.

"Agreed," she said. "I have an intuition about this, or perhaps just a prejudice: I find Euwen's gallant and curiously convenient rescue of Alexandra to be suspicious. I distrust coincidences, especially convenient ones like this."

"I share your distrust," Borrington said. "As two old conspirators, we may be a bit jaded, but I agree this deserves special attention. You will be pleased to know my inquiries began as soon as we knew Euwen had Alexandra."

Elizabeth smiled at her old friend.

"I had no doubt."

> *Rain falls against my window. A bird is there, crouching on the sill, buffeted. I hold a candle to the glass. My bed is dry. This is the divinity of the ordinary.*
>
> FROM "DIVINITY OF THE ORDINARY" BY MASTER BRADYN ARISTARCHUS

It was Sunday, the day Alexandra would be fitted for her wand. The previous day's outing had been a delightful departure from the seriousness of Byrnhelen. Mathias Wilamsfeld in particular had been a welcome break from her aunt's stilted formality. Alexandra looked forward to meeting him again.

Mathias and Darien arrived precisely at 10:00.

Mathias asked Alexandra to stand in the middle of Elizabeth's office and hold her arms out to her sides. Alexandra did as he instructed.

"We will be taking certain measurements and conducting certain tests. None of these will be painful. You need only follow my instructions. Your aunt will observe. Are you ready?"

Alexandra nodded shyly.

"Good. You may drop your arms. Please remove your shoes."

Mathias called Darien to him, and the two began their work. They measured Alexandra with different types and colors of strings and complex instruments. They seemed to give their attention not to absolute sizes and lengths, but to proportions and various relationships (the difference in the length of her index finger and her little finger, for example). Samples of skin and saliva were obtained. Darien took careful notes as Mathias whispered his findings. This went on for about half an hour.

When this phase was completed, Mathias asked Alexandra to sit on a chair he had placed nearby. It was floating in the air about half a meter above the floor. This chair was next to another just like it, also floating, so when one moved, the other did also.

Mathias assisted Alexandra onto the chair. He asked her to hold various stones and metals and other objects. He directed her to hold this or that object in a certain hand, then the other hand. Sometimes he had her holding objects in both hands. All the while, Darien appeared to be matching what Mathias was doing by adding, subtracting, and rearranging objects on the other chair.

Occasionally, Mathias paused and appeared to recheck an earlier measurement. The chair process, with re-measurements and the taking of some additional samples, ended in about an hour.

"We are nearly done, my dear. You have been very patient. There is one final thing."

Mathias reached up and gently teased some strands of Alexandra's hair away from her head. Darien snipped them off with a pair of scissors. Mathias wound them together, formed them into a loose overhand knot, and carefully wrapped the hair in a piece of black cloth. Darien took custody of the cloth and the other samples.

"All done," Mathias said, beaming.

He helped Alexandra out of the chair.

"You may put your shoes back on."

"You bore up well, Alexandra," Elizabeth said. "Feel free to relax, explore, enjoy yourself. The real work begins tomorrow night."

Alexandra understood she was being dismissed, and she was glad of it. She thanked Mathias and left the office.

"What is it?" Elizabeth asked the Mathias after Alexandra left the room. "I can see you're concerned."

"There were unexpected...complexities," he said in a whisper Darien could not hear.

"I knew there would be," she replied.

"It may take some time. The content of her character is exceptionally rich. Creating the space for it in the wand will be difficult."

"I understand."

Elizabeth reached into a pocket and withdrew a small satin pouch. She handed the pouch to Mathias. There was the soft tinkling of coins as Mathias deposited the bag into a pocket of his tunic.

"Guard her well," Mathias said.

"With my life."

"It may come to that."

"Yes, my old friend, it may."

43 *Dreams and Other Worlds*

*Some see without believing. They feel wind on their
faces and think they know the stratosphere. They dangle
their feet in ponds and think they know the ocean. They
do many calculations and think they know the stars.
They think too much, remember nothing of what came
before them, and die without experience.*

FROM "CHILD ON THE WALL" BY MASTER TOURIN ABDAL

Elizabeth had given no assignments after Alexandra's
fitting for her wand, so she was free to explore the
castle, the surrounding gardens, and the wilderness beyond
the gardens. She spent the remainder of Sunday and most of
Monday in these refreshing explorations.

All this came to an end Monday evening. After a simple
dinner (nothing like the extravagant affair of last Friday),
Alexandra followed Elizabeth up a winding staircase to a
circular chamber at the top of the largest tower of Byrnhelen.
A huge reflecting telescope was anchored to the floor of the
chamber. The telescope tube was some forty-six meters in
length and five meters in diameter. Elizabeth raised her arms
over her head and moved her hands outward. The dome
ceiling high above divided and gave a broad view of
thousands of stars.

Alexandra stared in wonder at the heavens.

Elizabeth nudged her.

"Follow me."

Alexandra followed Elizabeth in tight circles up an
enclosed metal staircase that ended high above the chamber

floor at a large platform enclosed in a metal cage. The platform swayed noticeably as they stepped onto it. On the other side of the platform was the top of the telescope.

"Don't be alarmed," Elizabeth said reassuringly. "The construction is sturdy. The Dyrisian astronomers like it this way. They call it 'rhythmic' and can sometimes be found dancing and singing with its movements. I don't disapprove as long as they stabilize the platform when necessary for the work." Elizabeth walked to a control panel near the stairway access and pulled down a lever. The platform instantly stabilized.

A large desk, bookshelves, and a bank of wooden filing cabinets occupied one side of the platform. Chairs and a long conference table were on the other side. Between them was access to the viewing chair mounted on the telescope tube near the focuser and eyepiece.

Elizabeth led Alexandra to the viewing chair and invited her to sit.

"Look through the eyepiece while I make some adjustments. Tell me when an object is clearly resolved."

Alexandra saw only indistinct blotches of light at first, but as Elizabeth made adjustments, distinct orbs, star clusters, disks of speckled light, and luminous clouds filled the field of view. Alexandra was stunned. She held her breath. She had never seen anything like this. She raised her hand when one of the larger images came into focus.

"Amazing," she exclaimed.

Elizabeth consulted charts, diagrams, and textbooks that lay about on the desk. She adjusted the telescope now and then, directing it to a new part of the heavens and explaining what Alexandra was seeing. This went on for the next three hours, with frequent pauses for Alexandra to take notes.

"It's late," Elizabeth said finally. "This has been an

introduction. Your study of astronomy will begin in earnest tomorrow morning, and it will continue for the rest of the week. You should rest now. You will need to be fresh in the morning."

Alexandra followed Elizabeth down the platform's metal staircase to the floor of the chamber. Elizabeth stretched her arms up and slowly moved her palms together. The ceiling closed. Alexandra followed her aunt down the winding stone staircase and through the labyrinth of hallways leading to her bedroom.

"You have begun well," Elizabeth said. "Now, enjoy a good night's rest."

***

Alexandra slept fitfully. In her dream (as in dreams before) she played a frustrating game of hide and seek with Daniel. He urged her to find him, but he offered no clues. He seemed not to know where he had hidden.

Alexandra drifted out of the dream and lay awake on her bed. She tried to remember the details, to resolve them into some meaningful pattern. She asked herself questions: Where was Daniel? Was he safe? Were these dreams a warning of something that had already occurred or a phantasmagoria of old memories. Or were they premonitions?

Her efforts to make sense of the dream were as frustrating as the dream itself, so she gave up. She arose, dressed in the red turtleneck sweater and khaki pants Elizabeth had purchased for her in Wilamsfeld, and went down to breakfast.

She ate alone in the vast dining hall. Candra, Elizabeth's personal assistant, appeared as she had the day before and escorted Alexandra to the main Byrnhelen library. Alexandra took two steps into the vast chamber and became transfixed by the grandeur of it. The Dyrisian gave a slight bow and departed.

Thousands of books lined the walls in three vertical tiers, each tier three meters high. Two circular staircases, one at each end of the room, gave access to the balconies of the higher tiers. The room was eighty meters long and fifty meters wide.

Alexandra obtained the astronomy books that had been assigned to her and sat at one of long tables near the center of the room. Elizabeth came and went, while a staff of Dyrisians instructed, demonstrated, tested, and gave other learning assistance. These were teachers like no others Alexandra had known. They did not so much teach as reveal. The revelations seemed more like old knowledge being uncovered than new knowledge being added. The Dyrisians gave answers before Alexandra could fully form questions. Sometimes the answers were given in natural language, sometimes by demonstration, and often by mysterious substitution: Where before there had been a question in Alexandra's mind, now there was only knowledge.

When the Dyrisians detected a mental blockage (as they did when Alexandra encountered the mathematics of astronomy), they joined in caressing her head and her face and gently covering and uncovering her eyes in hypnotic gestures that lifted her up, as on the wings of an osprey rising over a lake. She found herself looking down on the blockage as it broke apart and transformed into an arrangement of elegant mathematical formulas, equations, and solutions. She swooped down on the formulas and equations and solutions and took them in as the osprey takes in the fishes and makes them part of himself.

This experience, and others like it, were repeated throughout the day, until Alexandra's knowledge of the

Astronomy textbook, *Unlocking the Secrets of the Universe*, by Bradyn Aristarchus, was complete.

This accelerated learning was not without cost. Alexandra felt drained, mentally and physically. Elizabeth saw this and called a break. It was five o'clock.

"It is difficult," Alexandra said.

"You did not expect it would be easy, did you?" replied Elizabeth.

Alexandra did not answer. Any answer would have been a complaint, and she refused to complain or show any weakness.

"Dinner at seven, and after dinner, three hours at the telescope. I expect it will mean much more to you now. I will not be with you, but my Dyrisian teachers will. New ones. Males, who have a different way of teaching; they are a bit more direct. You will benefit from this."

Alexandra gave her aunt a steely look.

"I am doing my part, Aunt Elizabeth. I trust you're doing yours. Is Daniel on his way?"

Elizabeth stiffened.

"Assignments have been made. All that can be done is being done."

Alexandra studied her aunt's face.

"Good," she replied without emotion.

***

Alexandra had an hour before dinner and wanted to spend it alone. She lay on her bed, intending to rest only for a few minutes. Exhaustion soon dragged her into a deep sleep.

The same dream came: the hellish game of hide-and-seek with Daniel. She was bound, confined to movements in slow motion, and Daniel was not just hidden, he was lost. He cried out to her, and his cries awakened her.

"It is only a dream, only a dream," she murmured. The

intensity of the dream was past, but not its residue of dread.

***

She ate dinner alone. As she was finishing her meal, Candra appeared and sat next to her.

"Are you rested," the Dyrisian asked.

"Well enough. I have dreams that aren't restful."

Candra was silent, waiting. She did not ask for the details of Alexandra's dreams, at least not in words.

Dyrisians are like that, Alexandra thought. *They make you feel what is wanted, not as their demand, but as your own desire. And always gentle, so very gentle...and yet so compelling. A little spooky.*

Alexandra told Candra about her dreams.

"You should tell Elizabeth," the Dyrisian said.

Alexandra considered this.

"You should tell her," Candra repeated. "You, not I."

If I don't tell her, Candra will, Alexandra decided. She nodded and pushed her empty plate toward the center of the table.

"Can you find your way to the observatory?" Candra asked.

"I'm not sure."

"I will show you."

***

"There are some 9,000 stars visible to the naked eye," said Siala, one of the two male Dyrisians with Alexandra on the viewing platform. "But it does no good to count them. As the earth turns, new stars appear on one side while the ones we viewed only moments before disappear on the other. The sky is always changing; we see it as we might see a merry-go-round while looking through a keyhole."

Briel, the other Dyrisian, consulted a book of tables and made some adjustments to the telescope. He pressed a button and the telescope—or rather the whole chamber—rotated several degrees counterclockwise.

Alexandra marveled at Briel's deft manipulation of the giant instrument. She felt mounting excitement as she anticipated matching direct observations through the telescope with what she had taken in during the accelerated learning session earlier in the day.

She had done the arithmetic, learned the higher mathematics, and calculated size, age, and number. She had learned that stars are grouped not as constellations but as galaxies; that constellations are a human projection on the uncaring stars, a navigational device or a sort of astronomer's shorthand; that some galaxies are small, about eleven million stars, while others are large, nine or ten trillion stars, or more.

Still, these were just numbers.

She had learned the sun is one of about 200 billion stars in her little galactic neighborhood, the galaxy called the Milky Way. She had learned there are perhaps a trillion such neighborhoods, some larger, some smaller than her own. Thus, there are around ten sextillion one septillion stars in the known universe.

Again, just a number, a very big and difficult-to-pronounce number, but still merely a human way of expressing a quantity. She wanted to see for herself.

"Look into the eyepiece," Briel said.

Alexandra did as he directed. In the center of the optical field she saw a circular mass of stars enclosed within a glowing cloud of dust and gas. In the center of this circular arrangement was a spherical bulge, also made of stars, dust, and gas. Spiral arms stretched out from the central bulge and curved counterclockwise. This made it appear the mass was spinning clockwise. But nothing moved in the optical field;

the object appeared fixed in space, hanging there, lifeless.

"A galaxy," she murmured.

"MC1361," Briel said. "Discovered two months ago by astronomers here, at Byrnhelen. It is 13.5 billion light years from us and thus the most distant galaxy we have yet discovered. Do you understand the implications?"

Alexandra sat up, crossed her arms, and considered Briel's question.

Implications? What implications?

She went over in her mind what she had learned earlier in the day about galaxies and stars. She broke her new knowledge down into manageable parts:

The speed of light is a universal constant: 299,792,458 meters per second or, in imperial units, 186,282 miles per second. Time, space, mass, and energy are interrelated, according to the Theory of Relativity. $E=mc^2$. The speed of gravitation, gravitational waves, is the same... Stop! I'm being too complicated. What are the implications? That was Briel's question. Implications.

She concentrated on the fact of the speed of light. She then concentrated on what Briel had told her: This galaxy is 13.5 billion light years away. What are the implications of that?

It's not real!

The thought seemed not her own. She had not arrived at it deductively. It just appeared.

She looked again through the eyepiece, studied MC1361 closely, then leaned back in her chair. She smiled and said to Briel:

"It's not real. This galaxy could have disappeared 13.4 billion years ago or it could have disappeared an hour ago or it could still be there. I am not 'seeing' the galaxy; I am only seeing the light from it, and that light is 13.5 billion years old. I am seeing a 13.5-billion-year-old picture of something that might be long gone."

"And the implications of that?" Briel asked.

Alexandra thought again, but nothing came. She could see no deeper meaning, and she was tired.

"I don't know," she replied.

"You are almost there. Don't give up. You see that you are looking into the past, 13.5 billion years into the past. As you said, what you see, or think you see, may have ceased to exist billions of years ago...or yesterday or a few minutes ago. It took the image of that galaxy 13.5 billion years to reach your eye. You are reading old news, ancient history. The galaxy you see is not real. You see evidence of it, but you do not see the thing itself. Now, tell me what that means about everything else you perceive with your physical senses. There is a great problem here. Tell me what it is?"

Time, thought Alexandra, *the great problem is time. Time is the essence and time is an illusion.*

"Time," Alexandra said.

"Yes," Briel said, beaming. "The great problem is time. I am more real to you than MC1361 only because I am more recent. You would be tempted to say closer. But it is not space that stands between us. Time stands between us, however small its increments. Time is the great problem, Alexandra, and the great solution. What you and others call magic is, in its simplest essence, the mastery of time. Everything else is just method."

44 The Pit

It had been days. Daniel did not know how many, but enough for him to have emptied the waterskin. The candle had long been used up. Darkness, thirst, and hunger had become his world. They combined with his solitude, and Daniel became, by steps, less Daniel and more just this thing in the darkness, a creature of unknown origin, having no past or future.

The sound of clanking, as loud as gunshots in Daniel's ears, burst into the void he was becoming. It took several moments for him to connect the sounds with the disengagement of the lock securing his cell door.

A narrow shaft of light cut into the inky blackness of the cell. His eyes adjusted painfully to the light. He saw a cloaked figure in the doorway. Daniel stood and backed slowly into the shadows as the figure entered the room.

"Don't know why Master wishes to keep you alive," the man muttered as he leaned over and placed a new waterskin and a metal plate of food on the floor near the edge of the shadows. Displaying no fear of the prisoner, the man reached casually into his tunic, withdrew a small candle, and placed it within the candle lantern near the food. He stood upright, pointed his wand at the candle, and spoke.

"Ignatium."

The candle ignited. The man left the way he had come. The heavy door was pulled closed by unseen hands, and Daniel heard the sound of the lock mechanism as the key was turned and the bolt slid back into place.

The candle bathed the cell in an eerie flickering glow. After being so long in the dark, Daniel was momentarily dizzied by the dancing light. He steadied himself and stared at the food and drink on the floor. Hunger and thirst overwhelmed caution, and he sank to the floor, retrieved a chunk of hard bread from the plate, and bit off a piece. He ignored the bread's stale flavor. He considered saving some of the meal for later, but abandoned the thought and consumed the remainder of the stale bread, a block of moldy cheese, and an overripe apple. These he washed down with water. No food was left for later, and he did not know if more would come.

He pushed backward against the wall and stared at the candle flame. He appreciated for the first time how difficult it must be for the blind. The dim light cast by the candle was precious to him. It gave him sight, even if just a little. But it was a false promise, burning down; he would soon again be enveloped by the dark.

Escape.

The thought drifted through his mind like a wraith beckoning and denying, promising and forbidding like a song sung in rounds.

Row, row, row your boat...row, row, row your boat...gently down the stream...row, row, row, row...

He shook his head.

I don't know where I am. I don't know this place—not just this cell but the building I'm in and whatever surrounds it. I don't know these people who hold me here or why they do. Escape from what? To what? I might as well be on the

*dark side of the moon. But even on the dark side of the moon
I could move, I could act, do something, or I could just sit
here and wait.*

Daniel looked around him, studied the uneven surface of
the rock walls. He picked up the candle lantern and held it at
arm's length in front of him. He saw the cell was large and
seemed to have been excavated from the native rock, which
appeared to be granite. He walked to the door and closely
inspected the wall surrounding it. Seeing no cracks, no
weaknesses there, he moved slowly to the right, along the
wall, studying it carefully as he advanced. He continued to
the corner, turned, inspected the adjoining wall to the next
corner, turned, and continued his inspection to the edge of
the pit.

As the candle wavered, nearly extinguishing itself, he
peered over the edge. The candlelight illuminated only the
first meter of the pit walls. He worked a rock loose from the
wall, held it over the opening, and dropped it. He soon heard
the rock strike the near side of the pit. There was a silent
interval, then another collision, more faint, distant. And then
another, barely audible. Then silence. There was no
concluding thud; no evidence came back that the rock had
hit bottom.

No way out down there, Daniel thought. *The pit nearly
killed me once. A second attempt would be the end of me.*

Daniel lay prone at the edge of the pit. He held the candle
lantern as far down as he could. The candle cast only a dim
light on the walls, but enough for him to make out the root
he had clung to in his earlier fall. It was around a meter to
the left of where he lay. He crawled in that direction and
searched for the ledge above the root. He saw it, around four
meters down and directly below.

He swung the lantern to his left, hoping to get a better

look at the ledge. The move was too abrupt. The candle fell over within the lantern, gave one last rebellious flicker, and went out. Daniel could see nothing.

A combination of loneliness, desperation, and fear washed over him like the wave of a cold northern sea. He shivered. He placed the lantern on the floor to his right. He rested his chin on the cold stone and stared into the blackness below.

The blessing of light, however dim, was gone, as was the tiny projection of heat that had touched his hand.

What do I do now?

As if in answer to his question, an unnatural glow appeared in the opposite wall of the pit, about four meters down. Daniel stared directly at the light and saw a face shinning in the middle of it. He remembered the face from earlier, before Croft had lifted him out of the pit. It was the face of a girl. The girl looked down, right, left—searching.

Daniel held his breath, wondering if the face was real.

Have I fallen asleep? Am I dreaming?

The face looked up.

And then, just as quickly as it had appeared, the face was gone, replaced by the never-ending black.

"Hey come back! Whoever you are, please, come back. Help!"

Daniel received no answer. He heard only the distorted echo of his own voice, ever diminishing:

Help...help...help...help...

Daniel closed his eyes and drifted into peaceful slumber. He dreamed.

Alexandra was laughing as they stood together on the Wards' back patio. She ran away laughing and Daniel gave chase. Lightning flashed, and the night sky was fleetingly illuminated. "Are you alone?" Alexandra called out to him as she looked back over her shoulder. The lightning flashed again. Daniel continued to run after her.

"Who are you?" Alexandra asked him, just out of reach.

"You know who I am," Daniel murmured to the stone floor.

The lightning flashed a third time. It illuminated the dream sky, brilliantly, and awakened him.

"Who are you?"

It was not Alexandra's voice.

It was another voice, and it came from the darkness below.

45 Alea

Lightning flashes in a dark sky, a lifetime.

SIGVARDR

Daniel peeked over the edge of the pit and found himself gazing into the eyes of a young girl with delicate features and flaxen hair.

"Are you alone?" she asked.

"I thought I was. Who are you?"

The girl ignored his question.

"Are you a wizard?" she asked after a few moments.

Daniel pondered the question. Aedan had called him a warlock. Wizard, warlock: Same thing. He, Daniel Sutton, had made no such claim, to himself or to anyone else. Did his unusual powers and strange thoughts make him what Aedan said he was, what this girl now asked? He had not declared it. What others said was what they said. But somehow he knew if *he* said it, it would be true, and the course of his life would be altered.

"Yes," he whispered, "I guess I am."

"Why does Aedan want you?"

"I don't know. He hinted at my playing some part in a drama. Then he said I could play my part alive or dead. I thought he meant to kill me then and there."

"He gives clues," the girl said, "he manipulates. For all I know, you may be his agent. How did you get here?"

Daniel considered her comment in reverse. She might be Aedan's agent. Still, what did he have to lose by engaging her? Whatever she was, she might give him some idea of what was going on.

"I was in the woods near my home in Simsbury," Daniel continued. "That's in Connecticut. The next thing I knew I was here. Bam, just like that. Here, in this cell."

Simsbury? Alea thought. *Could it be?*

"What is your name?" she asked.

There was urgency in her question, and Daniel became suspicious.

"Please, let me see your face," the girl said.

What does it matter, Daniel thought. *She sees me, I see her. We both learn something.*

He edged forward and rested his chin on the edge of the pit. He saw shock in the girl's face and heard her take in a sharp breath.

"What is it?" he asked.

The glow brightened around the girl's face.

"You're Daniel Sutton!" she declared.

Daniel became as alarmed as the girl seemed to be. He shoved back from the edge of the pit so only his eyes and the top of his head could be seen. His thoughts raced:

How does she know me? If she knows me, she knows Alexandra and she might know what happened to her. Or is she with Aedan? Is she playing out her part in some sort of ruse?

"Can you climb down?" the girl asked breathlessly. "There's a ledge in an alcove across from me. You'd be comfortable there."

Climb down! Be comfortable. I almost killed myself last time I tried.

"Please, come down. We can't talk like this. We might be overheard."

Daniel heard earnest concern in the girl's voice. She

seemed as much a prisoner as he. Yet he could not discount the possibility that this was a trap.

"Talk to me from where you are. I can hear just fine," he said evenly.

"And so can anyone who might be standing outside your cell door, or mine," she countered. "Please, climb down."

"First tell me who you are and how you know me."

There was a long pause.

"I am Alea of Byrnhelen. I'm Dyrisian. I know you because...I just know you, and I know Alexandra."

Daniel felt a new wave of apprehension when Alea spoke Alexandra's name. The situation for him could not be more dire. He imagined Alexandra in similar circumstances, or worse. He decided it didn't matter who or what Alea was. She offered a sliver of hope in his otherwise hopeless world. That was enough. Doing something was better than doing nothing.

"How do I get to you?" Daniel asked.

"Climb down to the ledge where I first saw you, when you fell before. You can do it if you're careful."

"I can't see it from here," Daniel said.

Alea withdrew from the opening in the wall of the pit. A moment later, she extended her right arm and released something into the void. For a moment Daniel thought it was a lighted candle, but it did not flicker or fall, and it was brighter than a candle. It was a sphere of bluish light suspended in space. Daniel watched it drift across from her side of the pit to his, and he saw the ledge clearly in its light. A thick root curled out of the wall about one and a half meters below him. If he could step onto the bend in the root, or catch hold of it with his hands, he could reach the ledge. But he couldn't be certain. It would be a risky venture.

Fear gnawed at him and made his hands feel weak.

If I think too much about this, I won't do it.

Daniel turned onto his stomach and dangled his legs over the edge of the pit. He let himself down, slowly, gripping the edge with his hands and feeling for the root with his feet. He found it with his right foot. It felt secure. Keeping his grip on the edge of the pit with his left hand, he reached down with his right, hoping to find the root.

This was a mistake: His foot slipped and he lost his grip on the edge of the pit. He clawed frantically at the side of the pit as he slid downward. He grasped the root; held it for a moment, breaking his slide; then lost his grip and tumbled onto the ledge. His heart pounded as he scrambled frantically backward into the alcove behind the ledge. He looked across the four-meter diameter of the pit and found himself eye-to-eye with Alea.

"Okay, now what?" Daniel said with more bravura than he felt.

Alea studied him for a moment.

"I serve the Guardian," she said. "I've watched over you and Alexandra for the past six years. The Guardian ordered it. Aedan captured me a week ago, two weeks, maybe longer. I've lost track. Now they bring you here. What's happened to Alexandra? Is she safe?"

The Dyrisian spoke in an urgent whisper, deliberately varying her tone. Anyone a short distance away would have heard sounds, like a series of sighs and indistinct vocalizations; they would not have been able to make out words.

"I don't know what happened to Alexandra," Daniel answered. "She disappeared a few days ago. I was searching for her when I was...brought here. I don't know how that happened. I don't know anything."

"Not exactly," Alea said. "You know some things. I

know some things. Maybe we can piece this together."

"Maybe," Daniel responded, his tone conveying a combination of suspicion and resignation.

Neither spoke for several long moments. Then Daniel asked:

"Who's this Guardian?"

"Her name is Elizabeth Shaw. She is a very important leader."

"Whoa! Do you mean the woman who claims to be Alexandra's aunt? I met her. Is she the one who's behind all this?"

Alea stared at him.

"She *is* Alexandra's aunt. But how did you know of her?" Alea asked. "The Guardian would not reveal herself...unless...when did you meet her, and where?"

"A few days ago, maybe five days ago. She came to the house. Alexandra met her too. Some big deal about Alexandra. The Wards were pretty upset. Is Elizabeth Shaw a big deal?"

"Yes, a very big deal, as you say. She is the Guardian. That she came to you personally is also a big deal. It explains a lot. Important things are happening."

"Alexandra's a part of it, isn't she?"

"Yes. She too is, as you say, a big deal."

"Why?"

"It is believed she is the successor."

"Successor to what?"

"The Guardianship," Alea replied.

"I don't get it. Why is all this happening now? You said you've been watching over us for six years. What changed? Why are you here? Why am I here?

Alea heard irritation creeping into his voice.

"I don't know," she said again. "Aedan's men captured

me and brought me here weeks ago, well before Elizabeth came to you. They haven't tortured me or interrogated me or asked a single question. I'm guessing Aedan just wanted me out of the way, unable to observe or report anything to the Guardian. That you and Alexandra met with the Guardian five days ago and were unharmed is a hopeful sign. That Alexandra then disappeared and you were brought here..."

"She's probably dead," Daniel interrupted, his voice flat, emotionless.

"What makes you say that?" Alea asked, clearly alarmed.

"There was a huge storm," Daniel said. "Alexandra's father got real mad, fired my mom, and kicked us out of the house. Alexandra chased us and got lost in the woods. It was really cold. There was a big search, for days. No one could find her. I tried to find her when everyone else had pretty much given up. That's when I got snatched into this place. Except..."

"Except what," Alea whispered.

"Except they never found her body."

Daniel stared down into the pit.

"But they won't find mine either, will they, and I'm not dead."

He and Alea sat in silence for a few moments.

"She's alive," Daniel said, hope overcoming fear.

Alea joined in:

"I think you're right, and I don't think Aedan has her."

"Why? He grabbed me. She disappeared the same way I did, without a trace. He took you before that. Aedan appears to have had a hand in taking us all. If he didn't take her, then who did?"

"Not Aedan. It's too much to explain now, but it would not serve his purpose to take her. It would be...premature. No, if she was taken as you were—and I strongly believe she was—it was not Aedan who took her. I think it was the Guardian. She visited you five days ago. She would have done that only if she was preparing to take Alexandra. Taking her would have been check in their game of chess. To get himself out of check, Aedan takes you. They are playing a game and we are the pieces."

Daniel watched Alea's face brighten.

"I think Alexandra is safe and at Byrnhelen!" she said.

"Where's that?"

"Far from here but in Second World. Byrnhelen is the Guardian's fortress."

"Elizabeth Shaw has a fortress?"

"She has much more than that."

"Tell me about this Guardian stuff," Daniel said.

"Elizabeth is Guardian of the Two Worlds," Alea said. "She believes Alexandra is her successor."

"I understand successor, but what is this two-world stuff?"

Alea studied Daniel's face for a moment, then went on:

"Here on Earth there are two worlds that coexist in separate dimensions. Time, the weather, all things of the natural world are the same in both dimensions. The only differences are in anything human-caused. Each dimension filters out what is human-caused in the other. The Guardian protects both dimensions."

Daniel looked skeptically at Alea.

"Is there a Paris, France, in this world?" he asked with marginal sincerity.

"No, but there is a beautiful city called Lucernia in about the same place."

"So all the names of things are different here."

"Many, not all."

"Two worlds, two dimensions, filters; it all sounds made-up."

"I warned you it would," Alea said.

Daniel nodded.

Alea continued:

"Because of the centuries-long exodus of magical beings to Second World, mostly non-magical people now reside in First World, where you came from. Magical people mainly reside in Second World, where we are now."

"So there are two guardians?"

"No, only one."

"Okay," Daniel said, "so Elizabeth Shaw is the one-and-only guardian, and she thinks Alexandra is the one-and-only person who can do her one-and-only job when she dies, which she thinks will be soon."

Daniel folded his arms and gave Alea a defiant look.

"Please Daniel, this is serious," she said. It's nothing to joke about."

"I'm not joking. I'm just having a hard time believing. So tell me this: If Alexandra is supposed to be the successor to this Guardian, what makes me important? Why has Aedan brought me here? And why does Elizabeth think Alexandra is her successor anyway?"

"One thing at a time," Alea replied. "Let me think, please."

A long silence ensued.

"I think I see what his plan might be."

"Whose plan?"

"Aedan's. Remember the drama he spoke of, the one in which he said you play a small part. I think I see something of the plot. Your part is not small; it's huge. He plans to use you to control Alexandra. She cares about you. Aedan knows this, and so he imprisons you."

"He's going to be disappointed if that's his big plan,"

Daniel said. "I won't do anything to hurt Alexandra, no matter what he does to me."

"You won't have to do anything. You are the hostage. As long as you remain a hostage, you are his tool against Alexandra."

Daniel pondered this.

"So why is Alexandra so important? She dies; someone takes her place."

"It's complicated," Alea said.

"Uncomplicate it for me."

Alea ignored his contentious tone.

"There's evidence Alexandra is the natural daughter of Elizabeth's sister, Katherine Shaw."

"That's nuts," Daniel interjected. "Alexandra and I were raised together from before we could walk. My mom was our nanny. She was there the whole time. Alexandra is John and Mary Ward's daughter, period. What you're saying is someone's fairytale."

"Perhaps," Alea admitted, "but there is compelling evidence it is not."

"Okay. Forget that. How does Aedan expect me to influence Alexandra?" Daniel asked. "She pretty much thinks for herself."

"Not if you are in danger. She will give up her birthright, her place in the line of succession, to save you."

"Big deal. Aedan doesn't need me for that. I know Alexandra. She doesn't care about that stuff. I'll bet she'd be happy to let the next in line have it. Who is next in line, anyway?"

"Aedan Shaw," Alea replied, speaking the name very slowly.

"The Aedan keeping us prisoner?" Daniel asked.

"The very same."

"It wouldn't be good if he became the Guardian, would it?

"It would be unthinkable."

"Aedan Shaw, Elizabeth Shaw: same last name," Daniel observed. "How are they related?"

"Elizabeth is the eldest sibling; Aedan, the youngest."

"Same family stock. I hope Elizabeth is kinder than her brother."

"Her brother is insane," Alea said bitterly. "Elizabeth has been protecting us from him for many years."

"Why doesn't Aedan just kill his sister and take over?"

"He's tried, but Elizabeth is too well guarded," Alea replied, "and her powers are more than a match for his. Even if he succeeded in killing her, it would avail him nothing. There would still be Alexandra, and her protection is absolute until she reaches twenty-one years of age or until she passes through the Culling and relinquishes her birthright. If Aedan harms her or causes harm to come to her before one of these conditions is met, he will forfeit his place in the line of succession."

"The Culling sounds important," Daniel said. "What is it?"

"It's an ordeal, a test that concludes the first year of training. If Alexandra survived the storm and if she's been taken to Byrnhelen—and I think she has—she will have begun her training. I'm familiar with the training schedule. The Culling is months away. Aedan has no reason to move until after the Culling. In fact he has every reason not to move until then, for only then could his threats against you have the desired effect on Alexandra. Only then could she renounce her birthright. The Guardian and her brother are aligned in one thing: They both want Alexandra to pass through the Culling as soon as possible, but they want this for very different reasons."

"What can we do?" Daniel asked.

"Nothing, together, but there is one thing you can do."

"What?"

"Escape."

She might as well invite me to fly to the moon, Daniel thought. *I've nearly killed myself just climbing down a few meters into this pit.*

"Despite my fervent attempts, I've found no way to escape," Alea admitted. "My powers are limited by something in the design or materials of my cell. I can be of little use as long as I'm confined here. Have you felt anything limiting your powers?"

"I don't know much about what you call *my powers*," Daniel said. "Alexandra and I played around with the weird stuff we could do, but I can't unlock doors or walk through walls, that kind of stuff."

"You say you are a wizard, but you have had no training. Am I right?"

"I'm different, OK, like Alexandra. But the wizard thing I have to pretty much take from what people say about me. I just don't know what it means. I'm pretty useless as a wizard."

A long silence ensued between them, broken finally by Alea.

"There are stories about Durnakk, legends really. Some say no one has ever escaped from here. But the story of an escape is still told. The facts change, but the story always includes a pit like this one."

"Legends are of no use," Daniel said. "Tell me some facts."

Alea abruptly inclined her head and stared into the dark above.

"Listen!" she whispered.

"What is it?"

"Someone's coming."

Daniel heard it: faint voices from above, voices in the hallway outside his cell.

"Quick!" Alea said. "You must not be found here."

Daniel stood. He searched the wall for hand holds and foot holds. The root was there but it was too high for him to reach.

"If they find you down here again," Alea said, trying to suppress her panic, "they'll suspect some purpose, not just a fall, and they'll find the opening I've made into the pit and they'll move me and we'll be separated and I have more information you need...just go! Now! Please!"

Daniel found a foothold and shallow handholds above it. He climbed up about two meters before the highest hand hold crumbled and he slid back down to the ledge. He tried again with the same result.

"Wait, I have an idea," Alea said in a burst of excitement. "Most of my powers are gone because of this cell. But if I can push my arm out far enough, maybe I can help."

Alea disappeared into her cell. A moment later, her arm slithered through the opening. She pushed hard and got part of her shoulder through the opening before she was blocked.

She moved her arm in a precise pattern.

Nothing happened.

It didn't work, Daniel thought. *They're going to find me here!*

Alea moved her arm again in the same pattern and from her hand released a ball of light. The ball reshaped into a square about a meter on each side and around five centimeters thick. The object drifted across the pit to the ledge where Daniel stood. It hovered at his feet.

The guard's footsteps stopped abruptly. Daniel heard the jangling of keys.

"Stand on it; stand on the tile," Alea said, her voice muffled by the thick wall of her cell.

Daniel hesitated. The tile was transparent, unsubstantial. It glowed an eerie yellowish-green. He heard a muffled voice above and the sound of a key turning in the lock.

Daniel stepped onto the glowing tile. It held him.

He heard a door bolt sliding back.

The tile rose slowly, carrying him upward. He stared into the abyss below him and nearly lost his balance. The tile continued to rise. His head cleared the top of the pit just as he heard the groan of door hinges. He saw the door beginning to open as the tile reached the level of the cell floor. He leapt from the tile and took several quick steps away from the edge of the pit.

The door of the cell swung open. A slash of light fell across the space where Daniel lay prone and absolutely still on the cool stone floor.

46   The Wand and the Way

*Power lies within power, hidden. One must have power
to acquire it. This is the mystery.*

FROM "THE WAND AND THE WAY" BY MATHIAS WILAMSFELD

The summons to Elizabeth's office came after dinner on
Friday evening. Alexandra had just completed the five-
week astronomy master course in a single week and was
mentally and emotionally exhausted. The summons irritated
her. She had been looking forward to a relaxing evening.
Now it appeared this was not to be.

She entered the office and saw Mathias Wilamsfeld and
Elizabeth standing in front of the fireplace

Elizabeth was smiling.

"Mathias has something for you," she said.

Mathias held in front of him a rough-hewn wooden box.
It was rectangular, about forty-five-by-ten-by-ten
centimeters. He held it by the ends, the long side facing
Alexandra. When she was within a meter and a half of the
box, the cover rotated backward with no visible assistance
from Mathias. Within the box, lying on a maroon pillow,
was a wand.

"It is yours alone," Mathias said.

Alexandra reached out hesitantly. When her hand was a
few centimeters from the box, the wand changed from dark
ebony to glowing purple, and a faint hum filled the air. She
jerked her hand away. The wand returned to its original
color, and the hum subsided.

Not daring to reach again, Alexandra kept her arms at her sides and leaned forward to take a closer look. The wand again turned from ebony to purple. The hum returned.

Mathias's expression reflected tender amusement.

"It is safe to touch," he said. "It is yours, as nothing before has ever been so completely yours. It knows you. As you see, I hold it (he lifted the wand out of the box) and it is colorless and without voice of any sort, but when you approach, it comes alive. Take it now, gently. Don't be afraid."

Mathias returned the wand to its box and held the box out to her. She reached forward with her right hand. The wand went through the previous color cycle and the hum returned. Her hand closed over the instrument, and Mathias deftly pulled the box away.

The wand felt comfortably warm. It cycled slowly through the entire color spectrum as its hum became fainter and fainter until it could be heard no more. The color cycling also ceased, but the warmth remained. Alexandra noted the appearance of the wand was not quite as it had been when Mathias presented it. It was still nearly black, but other colors were subtly revealed within the wood.

"You see it, don't you," Mathias said with a knowing smile.

"What? The colors?"

"Yes, the subtle ones. You see them under the surface of the polished wood?"

"Yes."

"The Guardian and I see nothing but a finely finished black stick. We see no unusual colors within the wood. This is because we are not who the wand seeks, who it will always seek. You are the one. The wand finds in you its perfect match. This is by design; this is what all my measuring of you was about. I built you into the wand. Now the wand has found you and linked the "you" I built into it with the you holding it. The bond is unbreakable and unfathomably powerful. The wand will serve no one but you and reveal its secrets to no one but you for as long as you live. Upon your death, the wand will become a useless stick. It will be buried with you if that is your wish and circumstances permit."

Alexandra fingered the wand's smooth irregularities as she struggled to comprehend the relationship Mathias said she had with this piece of wood. It was too much, so she retreated into the mundane.

"What kind of wood is this?" she asked. "I've never seen any like it."

"*Dalbergia nigra,*" replied Mathias, "commonly known as Brazilian rosewood. It is a dense hardwood with beautiful variation in hues and a distinctive floral scent. It is highly sought after for its beauty and strength. It is a wood that matches you perfectly."

Alexandra blushed.

Mathias saw this, smiled, and went on:

"I've presented many wands to many apprentices," Mathias continued, "but I have never seen one so swiftly and so completely bond to its owner as yours bonded to you. Did you see it, Elizabeth?"

"Indeed I did," said the Guardian.

Alexandra passed her finger over the gilded Wilamsfeld name etched into the wand.

"It's beautiful," she murmured.

"Yes, and in more ways than you can yet imagine," Mathias said in a matching whisper. "But remember, the source of the wand's power lies in you, not in the wand."

"I don't understand."

"Yes, because you think I am speaking only of wands."

He's teasing me, testing me, thought Alexandra.

Mathias continued:

"Your wand is hollow. Tiny particles of your hair and saliva are imbedded in the walls of this hollow. Over your lifetime, you will add other essences to the hollow within the wand. The wand will fill as you are filled. You are in the wand, and your presence there will grow."

"Sounds a little creepy."

Mathias laughed.

"I can see how it would. I fear I have made it sound like a living thing. It is not, at least not in the biological sense. Think of it this way: You read a book, a really good book, one you will want to refer to in the future, one you will want to read again. Where do you store such a book when you're not reading it?"

"On my nightstand?"

"That's a good place. Where else?"

"In my head, my memory?"

"That's an even better place. Now, you read another good book, and another, and yet another. Many books over a lifetime. And you have experiences. Where do you store them?"

"In my memories, and the books in a library."

"Which is the more important place?"

"My memories."

"Yes, and the wand is your library, Alexandra. I created a wooden shell, a library with a small collection of books in it and some saliva and a bit of hair. The rest is up to you. The wand is a powerful tool if you are powerful. It is a wise tool if you are wise. It will do good if you are good. It will do evil if you are evil."

"What about spells and curses and all that stuff,"

Alexandra inquired.

Mathias turned quite serious.

"There is that," he said somberly. "The wand is also like the barrel of a gun. It concentrates and directs energy. This energy and the rest of the weapon's mechanism and its ammunition are within you. One day, perhaps, the entire mechanism, including the barrel, will be within you. The wand will then be merely an amplifier of your powers. But that should not concern you now."

"What *should* concern me?"

"That you not use your wand to amplify powers that have not yet matured in you. That you not use it to enhance flawed or incomplete or undisciplined capabilities, and thus harm yourself and others."

"How do I know what's mature and all that? I don't want the thing to blow up in my face."

Mathias remained serious. He glanced at Elizabeth, then spoke for the last time:

"I made the wand. Teaching you how to use it is the province of others."

***

Alexandra awoke from yet another disquieting nightmare. She had dared hope the presence of the wand might have some magical effect on her sleep. It was not to be. The nightmares had continued as before, though with slight, progressive variations. Once a variation was added, it remained part of the repeated plot in following dreams. There were exceptions to this, but they were rare. The core of the dreams remained the same: Daniel lost and she trying to find him. This disturbing consistency made the dreams all the more unpleasant.

Alexandra rolled onto her side and stared at the wooden box on her nightstand. In it was the wand Mathias had made for her. He had warned her to store the wand in its container whenever it was not on her person. The box was immovable, unbreakable, and unrevealing of its contents to anyone other than Alexandra. The wand performed as the magical amplifier it was intended to be. Away from her it was nothing more than a pretty stick.

Alexandra's thoughts turned to the coming week. Tomorrow she would begin her first five-week master course. She would be with the other apprentices for the first time, and she would not have the direct assistance of the Dyrisians, as she had during the accelerated course in astronomy. She would be on her own, just like the others.

The apprentices would travel to First World, a prospect that delighted Alexandra despite Elizabeth's assurance there would be no chance for her to visit her parents or Daniel. The subject of the master course would be cryptozoology. She'd had never heard of it, but, not wanting to appear stupid, had asked no questions. She also didn't ask how the apprentices would be transported between the worlds. This would have emphasized she was the new kid, and she didn't need that either.

Nagging thoughts about Daniel arose in the background of her other concerns. She had asked Elizabeth about him in different ways and at different times. The Guardian had been steadfastly non-committal, even evasive.

Alexandra studied the rough wood grain of the box that contained her wand.

Something is wrong, she thought. *Elizabeth knows more than she's saying.*

In this thought she was more correct than she could possibly have imagined.

47 Cryptozoology

All paths are new. Old paths are not paths at all; they are merely records, like books in a library.

FROM "DIVINITY OF THE ORDINARY" BY MASTER BRADYN ARISTARCHUS

Alexandra donned the backpack that contained everything required for the five-week master course in Scotland. She took a deep breath, opened the door of her room, and stepped into the corridor.

Byrnhelen was transformed.

The corridor that had been deserted for more than a week was now crowded with apprentices scurrying back and forth. "Alexandra!"

Alexandra turned and saw Becca running toward her.

"Kind of crowded this morning, huh?" Becca said. "Did you miss me?"

"I did," Alexandra said.

"Well, I missed you too. My brother is four years older than me. He is in an apprenticeship in Heidelberg, by where we live. It's not Byrnhelen, of course, but it is not nothing. Right now he thinks he knows everything there is to know about spells and potions. He wants to be a 'potioneer.' That is what he calls it, 'potioneer' (Becca pursed her lips and punched the p to make the word sound even more silly). He says he got an award for the most promising 'potioneer' in his class and he made it into this 'special club'(Becca curved her fingers on each hand to simulate quotation marks) and he created this new potion to make the voice of anyone who takes it sound like a rock star."

"Your brother sounds cool," Alexandra said.

"No! Not cool! Really annoying! Severely annoying!"

Becca took a breath, let out a sigh of exasperation, and chattered on, much to Alexandra's delight:

"All I hear is singing, singing, singing! The next song I hear I'm going to scream! All of his friends were over during the break having fun doing rock star impressions and my family just encouraged it by requesting songs! I swear it is so annoying! It's not even like the potion is so great. It only lasts for about an hour and you can only take it three times in a day or you sound like a frog. Now that's funny! Ribbit! I can't wait till I finish my apprenticeship here. I will know so much more than him and then I can wipe that snotty expression right off his face when I do something totally cool!"

Alexandra laughed.

"I'm going on and on, aren't I," Becca said.

"Yes, you are and I love it."

Alexandra put her arms around her friend and hugged her tight.

"Ditto," Becca said. "Your turn. How's it been, having the place all to yourself?"

"Long and tough," Alexandra said, "but I got through astronomy."

"What do you mean, 'got through'?," Becca asked.

"I finished the course."

"You what?" Becca said. "No way!"

"Yes, 'way'," Alexandra said with an impish smile.

"Wow, I'm impressed."

"Well, don't be. I had a lot of help from Dyrisian teachers, and I was the only one so I got the full blast all the time."

"Still, that's amazing," Becca said.

"I wasn't bragging, Becca."

"Of course you weren't. This is Becca you're talking to. I asked, and you answered. I love to hear about your accomplishments. What else did you do?"

"I went with my aunt to Wilamsfeld. Master Wilamsfeld fitted me for a wand; that was pretty weird. Aunt Elizabeth gave me the wand just three days ago, on Friday. Do you want to see it?"

Alexandra didn't wait for an answer. She reached into her robe, withdrew her Wilamsfeld wand, and held it out for Becca's inspection.

"Wow," whispered Becca. She leaned over to inspect the wand.

"Can I touch it?" Becca asked.

"Sure."

Becca ran her finger over the gilded letters etched into the base: Wilamsfeld.

"I've never seen a Wilamsfeld wand, except for your aunt's. I don't know anyone who has one."

"Really?"

"Yeah. They're expensive, but I've heard that even people with a lot of money, I mean a lot of money, have been turned down. Wilamsfeld has some weird requirements, and he doesn't tell anyone what they are. That's what I hear anyway. I suppose your aunt helped. I'm glad you got it. Oooops! Gotta go. Never be late for two-oh-eight."

Becca laughed at her rhyme. "I'm a poet and don't know it," she added.

"Pretty bad poetry," Alexandra said as she returned the wand to its pocket in her robe.

"Right, well I made it up on the fly," Becca said. "We assemble in room 208, two-oh-eight, get it?"

Alexandra rolled her eyes.

"I get it," she said.

"Good!"

Becca laughed again, thoroughly entertained by her alliteration.

She led Alexandra at a fast walk through corridors, down winding staircases, up winding staircases, across landings, in and out, up and down until they arrived at room 208.

Becca opened the door. Alexandra entered and Becca followed, closing the door behind her.

Four apprentices, three boys and a girl, stood under a large oil painting, studying it and conversing among themselves. They turned when Alexandra entered and gave her a curious look. The boys nodded and turned away. The girl gave a shy wave and returned to her conversation with the others.

"They're a little afraid of you," whispered Becca. "You are the Guardian's niece, from the other world and all that. They'll be nicer when they get to know you, like I have."

"Thanks, Becca. It's good to have a friend."

Alexandra felt a chill. There were no desks, chairs, tables, or any other furnishings. The stone walls held no decorative objects other than the large oil painting that so interested the other apprentices. The room seemed wholly dedicated to the painting, which depicted a forest, deep and dark. Black Elder, Alder, and Scot's Pine trees seemed to beckon to her to come closer and explore the secrets they held. Tiny white and yellow flowers peeked out from behind leaves that littered the forest floor.

The artist had captured the forest in early morning. On one side of the painting was a small stone cottage constructed of large boulders fitted together to form masonry walls. Wooden shutters framed the windows and pine needles and leaves covered the thatched roof. A golden glow came from the windows and blended with the early morning light.

Alexandra leaned forward to study the thatch roof of the cottage more closely.

So realistic, she thought, *and the smoke from the chimney...*

She stepped back, startled.

"Do you see that, Becca? There's smoke, real smoke!"

"Remember the murals in Wilamsfeld," Becca reminded her. "Same kind of thing here."

The other apprentices had stepped back so Alexandra could study the painting more closely. An unfelt breeze blew some leaves off the roof of the cottage. Alexandra watched in amazement as the leaves turned and twisted and tipped in the air as they settled to the forest floor.

"This is so bizarre," she whispered.

"It's a portal," said Becca.

Alexandra touched the ridges of dried paint that depicted the new-fallen leaves. The paint was hard and the leaves did not move. The painting was once again just a painting. The smoke from the chimney no longer drifted up; it was just a smudge of gray and blue.

"He's coming," Becca said.

"Who?" Alexandra asked.

"Master Asherton."

"And you know this how?" Alexandra asked skeptically. "I don't hear anything."

"It's not in the hearing," Becca said, suppressing a smile.

Before Alexandra could ask another question, the door of room 208 flew open. A short, rotund man with gingery blond hair and a huge mustache strode into the room. He was followed by the last apprentice, a girl who had the sheepish look of one recently reprimanded.

"Well then," the man said, "now that we are all here (his head bobbed as he completed his head count), we shall begin."

Becca leaned in to Alexandra and whispered:

"Master Corneilus Asherton. Don't forget the master. He's rather attached to his title."

"Gather in, gather in, apprentices," Master Asherton ordered, hands flapping. He stood with his back to the painting.

All seven of the first-year apprentices crowded forward.

"Let's see," Asherton said, pulling a folded piece of wrinkled paper from his pocket. He studied the paper.

"So, I see that this group is going to Scotland, for cryptozoology. Is that correct?"

He looked up.

Everyone nodded.

Asherton gave Alexandra a hard look and said, "Young lady, I'm afraid I do not know you. Please wait outside."

Alexandra hesitated.

Becca spoke, gently and respectfully:

"She's with us from now on, Master Asherton. Alexandra Ward, the Guardian's niece. She's just starting."

Master Asherton's expression turned from stern to quizzical to embarrassed. He consulted his crumpled notes, then looked up.

"Oh, my. Of course, Miss Ward, Miss Alexandra Ward. Yes, I have it right here, in my notes. I'm pleased to meet you, very pleased, very pleased indeed. The Guardian spoke to me. I can be so forgetful. Please forgive me, but I must be most careful in guarding the portal."

The man was blubbering and Alexandra could not pick out a reply that would fit, so she made none.

Asherton cleared his throat and went on.

"I will assist all of you through the cryptozoology portal. When I call your name, please say 'here.' Not 'yes', not 'ah-huh', not 'yeah' or anything else that comes into your dear little heads."

Alexandra folded her arms.

There are only seven of us, she thought. *Why all the fuss?*

Asherton began calling out the names on his list:

"Jonathan Eaten,"

"Here"

"Mariah Griffith."

"Here."

"Alexandra Ward."

"Here."

"Rebecca Vogel."

"Here."

"Katrina Thomas."

"Here."

"Rondegal Demperton."

"Here"

"Trenton Rigby."

"Here."

"Good, it appears everyone is here. Now, arrange yourselves in a single file behind Mr. Rigby."

The apprentices began shuffling into a line, Trenton Rigby in front closest to the painting. Becca stepped in behind him and Alexandra slid in behind her.

"That's good. That's right. No pushing. Good, good."

The shuffling stopped. The apprentices looked expectantly at Master Asherton.

"I will open the portal," he said with great seriousness. "Once I do, you will have one minute to get through. No more. Pay close attention and no lollygagging."

Lollygagging: That's one I haven't heard for awhile, thought Alexandra.

Asherton turned toward the painting.

"Alterraina Porticalis," he said with ceremonial formality. He immediately tapped all four corners of the painting with his right index finger, gave a final tap on the cottage door, and stepped back. The painting became a blackness and the blackness morphed to the width and height of a narrow doorway. The threshold of the blackness was a meter from Rigby's feet.

"Forward, Mr. Rigby," Master Asherton urged. "No time for stalling. Everyone follow Mr. Rigby."

Trenton Rigby stepped over the threshold and was instantly swallowed up in a black fog. Becca followed.

Alexandra hesitated.

"Come, come, quickly now, Miss Ward."

She felt Master Asherton's hand on her back, gently but urgently pushing her forward. She yielded and crossed the threshold. Darkness. More than darkness. A sensory wasteland: all light, all sound, all sensation swallowed up in nothingness. She felt paralyzed, the pounding of her heart and the working of her lungs the only evidence of her being, of her continuing to exist. The moment passed and she stepped forward. She looked down and saw sunlit grass at her feet. She was standing in the forest near the cottage depicted in the painting. A cool breeze caressed her cheek.

Becca was ahead and to the right, waving her on.

"Get out of the way," Becca said urgently.

Alexandra stepped aside and walked to Becca as the others arrived.

"Wow!" Alexandra exclaimed.

"First time is freaky, for sure," Becca responded. "But you'll get used to it. Let's go. We can't be late."

Becca took Alexandra's hand and led her through the open cottage door.

"Come in, come in!" said a middle-aged man standing with his back to a massive stone fireplace. A warm fire crackled invitingly behind him. The man's hair and beard were mottled red, and his eyes were pale amber. He wore a forest green shirt, breeches, and a long robe woven of thick strands of moss. The man gestured for them to be seated in wooden chairs arranged in a semicircle facing the fireplace. Alexandra took a seat on the right end of the semicircle; Becca sat next to her. The rest of the apprentices filled out the row to Becca's left.

"Welcome to Scotland, people. I'm Gregory Travits. The records at Byrnhelen call me master of cryptozoology. It is a good enough title, I suppose, as far as titles go. Doesn't mean much to me. A master is what a master does, not what someone writes on a piece of paper. I spend my days and sometimes my nights in the woods. I watch, I listen, I measure, and I record. You will do the same. You will read to help give meaning to what you see, hear, measure, and record. Thus you will advance, more by blisters on your feet than by tired eyes from reading books, even my books—which are very good."

Travits smiled to let the apprentices know this was a joke on himself and all academics.

"You will learn some answers; you will then leave them behind like steppingstones you might use to cross a stream. Always your search should be for the next right question, and the next and the next—leaving the answers behind."

They grasp little of what I say, Travits thought, *because they are school taught. No matter. They will come to an understanding.*

"Enough of my learning philosophies. Let's begin with

some basics. Prepare to take notes."

He glanced at Alexandra as she and the others withdrew note-taking materials from their backpacks. When the apprentices were ready, Travits continued.

"Animal cryptids, including human and humanoid forms, are my specialty. They will also be yours for the next five weeks. We will touch on general zoology, biology, physiology, and related disciplines; however, cryptozoology will be our primary focus."

Rondegal Demperton raised his hand.

"Kindly hold your questions until later," Master Travits said, not unkindly.

Rondegal jerked his hand down.

Travits continued:

"We will begin with definitions: Cryptozoology is the study of the origins, biology, physiology, character, behavior, and roles of animal cryptids. A cryptid is any animal that has escaped discovery or scientific verification in First World. There, such animals are thought of as being on a scale from pure fantasy to unverified possibility. We do not seek to dispel this thinking; it helps keep cryptids safe. We have verified the existence of many cryptids that are thought of as fantastical in First World. In fact, our list of true cryptids is quite short. Our work in Second World is far advanced over that in First World. Still, there is more work to be done; some species remain elusive."

Master Travits cleared his throat. The apprentices scribbled. The fire crackled.

"We will study the eating, sleeping, growing, eliminating, and procreating habits of verified cryptids," Master Travits said.

A wave of tittering passed along the line of apprentices.

He looks like a toadstool, Alexandra thought. *A red*

toadstool! Travits folded his arms and gazed steadily for a few moments at each apprentice.

"Do not waste my time, or yours, with adolescent imaginings," he said to the group. "Time is short. Five weeks is nothing. Intense concentration and hard work will be required for you to gain even the beginnings of the knowledge you require. Please set aside any squeamishness from which you may suffer, and do not bore me with your titillations. Am I understood?"

Every head nodded.

"Good."

He made an elaborate gesture with his left hand and a large map appeared next to him. It hung without visible means of support in front of the fireplace.

"You are in the mountains of northern Scotland...here."

He pointed to a place on the map.

"I have built a cryptid preserve in this place."

He traced a large area on the map.

"It took many years and much patience. The preserve is shielded from the usual extremes of weather and from prying eyes of the locals and of satellites above. (First Worlders love satellites.) First Worlders see here only what I want them to see. This ensures safety for me and my creatures, and for you also."

Travits used the map to describe the terrain of the preserve, its boundaries, and the locations of various ecosystems. He pointed to where specific cryptids were most likely to be sighted. A few questions were asked and answered. Travits then made the map disappear and went on with his lecture.

"In a school, you would learn about animals from books and lab study and perhaps an occasional visit to the zoo. I am not a schoolmaster, and the preserve is not a zoo. Your book study and laboratory work will be limited. You will spend most of your time in the field with the animals, very close to them, living with them."

Several apprentices exchanged anxious looks. Others beamed. One or two showed no reaction. Travits noted the differences and catalogued them for future reference.

"You will study the attributes and abilities of certain cryptids. You will also work with a few common animals to discover their hidden cryptid powers. My emphasis will be on the husbanding of these creatures, cryptid and non-cryptid alike, and on understanding and using their powers."

Travits saw that several apprentices had begun shifting in their seats and looking down at their feet. Others glanced diffidently around the room or stared at the fire. Two or three, including Alexandra, kept their attention on him.

Dry stuff, Travits thought. *I'm tired of repeating it myself. What they need is an example, and there is no better one than...*

"Dragons," Master Travits announced.

All shifting in seats stopped, interest in the furnishings of the room vanished, and fascination with the fire ended. Master Travits again had their full attention.

I always get them with dragons, he thought. *It is the best place to start.*

"For years I wondered how dragons made themselves invisible. I brought several of them here and observed them closely, and, as you might expect, quite cautiously. I won their trust and tested them every which way over five years.

"The invisibility question was difficult. Was it an autonomic response to fear or aggression or some other physiological stimulus? Did they have no more control over it than we do over how fast our hearts beat? Or was it something the dragons controlled consciously? I had many questions, and the answers did not come easily or swiftly. But they came, a step at a time.

"The unusually complex molecular structure of their scales intrigued me. Through much study and a chain of lucky accidents, I discovered that the oil secreted from these scales held the answer. It was many more steps from that discovery to the creation of invisibility cloaks and other clothing and even invisible rooms. All are now created using this secretion."

The apprentices sat in rapt attention.

Master Travits smiled.

"Any questions?" he asked.

A few hands went up, tentatively.

"Yes, young man," Travits said, pointing at the boy to his right.

"Master Travits, what can..."

"Please stand, young man, and state your name. All of you, please stand when you are addressing the group or me. It helps us to focus on the question or the information being delivered. It is also an endangered species of courtesy. We shall preserve it here."

Master Travits did not issue this instruction unkindly, nor did the apprentices receive it resentfully. His regimen was being accepted, especially since he had brought up dragons.

The boy stood.

"Rondegal Demperton, sir. Will we get to see dragons?"

Travits fixed his gaze on the rather plump young man with mousy brown hair.

Rondegal squirmed.

"Perhaps dragons," Master Travits said, "and certainly other creatures you will find just as interesting."

Travits pointed to another apprentice with a raised hand. The apprentice stood.

"Jonathan Eaten, sir. Five weeks doesn't seem like enough time. Will we be able to come back?"

"You are correct. I have been at this for many years, and feel I have barely scratched the surface. However, if you work hard and with serious intention, five weeks will be enough for our purposes. By then you will need to rest, and you will need time to ponder what you have learned before you can advance to further study. As to returning, that may be possible, but not until your entire apprenticeship is completed successfully."

Eaten sat down.

The fire behind Travits found a pocket of pitch in one of the burning logs. There was a hiss and a loud pop.

The apprentices flinched in unison.

Travits smiled.

The young, he thought, *one moment half asleep with boredom; the next moment alarmed by the natural sounds of a fire. Experience stills the mind and balances the heart. I will give them experience.*

Travits continued his lecture:

"During the first four weeks of this course, you will work together in the study of eight cryptids, two per week. I will choose them for you. During your fifth and final week, each of you will make your own choice of a cryptid to study. You will work alone. I will monitor your progress, but I will not be physically present, unless a serious problem arises. At the end of this final week, each of you will describe to me and your fellow apprentices why you chose the cryptid you did, what you learned about the selected creature, and what you learned about yourself. Are there any questions?"

There were none, so Travits went on:

"Be attentive during your first four weeks so you can make a wise choice in your fifth. Take manticores, harpies, dragons, and trolls, for example. While they are interesting, they are also stubborn, illusive, and sometimes dangerous. You might be wise to spend your week of solitary study with a cryptid more...docile. But the choice will be yours. That is the outline. Now on to the specifics."

Travits paused to clear his throat.

"This week we are going to study two species of fairies. There are several species living abundantly here in Scotland. Can anyone name three?"

Six hands came up.

Becca was so eager that she bounced up and down in her seat.

"You there," Travits said, pointing to a petite girl with shoulder- length red hair.

The girl stood.

"Katrina Thomas, sir. There are Leprechauns, Redcaps, and Chantillas."

"Very good," said Master Travits, giving Katrina a quick smile.

The girl sat down.

"I have chosen Chantillas and Leprechauns for your study this week. Redcaps are too dangerous."

Alexandra raised her hand.

"Yes," Master Travits said.

Alexandra stood.

"Alexandra Ward," she said. "Why are they too dangerous?"

So this is the one, Travits said to himself. *She challenges me already.*

"Do you question my decision?"

"No, sir," Alexandra said. "I would just like to know more about any cryptid too dangerous for study."

Like a moth to the flame, thought Travits, *she is drawn to*

the dangerous, the difficult, even what others would label
impossible. I can see what the Guardian sees in her.

"Traouxsiousrexa," Master Travits said, "more commonly known as Redcaps, haunt castles where particularly bloody battles were fought. They are nasty, murderous buggers. They appear in many different forms. Some say they have bright red hair and sharp jagged teeth. Others say they appear as beautiful, voluptuous women with flowing red tresses. They usually carry a weapon of sorts, perhaps hidden. The one thing they all have in common is the wearing of a bright red cap that appears black under the moon. Quite innocent enough you may think (the wearing of a red cap), until you realize it has been stained red by soaking in fresh blood. Redcaps lure their victims to a ruined castle, where they kill them and renew the day-time brilliance of their caps. There are several ruined castles on the preserve. If you come upon one, give it a wide berth."

Alexandra sat down.

"Has anyone here ever seen a Redcap?" Master Travits asked.

Becca raised her hand.

"Go ahead, miss"

Becca stood.

"Rebecca Vogel," she said. "I haven't seen one, but my brother, Edvard, said he saw one while we were visiting our grandparents in Bavaria. He was walking past a ruined castle. He said the Redcap looked like a woman with long red hair. She beckoned to him, but he ran. As soon as he started to run, the Redcap changed into a hairy beast with red eyes and chased after him until he made it past the ruins. I don't know if this really happened; my brother likes to tell stories. But I stayed away from that old castle, that's for sure."

"Thank you, Miss Vogel," Master Travits said. "Enough about Redcaps. They will not be the object of our study. Chantillas and Leprechauns will be."

Master Travits put another log on the fire.

"Most Leprechauns live in Ireland," he said over his shoulder, "but here in Scotland we are fortunate to have a small population of them. Leprechauns grant certain wishes to those who capture them. They are exceedingly mischievous, but not seriously dangerous. In watching them dance, I noticed that every time their foot stomped the ground, tiny specks of gold dust flew into the air and then settled to the ground. I carefully gathered up some of this dust and spent days analyzing it before I made a fascinating discovery: If this dust is sprinkled over a cut, the cut mends itself and disappears. The dust can't give you all the things a Leprechaun can; it can only fix the things that obviously need to be fixed. I am not sure what all those things are. I have sent some Leprechaun dust to Albumter Drouse. He is studying how the dust can be used in potions."

Travits could see his excitement about Leprechaun dust was not shared by his apprentices. No matter; they would acquire their own excitements, each in his or her own way.

"Enough of Leprechauns," Travits said. "Let's move on to Chantillas—
unless there are questions?"

He waited. No hands went up.

"Very well. Chantillas are delicate winged creatures. They can be both kind and mischievous. So far I have not discovered much about them, other than that they live in family groups in forest meadows. Some of them live in flowers while others live in trees. They are shy and quite elusive. I have collected their wings, which they shed every spring, and I am working to discover whether their wings are useful in potion making."

Master Travits again sensed restlessness in the apprentices.

Their brains can absorb only as much as their bottoms can bear. I have said enough. Time to move on.

Master Travits waved his wand. The front door flew open and slammed against the inside wall.

Katrina Thomas fell out of her chair.

Sunlight streamed in through the open door.

Master Travits stood to one side and bowed to his apprentices. He swept his arm through an arc that ended with his wand pointing toward the doorway. The apprentices scrambled through it in quite disorderly fashion.

Travits chuckled.

48   *Field Work*

> *I wonder what we might find if we journeyed deep within ourselves, taking nothing with us, leaving behind all we find so necessary in the life we know. There may be dragons. But beyond the dragons, there may be wonders undreamed of in our encumbered hours.*

FROM *"THE AWAKENING"* BY ELIZABETH SHAW

Alexandra had never heard of most of them: titillas, mentiers, magical salamanders, and many others. The list of cryptids went on and on. Others she had heard of: dragons, fairies, Leprechauns, Amphisbaena, and so forth. Before now, these had been the subjects of children's stories; here, they were real.

Master Travits lectured, led long hikes to prime locations in the preserve. He pointed out the habitats of various creatures, and set up well camouflaged observation blinds and tree stands in each. The apprentices spent hours in hides, observing cryptids and other creatures. Many of the creatures were nocturnal, so field studies were often conducted at night. For nighttime research, Alexandra and the others went to bed right after dinner, were up at midnight, hiked with their research gear to the designated blinds, and worked through until dawn. Laboratory work was done immediately after the field work to preserve samples, flesh out notes, and correlate data.

The apprentices slept whenever they could, night or day. Their normal sleep cycles were thoroughly disrupted by the end of the first week. They found themselves in various states of exhaustion, and by the end of the fourth week they were clearly in need of rest. For Alexandra the broken patterns of sleep had brought a blessing: She had occasionally been spared from her usual nightmares.

On Friday of the fourth week, dinner was served as usual in the cottage. The apprentices had finished dessert and were engaged in relaxed conversation. Master Travits stood, and the chatter, already subdued, faded into silence.

"You have done well, people," he said. "Many of you have made discoveries that would have taken me years of working alone. For this I am deeply grateful. It is Friday. You will rest. Monday will begin your fifth and final week, and for that week each of you will work alone. You have each submitted your choice of creature to study during this final week. I have approved those choices, but I forbid you to begin until Monday. Rest and play. You have earned it, and you will need it for what lies ahead."

Alexandra welcomed these orders, but she harbored a fear that any return to normal sleeping hours would end her occasional reprieve from the nightmares about Daniel. She often wondered what progress Elizabeth was making in finding him and bringing him to Byrnhelen. Any hope of him joining her here, in Scotland, was gone. It was too late in the course for that. But maybe he would be at Byrnhelen when she returned. This hope had arisen in her repeatedly over the past weeks. It had buoyed her spirits and allowed her to concentrate on the work at hand. Her research had therefore been singularly productive.

She recalled Master Travits' reaction to her choice of creature for solitary study during the upcoming week.

"Unicorns! Foolishness!" he had exclaimed. "You've read too many First World fantasy books."

"You mean they don't exist?" she had countered.

"I didn't say that. They do exist, but they might as well not for the purposes of study."

"Yes, sir, you did. And you said they were 'exceedingly reclusive and preternaturally aware'."

"That's right, young lady, and I said all five of their senses are highly developed: the eyesight of an eagle, the hearing of a great whale, and a sense of smell exceeding that of the wolf. But I was guessing. Their true powers I have never measured. In all my years here, I have caught only glimpses of them, flashes of white, fleeting and partial, between the trees and heavy undergrowth of the deep forest. The unicorn chooses you; you do not choose the unicorn. Choose something else to study."

"But what if I *have* been chosen, Master Travits?"

She remembered his expression, a mixture of shock and something else. Hope perhaps? Wonder? She recalled her thoughts, then and now:

Impossible to study...not permitted...unverifiable...never measured...least known. Why am I drawn to such things? I guess the "why" doesn't matter. I want the unicorn, and I do feel chosen. I want what others call impossible. For that too I feel chosen.

She remembered her words to Master Travits:

"Sir, is it your choice or mine?"

Travits had given her a long, hard look.

"It is yours."

"I choose the unicorn," she had said again.

"And you shall have it, Alexandra Ward. Whether it will have you is another question entirely."

49 Escape

There is no small talk when Daniel is challenged. He becomes silent. He listens, as the cheetah listens for the gazelle. He watches, as the osprey watches for the fish. He does not rise to the challenge. He is risen before the challenge appears. He considers only when to strike.

FROM "CHRONICLE OF THE SUCCESSION" BY MASTER BRADYN ARISTARCHUS

Daniel's unique sense of time informed him his meager meals arrived ten to twelve hours apart. Thus he knew he was being given two meals a day. The guards brought with each meal new container of water and a candle for his lantern. The candle never lasted until the next meal, so much of his time was spent in unrelieved darkness. He recorded each meal with a shallow scratch in the wall of his cell. Two meals equaled a day. He imagined one of the meals to be his "breakfast" and the other his "dinner." He could only imagine this, since the meals were exactly the same—a bit of stale bread and a piece of foul tasting meat—and he had no way of knowing the rising and setting of the sun. He created morning and evening in this way and knew the passage of days. By these and other small means he ordered the dark universe of his cell.

His calculations told him he had been imprisoned at Durnakk for about a month. It seemed far longer than that. Counting meals, counting days, scratching on the wall helped, but it was the company of Alea, the Dyrisian imprisoned in the cell below, that preserved his sanity and perhaps his life. Their visits across the pit made his dark confinement bearable.

They talked of the Two Worlds. She delighted in hearing of Daniel's life in First World, and he took equal delight in her accounts of life in Second World. She told him of the persecutions of magical people in his world and of the secret exodus Andronius Caledon made possible through his discovery of the dimensions. She spoke reverently of the earth, how it was home to both worlds.

And always they talked of escape: his escape, not hers, for she denied that possibility. He rejected her denial, but still she denied. She would not tell him why. She told him stories of escape from Durnakk, legends really, but in them were no facts, no clues how to make a real escape. Legends were legends. Still, they talked of it, of escape. The talk alone gave them hope. They did not speculate on probability. There was no hope in that.

***

The door hinges groaned and a shaft of light cut through the dark of Daniel's cell.

It was "dinner" time.

Escape time.

In a month of considering it together, he and Alea could come up with no better plan. It was a simple one because there were no facts. The last obstacle to its execution was Alea's insistence that Daniel leave her behind. Daniel had objected for days. In the end it became obvious. He could return to rescue her, but he had no way to take her with him now.

"Back," the guard snarled.

Daniel held his arms over his head protectively, as though afraid, and retreated backward into the darkness. The guard entered and reached down for the candle lantern. Daniel lunged forward, toppled the guard, and sprinted through the open door. He pulled the door closed and slid the bar into its slot in the door frame. The guard cursed and howled and beat his fists against the door.

Daniel looked left and right. He could not see or hear anyone in either direction. He had no idea which way might lead to freedom. Left was the direction General Croft had taken him for his chat with Aedan.

Not that way.

He sprinted down the corridor to his right. The corridor curved left about ten meters ahead. Daniel slowed his pace when he heard voices coming from around the corner. There was a door on the left side of the corridor, just before the turn.

Probably locked, he thought. *They'll catch me for sure.*

He reached the door and found it not only unlocked but ajar. He stepped through into the darkness and eased the door closed. As he did, the latch plate scraped against the jam.

"D'you hear that?"

It was a man's voice just outside the door.

"Hear what?" another man asked.

"Listen," the first man said.

"Listen to what. I don't hear nothin. Let's go."

Daniel heard the rattle of the latch and braced himself against the closed door.

"Is it locked?"

"Don't know. Won't budge."

Daniel's blockade was holding.

"Let's go," the first man said.

"Yeah, okay," said the other.

Daniel listened to the fading sound of the men's footsteps. Soon he could hear only the pounding of his heart.

He allowed himself to breathe, opened the door, and stepped cautiously into the corridor. He saw no one to the right, the direction from which he had come. To his left, two meters ahead, the curve to the left began. No voices from there now. It was too wide a curve to see around, but he heard nothing, so he risked moving into the curve.

The corridor continued curving to the left. Daniel increased his pace until he was running again, on the inside of the curve. He did not see the cloaked figure until it was too late.

They collided.

The cloaked figure fell backward, Daniel on top. In the ensuing struggle, the figure's hood slid back, and Daniel found himself staring into the face of a raven-haired girl with brilliant green eyes. She issued a guttural snarl as she reached into the folds of her robe and withdrew a shiny black wand. Daniel knocked it out of her hand. The wand rolled away, across the floor of the corridor. The girl lashed out at his face, raking her nails across his right cheek. Daniel grabbed her wrists and pinned them to the floor. He held her there for a moment, then jumped up, stumbled forward a few steps, scooped up the fallen wand, and sprinted ahead through the rest of the curve in the corridor.

"Guards, Guards!" he heard the girl scream.

Daniel kept running, the wand clenched tightly in his right hand. The corridor was straight for a few meters, then began twisting to the right and left.

So, Daniel thought, *I have a wand. But what good is it? I don't know how to use it.*

He rounded a corner. Fifty meters ahead were three guards, wands raised. Three spheres of light, one from each wand, hurtled toward him. He dodged. The guards cursed. Daniel turned and sprinted back the way he'd come.

Rounding a corner, he saw another four guards running toward him. They were further away than the first three, maybe a hundred meters. This time there was no convenient door to hide behind; he was trapped. He turned back and halted in a curve of the corridor, out of sight of both groups of guards.

What now?

He looked at the wand in his hand, and memories of Alexandra and their experimentations with magic came to him in a rush. They had moved things with their thoughts. It was just play. He looked again at the wand in his hand. He and Alexandra never had wands. Maybe with the wand there was greater power...

Daniel ran left, in the direction of the guards he had first encountered. The corridor straightened and he saw them. When they saw him, they halted. Daniel did not stop; he ran harder, his arm extended, his wand pointing forward.

The rest seemed to occur in slow motion.

Daniel and the guards were some sixty meters apart. One of the guards broke and ran in the opposite direction. The other two held their ground and cast the same spells as before, spheres of deadly energy issuing from the tips of their wands. Their aim was poor and their target, hurtling toward them in a zigzag pattern, was difficult to acquire. Their spells shattered portions of the walls, floor, and ceiling around Daniel. Dust and particles of stone rained down on him. He could distinguish each particle, each fleck of dust— all descending over him with exquisite slowness. He glided through the cloud of destruction. It was like the tricks he and Alexandra had practiced, but intensified now by the threat before him.

And the wand.

I've never had a wand before.

For a moment he separated from himself. He was above, observing himself, approving. Then, in an instant, he was again himself, gathering power, spinning up like a laser cannon preparing to fire.

The wand in his hand glowed and changed from black to a mixture of purple and red. He felt its heat. He became the wand, and he felt electric, on fire.

He aimed at the taller of the two guards.

"Fire."

It was all he knew to say.

The wand understood.

A deadly sphere erupted from its tip. The sphere slithered toward the guard and struck him center-mass. The man's body disintegrated. Daniel, still charging, took aim at the second guard and again gathered his power. He was about to give the command when the wand, anticipating him, discharged another deadly sphere, vaporizing the second guard.

Daniel halted. His world became real-time again, in increments. He felt like he was coming out of a trance. He heard shouting coming from just behind him.

Too close, he thought. *It has all been for nothing.* They were upon him now. He knew he should care, but he didn't. He didn't bother to turn and face them. He let the wand slip from his hand. It clattered to the stone floor, rolled to the wall, and disappeared into a crack. He could see its glow, slowly fading. His last thought, before all went black, was of Alexandra and of the raven-haired girl with the brilliant green eyes.

50   The Interview

The curse of human consciousness is to know beyond itself. The other animals expand their territories as they are able and according to their kind. They do not engage in conquest beyond their needs. They do not contemplate the stars. They do not fear death.

FROM *"ANIMAL TEACHERS" BY MASTER GREGORY TRAVITS*

Monday of the fifth and final week came too soon for the cryptozoology apprentices, but everyone was grateful for the weekend rest they had been allowed.

Much of the conversation over the weekend had been about choices the apprentices had made for their individual research this week. Alexandra had avoided telling anyone of her choice by deflecting questions with other questions, showing an intense interest in the choices of others, or simply changing the subject.

But this was Becca.

"What's the mystery?" Becca asked with a mischievous grin. "Which of the cryptids did you choose?"

"None of them," Alexandra replied.

Becca's eyebrows went up.

"Don't give me that look," Alexandra said.

"Well, then tell me. No more suspense. What's your plan?"

"Unicorns."

"WHAT?!"

"See!" Alexandra snapped back. "This is exactly why I didn't want anyone to know. Master Travits knows. He approved it, but he wasn't happy about it. I asked him not to mention it to anyone, and he promised he wouldn't."

"Wow!" said Becca, her surprise tinged with wonder. This reaction soon faded, however. Becca folded her arms tightly across her chest and gave her friend a look of deep concern.

Alexandra chastised herself.

I knew I shouldn't have told her.

"Master Travits said no unicorns," Becca said. "So we didn't look for them, didn't do any research on them. Nothing. Now you tell me you're making them your project. What kind of sense does that make?"

There was an awkward silence.

"Alexandra," continued Becca, speaking more gently, "you'll fail this course if your project is not completed to Travits' satisfaction. Tell me how he can be satisfied when he warned you, warned all of us, to leave the unicorns alone? How can he be satisfied when you come back with nothing? It's like you are setting yourself up for failure. It doesn't make sense!"

"That's why I kept quiet, Becca, I knew it would be the unicorn as soon as Travits issued his warning at the beginning of the course. I don't know how I knew, but I knew."

"You are so contrary!" Becca said, clearly frustrated. "And so stubborn."

"Sometimes, I am," Alexandra admitted, her voice barely audible, "but not this time. This is something I must do. I don't know why and I certainly don't know how. But I must do it. I was called to this. I know it makes no sense. I can't explain it, but please be my friend: Don't turn me away from this."

Becca stared at the oak floor boards beneath her feet. A

full minute passed in silence while her countenance slowly changed: Frustration became compassion. She put a hand on Alexandra's shoulder. "I am your friend, not your critic. If there's anything, anything at all, I can do to help, you must promise to ask."

"And you won't say anything to the others?"

Becca pinched her thumb and index finger together and drew them across her mouth as though pulling a zipper.

"My lips are sealed."

Alexandra hugged Becca. "Thank you."

"If there is anyone who can do this, it's you," Becca whispered in reply.

***

After breakfast, Master Travits began a series of private interviews with the apprentices. Alexandra was scheduled last. She waited alone on a bench outside Travits' office. Apprentice Mariah Griffith emerged from the office, closed the door behind her, and walked past Alexandra without saying a word.

It was Alexandra's turn. She walked to the closed door and hesitated.

"Come in," Master Travits said from the other side of the door.

Alexandra had not knocked, but she was not surprised he knew she was there. People of Second World often seemed to know things without physical indication of them. This ability and others like it were uncommon, even freakish, in First World; they were common, assumed in Second World.

Alexandra opened the door and walked in.

Travits was scribbling something in a worn file on his desk; he didn't look up.

"Please take a seat, Miss Ward."

A straight-back wooden chair had been arranged in front

of his desk. She sat in it, took out her notebook, and prepared herself. Her heart was pounding.

"So, it is to be the unicorn," he said, still scribbling, still not looking at her. His words could have been a question or an affirmation. Alexandra's answer was the same to either."Yes, sir."

Travits finally looked up, his intense amber eyes fixed on hers.

"You're sure," he said.

Affirmation or question again; answer the same.

"Yes."

"If you come back with nothing, you will get nothing. I make no allowances. Failure in your fifth week is failure in this master course. Your friends have chosen...carefully. Each selected a creature which our research touched on in the first weeks. Some will do well with their choices; others will just get by. But none, I venture, will fail. All will complete the course. All but you."

Alexandra felt suddenly short of breath.

Is he going to kick me out now? Not give me a chance? All because I want to try something he failed at?

She did not reply to his threat.

"You chose differently from the rest," Travits continued. "You did not choose the safe path. You chose the other path, the one less traveled, as one of your First World poets once said. You are brave, and great risks can bring great rewards. They can also bring crippling failure...and regrets that last a lifetime."

Master Travits paused to allow Alexandra to consider this.

She found she had been holding her breath. She made herself relax, exhaled slowly, and began to breathe again.

Travits went on:

"But the choice is not mine and neither, in a strange way, was it yours. You are who you are, Alexandra Ward, and I have been brought to the realization that any other choice would have been beneath you."

Alexandra observed with surprise that Master Travits' eyes were glistening. He was holding back tears! This brought a similar response from her. Her throat became tight and she felt tears welling in her eyes. She gritted her teeth.

I am not *going to cry*, she promised herself. *I am* not*!*

Travits looked at the file on his desk.

Alexandra looked down at her hands.

"I have something for you," he said.

Alexandra looked up. Travits was holding out the thick, hand-worn file he had been scribbling in. She hesitated.

Travits scowled and gestured impatiently with the file.

Alexandra stood, took the file from him, and sat back down with it in her lap.

"I have given you the work of a lifetime, my work. No one knows of this, my obsession."

Alexandra ran her hand over the faded file jacket, read the label. It named the creature she had chosen. Under the name was a date. Alexandra calculated.

More than twenty years ago! This is his work, this is everything!

"No one has seen my foolish notes. They document failure after failure, dead-end after dead-end. They tell a story of rejection, the beast's rejection of me. I am not the great cryptozoologist they say I am."

"That's not true" Alexandra said.

"It is true. You hold the evidence. But this is not what's important. What is important is that you do not let my obsession become yours. Seek the unicorn, but do not be consumed by your seeking."

Alexandra did not know what to say; wisely therefore, she said nothing.

"My notes can help in your search. Because they are a record of failure, they can tell you what you need *not* do and where you need *not* go. That is no small benefit. But the notes and your best efforts will come to nothing if the great question is not answered in your favor."

"What do you mean? What question?"

"You have chosen the unicorn," replied Travits, "but has the unicorn chosen you?"

Alexandra thought about that.

"I feel it," she said, "but how will I know?"

"The knowing is in the seeking to know. The beast will answer. Perhaps it already has."

Alexandra nodded.

"Passing my work on to you is my redemption," Master Travits said, leaning back comfortably in his chair. "I never want to see that file again. It is yours now. I am finished; you, my dear, are just beginning."

51   Last Words

*You wake up on a certain day. You have a chance
meeting with a stranger, lose your favorite pen, or find
a baseball cap on a fence post...and everything changes.
The smallest drop of rain alters the plane of the ecliptic.*

FROM "CHILD ON THE WALL" BY MASTER TOURIN ABDAL

Alexandra had just placed Travits' unicorn file in her
backpack when Becca burst into the room they shared.

"Well, what did he say? You've got to tell me all of it."

Alexandra did not look up. "He said I was not to say what
he said."

Becca giggled.

"Say that again, real fast."

"No, I mean it: He said not to talk about it."

"Well, he sort of said the same thing to me, but if we
don't tell anyone but each other..."

"I think he meant anyone," Alexandra said.

"I guess you're right. I'm just so excited!"

Becca ran to her closet and began her own packing. She
pulled down a large wooden box and placed it on her bed.

"Will I see you later?" Becca asked.

"I don't know. Maybe. I might have to stay late. Don't
wait up for me."

She did not tell her friend that she alone among the
apprentices would not be returning to the cottage each night,
that she would only return at the end of the week—if she
returned at all. She felt bad about keeping this from Becca,
but Master Travits had been quite emphatic. No one was to

know.

Becca gave her friend a concerned look. "Be really careful, Alexandra."

"I will," Alexandra replied as she hefted her pack.

"Wait. Do you remember the spell Master Travits taught us?"

"I know. Don't say it now or he'll show up. If I need him, I'll use the spell. I don't think I'll need it, but how could I forget it after all the drilling he made us do."

"You never know," Becca said. "I just want you to remember it. I don't want to spend all my time worrying about you."

She knows, thought Alexandra. *I don't know how, but she does. Still I must say nothing.*

"I'll remember, Becca. Don't worry about me."

Becca walked over to her friend and hugged her tightly.

"Take care of yourself," Becca whispered.

"You too," Alexandra whispered back.

I take no side. I wait. I watch. I listen. I speak only when the truth requires a friend.

SIGVARDR

A lexandra rested against the thick trunk of a fallen pine tree. It was mid-morning. Sunlight streamed through the trees and formed patches of light and dark that lay over the tall grass of the meadow before her. A light breeze parted the grass in random patterns, gently leading the yielding blades in a slow waltz, back and forth and side to side. Sunlight penetrated the swaying grass, deeply here, shallowly there, creating the appearance of vertical movement as the grasses swayed side to side.

Alexandra had walked briskly, with few rests, for at least three hours to get here from the cottage. She calculated that she had covered sixteen kilometers. The file Master Travits had given her lay in the grass at her side. She studied the large hand-drawn map he had pulled from the file and gone over with her during their interview.

"This is the least explored part of the preserve," he had said, pointing at the southeast quadrant of the map. "This is where you should concentrate your efforts. Don't bother with the places you know. Cryptids are in those places. That is why I led you to them. But the unicorn is not there. You must go south and east. You must go where I have never been."

He had paused after those words, and become pensive.

"Let me tell you a great truth," he had said. "We think we lead our lives by making choices; in fact, we choose and then are led by the unimaginable consequences of our choice. You must not pursue the unicorn; you must be led by him. If you follow, he will find you."

Master Travits had then pointed to this meadow on his map, and had run the tip of his finger over the trail that led to it. He had warned her sternly not to stray left or right of the trail:

("There are dangers there that have no part in your search.")

Alexandra rested her hand on the unicorn file next to her. She considered the paradox Travits had presented.

Follow a thing to be found by it?

Follow a question to be found by the answer?

Seek and ye shall find.

She saw the meaning, and she smiled.

It doesn't matter, she thought. *I am here. I can follow the signs, if there be any, and if there are no signs—if there are no markers, no flags, no hints, no tufts of fur or broken branches or trampled leaves—then I will lean into the wind. I will wander the unknown quadrant as Master Travits told me to. I will lean into the wind. I will go forward.*

The breeze caressing the meadow shifted and came out of the north. It moved Alexandra's hair away from her face—as the hand of a friend might do—touching her, gentling her thoughts. She recalled this morning's final instructions to all the apprentices:

"Today will be the start of an exciting week," Master Travits had assured them. "Each morning you will start out early to follow the creature of your choice. Each evening you will return to the cottage for a late-night supper followed by studying your findings and testing whatever hypotheses you have formed about your creature. By Thursday evening all of you should have a clear idea of what your creatures are like and what powers they possess. On Friday, we will listen to each of your reports. You will then depart through the portal back to Byrnhelen, where you will await my decision. If you experience an emergency while you are away from the cottage, use the Raportio spell to summon me. I will appear moments later, wherever you are. Remember, "emergency." The spell is not to be used for anything less. Now, be on your way."

Alexandra had heard the instructions, but she knew they were not for her. Her path was not their path. Master Travits had made this perfectly clear in their interview, and he had given her altogether different instructions. Now she was on that path.

She folded the map, tucked it into her shirt, and shouldered her pack. The meadow was a beautiful resting place, but there was much ground to cover. She walked back a few meters to where the trail ended and from there continued south cross country.

***

The sun moved through its inexorable arc toward evening as Alexandra made her way into the southeast quadrant. The details for this quadrant were sparse on the map Travits had given her. She began building a picture of the terrain in her mind: an unusually tall Birnam oak here, a moss-covered cliff there, a ridge to the west, a saddle between two summits on the east, water sources, stream crossings, ponds, meadows. She connected things, began to see the shape and clothing of the land. She made notes or drew symbols on the map to mark significant features she encountered. Her notes and symbols would guide her back when the time came. Without them, without the map, she would surely become lost in this trackless wilderness. Then she would have to use the emergency spell to summon Travits. She didn't want to do that; it would be an admission of defeat.

She left the meadow far behind. There were no trails. Travits had given her a compass, a device he had obtained long ago from a First World visitor, and he had instructed her in its use. Its use now was to keep her moving south and a little east. Unlike the other apprentices, she would not return to the cottage this night or any night before the end.

"To have any chance you must go deep into the quadrant," Master Travits had said. "You will have no time for back and forth like the others. You will not share meals with us or sleep in your soft bed. You have chosen a different way. I will give you what you need for your quest."

In her pack, Alexandra carried ample food, a bundle of shelter cloth so light she could hardly feel its weight, blankets as thin as rice paper, and a few other necessities. Travits had promised that the blankets, as thin as they were, had special properties that would measure her temperature against that of the air around her and adjust to keep her warm. He had instructed her to spread the bundled cloth over her at night or whenever foul weather stopped her progress.

"It will do the rest," he had said.

Her problem was not the gear. Her problem was getting back. She knew this, and she therefore paid close attention to map, compass, and the terrain.

***

Dusk settled over the land. Alexandra came to a flat spot concealed between two stands of saplings above and fifty meters west of a small stream. She laid out her blankets and placed on them the food she had selected for her evening meal. Before eating, she dropped down to the stream and filled her leather water bag. She drank deeply, returned to her blankets, and ate.

The forest around her shifted gradually from a place of day creatures to a place of night creatures. The night creatures watched as she unfolded a three-meter by three-meter square of double-layer cloth. As Travits had instructed, she slid herself and all her gear between the layers. She lay on her back and watched as the upper layer rose and magically linked itself to the sapling trunks on either side of her campsite. The cloth continued to shape itself into a simple tent. Alexandra poked at the canopy: it was stretched tight and the material seemed quite strong, certainly proof against any weather that might come as she slept.

She fluffed one of the blankets and settled it on the ground. She lay on it and pulled the other blanket over her. She felt a nearly imperceptible uplifting as the blanket beneath magically cushioned and insulated her from the cooling earth. The blanket over her seemed to know how warm or cool she needed to be.

This is way better than First World camping, Alexandra thought.

She was glad she would not have to go back to the cottage with the others each night. The solitude of the wild was imbedding itself in her. Ancient memories arose, memories of ancient people huddled around fires, listening to the night. She listened to the gentle babbling of the nearby stream. The night sounds faded. The moving waters became silent.

Alexandra slept.

The night creatures peered at her. They knew who she was and they were comforted by her presence. They were content, and they sent the signal, the long-awaited message.

She is here.

53   The Lavertanian Unicorn

Lavertanian Unicorns swim through history like great whales taking in plankton. They store events in their tissues and note carefully the warp of opinions, beliefs, dreams, and hopes. Roiling in the caldron of their racial memory are the birth, evolution, and death of every animal species. Computers of First World can model the future of a railroad trestle or a spacecraft or a disease epidemic. Lavertanian Unicorns can do this and more. They can predict with high reliability the long-term effects of possible futures on every species of animal, including man.

FROM *"HISTORY OF THE TWO WORLDS"* BY MASTER BRADYN ARISTARCHUS

The morning sun was not yet visible above the mountains to the east, but its diffused glow appeared there. The day creatures were making themselves heard. The night creatures were saying their goodbyes. A Tree Pipit announced the beginning of its day, while a great horned owl hooted, calling out the end of its nocturnal hunt.

Alexandra awakened in the midst of this transformation, grateful her sleep had been deep and dreamless. She felt fully refreshed for the first time since arriving at Byrnhelen.

It was cold.

She decided not to eat before the sun appeared over the mountains. Instead she broke camp in the semi-dark, donned her pack, and followed the nearby stream as it meandered south and then east toward the base of the mountains. The stream became a rivulet, then a trickle, and finally a patch of moist green earth at the base of a ridge that linked two grassy summits, one north of her and one south. The ridge dipped to a saddle about 250 meters above where Alexandra stood.

She climbed. When she reached the saddle, she encountered a landscape for which neither the map nor Master Travits could have prepared her. Below and stretching east was a wide valley enclosed on all sides by high mountains. The valley was hidden from anyone who did not climb as she had. The morning sun had risen above the mountains at the east end of the valley. It bathed everything in golden light and warmed Alexandra's face.

She stepped onto a rock outcropping overhanging the steep east face of the ridge. She found a comfortable niche, took off her pack, and settled herself against a large boulder. She pulled her pack onto her lap and reached into it for a piece of bread. The sun broke the eastern horizon as she did this. It was as though a great king had arrived, arrayed in the golden vestments of his rank. One did not fidget with food in his presence; one did not move.

The moment passed. Alexandra relaxed but remained quite still. The sunlight softened and calmed her and blurred her memories. There was only this hidden place and her in it. There was no other place, no other time, no other anything but this now and the great valley stretching to the jagged horizon and the rock pressing against her back.

That was when she saw it: a distant speck of white breaking up the mottled gray and green near the base of the ridge.

She stared.

The speck moved and Alexandra dared to hope.

***

The messages had come to him the day before: reports of her route, her encampment, her sleeping, her waking, and her climb to the saddle.

She was cared for and did not know it. She was guided and did not know it. She did not know the animal ways. That would come later.

He had waited in the valley until he knew she had reached the saddle. He wished her to see him coming. He wished her to have time to prepare. He observed from afar her questions, her hopes, her expanding awareness. He observed her interior preparations, her making herself ready. How she received him would tell him much of what he needed to know.

He was a Lavertanian Unicorn, and he had no desire for the company of men. Their thoughts were jumbled and unbalanced. They had no center. They were ahead or behind themselves, never present. He had never met one who could see clearly.

The child was different. In what way he did not know, but the difference was worth exploration.

And he had promised the Guardian.

***

Alexandra sat perfectly still. She held the piece of bread in her hand inside her pack. She did not lift the pack from her lap. She did not move her hands or shift her feet or do anything that might make a sound or break the visual plain. In obedience to a long-buried predatory instinct, she sniffed the air, and her breathing became shallow, measured, and quiet.

The thing, clearly an animal of some sort, reached the base of the ridge-wall and began ascending a switchback trail leading up the wall. Alexandra's view of the animal was intermittently obscured by bulges in the wall, but she could see it was some kind of horse. She strained to see the tell-tale horn of a unicorn, but the animal was too distant. She would know soon enough. It was coming to her.

The animal finally reached the last switchback, far to Alexandra's left and some thirty meters below. A wave of elation passed through her when she saw the beast clearly for the first time.

Unicorn!

Alexandra remained as still as a statue while the unicorn passed below her, left to right, heading toward the end of the trail. The animal seemed not to notice her—clip-clop, clip-clop, slowly, steadily walking, walking.

The unicorn was a stallion, very tall, at least eighteen hands at the withers. Its coat was luminescent white with patches of gold formed by reflections of the morning sun. The shape of the patches and the intensity of their golden reflections varied with the working of muscles beneath the stallion's coat. A sixty centimeter horn protruded from its forehead.

The unicorn achieved the ridge and turned north, toward Alexandra, without pausing or looking up. He continued his silent, steady walk. Thirty-five meters, twenty meters, seven, four, two, one, and...stop. It was as though they had an appointment, and Alexandra's perch was precisely where they had agreed to meet.

Alexandra did not move. Her hand was concealed in her pack, holding the bread in a crushing grip. The sun beamed warmth down on her. There was not a breath of wind. Far to the east and high over the valley, a White Tailed Eagle spied her and the unicorn. The eagle called out in a thin screech to the creatures in the valley and below:

They are met.

The Lavertanian Unicorn looked at Alexandra. She gazed back into his large golden eyes. The unicorn bobbed his head.

Show me your hand.

The words formed in her mind as a thought, her thought but not her thought—strange, compelling. She looked down at her left hand, the hand that held the bread concealed within her pack. She smiled and slowly withdrew the bread. She held it just above the opening of her pack. She did not make an offering of it, but neither did she deny it.

The unicorn bobbed his head upward, then, slowly, brought his mouth down to Alexandra's hand. He did not wrest the bread from her. He pressed his warm muzzle gently against her hand, breathed on it. It was a greeting, not a seeking for food. Alexandra made a slight gesture upward with the bread, and the unicorn took it. He ate the bread without lifting his head. There was no eagerness in this; it was a sacramental offering and a sacramental acceptance.

Alexandra raised her right hand from her lap. The unicorn did not move. She placed her hand gently on the animal's nose. The unicorn allowed it. She moved her hand to the animal's forehead, stroked it just beneath the horn. Her fingers brushed the base of the horn and it began to glow as though illuminated from within by a bright golden light. She did not pull her hand away. Still the unicorn did not move.

An understanding flowed into Alexandra. She was *not* here to study, to experiment, to collect samples, or to engage in any of the activities assigned to the other apprentices— though she would do some of these things. She was here for something more. A vision came. Inside the vision, she heard a cacophony of voices covering voices; words covering words; jumbled sentences begun in hope and finished in despair, all rising and falling on a tide of hints and whispers. She saw, as through a fog, the acting out of high purposes, base desires, courage, cowardice, love, hate, vicious conflict, triumph, and devastation. The vision resolved into two essences: domination and darkness on the one hand; freedom and light on the other—coexisting eternally. Alexandra felt crushed one moment by a wave of despair, then lifted up in the next by an opposing wave of hope. When she struggled for hope, she found in it tendrils of despair. When she was thrown back into despair, she found tendrils of hope. The waves of hope and despair crashed into each other, became one, and there was calm.

The unicorn had delivered his first lesson.

Alexandra pulled her hand away from the horn. Its glow faded. The animal backed up a step and slowly turned its side to her. She knew exactly what to do. She reached down, cinched her pack closed, and pulled it onto her back. She climbed onto the rock where she had been sitting and faced the side of the unicorn. He sidled toward her. She grasped a large tuft of his thick mane just above the withers, and pulled herself onto his back. When she was settled and sitting upright, the unicorn turned, walked south to the trail, and began a slow descent into the valley from whence he'd come.

***

Days passed. The unicorn took her far and wide, but always southward. He introduced her to places and to cryptids that were not on Master Travits' list (or any list). Storms came and went. The unicorn never left her. He guarded her at night and made shade for her in the day. When she looked at him, he turned away, unable to bear her gaze. But he never left her.

It thrilled Alexandra to know she was in uncharted territory, making new discoveries far beyond the scope of the master course. She felt a passing concern for the anxiety her extended absence might be causing her fellow apprentices, but Master Travits had promised he would explain to the others, especially Becca, that she was safe and operating on orders from him. Travits could not have known how far those orders would take her or how unfounded his promises about her safety would become. The unicorn took Alexandra far past the boundaries set by Master Travits. She did not care. Her trust in the unicorn had become complete.

Eventually, Alexandra did not require the medium of the unicorn's horn to call up the vision he had implanted during their first meeting. Any gesture of affection would do: leaning against his side, laying her arms over his back or wrapping them around his neck, lying forward against his thick mane when she was mounted.

She tried to enter the vision, sought for its meaning. But it was gossamer, a teasingly transparent window one moment and an opaque barrier the next. Messages were being passed into her, but she could not decipher them or retain them for long in her conscious mind.

Alexandra made notes and marked Master Travits' map until the unicorn took her beyond its edges. On the back of the map, she scrawled a new map based on her guesses and fragments of evidence she collected: the husk of a horn shed by her unicorn or another, the cast-off wings of a previously unknown species of fairy, blossoms and seeds of unknown plants, bark shaved from trees she could not identify. She became a collector of samples of her ignorance.

Early Thursday morning the unicorn turned north. His pace quickened, and he no longer stopped to allow Alexandra to explore. He sensed his mission was nearing its end. The child had seen enough. He had sent the messages, implanted the vision deeply in her. If he did not return her now, while he had the will, he might never return her.

Such was the bond.

So he pressed on, through forests, around lakes, over

ridges, across streams—urgently and against his deepest desire.

54 Parting

There are no constants. Light, dark, the touch of a friend's hand, the whisper of a lover waiting outside our door, these are but pulses, the weaving movement of light or air or atoms. We do not see the world as it is; we see it as we wish it to be, and sometimes we wish poorly.

FROM "THE AWAKENING" BY ELIZABETH SHAW

A lexandra studied the meadow and the trees surrounding it. She checked the map and smiled.

He knew. He brought me to the meadow where I started, and just in time.

It was late afternoon. The long return journey had been long, and Alexandra felt exhausted. She imagined the awe and admiration of the other apprentices when they saw her arriving on the back of the unicorn. She had succeeded where the great Master Travit's had failed. She had risen above him, above them all.

She relished these thoughts. And then, with cold suddenness, they were gone, erased like chalk sprayed off a chalkboard with a fire hose.

This becomes you not!

The unicorn's chastisement startled her. She had become accustomed to his promptings appearing as her own thoughts, and she had learned from him how to send her thoughts (though sending was unnecessary with him; he knew her thoughts before they were fully formed). He had taught how to protect her thoughts from being read and, finally, he had taught her how to read the unprotected thoughts of others. But never had his communication with her been so forceful, so implacable, as this one.

She had disappointed him, and there was pain for her in this. Tears came. His pain was her pain; his disappointment, her disappointment; his joy, her joy. He had shown her how to do this, how to bond so deeply, but he had not shown her how to protect herself from the effects of such bonding. Unicorns used avoidance. They stayed hidden to avoid the pain of bonding with humans.

This protection was not available to Alexandra. She could not hide from people. The unicorn had said he would help if he could, but, in the end, she would have to find her own way of protection.

The unicorn's chastisement soon dissolved into something else. Her emotions, even her pride, were as strong as before, but the need for outward expression felt diminished. The unicorn's words became a gentle assurance:

You have no need for prideful displays or for approbation. They weaken you. They make you dependant on others.

The pain of his disapproval was gone. The unicorn's thoughts came to her again:

It is finished. I can go no further. I must go. I must go now.

Somehow, Alexandra already knew this, though the knowing did not diminish her sadness. She slid down from the unicorn's back and leaned against his warm, sweat-drenched flank. She walked forward and put her arms around his powerful neck.

More silent tears came.

The unicorn lowered his head.

"Goodbye," Alexandra whispered, her cheek pressed

close to his ear.

The unicorn's head came up, and he pulled away, out of her arms, as though with that terrible word she had thrust a sword into him. He stamped the ground with his right forefoot, snorted, turned his back to her and high-stepped away to the edge of the woods bordering the meadow. There he halted, turned around and presented himself obliquely to her. He did not look at her. With sudden violence, he reared, stood nearly upright on his powerful hind legs, and clawed the air with his forelegs. His horn glowed more brilliantly than Alexandra had ever seen it glow. He whinnied, dropped to a rigid stance on all four legs, and then leaped into the concealing forest.

Alexandra stared after him. Flashes of white between the trees marked his retreat from her. She felt the pounding of his hooves. In a little while, there were no more flashes of white, and the pounding of the unicorn's hooves merged with the sound of distant thunder. A light wind came into the meadow and the tall grass moved in confused patterns and the trees around the meadow spoke to the wind in the special language they had between them. A storm was coming.

I never knew his name or if he even had one, Alexandra thought. *If he didn't have one, I should have given him one.*

She shouldered her pack and set off along the trail leading back to the cottage. She pictured a warm fire there, and she thought of her friends, of Becca and the others. It was good to be going back. What a time she would have tomorrow. What stories they would all tell.

She pondered what story she would tell or whether she would tell any story at all. The unicorn had not forbidden it, but telling the essence of her experience with him would not be possible in words. It was sacred, untellable. Perhaps she would tell only of the lessons she had learned.

55   Sigvardr

Habitat, species, family, and self are the essences. All else is an elaboration.

FROM "DIVINITY OF THE ORDINARY" BY MASTER BRADYN ARISTARCHUS

Sigvardr reached the saddle between the two great mountains and gazed down on his beloved valley. In the quiet of dusk, he thought of his many children and of their mothers. He saw the many generations that would flow forward from him. Looking backward in time, he saw his mother clearly, and something of his father. He looked beyond them and saw the ancestors that had made his life.

Sigvardr saw he was a bud in the tree of life. He had once, for a moment, been the bud at the tip of the highest branch of that tree. That was long ago. Now his cells were deeply imbedded in the tree. New buds formed above him. The tree grew by this process, even as he, Sigvardr, faded away. The ancients within the tree whispered to him.

He faced south and pawed the rocks with his right forehoof. Behind him was the easy track along the ridge to the northern summit. He had achieved that summit many times. In front of him was the southern summit. He had never achieved it. The ridge leading to it became a steep knife edge, an arête, for the last seventy-five meters. The arête fell away steeply five hundred meters on either side. It was too narrow and too steep for a unicorn.

In his youth he had often plodded to the base of the arête. He had studied it for hours, wondering if it was truly impassable. He had imagined he was a man, small and supple, with clever hands and fingers to take him over those last few meters to the summit. Somewhere along the path of his existence he had given up going there and staring and imagining he was a man. In his maturity, he had become ruler of the valley below. The valley was his place. Nothing there was impassable to him. There he was king. He forgot the southern summit.

But now he was here, the impossible summit towering above him, beckoning to him as it had when he was young. He thought of Alexandra again and felt the pain of separation. Behind the pain he sensed a mystery, something in his future, and hers.

Before he had been whole, as unicorn. Now, because of the bonding and the separation, he felt he was something less than whole. He had been cleaved. He had laid down his life for her and she knew nothing of his sacrifice. This had always been the risk in agreeing to mentor Alexandra. This had been the risk in opening his psychic gates to her. Passing the vision to her required this. Granting her his powers required this. Preparing her for the Guardianship required this.

He was unicorn. He had been born into a place, into a time, and into a purpose. Unicorns could not live without purpose. His purpose now lay within the child. The hidden valley of his birth and his youth and his maturity was becoming just a memory even as he gazed down upon it. He had fulfilled his purpose there. He had a new purpose, and it resided elsewhere.

One thing was left undone here, one knot was not tied off. It was a personal thing, covered over in the rapids of his life. But the river was now wide. Its waters were smooth and slow, and the great ocean was not too distant. The undone thing rose out of the waters.

The south summit.

The Ancients saw it and whispered their approval. And something more they whispered, something he did not understand.

Sigvardr walked south along the ridge. He could see the beginning of the arête, high above and distant. There was something different about it, a golden glow from the setting sun and something more he could not discern. The pain of separation from Alexandra was still there, but the ancestral voices directed his attention to the knife edge and the summit above. The years of imagining were over. All that was left was the doing of this last thing.

His slow gait became a canter. The canter transitioned into a full gallop. The ridge steepened, and his gallop became a mighty scramble. He charged upward, passing all limits of muscle and sinew and heart. He saved nothing. He obeyed the ancestral voices. He reached the beginning of the knife edge. He did not stop. He did not doubt. His hooves clattered onto the knife edge. With each step he flattened the arête just a little and sent debris tumbling down both sides. Ten meters, twenty meters, thirty, forty he continued upward, attacking the mountain, pounding it into submission.

It is all as I imagined it would be, as I saw it when I was young. I encounter each rock in its proper place. Each depression, each bulge where I remembered it. I change it as I pass over it, and it changes me.

His right hind leg slipped downward as rock fell away on the west side of the arête. He dug in with his left hind leg. He twisted, reared up, teetered precariously for a moment, then found footing again. He lunged upward with both hind legs, found purchase for his fore hooves, and mounted the summit.

Sigvardr snorted and shook his sweat-saturated coat. He turned and looked down at the route he had taken. Dust was still settling over the arête. The top of it was flattened, forming a steep but passable path for his safe return, and for later climbs by others long after he was gone.

Something wonderful revealed itself to him then. With preternatural clarity, he could see, hear, sense in every way the finest details of distant life in the valley below: a glittering stream, wildflowers, grass, a hummingbird drawing nectar from a bright red blossom, a squirrel darting beneath a rock. He perceived sounds in infinitesimal snippets: a faint breeze caressing the tall grass of a meadow far below, water sliding over a rock, an insect chewing on a leaf five kilometers away, and the call of a raptor in a distant canyon. It was the Ancients who had magically enhanced his senses, and they reminded him again of their purpose:

The child.

Sigvardr concentrated his enhanced senses northward. Alexandra was there, beneath the forest canopy, making her way back to the old man's cottage. Sigvardr's augmented sensorium diminished the pain of separation; it placed him near her even though she was far away. She was unaware of this, and it was important she remain so. The bond must not compel her as it did him. For her to know of his presence would be a distraction, a weakening dependence. It was his burden to know and not be known.

The truth-teller cannot hear the lies; the liar cannot hear the truth. Reach through illusion to the open sky.

FROM "MANUAL OF THE TRUTHSEEKERS" BY ANDRUS MAXWELL

Alexandra was confident she could reach the cottage before nightfall. Sixteen kilometers, three hours. She could do that. The storm might be a problem. Gathering cumulous clouds were already passing in front of the sun, intermittently blocking its warming rays. Thunder sounded in the distance.

Suddenly lightning struck. Pure white light, momentarily blinding, and immense, deafening sound came together in a single instant one hundred meters to her right. She stumbled backward. Smoke rose in a spiral along the massive trunk of a nearby fir tree, taller than the rest. She smelled the burning wood, but saw no flames. She had never been so close to a lightning strike, and she knew nothing of dry lightning. It seemed other-worldly to her, this bright finger of destruction coming out of nowhere.

An unsteady breeze came up, first from one direction, then another, uncertain, agitated. Heavy raindrops began to fall in scattered patches over the thick forest canopy. Soon the patches merged and the rain fell hard in sheets that parted the canopy and sliced heavily to the forest floor. Alexandra was glad she was moving into the tallest and most closely-growing trees. They gave some protection from the rain, though they also blocked what little light the storm allowed.

Flashes of lightening—none so close as the first—were followed more and more closely by thunder. The storm was creeping toward her from the south. She pressed on more urgently than before.

She thought of the unicorn:

He took away fear, she thought, *and now fear is back. He made me forget fear. I should have given him a name...*

Lightning flashed again, followed almost immediately by thunder. Alexandra heard the crashing of branches, a tree falling. Another flash illuminated the swaying trees—then another and another, followed at shortening intervals by explosions of sound.

Despite the protection of the deep forest, Alexandra was soon drenched and shivering. She thought of stopping to drape the tent over her, but she felt more strongly the need to keep moving, to reduce the remaining distance to the cottage. She had to stay ahead of the advancing darkness.

Several bolts of lightning arrived in near unison, illuminating the wilderness on all sides. Alexandra saw the unicorn on the trail ahead: at first a near certainty, rearing up, tossing its mane in the wind; then a vague, shimmering apparition; then a nondescript shape made by the windblown rain swirling in the descending darkness. She finally decided she had seen nothing at all.

Heavy rain, violent thunder and lightning, and the cold became her overriding concerns; this was not going as she had expected. She spied a rock overhang at the base of the steep granite wall on her left. She skidded down an embankment beside the trail and threaded her way through the trees to the overhang. She had just ducked under it when lightning struck the rock face high above. Giant shards of granite cascaded to the earth in front of the overhang.

That was close, she thought.

While it had protected her from the falling rock, the depression beneath the overhang was too shallow to shelter her from the pelting rain. She shuffled to her right along the back of the depression and came to a tall fissure in the rock wall. She removed her pack, turned sideways, and squeezed through the opening. She dragged her pack behind. The fissure widened, and she soon found herself at the entrance of a tunnel. The light coming through the fissure was enough for her to see the tunnel was not a natural widening of the fissure; it was clearly of human construction, the fissure serving to hide it.

The storm raged outside. She had no intention of going back into it, at least for now. The cold was reaching into her, and she had begun to shiver. She dropped her pack and took off her rain-soaked shirt. She pulled on a dry shirt taken from her pack, threaded her wet shirt under the top flap, and put the pack back on.

She took a few steps into the tunnel. It felt warmer there. With her right hand on the side wall, she began feeling her way forward into increasing darkness. She had gone about seventy meters and through a wide turn to the left when she detected light ahead. The light provided weak illumination of the tunnel and the ground around her, but it was better than the absolute dark she had been negotiating by feel. She continued toward the light. It brought her to the base of a steep, narrow stairway. The light came from the top of the stairway. She climbed one-hundred or more rough-hewn rock steps to a massive archway. The archway was set in a rock wall two meters thick. She walked through it and all at once the sky was clear and blue. The afternoon sun felt warm on her skin. Only the time of day, late afternoon, seemed the same. The tunnel had taken her into a world completely apart from the stormy one she had just left.

Before her was the most peculiar castle she had ever seen. It rose some eighty meters above the moat surrounding it. The builders had not made the least effort to make horizontals horizontal or verticals vertical. Nothing appeared to be parallel with anything else. The castle was constructed from a hodgepodge of materials: glass fragments of many colors were imbedded in the stone walls. Filigreed metal supports held up wooden ramps that wound upward around gigantic towers. The towers tilted and twisted like giant arthritic fingers pointing skyward. Like the castle, the surrounding landscape had neither the symmetrical beauty of a manicured garden, nor the natural splendor of a wilderness. It was in between, a failed effort, more dead than alive.

Alexandra could see no evidence of the storm, no pooling of water anywhere, no moisture on the leaves or grass, no wet walls or pavement. A rickety drawbridge extended over the turbid waters of the moat. She crossed it, being careful to avoid jagged holes in the decking and broken timbers. She walked up to the massive castle gate. It was partially raised, the ten-meter-wide base hanging three meters above her head. Long spikes were arrayed across the base, like teeth in the upper jaw of a monster poised to bite down on whatever (or whomever) dared to pass under.

Alexandra considered turning back. Master Travits had warned, seriously warned, against exploring off-trail between the cottage and the meadow, but she wasn't actually, exactly, precisely off-trail between the meadow and the cottage; she was somewhere else entirely. The sky was clear and the sun was bright, though low in the sky, and if she turned back now, she would forever wonder what she had missed.

Alexandra crossed under the gate and entered a large courtyard strewn with rubble, most of it from breaches in the castle sidewalls. The walls that still stood were enough to block the late afternoon sun and leave the courtyard in deep shade. Nothing stirred. Alexandra experienced an eerie whipsaw of emotions: wariness, bordering on terror, followed immediately by a deep, mesmerizing, calm. The calm urged her on.

Alexandra picked her way through the rubble to the main entrance of the castle. The entrance was protected by a massive double door, the right one closed, the left dangling from a single rusted hinge. She squeezed past the precariously hanging door and found herself in what had once been a lavish entrance hall. The hall was open to the sky. The remains of its ornate ceiling formed a mosaic of rubble covering the floor. Alexandra spied another door on the other side of the hall. She made her way to it and tried the handle. It released when she pushed down, but the door would not budge. She leaned into it and pushed harder. The door dragged a few centimeters over the gritty stone floor until it was half open. She stepped through and beheld a sight that took her breath away.

There was no sign of decay or destruction. The chamber reminded Alexandra of pictures she had seen of the interior of gothic cathedrals. The lofty ceiling was an elaborate fresco of gargoyles, angels, men, and dragons. Tall, brilliantly colored stained-glass windows were set in the side walls. The chamber was about 120 meters long and seventy wide, and the ceiling seemed as high as the room was wide. Alexandra stood on a narrow red carpet that extended to the base of a massive stone dais. Ten carpeted steps led to the top of the dais. There, near the center, sat two empty thrones, one larger than the other. A thick drapery of brilliant red hung across the wall behind the dais. The drapery seemed to be hanging in midair, attached to nothing.

Alexandra walked toward the dais. As she neared the center of the cavernous chamber, she stopped and turned in a slow, complete circle to take in the wondrous beauty of the place. When she again faced forward, she was startled to see the thrones were now occupied. A skeleton sat on the throne to her left; a beautiful woman sat on the one to her right.

Alexandra felt a wave of cold, immobilizing fear sweep over her. Her fear was immediately neutralized by an unnatural calm. She became suspicious. She did not process fear in this way. She did not go from terror to narcotic serenity in an instant, but twice in the last few minutes she had experienced this. She was experiencing it continuously now.

Someone is manipulating my emotions, she thought. *The unicorn? No, the feeling is wrong. Someone in this place is doing it.*

She concentrated on the skeleton. A jeweled crown rested at an awkward angle over the skull. Cobwebs and a few strands of red hair descended from beneath the crown to other parts of the gruesome remains. The skeleton was clothed in royal garb, faded and shredded by time.

This was once a king, Alexandra thought.

The dead king's cavernous black eye sockets seemed fixed on her. She shuddered and turned her attention to the woman.

She too wore a crown.

This must be the queen, Alexandra thought dreamily, *and she is definitely not dead.*

The woman's eyes were deep blue, almost black. Her long red hair framed smooth, perfectly formed ivory cheeks and spread over her bare shoulders. She wore a bejeweled scarlet gown, and she was stunningly beautiful.

The queen returned Alexandra's gaze and smiled at her.

The smile was wrong, somehow incomplete. The queen seemed to know this, and tried to fix it by making it broader. The effect was garish, unnatural. The queen beckoned for Alexandra to come forward.

A dead king sits next to his living queen. The queen makes a smile, constructs it, and does it poorly. What does this mean?

The unnatural calm visited earlier upon Alexandra swelled into elation. Emotion dissolved skepticism. Through a languorous mental fog, she marveled at the queen's great beauty, the perfection of her attire, the gentleness of her gestures, the depth of tenderness in her eyes, the bejeweled gown flowing over her perfect form, her golden crown resting lightly over her flowing red hair, the bright red cap set within the circle of her crown.

Alexandra halted at the base of the dais. Something about the red cap set within the crown was important. Something just out of reach. Something...

Divide your awareness, child. Look upon yourself from outside yourself. Observe carefully, you and this thing before you. Nothing is as it seems. Everything is a test. Beware, little one. I will say no more.

It was the unicorn. She was sure of it. His thought projections, his way of influencing was different from all others. There was no coercion in it. He only pointed. He did not interfere. He left her whole, even when the danger was great.

Alexandra broke through the numbing trance that had lured her to the dais. Redcap!

Millions of tiny lightning flashes passed from synapse to synapse in Alexandra's brain.

Redcap!

Alexandra pivoted as she saw the beginning of the

Redcap's transformation. Her feet dug deep into the thick carpet as she sprinted toward the door through which she'd entered. She could hear the sounds of the Redcap's pursuit, its wet snarling and its pounding strides.

What followed seemed to occur in slow motion. Free of the Redcap's narcotic, Alexandra felt un-blunted terror. With it came intense focus and a kind of precision Alexandra had never experienced. Thoughts came and elaborate plans were made in particles of seconds. Thought and action merged. She reached the door through which she'd entered. She slowed only enough to grab the iron handle with her left hand, the door's edge with her right, stiffen her arms, and let her momentum take her in a narrow arc around the outside edge of the door and through the opening. She glanced back just before disappearing behind the door. The Redcap was nearly upon her. It had completed its transformation from enticing bait to loathsome killer. Gone was the beautiful queen; fully present was the hairy red beast, jaws agape, dagger-like teeth flashing, lizard legs pumping. Alexandra lost sight of it as she swung through the doorway into the destroyed entry hall.

Blinded by its killing frenzy, the Redcap miscalculated. Its speed was too great and its estimate of distance was a few centimeters off. The beast grabbed for Alexandra on the other side of the door just as it crashed against the face of the door, slamming it against its own arm. The Redcap's roar of pain echoed through the ruined castle.

Alexandra dashed across the destroyed entry hall. She could hear the Redcap shredding the door behind her as she slid beneath the precariously hanging courtyard door. She tumbled into the courtyard and ran toward the castle gate. The Redcap queen crashed into the courtyard and caught a glimpse of Alexandra running toward the castle gate. The

Redcap threw its head back and unleashed a guttural shriek. The shriek was answered with other shrieks from within and outside the castle.

Ahead of Alexandra, the castle gate began to descend.

I'm not going to make it.

In shuddering confirmation of this thought, the gate met the ground. Still running toward it, Alexandra calculated the size of the spaces in the heavy metal latticework of the gate.

I might be able to squeeze through, she thought with renewed hope, *and it may slow down the thing behind me.*

There came a response.

Might, may! This is not the time for speculation. This is the time for confident action!

"Quiet!" Alexandra yelled out loud, "I'm working here."

Good, the unicorn replied.

Alexandra reached the gate and knelt by one of the openings. She pushed an arm and shoulder through the opening; then her head; then, with her other arm held flat against her side, she wriggled her whole body through the opening. *She ran across the drawbridge and was on the path leading to the archway when she saw them. Redcaps! Two emerging from the forest on her right, three or more from somewhere on her left, all converging on her.* A vaporous cloud, smoke or steam, billowed out of the tunnel and through the archway, obscuring it and everything in front and on either side. It rolled toward her, obliterating from sight everything in its path.

Alexandra glanced over her shoulder. The nearest Redcap was no more than twenty-five meters behind and closing fast. She could no longer see the archway. She was caught between the billowing cloud in front and the Redcaps behind and to the sides. She ran blindly into the cloud, stumbled, and fell. The nearest Redcap galloped past. Alexandra rolled into the tall grass beside the path and lay as still as death. The mist thickened until she could barely see the grass in front of her face. She heard the Redcaps roaring in frustration as they moved back and forth, searching for her in the ever thickening cloud. She heard a loud thump followed by roaring and screaming, the sound of blows, and the rending of flesh.

They are attacking each other! she said to herself.

She knew the arch was at the end of the path next to her. She could see the edge of it. She rose to a low crouch and skittered forward. The roaring and screaming and fighting were on all sides, loud, nearby, but invisible.

I can't see them. They can't see me. It's a good relationship.

The grass ended. The edge of the path ended. She got down on hands and knees and made her way forward over the gravel and soon arrived at the wall.

Left or right to the archway? she asked herself.

She chose left but soon encountered thorny vines that covered the wall.

Wrong way.

She turned, crawled along the wall in the opposite direction, and found the archway. She rolled through the opening just as a Redcap lumbered past. The Redcap passed by the archway as though it wasn't there.

They can't see it! They don't know the archway is here. It is invisible to them!

The thought brought Alexandra tremendous relief, but she was not going to wait within the archway to test her theory. She descended the stairs as rapidly as her weakening legs permitted, followed the tunnel to its entrance, and squeezed through the fissure in the rock wall. Heavy rain was still falling, but there were no flashes of lightening. She made her way to the trail and hid herself in the tall grass beside it. She listened to the falling rain, to the wind, to the pounding of her heart. She then made a terrible discovery.

She reached up for the strap of her pack. There was no strap. There was no pack. She scanned her memory and found it. She had shed it to escape through the castle gate. She could not go back. The pack was lost. Her equipment and clothing, her notes, Travits unicorn file—all lost.

She wept as minutes passed without the sound of thunder. Finally, she dug through her pockets, hoping she might have salvaged something from her disastrous excursion. In its special sheath stitched into her right pant leg she found her wand.

Anger and disgust welled up in her.

Stupid! Stupid! Stupid! Through all of this, I never thought of my wand. I forgot all about the Raportio spell, any spell. Everything gone because I am a stupid girl!

Alexandra flipped her wand carelessly into the air and watched it land in the wet grass. What would Master Travits say? All evidence of her adventure was lost. Who would believe her?

The rain fell on her accusingly. She took a deep breath, picked up her wand, and headed north.

57   The Message

Everyone lives by assistance. Affection can be attached to it, but affection is not necessary. Credit can be claimed for it, but no credit is due. A tree can give it, or a rock, or an elf, or a man. The sun gives it, the shade from the sun gives it, the warmth of the fire gives it. The generous giver and the generous receiver do well together.

FROM "WISDOM OF THE ELVES" BY MASTER BRADYN ARISTARCHUS

The guards dealt with Daniel mercilessly, taking turns so all might have the pleasure. They were under strict orders not to kill or maim him, but these were jailors of the dungeon of Durnakk, experts in torture both gross and subtle. Leaving no visible marks was an insignificant challenge; internal injuries were allowed. There were many ways to inflict pain.

Alea heard what they were doing to Daniel, heard his screams. From the depths of Dyrisian empathy, she felt his pain as if it were her own. Whenever the guards left, she called out to him, often receiving no answer. Only when she heard him stir or groan or make any sound, did she stop calling out.

Eventually, the guards stopped coming. The wrath of Aedan would descend upon them if they killed the boy, and they had come dangerously close. It was enough.

***

Alea waited. After some time—hours, maybe a day—she heard the familiar sound of gravel falling into the pit. She put her head through the opening she had made in her cell wall and saw Daniel crawling down to her. He was carrying the waterskin and using the hand and foot holds he had painstakingly carved into the side wall. When he reached the ledge, he lay down and was silent.

It was his first visit since cessation of the beatings.

Alea wept.

Daniel heard her sobs. He propped himself against the wall at the back of the ledge.

"It's OK, Alea. I'm OK," he said soothingly.

Alea stopped crying.

For a long time neither broke the silence. Daniel drank from the waterskin occasionally. Alea watched him.

"I'm so tired," Daniel said finally.

"Go back up," Alea said. "You might fall if you sleep here, and the guards might come. Go back up but lie near the edge of the pit. I will sing to you."

Daniel did as she bid him to do.

She sang him the Dyrisian healing chant, repeating its curative phrases over and over long after he had fallen into a deep sleep.

***

Though the beatings had stopped, Daniel's captors did not replenish his food, water, or candles for what he guessed was three days, maybe longer. Alea tried to share her food, but he refused. The thinness of her face told him she was barely surviving on what they gave her.

The only relief from the darkness was Alea's glow. He sat on the ledge for hours, watching her, listening to her. She talked to him about magic, his abilities, and Dyrisian wisdom. She talked about her life and her work before she was captured. Sometimes she talked about her family, her mother, father, and two younger siblings. Talk of family made her voice thick with emotion. Alea talked and Daniel listened, often half asleep, comforted simply by the sound of her voice.

Alea would also sing. She would sing strange ballads with names Daniel had never heard and words he did not understand. But the songs brought comfort.

Occasionally, Alea would extend her hand out of the hole in the wall of her cell and float a ball of light to him. The light rolled gently over his body, pausing at his wounds. It felt like a mother's touch. He healed rapidly, but he sensed his healing came at a cost to Alea. Each time she sent the light, she withdrew afterward into her cell, where she stayed quietly for about half an hour. Daniel noted her glow was diminished each time she reemerged. When he asked about this, she said it was nothing, a normal fluctuation of energy. Daniel sensed it was more than this. She was giving up something to heal him; he hoped it was not too much.

***

"Daniel, wake up!"

Daniel had fallen asleep on the ledge. He opened his eyes sleepily.

"I hear footsteps," Alea said. "You need to get back up to your cell."

Daniel pushed himself to his feet. His muscles were stiff, but thanks to Alea's ministrations his pain was almost completely gone. He felt for the hand and foot holds in the wall and climbed back out of the pit. He heard the key turn in the lock and the bolt slide back. The door hinges groaned and a shaft of light cut through the dark of the cell.

Daniel backed against the wall as three hooded guards advanced into the room. One of the guards was shorter and of slighter build than the other two and was carrying a plate of food and a waterskin. This guard placed the waterskin and food on the floor while the other two guards watched silently, poised to repulse any attack. When the smaller guard backed away, the guard on the left walked over to the candle lantern, placed a candle inside, withdrew a wand from his cloak, and whispered a spell. A small flame appeared at the tip of the wick.

Daniel noticed the smaller guard was staring at him with unusual intensity. Two green eyes reflected the candles flickering light, and a lock of shiny black hair protruded from beneath the guard's hood. There was something familiar about the hair and the eyes.

The three guards backed cautiously out of the cell and closed the door. As soon as Daniel heard the key turn in the lock, he hurried to the plate of food and devoured all but a last piece of meat. He picked up the meat and spied a folded scrap of paper concealed under it. He lifted the paper gingerly from the plate, unfolded it, and brought it close to the candle lantern.

The writing was spindly and the ink faint. Daniel squinted to make out the words.

"Talk soon" was the message.

58   Priorities

It is not an evil saw that cuts the table leg too short; it is the incompetent carpenter. It is not an empty gas tank that strands a family, it is the driver who did not fill it.

FROM *"UNCERTAIN JOURNEY"* BY JOSHUA TURNER

Borrington sat erect in an ornate wooden chair in front of Elizabeth's desk. His hands were relaxed, folded in his lap. His amber eyes were fixed on her. She returned his gaze with matching intensity.

"What should I do, Andrew?"

"Nothing more than you are already doing," he said.

"Do I tell her?"

"You must. She will not forgive you if you don't. The boy isn't the first casualty, Elizabeth, and he won't be the last many great wizards have fallen in the quest for peace in Second World. First World has all but given up on this quest. War is a constant in that world. What we're seeking to do here does not come without a price. Alexandra needs to know this."

Elizabeth allowed herself a moment to enjoy the sight of him. He wore a simple purple and black tunic. His lean body, lined face, and thick white hair spoke of his years of experience and of his role as her most trusted counselor. She wondered if he knew what a distraction he was. Sometimes she resented him for it—his soft voice, his mouth, his steadiness. It seemed so...deliberate. She wondered if he could see the effect he had on her and the embarrassment she felt for it. He was, of course, too much the gentlemen to tell her either way.

Enough of this, she thought. *I am the Guardian, not some school girl. He is my general. There is work to do.*

"She's but a child, Andrew. I abducted her from the only life she knew, separated her from her parents, her loved ones, her friends, and most importantly from Daniel. I brought her here to train for a role so demanding that I dare only hint at it when I'm with her. Now you advise me to tell her that her dearest friend might be imprisoned by Aedan or even dead? That seems a cruelty."

Borrington's gaze remained steady.

"You may have it backwards," he said. "I think the cruelty would lie in not telling her.

The two sat for some time without speaking.

So much history there, she thought. *He is wise, but he does not have to deal with the consequences, at least not in the way I do.*

"The thing is complicated," Elizabeth said. "Alexandra said she would not continue without him. I promised to bring him here. Who knows what she'll do when she hears all this!"

Borrington leaned forward.

"You take too much on yourself, Elizabeth." Borrington's voice was almost a whisper.

"You did *not* abduct Alexandra. Others did. Whether by chance or design, she is now with you. Whatever happened to Daniel was not your doing. There are powers greater than ours at work here. Your brother is as subject to them as we are, but he is rigid. We must be flexible, ride the wave of random combinations better than he, see where it takes us. Let me take care of this for you."

Elizabeth relaxed. She welcomed Andrew's perspective, the peace and clarity of mind it brought. Ride the wave? It was more like a dragon and Andrew was telling her to ride it in the direction it was flying.

"Do I tell her the rest? Do I tell her the seriousness of our situation?"

Borrington smiled.

"Not quite the same question, Guardian, but my answer is still yes."

"And let the chips fall..."

"...where they may," Borrington said, completing her sentence. "A quaint wood-chopping idiom of First World that is quite apt in this case. You believe in Alexandra. Exercise that belief."

Elizabeth pondered how the chips might fall and whom they might strike:

Alexandra is young and impetuous...and in so many ways fragile. She has magical powers, but lacks experience, discipline. The Protectors are doing all they can to strengthen her, to give her experience and discipline, but will this be enough? Will it be in time? How much can she bear? The fate of the Two Worlds rests on her shoulders. The situation of her friend, Daniel, is unknown. Exercise a little faith, Andrew says to me. This requires more than a little faith.

Borrington did not interrupt her thoughts. He waited.

"Increase the guard at Byrnhelen," Elizabeth said finally, "and make sure no more letters fall into the wrong hands. Our communications must be secure. I will tell Alexandra. Now tell me what you've learned of young Mr. McConnelly."

Borrington furrowed his brow.

"I can tell you very little about him. My people continue to investigate. Inquiries so far have turned up nothing out of the ordinary."

"How long has the family lived in East Valley?" Elizabeth asked.

"Not long, by standards of the region. Euwen's father, Ian McConnelly, acquired the Wilacross estate after the East Valley fire sixteen years ago. The estate had been heavily damaged in the fire. Records show he purchased it for little more than the land value. McConnelly must have had considerable means. The estate had to be rebuilt from the ground up."

"Not unusual," Elizabeth commented. "Wealthy man purchases a distressed property at a considerable discount. Rebuilds. Do you see something in that?"

"You rely on me to be suspicious," Borrington replied. "The buildings of the McConnelly estate are massive, four stories high with walls of thick stone. Yet construction was completed in just under six months. That kind of haste costs a lot of money."

"Still, not unusual," Elizabeth repeated.

"True, but the rebuilding of the other fire-ravaged estates, all sold to outside buyers, was also completed in six months."

Elizabeth thought about that.

"Coordinated?" she asked.

"Perhaps. Maybe some sort of consortium. Or perhaps the concentration of engineering and construction resources required for the McConnelly project contributed incidentally to the swift completion of the others."

"All this within six months of the fire?" Elizabeth inquired.

"Some more, some less, but all close to that period of time," Borrington replied.

"What do we know of this fire?"

Borrington leaned back in his chair and clasped his hands

behind his head.

"The cause was never determined. Families who had lived there for generations could not afford the cost of reconstruction. Almost all had to sell. Wealthy buyers came in with cash just at the right time. Then there is the speed of re-construction. Interesting. Euwen's rescue of Alexandra, if that is what it was, is interesting. Interesting but not conclusive."

"What about the family?"

"Euwen has a younger sister. The mother is deceased. It appears to be just the three of them and some domestic staff."

"Tell me about Ian McConnelly."

"He is a landlord who, along with his two children, is often absent. Little about him is known or admitted to by the locals. They say he is a business man, but stories differ on the nature of his business. His name, both first and last, is quite common in the area. This adds to the difficulty of my inquiries, especially since this all goes back more than sixteen years."

"So we have nothing."

"So far. Yes. There is no hint of impropriety. There is no hint of anything. I am sorry so short on specifics. My investigation continues, however."

Elizabeth looked concerned.

"Could he be an agent for my brother?"

"Anything's possible, but I see no evidence of that. If he or anyone from East Valley were actively operating against you, I would know something. There would be signs. There are none. Maybe they wait, conspire. Or maybe they do nothing of the sort."

"Euwen's story. Does it hold up?"

"So far, but I'll keep shaking the tree. Something may yet

fall from its branches."

"Breadcrumbs: My letter to you was stolen. That letter had details of Alexandra's last known whereabouts. Then comes Euwen to rescue her. I'm glad of it, but not blind to how unlikely it seems. Storm chasing? Too convenient for my taste. And I have a bad feeling about the absent and unknown father."

"As do I, Guardian. I'm following the breadcrumbs. We shall see where they lead. Time settles all mysteries."

"And time is in short supply, Andrew. Are we done here?"

Borrington made no immediate reply. He stared up at the ceiling and became adrift in thought, his great intelligence silently at work, probing, measuring, sifting, testing hypotheses. It troubled him that he did not know the location of Aedan's headquarters or the identities of members of his general staff. This was basic intelligence necessary to gauge the strength of one's adversary. Aedan had been quite effective in thwarting his efforts to acquire it.

Terror is the great silencer, he thought.

He let go of this thought, looked at Elizabeth, and spoke of another matter on his mind:

"Regardless of what we learn about Euwen, you must put a stop to this 'friendship' he has with Alexandra. She is vulnerable to him. He rescued her, nurtured her back to health, and brought her to you. He has the power to charm her, perhaps already has. I trust your misgivings about him. *You* should trust them. How you separate them may not be as straightforward as the other matters we've discussed."

Elizabeth nodded.

Borrington stood and walked slowly around the desk.

Elizabeth stood to meet him.

He took her right hand in his and brought it to his lips.

Tears welled up in Elizabeth's eyes. The old feelings, the ones she kept locked away in the most secret cell of her heart, rose up. She slowly pulled back her hand and turned away from him.

"This must not be, general."

Her voice was unsteady and distant, and she had called him by his rank. General Borrington was the commander of her armies. Andrew was someone else, someone she was asking to leave.

He backed away from her, gave a slight bow, and departed through the secret door by which he had entered.

She did not see the sadness in his eyes as he retreated, but she knew it was there.

I am the Guardian. Some things can never be.

As soon as the thought came, she knew it was a lie. It was not a matter of possibility; it was a matter of price...to her, to Andrew, and to the Two Worlds.

Up to now she had been unwilling to pay that price.

59 Closure

Years, days, moments: They are the same. Fools count the stars and ask what time it is.

FROM "VESSELS OF DESTINY" BY MASTER MAREK AVALARD

Everything that had happened was gone. Alexandra told Master Travits most of it, leaving out only what she had promised the unicorn she would not tell. Master Travits sensed this but did not pry.

"I lost the unicorn file, all your research," she said.

"I gave it to you. It was yours to lose. Your encounter with the unicorn accomplished the purpose of my research. The file is of no importance."

"The final exam...," Alexandra began.

"It is enough," Travits interjected. "You did in a week what I have sought to achieve my entire life. You far exceeded my requirements."

Tears welled up in Alexandra's eyes.

Master Travits pulled her close in a bearish hug.

"You are so much," he whispered, "a gift to us all. Guard yourself well. Guard us all. Now go."

Alexandra left the cottage and walked to the portal. The others had gone ahead, eager to return to Byrnhelen. Alexandra was not so eager. She looked back at the cottage. Master Travits stood in the doorway, his hands in his pockets. There was the hint of a smile on his face. Alexandra gave a shy wave. He did not wave back, but he nodded and his smile broadened.

Alexandra entered the portal and seconds later found herself back in Room 208 at Byrnhelen. What had been a portal was now just a painting hanging on the wall. She looked back at it for a moment and thought she saw a flash of white in the trees behind the cottage, but it was gone before she could organize it into what she wanted it to be. The unicorn had said he could go no further, yet he had gone further. He had come to her aid against the Redcaps. She wondered if he would do that again. Then she doubted; perhaps it had been no more than her own imaginings rolling around in her head. Maybe the unicorn spoke truth: He could go no further.

Her ruminations turned to the past, to the backyard of her home in Simsbury, Connecticut. It was early morning. It had rained the night before and the ground was still wet. She was kneeling in the wet grass, studying a small boulder in a flower bed. She pushed the top of the boulder. It wobbled. She pushed again, much harder, and overturned it. Within the shallow crater where the boulder had previously rested was a world teeming with tiny alien creatures. She wondered what they thought of her, the great disruptor of their world. Did the scattering insects see her? Did they know she was there? Did they think she was a god? Or did they merely register in their various ways that the cool dark had been suddenly blasted by light.

Does some being look down on me as I now look down on these tiny creatures?

She remembered how she and Daniel had often shared such thoughts and imaginings. It was a thing linking them, this imagining big things from little things. They rearranged the universe together.

She missed him.

Alexandra left Room 208 and made her way through the

halls of Byrnhelen to the comfort of her own room. She
entered, closed the door, tossed her bag on the floor, and
flopped onto her bed. Her thoughts merged into a comforting
fog that lay over her concerns about Daniel; her fear of her
disturbing dreams; and her speculations about what she
would face in the next master course. She closed her eyes
and drifted into a deep sleep.

60   *Dream Making*

Good and evil are distinctions made by the weak. Sheep make these distinctions. They crudely label the shepherd who cares for them as good and the wolf that eats them as bad. Men who take action on a grand scale do not do this. They do what is necessary, giving no thought to right or wrong.

FROM "ESSAYS ON SUPREMACY" BY AEDAN SHAW

Expressionless men huddled around a rough granite basin. The basin was chest high, three meters across, and filled with dark, roiling water. Viscous streaks of red floated to the frothy surface, giving the impression some poor creature was being slaughtered beneath the waters.

One of the men held a brown leather pouch over the churning water. He turned the pouch over with ritual slowness. Gray dust drifted down and was absorbed. The water calmed. Its surface transformed into a black mirror without blemish or feature, a perfect reflector with a dark void at its center.

The men surrounding the basin began to chant, their resonant voices rising and falling in haunting modulation. The candlelight illuminating the circular chamber pulsed in cadence with the chanting. Mist billowed ponderously out of the center void and formed a translucent dome over the basin. The glow of the dome cast shadows of the chanting men onto the walls of the chamber. The glow dimmed and figures appeared within the dome. The figures were vague and ghostly at first, but gradually became more defined.

In the darkest shadows of the chamber, well away from the basin, stood a man alone. He was tall, robed and hooded like the others but not one of them. He leaned against the cool stone wall, watching, evaluating.

One of the men at the basin stepped away when an image within the dome became clearer. He approached the tall man in the shadows and whispered, "She dreams, Lord Aedan."

Aedan pushed the man aside and approached the basin. The others pulled back, but they continued to chant.

Aedan peered into the dome.

An evil smile twisted his thick lips as he leered at the image of Alexandra lying on her bed. Her blonde hair lay in sensuous tangles over her pillow. The girl's eyes were closed, her face twisted in a grimace. She rolled back and forth, as if trying to awaken.

"Show me her dream."

"Yes, My Lord."

The Dream Master pointed his wand at Alexandra's image and murmured a spell. An image of Daniel appeared. He was standing on a garden path. Elizabeth Shaw was standing nearby on the same path. She gave a forceful snap of her wand in Daniel's direction, and he fled in terror. The image faded. In a few moments Daniel appeared again with Elizabeth exactly as before. The entire sequence was repeated over and over, exactly the same.

"The repetition frays her psyche, My Lord. Her mind tries to complete the sequence, but we prevent that. Very damaging, delightfully damaging. A deep-seated distrust of the Guardian will grow in her. Distrust will turn to hatred."

"Is she pliable enough for that?"

"Ah, well, yes," the Dream Master said hesitantly.

"There is a problem?" Aedan asked, detecting the hesitance.

"Ah, no, no, Sire, no problem, just an unexpected, ah, element. All part of the process, part of the work."

"What element?"

"Oh, nothing we can't handle, My Lord."

"You answer a question I did not ask. What is this unexpected element?"

"The element, yes, well, we do not as yet, ah, know, that is, know precisely. There is a force: not a spell, but definitely something we have not seen before. It limits us. We can introduce the images into the girl's dreams, but they do not have the usual power. Something interrupted our dream sequence the last week she was in Scotland, and has remained with her. It is not Travits who protects her, nor your sister, Sire. But we will know soon and make an end of it. A small problem, very small, very, very small."

Aedan sighed.

"How long to fix this?" he asked.

"We don't know, Sire, but...

"Idiot!" shouted Aedan.

A shudder went through the Dream Master. Aedan's rages had unpredictable outcomes. Men had been killed for small mistakes. The Dream Master had made no mistake, only an unpleasant discovery. He hoped Lord Aedan could see the distinction. He thought of pointing it out, but immediately thought better of it. Better to remain silent and ride out the storm.

Aedan waved the Dream Master away.

I will tell Euwen to continue his efforts, Aedan thought. *It is a risk. Elizabeth is wary of the boy. But seduction has magic this Dream Master cannot match. It is worth the risk.*

With startling swiftness, Aedan plunged his fist into the mirror-smooth water. The chanting stopped and the dome over the basin collapsed.

61   Breeanna

Talk soon."

This was the message Daniel had found on a scrap of paper hidden in his food.

Talk soon?

Who wanted to talk to him and, more important, why?

He sat against the wall next to his cell door, waiting, listening. After a few hopeful minutes he realized he had no idea when "soon" would come. It could be minutes or hours or days...or never. Was he going to sit here, just waiting? Madness. Perhaps that was the purpose of the message: to drive him closer to madness. To give him hope, then withdraw it. To punish him.

Daniel shook his head, stood, and walked to the pit. It was time to tell Alea. He had not told her immediately because the note was hope, probably false hope. He wanted to protect her from disappointment.

Daniel was easing himself into the pit when he heard someone unlatching the view port in his cell door. He scrambled out of the pit and into the shadows just as the view port slid open. Keeping to the shadows, he made his way to the hinge side of the door and stood against the wall, listening, hardly breathing. Below, through her opening in the pit wall, Alea listened also.

"Come to the door. I don't have much time."

It was a girl's voice, insistent but not unfriendly.

Daniel moved in front of the view port. He saw a pair of bright green eyes staring at him. He knew immediately who she was.

"Come to gloat?" he said bitterly.

"No, I came to talk."

"I would love to come out and chat, but I'm quite busy and fear I have lost my keys. Do you happen to have an extra set you could loan me?"

"Cute," the girl responded cynically.

"Well then, come in and we'll talk. I don't get many visitors. Oh, I forgot, you need your muscle-men to protect you while you leave stupid notes."

"I can protect myself, and the note wasn't stupid. I'm here, aren't I?"

"Well, come in then. Let's talk."

"I think not," the girl said. "You will try to escape again. Where's the wand you stole from me?"

"I stole nothing."

"Yes you did, and I must have it back."

"Sorry, can't help. As you can see, I'm being detained."

"And you're being stupid, Daniel! It will go badly for both of us if I'm caught talking to you. Don't waste our time."

"As I said, I get few visitors. You would be safer in here than out there, if what you say is true, which I seriously doubt."

The girl's eyes narrowed as she held his gaze.

"Would you give me your word of honor?" she asked.

"What makes you think I have any honor left?"

"I have reason to believe."

Daniel thought that a strange thing for her to say.

"Come in or don't come in," he said, petulantly. "I'm not standing around waiting for you to decide."

He stepped away from the viewport and took his former position against the wall where she couldn't see him.

"Will you promise not to try to escape? It would destroy us both. They would think I arranged it. And you would not be successful, not that way."

Her voice had lost its defiant edge.

"Yes," he responded, "I promise."

The view port slid shut. Daniel stood absolutely still. He heard a key turn in the lock and the bolt slide back. The door opened. The girl slipped quickly into the cell, closed the door, and stood with her back against it. He could see her silhouette dimly outlined in the candlelight. He could hear her breathing. Something stirred in him, pushing through the harsh inhumanity of his present existence, something warm and promising.

Daniel walked to the candle lantern, seated himself near it, and motioned for her to join him. She shook her head and put her forefinger to her lips and her ear to the door. Daniel sat in silence, staring at her. The girl finally left the door and approached him, stepping carefully, silently, as though she feared the floor under her feet might fall away. She sat on the floor across from him. He noticed she kept one hand tucked inside the fold of her tunic. Probably holding her wand, he thought.

"Where can I hide if someone comes?"

"Over there," Daniel replied, pointing to the darkest and most distant corner of his cell.

"If they come," Bree said, "you must say nothing. They will only want to see you are still here. They will not want you to know they found your door was unlocked and they will not report it for fear of reprisal. You must act as if you know nothing. Best to pretend you're asleep."

"Nobody will come," Daniel said.

This is odd, he thought. *I am reassuring my captor, the person who prevented my escape. Now she's here, asking me how to hide from them.*

"My name is Breeanna," the girl said, "But everyone calls me Bree."

"Why are you here?"

She gave him a hard look.

"Not because I want to be," she said, matching his harsh tone. "You have my wand or you know where it is."

"Sorry, can't help you there," he snapped back.

The fatalistic part of him was in control, and he was angry. Bree dropped her gaze to the flickering candle between them. Her expression softened. Daniel studied her face and saw sadness—or the simulation of it by a consummate actress.

"My father is one of Lord Aedan's generals," Bree went on, taking a different tack. "He's been with Aedan for many years."

She paused, her gaze fixed on the flame of the candle.

"My father is a good man, but in some ways blinded by loyalty and his history of service. He's deeply troubled, and he is not a man easily troubled. I've never seen him like this. I think you're part of it. I want to know who you are and why you're here. I hear things, rumors. I want to know the truth."

Bree looked up into Daniel's eyes.

"That's why I'm here," she added simply.

Daniel returned her gaze, seeking in her face some clue to her motives. The strangeness of their conversation was disorienting. Why this intimacy, this thing about her father? What's going on here? Daniel felt suddenly out of his depth.

He reached into his anger to steady himself.

"Why should I believe you? I'm your prisoner, not the other way around."

"Your confinement has been a few months," Bree responded. "Mine, I am discovering, has been a lifetime."

"When did you decide that?" Daniel asked with a trace of derision.

"I don't know exactly, but when we met..."

"We did not *meet*! You and your henchmen captured me. It was you who made sure of that. It was you who put me back in this cell, had me beaten nearly to death!"

"I did not have you beaten! I had no part in that. I knew only that you were a prisoner when you slammed into me. Most prisoners here are vile and dangerous."

Her vehemence disturbed the flow of Daniel's anger, created a breach in his defenses.

Bree went on, speaking confidently. "Because I am the daughter of a great general, I am a very well-treated prisoner, but I am still a prisoner."

"Hardly a fair comparison," Daniel observed.

He looked at his captor. She was about his age, and she was beautiful: olive skin, long dark hair, brilliant green eyes. Her face was lean, well proportioned, and her tunic, probably "borrowed" from one of the smaller guards, did not entirely conceal her form. He took all this in, hungrily. He found himself storing her image to use later against the darkness and despair that threatened to overwhelm him in this place. She had an abundance of the life force that was dying in him. He would borrow from it. He would use the memory of the look of her, the smell of her, the shape of her to ward off the demons hiding in the shadows of all places of confinement, especially this one. He could use her this way even if all else about her was false.

"What about my wand?" Bree asked.

Ah, the wand, thought Daniel. *That is the purpose in all this banter.*

Daniel often dwelt on that wand and what he might do with it. It featured prominently in many of his escape fantasies, and he knew exactly where it was.

"I don't know what happened to it," he said. "Maybe one of the guards took it. I don't have it."

Bree smiled for the first time since entering his cell.

"You're a terrible liar. I like that."

Daniel felt it again, the strange stirring that her words, her voice aroused in him. She was making an opening in his barricade of anger. He knew this but seemed unable to stop it.

"Of course you don't have it," Bree continued. "You hid it. I want it back."

Daniel made no reply, so Bree went on:

"Durnakk is a fortress of rumors, and I overhear things, things you might like to know: meetings my father has with different people, discussions, orders he gives, rumors. And I see things. I don't even have to be sneaky about it because I'm a kid. So I know you were taken from First World and are being held here because of some girl, not because of any crime you committed or because you are a threat to Aedan."

She's talking about Alexandra, Daniel thought.

He tried to appear disinterested.

Bree smiled again.

"Nice try," she said.

"What?" Daniel replied, feigning confusion.

"You don't pretend very well, either; at least not with me."

She paused, thinking.

"You *know* this girl," she said. "And I think you know

why you are here."

"I don't know why I'm here," Daniel said honestly.

"But you know the girl."

Daniel did not reply.

"Your turn," Bree said. "Tell me why my wand worked for you."

"I don't know."

"Not good enough. Tell me something you *do* know. How about where you were magically trained."

It was Daniel's turn to smile.

"Nowhere," he said. "I live in what you call First World. We don't have magical training there. Just reading and writing and arithmetic and history and a bunch of other dumb stuff. No magical training."

"My wand is a Wilamsfeld wand," Bree retorted. "It was made especially for me. When Mathias Wilamsfeld makes a wand like mine, it works only in the hands of the person for whom it was made. I was measured for it, tested for it. I alone can employ its powers. What you did is not possible."

"But I did it, didn't I," Daniel said smugly.

"Yes, you did."

I can read him so well, Bree thought. *I can see truth in him even when he lies or pretends. Why? What is our connection?*

"Maybe the wand knows something neither of us knows," Daniel said.

"What might that be?"

"How should I know? You're the wand queen."

Bree ignored his verbal jab.

"So far, you've told me nothing," she said. "I think you would very much like to hear what I have to say when your turn is up. Your turn is not up."

"Do you know the girl's name?" Daniel asked.

"Alexandra."

Daniel felt as though Bree had cast a spell, so powerful was the impact of hearing Alexandra's name.

Bree saw this: the tightening of his jaw, the stiffening of his body.

So it's true, she thought. *Alexandra's the one; she's why Daniel is here. She's why all this is happening.*

The mention of Alexandra dissolved Daniel's anger and replaced it with clarity of purpose: An alliance was necessary, and acrimonious tit-for-tat did not alliances make. He knew nothing of Mathias Wilamsfeld or of the powers of Bree's wand or any other wand. Why the wand worked in his hand was as much a mystery to him as it was to Bree. No matter. It was time to make a friend, not add to his list of enemies.

***

Bree gave Daniel her rapt attention while he told his story:

"My mother, Ellen Sutton, is a nanny, cook, and housekeeper, all wrapped into one. She works for Alexandra's parents. My mother raised Alexandra and me from birth, so we're sort of like brother and sister, but more like really good friends. It's complicated. Anyway, my mother means as much to Alexandra as her own mother does, maybe more. I don't have any memory of my father; he died when I was a year old. Alexandra and I have...powers. We can make things happen. I don't know how to explain it; sort of like magic, but not rabbit-out-of-the-hat or rope tricks or sawing-people-in-half stuff. Different."

The two sat in silence for a few long moments.

"I met your Alexandra," Bree said finally. "My brother rescued her and brought her into Second World, to our home. She was near death in a storm."

"Is she okay?"

"Yes."

"Where is she?"

"She's at Byrnhelen, the Guardian's castle. She's safe and well there. Byrnhelen is not Durnakk."

Bree noted a shift in Daniel's expression.

"Do you know of the Guardian?" she asked.

"What is her name?" Daniel inquired, pretending to know less than he did.

Bree noticed the pretension.

"Elizabeth Shaw," she replied, watching him very closely now.

There was pause.

"Do you know her?" Bree asked.

"We've met."

It was Bree's turn to be surprised.

"Where?"

"She came to our home in Simsbury. That's in Connecticut. First World. Did you bring Alexandra here, to Durnakk?"

Bree allowed the change of subject.

"No, only to my family's estate. It's nowhere near here. My brother took her straight from there to Byrnhelen."

"As a prisoner?"

"Far from it. I told you she is safe and well. I know this to be true. I know also that she is important to the Guardian, but I don't know why."

Daniel *did* know why. Alea had told him. What Daniel had *not* known until now was that Alexandra was safe and well. This new knowledge swept away the part of his suffering that came from not knowing Alexandra's situation and not being able to come to her aid. A great burden was lifted from him.

"You may have your wand," he said, and told her exactly where to find it.

Bree left the cell and returned with her wand a few minutes later.

Daniel stood when she re-entered.

Bree took his hand.

"I can help you escape," she said in a throaty whisper. "I've studied all the ins and outs of this place. I have explored Durnakk. I know its rhythms: the comings and goings of important people, the changing of the guard, the places to sneak in and out unseen, stuff like that. I've made a game of it to pass the time and prepare in case trouble comes. And trouble is coming. I've sensed this ever since Aedan made my father and me live here instead of at our home. My father says it's because Aedan needs him close to make and carry out some new plan. I don't think that's the only reason. There are plots within plots in this place. I'm discovering them a little at a time."

Bree's confidence buoyed Daniel up, not to elation—he had suffered too much for that—but to a kind of peace and hopeful anticipation. Alexandra was safe and well. His escape was imminent, and he would soon be reunited with her.

Bree stepped into him, put her arms around his neck, and laid her head on his shoulder.

"I will visit as often as I can," she whispered. "Prepare as best you can. Be ready, but be patient. I don't know what lies ahead. You are not alone. You will leave this place. I promise."

Daniel let his arms encircle her waist. The gesture was tentative at first, then urgent. He pulled her hard against him, drawing strength from her. They stood like that, not moving, not speaking for a long time. When it was time to break the connection, they released each other at just the right moment.

They did not speak again.

Bree backed away from Daniel and found the cell door. She smiled at him, gave a tiny wave, and was gone.

Daniel felt a moment of the old hopelessness. But it did not cling to him as before. Breeanna had transformed his black ordeal—an empty and meaningless plodding toward death—into an adventure. She had returned his future to him. She held out the promise of blue skies and open air, and he knew that sometime in the not-too-distant future, he would follow her there.

BONUS MATERIALS

-THE ADVENTURE CONTINUES-

The Culling

Book Two

Chronicles of the Two Worlds

Exactly at the instant when hope ceases to be reasonable it begins to be useful.

G. K. CHESTERTON

SNEAK PEEK AT CHAPTER 1...

1   *Night Terrors*

Superstitions come into being when they are denied. The safest course is to know you do not know.

FROM "THE AWAKENING" BY ELIZABETH SHAW

The nightmares were back.

The golden half-light of dawn illuminated Alexandra's chamber. She stared at the ceiling and let memories of Scotland and her time with Sigvardr wash away the debris of the terrible dream. She had been spared from these nightmares while in Scotland. Now she was back, and last night an unknown hand lifted the latch on a secret door in her mind and delivered the same poisonous visions as before—with a change as disturbing as the dream itself. She had considered telling the Guardian of these repetitive dreams. Last night's change made her discard that idea.

Alexandra rubbed her eyes, folded back the thick down comforter that lay over her, and slid out of bed. The cool stone floor felt good against the bottoms of her bare feet. Despite the return of the nightmares, she was glad to be back in her own room within the protective walls of Byrnhelen.

The Guardian's castle was home to her now. Being the Guardian's niece and an immigrant from First World had made her at first—seven weeks ago—an object of curiosity and fear. The curiosity remained, but the fear was mostly gone. She had Becca to thank for this. Becca, one of the seven apprentices at Alexandra's level, had made a special effort to befriend her. When Becca didn't collapse into a pile of ashes at Alexandra's touch, the other apprentices relaxed. Life at Byrnhelen became easier.

Alexandra dressed quickly and made her way to the main dining hall. Candra, the Guardian's personal assistant, met her there.

"Good morning, Alexandra," said the Dyrisian with her usual formality. "The Guardian wishes to see you."

Of course she does, Alexandra said to herself.

She hated the special attention she received from the Guardian. She understood the necessity, but did not like being set apart from the other apprentices. She wanted to be normal, to be accepted. Her relationship with the Guardian made this difficult.

"Will there be breakfast? I'm famished!"

"There will be food."

The girl is always hungry, thought Candra, unable to suppress a smile.

Alexandra saw this and smiled back.

Her aunt's summons could not be ignored. Candra would see to that. But Alexandra would have complied even without an escort. Defying the Guardian was unthinkable. Becca and the other apprentices would have to wait.

Candra led her through a labyrinth of dimly lit hallways. Alexandra became lost in thoughts of her life before Byrnhelen and her new life here. A mere seven weeks ago she had been taken from Simsbury, Connecticut—abducted actually, though her memory of that event was unclear because she had been near death. People here said she came from First World and was now in Second World. It all seemed nonsense at first, but she observed undeniable differences. Some things were the same here as in her world. Time was the same, she had been told, and the natural world, wilderness, all that was not of human origin—the same. But the similarities ended there.

She wondered how Simsbury, the only home she had ever known, would appear here. The hills, streams, trees, and other natural features would be the same, but all else—her house, her school, the paved roads and covered bridges, the town—all that would be erased. She had difficulty picturing this.

Magic was the most fantastic of all the differences, yet it was the most comforting. The magical powers she and Daniel had spent a lifetime hiding in First World were commonplace here. She smiled at the thought of this. Here she was not a freak. Here she could let others see who she really was—up to a point.

She missed the familiar things of Simsbury: her school, her parents, Daniel—especially Daniel. Yet somehow, without her knowing it, this world, and Byrnhelen Castle in particular, had always been her destination.

Candra halted in front of a narrow wooden door; opened it; and stepped into a small, unlit janitorial closet. Alexandra followed.

"Close the door and lock it, please."

Alexandra complied and listened for the incantation she knew would follow.

"Alterraina," Candra said, placing heavy emphasis on the vowels: *auh, er, ae, ah.*

The wall opposite the door glowed yellow-green. A crack formed there and pulled back slowly, like a stone curtain, to form an opening into a spacious library. Alexandra followed Candra through the opening and saw the Guardian seated at a large desk some thirty meters away and to the right.

"Give me a moment," the Guardian said, not looking up.

She was going through a stack of papers, pausing now and then to scribble something, perhaps a signature, on whatever paper was before her.

Alexandra gazed at the Guardian and considered the part this woman played in her life. In the not so distant past, she had been merely Aunt Elizabeth. The shock of learning Aunt Elizabeth was the Guardian of the Two Worlds had diminished, but not the mystery. Uncovering the mysteries of the Guardianship seemed a part of everything Alexandra did now. Indeed, uncovering mysteries of all sorts had become her new life.

Alexandra looked around the Guardian's library. A fire burned in a massive stone fireplace to her left. Its flames leaped and danced beneath a stone arch as high as a man's head. The walls of the room were seven meters from floor to ceiling and lined with books, thousands of them on all sides.

Seemingly on command, Candra bowed in the direction of Elizabeth, and then, quite suddenly, vanished. There was no flash of light, no puff of smoke, no incantation: Candra was simply there one moment and gone the next. The necessity to enter by the closet was for Alexandra, not the Dyrisian.

Elizabeth scribbled something on the last of the papers before her and looked up at Alexandra.

"Come, come, my dear," she said, rising from her desk and crossing the distance between them. She took her niece's hand and led her to a large wooden table in the center of the room. The table was laid out with a sumptuous meal. Elizabeth gestured for Alexandra to sit at one end of the table, while she sat at the other.

"I don't understand why I have to come through that silly closet," Alexandra commented.

"A necessary precaution," Elizabeth replied with a dismissive wave.

"It's pretty weird," Alexandra said. "Why can't I come and go like Candra?"

"You are not Dyrisian. It is not possible," Elizabeth replied casually as she gestured toward the food.

"Please, eat."

Alexandra grabbed an orange roll and hungrily bit into it.

Elizabeth chatted about trivial events that had occurred during her niece's five-week absence. Alexandra only half listened. Her thoughts were on the Cryptology Master Course she had just completed in Scotland. Something wonderful had happened there, but also something terrible. She needed time to consider the polarities and what lay between them. So far her aunt was granting her that time with small talk that required no response, but Alexandra knew serious questions would come, questions about her "progress." It was always about that, even when the word was not used. The Guardian was investing in her for a purpose that was not clear, might never be. But the urgency was quite apparent, sometimes painfully so.

Alexandra considered what she had been told about her new home. Someone named Andronius Caledon had discovered the Second-World dimension of earth some sixteen centuries ago. He had led a great exodus from First World. Thousands of witches, warlocks, wizards, and others suspected of having magical powers entered Second World to escape vicious persecution. Many other thousands did not leave. They died at the hands of inquisitors who feared and hated them.

The Guardian had told Alexandra she had an important part to play in the future of Second World. Did she? Or was she just being used for some dark purpose of the Guardian? How much did she really know about her aunt or anyone here?

"Alexandra! My dear, are you hearing a word I say?"

"I'm so sorry, Aunt Elizabeth. I was just . . . thinking."

"Would you care to share your thoughts?"

Alexandra hesitated, then spoke in a low voice.

"I was thinking about time. I mean time here and in First World being the same. Everything else is so . . . different. And the Exodus sixteen centuries ago. Why does no one in my world know of it? Why is there nothing in the history books? How have you stayed hidden for so long? Why . . ."

Elizabeth lifted her hands, palms forward, in a friendly gesture signaling for silence.

"Enough questions, dear girl. Allow me to provide some answers."

Alexandra sighed and leaned back in her chair.

"We, and that now includes you, remain hidden in plain sight. The witches pursued and persecuted over the centuries have faded into myth in your world. Only among primitive tribes is belief still strong, and where it is strong the persecutions remain brutal. How many in First World would believe you spent a week in the company of a unicorn or that dragons and other cryptids are real? You spent the last five weeks studying creatures no one in your world believes exist—and you did it in that very world, under their noses, as First Worlders like to say. The inhabitants of our world and a few in yours are the stuff of fiction to First Worlders, and we do what we can to keep it that way. We hide behind the fictions that have taken the place of persecutions. We are entertainment now. Magic is an act performed on a stage in your world. It bears no resemblance to our powers or our beliefs. Witches, warlocks, wizards, and the cryptids you studied in Scotland—these are entertainment artifacts in your world, not real, not a threat."

Alexandra looked surprised.

"There are Second Worlders in First World?" she asked.

"A few, in key positions to maintain the separation of the two worlds."

The Guardian smiled.

"Enough for now, my dear. Please, finish your meal."

Alexander continued to eat, knowing the interrogation would soon begin. And so it did only a few minutes later.

"Master Travits told me of your unprecedented success in the fifth week of the course," the Guardian commented offhandedly. "But I would like to hear of it from you. I am interested most in what you did *not* tell him."

It's always like this, thought Alexandra. *Always she probes directly, never leads up to anything. Bam!—right to the heart of where I don't want to go.*

"I told Master Travits everything."

"Yes, yes, you told him what you told him. I do not wish to pry."

Alexandra was surprised. Aunt Elizabeth usually did not back off so easily, and she never advanced or withdrew without purpose.

"There is another matter I must discuss with you," Elizabeth said. She looked away from Alexandra and paused for several long moments.

"I sent General Borrington to make arrangements for Daniel to come here," she said finally, looking back at her niece. "He could not find him." The Guardian's voice became almost a whisper. "I am so sorry. I know I promised . . ."

Alexandra felt a sudden tightness in her chest. Daniel was the son of Ellen Sutton, the nanny who had raised them both from infancy. The bond between her and Daniel was not only one of shared upbringing, but also of shared magical strangeness. He was the piece of family and of First World that Alexandra desperately needed to be here with her. Elizabeth had promised to bring him to Byrnhelen, had solemnly promised it in writing! And now this!

"'Could not find him?'" Alexandra repeated, her voice rising.

"Everything that can be done is being done," Elizabeth assured her, still speaking softly. "Daniel was last seen entering the forest near your home in Simsbury, where you had disappeared. He was never seen again. A search as intense as the one for you turned up nothing but his backpack. General Borrington continues his own search, and he has considerable resources. I will keep my promise, Alexandra."

Alexandra pushed back her chair and stood.

"They didn't find me either, did they? Yet here I am!"

"Yes," Elizabeth said quietly, "and that suggests something."

Alexandra felt tears welling up.

I've got to think straight. I can't start bawling.

To be separated from Daniel while knowing he was home safe with his mother was one thing. To be separated from him and not know if he was alive or dead was quite another.

"What do you mean, 'suggests something'?" Alexandra demanded. "You speak in riddles."

"I mean he may already be here."

"Here? At Byrnhelen?"

"No, but somewhere in Second World. We can surmise

no more, given the scanty evidence."

"I think you can *surmise* more," Alexandra retorted angrily. "Much more."

"Take care how you address me, young lady."

Alexandra glared at her aunt.

Elizabeth ignored the look and went on:

"Your people in First World are beyond their abilities, especially if Daniel has been abducted as you were."

"I wasn't abducted; I was rescued. I would have died if Euwen hadn't found me and brought me here. It's not the same."

"Granted, what the McConnelly boy did qualifies as a rescue. I have questions about his motives, however, and about Euwen McConnelly himself. Whatever the case, Daniel's whereabouts are unknown. We are searching for him. I have made this General Borrington's highest priority. If Daniel can be found, General Borrington will find him. He commands all my forces. There is no better. I will keep my promise to you."

Alexandra muttered something to herself and began to pace.

"What?" Elizabeth inquired, leaning forward.

"I said the dreams were right."

"What dreams?"

"My nightmares, they were right."

"You've told me nothing of dreams."

Elizabeth observed her niece's pacing, the increasing tempo, the subtle rhythms. She studied Alexandra's facial expression, especially the eyes and the tightening of certain muscles.

She is spinning up, gathering her dangerously undisciplined magical powers. She could hurt herself . . .

and me. I must take control, but with precision and at just the right moment.

"I don't get up every morning and tell you my dreams," Alexandra went on, her voice rising steadily. "Is that so bad? They're just dreams! Aren't even my dreams my own!" Now she was almost yelling, on the edge of mania.

"I suspect they are *not* just dreams, Alexandra, and there is a good chance they are not your own."

Elizabeth paused as her own powers reached their peak. It was time.

"Take . . . a . . . seat," she thundered suddenly.

The words slashed across Alexandra's psyche. She stopped pacing but did not sit.

Elizabeth was amazed her command was not fully obeyed.

The child's powers are greater than I thought.

"Tell me of these nightmares."

"They're nothing."

"Do they repeat themselves? Does the story in them remain unchanged or changed only in small ways?"

"How did you know?" Alexandra asked, suddenly bewildered.

Ah, better, Elizabeth thought. *She is winding down.*

"Your nightmares may be the key to finding Daniel."

"How?"

"Dream manipulation is in its infancy in the world from which you came; it is quite advanced in Second World. I may be able to help."

Alexandra relaxed and took her seat at the table.

She pondered how Elizabeth spoke in neat little packets. Her aunt seemed to pull these packets out of hiding and deliver them at the precise moment and in the precise path of her argument. She did not sound rehearsed; she sounded preternaturally prepared. She always seemed to know what was coming. Alexandra did not trust her aunt's intentions with regard to Daniel, but she realized Elizabeth offered the only hope of finding him. She had to trust, if only a little. If the dreams could help, she would describe them.

"I have the same dream over and over, just as you said," Alexandra began. "It starts out with Daniel and me playing hide-and-seek. The dream ends with Daniel crying out for my help, but I can't find him. I cannot help him."

"When did you start having this dream?"

"When I first arrived at Byrnhelen. Maybe it was a few days after. I can't remember exactly. Does it matter?"

"It matters very much. Everything about the dream matters. The repetition is telling. Changes in the dream, sometimes very small, are also revealing over time. With close observation, patterns can be discerned. Do the dreams ever stop?

"Only when I was in the Scottish northlands, with the unicorn. I had no nightmares with him. I slept well. I thought clearly."

"Ah, the unicorn," Elizabeth murmured with a knowing smile. "Is it always the same dream? No changes in characters, action, anything?"

Alexandra considered the question. Something had changed in last night's dream, something important. She recalled the details and listed them to herself:

I was chasing Daniel, the same as before. But this time, for the first time, I found him, found his hiding place. We were walking toward each other. He was smiling and everything was going to be like it was before. Then Elizabeth appeared. She threatened Daniel. She chased him away.

Elizabeth interrupted her thoughts. "Were there any changes?" she asked again.

Alexandra looked speculatively at her aunt.

Is the manipulator of my dreams sitting across the table from me?

"I have a question," Alexandra said, "and I hope you will trust me with a truthful answer."

Elizabeth nodded.

Alexandra considered carefully what to say next. Then she continued:

"You tell me I'm important to you—my education, my progress, my purpose—or rather your purpose for me. Daniel is *not* important to you. So, do you want him to stay lost, to never come to Byrnhelen?"

Elizabeth marveled at the question. It was formed perfectly. It was timed perfectly. It was simple, innocent, honest, and starkly direct. And therein lay its power to elicit truth. Her niece spoke without guile, yet with an understanding far beyond her years.

She has the gift, thought Elizabeth. *She will need it.*

"My answer is both yes and no," Elizabeth replied. "No, because his being here will, I fear, bring you pain I can neither predict nor prevent. Yes, because you have chosen him to play a vital part in your destiny. That choice makes him a necessity, whether I like it or not."

Alexandra studied her aunt's face.

"There has been a change," she admitted, "last night."

"What was it?"

"You. You are in the dream now, and not in a way I like."

Alexandra told Elizabeth everything: about the change, about Elizabeth's banishing Daniel, about every detail she could remember in every dream leading up to that of last night.

Elizabeth probed expertly. Alexandra was quite aware of this, and yielded to it. She felt hope rising in her. She knew nothing of how this might work, but she hoped and she trusted. The trust was hard, but the necessity was great.

"You've told me enough for now," Elizabeth said finally. "We will go on with this later."

Elizabeth walked to her desk, reached into a drawer, and pulled out a small leather-bound book. She handed it to her niece.

Alexandra thumbed through the pages. They were blank.

"Leave this on the nightstand beside your bed. Do not take it from there; do not carry it with you. Leave it there. When you first go to bed and while still awake, recall the dream you had the previous night. Picture yourself in the dream. Picture the others in the dream. Picture the surroundings. Then, like the director of a play, make changes here and there in the direction you wish your dream to go. Nudge the players, the setting, the action. Do not push. Do not force. Rehearse the entire dream this way. Do this three times, keeping yourself awake. Write in the book after each rehearsal. Note the differences you were able to make, along with the things that stayed the same despite your efforts to change them. Above all, do not fall asleep until you have completed the third rehearsal and made careful notes in the dream journal."

Alexandra shook her head. "I hate these nightmares. Why must I rehearse them?"

"Because you cannot master a thing without first embracing it. You must embrace these dreams, cease resisting them, and then, a little at a time, you will master them."

Alexandra made a gesture of irritated submission. What Elizabeth proposed seemed impossible. The tools—this book, a pencil, and her imagination—seemed wholly inadequate. How would any of this help her? How would it help Daniel?

"You're not the author of these dreams, Alexandra. Someone else is. If we can keep the dreams going while you gain the ability to observe yourself in them and to influence people and events in them, we have a chance."

"A chance for what?"

"A chance to walk back through your dreams to their author, and then to spy on him as he has been spying on you."

Alexandra felt a chill.

"I don't like any of this," she said.

"Neither do I. But it is an opportunity. Consider this a step in your training. As you complete your notes on the third rehearsal, you will be fighting off sleep. The dream-maker, the manipulator, needs you to sleep. You will barely be able to hold your eyes open. Let them close. Picture a stage and you on it, playing your part, and you above the stage, observing and directing. Hold that picture and let sleep come."

"Sometimes the nightmares wake me up. What then?"

"Then you take your dream journal in hand and write down every detail you can remember. Do this immediately, before the details merge into incomprehensible mush."

"Where will all this lead?"

"To the dream-maker," Elizabeth replied, "and through him to his master. To discovery of why you are under psychic attack. And finally, for your sake and his, to Daniel."

-GUIDE TO THE TWO WORLDS-

AEDAN SHAW, *younger brother of the Guardian and second in the line of succession.*

ALBUMTER DROUSE, *master of potions in the service of Byrnhelen.*

ALEA, *Dyrisian bound in service to Byrnhelen, daughter of Candra.*

ALEXANDRA (ALEX) WARD, *only child of John and Mary Ward and apprentice at Byrnhelen.*

ANDRÉ DU BOURGAY, *abbot of Mont Saint-Michel.*

ANDRONIUS CALEDON, *Protector of All Magical Beings, Master of the Dimensions, and Creator of Second World.*

ANDREW BORRINGTON, *Protector of Second World Human Kind and senior general of the army of Byrnhelen.*

BRADYN ARISTARCHUS, *master of astronomy in the service of Byrnhelen.*

BREEANNA (BREE) MCCONNELLY, *daughter of Ian McConnelly and sister of Euwen McConnelly.*

BRIEL, *Dyrisian bound in service to Byrnhelen.*

BYRNHELEN, *fortress of the Guardian.*

CANDRA, *Dyrisian bound in service to Byrnhelen, personal assistant of the Guardian, and mother of Alea.*

CORNEILUS ASHERTON, *master of metamorphology in the service of Byrnhelen.*

DANIEL SUTTON, *son of David and Ellen Sutton, best friend of Alexandra Ward.*

DAVID SUTTON, *Second World expatriate, arranger of secret adoptions in First World, husband of Ellen Sutton, and father of Daniel Sutton.*

DARIEN WILAMSFELD, *Nephew and wandmaker apprentice of Mathias Wilamsfeld.*

DREAM MASTER, *a wizard who manipulates dreams.*

DURNAKK, *hidden fortress of Aedan Shaw.*

DYRISIAN, *humanoid species bound to the service of various houses in Second World. Intensely loyal to the houses they serve while assiduously neutral in all disputes.*

EDVARD VOGEL, *Rebecca Vogel's older brother.*

ELIZABETH SHAW, *the Guardian, Preserver of the Two Worlds and head of the Council of Protectors.*

ELLEN SUTTON, *housekeeper of John and Mary Ward, nanny of Alexandra Ward, mother of Daniel Sutton, and widow of David Sutton.*

ENNIS CROFT, *high-ranking general in the army of Aedan Shaw.*

EUDORA, *Pegasus used for pulling carriages at Byrnhelen.*

EUWEN MCCONNELLY, *brother of Breeanna McConnelly and son of Ian McConnelly.*

GREGORY TRAVITS, *master of cryptozoology in the service of Byrnhelen and creator of the cryptid preserve in Northern Scotland.*

GIDRAM HINBANTERFELD, *Dwarf bound in service to Byrnhelen.*

GUARDIAN, *Elizabeth Shaw, Preserver of the Two Worlds and head of the Council of Protectors.*

HENRY LUSK, *butler of John and Mary Ward.*

IAN MCCONNELLY, *high-ranking general in the army of Aedan Shaw and father of Breeanna and Euwen McConnelly.*

JACQUES VILLEDIEU, *friend of the abbot of Mont Saint-Michel.*

JOHN WARD, *husband of Mary Ward and father of Alexandra Ward.*

JONATHAN EATON, *fellow apprentice of Alexandra Ward at Byrnhelen.*

JOSHUA TURNER, *Protector of First World Human Kind and leader of the search for the Successor.*

KATHERINE SHAW, *younger sister of the Guardian and first in the line of succession. Wife of Nathan Thomas Greer and suspected birth mother of Alexandra Ward.*

KATRINA THOMAS, *fellow apprentice of Alexandra Ward at Byrnhelen.*

LAVERTANIAN UNICORN, *animal species with enhanced mental capacity, including telepathy.*

LAYTON HUNT, *chauffeur of John and Mary Ward.*

LUKE PATTERSON, *fellow apprentice of Alexandra Ward at Byrnhelen.*

MARIAH GRIFFITH, *fellow apprentice of Alexandra Ward at Byrnhelen.*

MARY WARD, *wife of John Ward and mother of Alexandra Ward.*

MAREK AVALARD, *master of guardero mentis in the service of Byrnhelen.*

MATHIAS WILAMSFELD, *master wandmaker and keeper of the secret of the Wilamsfeld wand. Uncle of Darien Wilamsfeld.*

MRS. MURPHY, *sister of Ellen Sutton.*

MRS. NOTTINGBATCH, *neighbor of John and Mary Ward.*

NARA, *Nepenthian. Protector of Rock, Water, Air, Fire, and Flora of the Two Worlds.*

NATHAN THOMAS GREER, *husband of Katherine Shaw and suspected birth father of Alexandra Ward.*

NEPENTHIAN, *humanoid species responsible for protecting the balance of natural systems that sustain all life in the Two Worlds.*

PETER KENDAL, *chief-of-staff of Joshua Turner.*

REBECCA (BECCA) VOGEL, *fellow apprentice of Alexandra Ward at Byrnhelen and her best friend among the apprentices.*

RONDEGAL DEMPERTON, *fellow apprentice of Alexandra Ward at Byrnhelen.*

SIALA, *Dyrisian bound in service to Byrnhelen.*

SIGVARDR, *Lavertanian Unicorn. Protector of Animal Kind of the Two Worlds.*

STANLEY TANNER, *police lieutenant in charge of the search for Alexandra Ward in First World.*

SUSAN FAERBER, *secretary of Andrew Borrington.*

THEODORUS WILAMSFELD, *deceased master wandmaker and creator of the first Wilamsfeld wand.*

TRENTON RIGBY, *fellow apprentice of Alexandra Ward at Byrnhelen.*

-Q&A-

NAOMI SAWYER

Was there any particular incident that inspired the plot of *The Successor* and the rest of the *Chronicles of the Two Worlds*?

Yes. When I was growing up, it was tradition for my sisters and I to write stories and read them to our parents and each other on Christmas Eve. This tradition continued into adulthood. During a Christmas season around seven years ago, I sat down and once again began to compose my annual Christmas story. I don't remember much about the story, but I do remember it being about a sad little orphan boy. (I was going for tears. Orphans usually work.) I remember quite clearly that in one of the scenes in my story, the boy was being chased through a wintry forest during a savage snowstorm. The boy became very cold and lay down in a forest glade and fell asleep. As his breathing became shallow and death drew near, two arms reached out, gathered him up, and took him into the Netherworld. I stopped writing at that moment. I had a strong impression that this scene was part of another story, a much larger story—one I had yet to write. I did write it soon after, the plot unfolding as I progressed. Chuck later joined me in a writing partnership, and we crafted the story into our first novel, *The Successor*, and its sequel, *The Culling*.

What motivated you to become a writer?

I love to read. When I was a child, my sisters and I were required to take a two-hour nap every afternoon during the summer. We could sleep or we could read. I read because I felt I was much too grown-up to sleep (only babies took naps). I learned to love those two hours. Often I didn't want to get up when my mom (the warden) finally came to release her prisoners. Another fond memory is of my father reading aloud to me. He read *Below the Salt* when I was but twelve, while on my own I read all the Nancy Drew books and was fast becoming hooked on Agatha Christie novels. Seeing this, he guided me to Schulenburg, Dumas, Costain, and others. I carry on the tradition of reading aloud to my own children. I have read entire series to them, including *Junie B. Jones*, the *Magic Tree House*, and, of course, *Harry Potter*. The strong influence of books in my early life led me to want to write them.

How did you meet your co-author?

It was 2010. I had recently finished the original version of *The Successor*, titled at that time, *Tessa Ward and the Guardian of Edom*. My original bad guy was "Darkevel." ("Dark" and "evil," get it? Fortunately, I now have Chuck to suggest more suitable names for our characters.) Chuck was a friend of my father, who had told him I had written a book. Chuck offered to read it. He had spent 40 years as an editor and ghostwriter, and was a published author. My father declined his offer. Chuck and I later met for the first time at a Halloween Party. We agreed to meet again to discuss my book's prospects. We did meet, and soon after, on 25 August 2010, we formally entered into a writing partnership. My book became our book.

How did you make the decision to collaborate?

When Chuck and I first discussed collaboration, I was skeptical. It was not clear to me how two people could write a book together, especially one I had already written and felt very possessive about. Chuck offered to do some sample editing on the first couple chapters so I could decide if there was value-added. There was that and more. Not long after, we agreed to become co-authors.

How do you settle disagreements?

Our disagreements are rare, but they can end in raised voices (I never shout) and tears (mine, not his). Sometimes the matter can only be settled by a strenuous hike or a few hours of outdoor photography or both—anything to break the deadlock. The same methods serve to prevent or put an end to writer's block or, on the other hand, writer's trash (too many words, too little meaning). Nothing breaks up these delays better than taking a timeout, climbing a mountain, setting up an antenna on the summit, and talking to people about nothing on a ham radio in whiteout conditions while 60 mile-per-hour winds hurl shards of snow into our eyes. In between we write. Whatever it takes, right? Beats excessive consumption of alcoholic beverages, which is the time-honored method employed by some very famous writers.

What are the challenges in a writing partnership? What are the benefits? How do the challenges and benefits balance out in your partnership?

The biggest challenge and the greatest benefit from working with a co-author is that neither of you is alone. The challenge is that important decisions require agreement between partners, and reaching agreement is sometimes difficult. The benefit is that artistic and business decisions are better informed by the process of achieving consensus. One partner shares an idea. The other partner adds to it or chips off a rough edge or proposes an entirely new idea. The idea-ball is tossed back and forth until consensus is reached. In this way, the partnership grows into something greater than the sum of the two partners. Together we share the work of writing and editing the book (and even the answers to these questions). Together we share the frustrations of the publishing process. Together we promote the book. Together, in short, we share the work. In our partnership, these and other benefits far outweigh the challenges.

What advice do you have for those who are thinking of writing a book?

First. Read every day. Good writers are born from good readers. Reading deepens the imagination. It informs as no other medium can. It strengthens one's grasp of language and the dynamics of crafting words into a story.

Second. Write every day. I build momentum when I write every day; the words seem to flow onto the page. When I miss a day, I lose a measure of this momentum. I have to back track and find where I left off. My flow threatens to become a series of spurts. It takes a while to get back into the groove, to regain the flow.

Do you see yourself in any of your characters or their relationships in the *Chronicles of the Two Worlds*?

It is interesting that readers who know me tend to see me in a particular character or relationship in the book. I don't see what they see. I have helped create all the characters and relationships, and only for moments (or minutes or hours) in my imagination am I any one of them. While writing the first two books of the *Chronicles*, I found myself being Daniel fighting to escape the dungeon of Durnakk, then Alexandra in awe of the new world being opened up to her, then Borrington commanding great armies, then Bree exploring and hatching schemes, then Elizabeth suppressing her feelings while being troubled by what the future might hold.

That is how the characters seem while I am creating them. Afterward, they take on a life of their own (like the story itself), and I see them from a certain remove, much as the reader does, but the additional knowledge I have as their creator. Then I see I am Alexandra in my determination and forward-thrusting rebellion against demands made on me. I respond to Joshua's directness and First World manliness: a good man on a dark night, as Chuck likes to say. I am Nara in my love of the natural world and of children. Borrington turns my head. I might flirt with him. Sigvardr is my rock, my constant companion, my defense against the storm.

Your turn. Read the books. Tell me who you are.

What is the hardest thing about writing?

The hardest thing about writing is writing. Then comes finding the time and stamina to do it. Then comes surviving the lacerations from the editorial knife of my partner. You must understand: my feverish brain thinks my first drafts are my final drafts. Every word, every sentence, every paragraph is a gem, a perfection of light and color and poetry (I would call them awesome, but Chuck forbids the use of that term). When the violence stops, I smile, wipe back a tear, and say, "I don't understand" or I'm confused." He ignores me.

I jest, of course, but only in part. It is hard work, this dragging scenes out of one's head and rendering them into words that do justice to the vision and the feelings of the imagining. It is even harder to "kill my babies," to spend perhaps hours forming my imaginings into deathless prose, only to discover that what I have written is redundant or outside the story line or trite or otherwise wrong or unnecessary. I stare in shock for a moment after this discovery, and then I put an end to them… It is horrible to behold.

What is your favorite scene in your book?

I must answer as a reader, not the writer. The funniest scene in *The Successor* is in the chapter entitled, "The Birthday Surprise." It delights me every time I read it. There is something so charmingly whimsical about flying hotdogs being jammed up people's noses while sticks of licorice whip their legs. Sorry.

The most intense scene in *The Successor* is in the chapter entitled, "Trouble on the Trail." Alexandra is being chased by Red Caps, lethal monsters who pursue her with the intent to kill her. My heart raced as I wrote the scene. I felt it was I who was being pursued through the ruined castle.

Favorites? There are many and there are none. It's rather like asking me which thread I like best in my coat of many colors.

Does *The Successor* end how you thought it would end?

The trouble with writing books in a series is that there are no endings, only (hopefully satisfying) pauses. Each of our books is part of a single story: *The Chronicles of the Two Worlds*. Similarly, *Lord of the Rings* is the story, while each of the constituent books is merely a part. Tolkien even calls his books parts.

Our original book combined *The Successor* and *The Culling* into a single epic. Thus the end of *The Culling* was the end of our original book. Publishing standards on word count, especially for earlier books in a series, demanded otherwise, so we made two books of one.

I see on your web site and on Facebook, Twitter, Instagram, and other social media pictures of you and your co-author hiking, climbing, and doing other things together. Is this just play time, as you mentioned earlier, or do these activities contribute to your collaboration as writers?

Yes and yes. In fact, these activities are vital to the success of our collaboration. Companies have team-building courses and retreats to revitalize employees, build moral, and iron out troublesome relationships. These exercises also lead on to greater innovation and increased efficiency. They make the company stronger. Our collaboration requires much the same thing. I cannot tell you how many scenes and plot lines were hatched while hiking down a mountain or navigating an icy ridge in high winds. Experiences, especially intense ones, are the fodder of the imagination. One must experience nature to write convincingly about it. I remember writing a scene in *The Culling* where my character is walking through a forest. A mild breeze is passing through the trees. In my artistically naive mind, I thought I had written the scene with great clarity. Evocative I think I called it. Soon after I found myself hiking through a forest with Chuck. A light breeze was blowing. He stopped me and told me to close my eyes and listen. I obeyed. He asked me to describe what I heard. I realized in the passing minutes that I had never listened, really listened to the play of wind in the trees. The wind sounded like a giant wave rolling over the forest canopy. He told me to listen for the variations in pitch (the musical kind, not the sticky kind) within the wind. I did. I heard for the first time that wind makes not one sound, but many as it passes. Chuck explained that the pitch of the wind was made by the length of the pine needles it was passing through. I looked. I saw. Each species of tree and each individual tree, depending on size and location, had its own song to sing. Chuck smiled and asked, "Does the wind make the trees or do the trees make the wind." I went back to the house that night and re-wrote the forest descriptions in my book. One cannot write what one does not know.

Are you sending a message in *The Successor*?

Yes...and no. In a literal sense, what people say and what people write is no more than a series of messages, some trivial, some profound. When the messages are combined with poetic skill, the result is a thing of beauty, measured more in the emotions than in the mind. I do have secret wishes for our readers, "messages" I hope they will receive, but I'm not always sure what they are. We began with a story in mind, but the story soon takes hold of its authors and sends its own messages. And there is something else: The reader, not the author, decides what the message is. Reading is an art form. We invite you to search in the *Chronicles* for your own meaning, a nugget here, a gem there. Consider where you are going and take what you can use. Leave the rest, perhaps to come back later in life and find meaning where there was none before. Or just move on.

We have written a story. Let it take you where you need to go. Let it be yours. As authors, we can ask for nothing more—except that you might tell us something of your journey. We hope you will.

CHARLES SALE

Was it always your dream to be a writer?

Nope. I wanted to be a cowboy like Roy Rogers. I didn't know it in the fifth grade, but that meant I wanted to be a police officer. There was much consternation when I came out of the closet with that. Mom and Dad went on a campaign to make me an attorney. Mom said I should be an attorney because all my life I had demonstrated exceptional skill in argumentation—most of it with her.

I took an aptitude test in college; didn't come out an attorney; came out a cop. More consternation. Wanting to please, I researched the best undergraduate preparation for law school. (Maybe I could go to law school and then be a cop. Writing still not on the radar.) Turned out the best majors were history, political science, or English. I chose English. Turned out I was pretty good at it. They put me in an accelerated program leading to a master's degree in the time usually taken to earn a bachelor's degree at the University of Arizona, Tucson. Then on to a PhD and a professorship in an English department somewhere. More pressure. Is no one hearing me? I want to be a cop!

Family tragedy struck, forcing me to leave college and help support my mother and four brothers and sisters. That did the trick. I applied to the Los Angeles Police Department, was accepted, and graduated at the top of my Academy class. Two and a half years later, after working patrol and accident investigation, I am back at the Academy doing—you guessed it—writing. Two years after that I'm a sergeant and back on the street. I got in about 11 years doing a wide variety of police work before I got pulled in to serve as a writer and editor in Planning and Research Division and the Office of the Chief of Police. I never fully escaped from that role. I retired after 30 years of service. I lived my childhood dream, but it wasn't writing. That just happened. Sorry.

Some say the fact that my grandfather, Charles "Chic" Sale, was a famous actor and somewhat less famous writer had something to do with my fate. I don't buy it.

What authors and literary works most strongly influenced you in writing the first books of the *Chronicles of the Two Worlds*?

Shakespeare's *Henry V* was an influence. Mountain climbing friends and I memorized King Henry's famous St. Crispin's Day speech (Act IV, Scene III, 18-67) and tortured our climbing companions by reciting it with gusto when the climbing became difficult. (Fun for us; irritating for them.) King Henry delivers his speech just before the famous Battle of Agincourt, where the English were outnumbered 6 to 1: 6,000 of King Henry's English troops defeated 36,000 French, and Henry made a wife of the French princess, Catherine of Valois. Valor, the moral burdens of a monarch, success against great odds, love, politics—*Henry V* has it all, a classic tale of ordeal and triumph.

Ordeal and triumph fascinates me, and there is much of this cycle in the *Chronicles of the Two Worlds*. Helen Keller, whose ordeals and triumphs were far from trivial, said that life is a great adventure or it is nothing. The characters in *The Successor* and its sequel, *The Culling*, do not lead nothing lives, and they do not go quietly into the night when their lives end.

Predictably, my other influences include Jack London (*Call of the Wild*), Rudyard Kipling (*The Jungle Books*), Garth Stein (*The Art of Racing in the Rain*), Ladislas Farago (*Patton: Ordeal and Triumph*), Charles A. Lindberg (*The Spirit of St. Louis*), Frank Herbert (*Dune* and its sequels), Robert Ardray (*The Territorial Imperative: A Personal Inquiry Into the Animal Origins of Property and Nations*), and J.K Rowling (the *Harry Potter* series). Ernest Hemingway, F. Scott Fitzgerald, Melville, Emerson, Thoreau, and others are in the foundations of my literary experience. There are others, but these will do.

Is it difficult to write a fantasy novel that is not derivative of the many others that have been written?

Exceedingly difficult. Perhaps even impossible. And in some ways not desirable. Fantasy readers, especially young ones, expect certain norms to be followed. Also, there is the matter of cultural "echoes." If one writes a certain way, the reader hears echoes of the familiar: great writers and great books of the past, historical events, universal life experiences, and the like. When they are not trite or painfully imitative, these echoes enhance storytelling. Sadly, the emphasis on being contemporary (even when telling stories about the past) is causing these echoes to fade or be blocked altogether. Being "contemporary" in some fashion is quite necessary, especially today. The period of doubling of all human knowledge has grown obscenely short: It is estimated now to be thirteen months on average. With advances in artificial intelligence and other computer technology, IBM experts say the period of doubling could soon be down to every twelve *hours*. We are in danger of having no past, of having technology overwhelm the magical nature of humanness.

This is a background theme throughout the *Chronicles of the Two Worlds*. We need our past. We need to repeat things: sayings, poems, music, memorized passages from our favorite books and movies—as well as our greetings to one another. A work of art that is purely and entirely original (an impossibility) is for that reason incomprehensible. We seek to make the books of the *Chronicles* both original and comprehensible.

Why do you collaborate with another writer?

I collaborate because it is what I know.

One of my heroes is William Maxwell Evarts ("Max") Perkins. He was the famous editor for Ernest Hemingway, F. Scott Fitzgerald, and Thomas Wolfe. His collaboration with these men was not easy. Hemingway and Fitzgerald were heavy drinkers, and Wolfe never wrote a word he did not love with all his heart. Perkins was fiercely devoted to all of them and fiercely critical of their work. It is widely agreed that he contributed mightily to their literary and commercial success.

I have been a writer and a copy, content, and executive editor off-and-on since 1965. During the final years of my 30-year law enforcement career, I was the executive editor of a research and writing team and was the speech writer for the chief of police and other senior officials. I wrote, trained others to write, edited, and re-wrote countless pieces of non-fiction. Although I wrote on my own for sensitive projects, circumstances and my abilities more often put me in the company of other writers, both in an institutional setting and a freelance capacity.

So, when I learned of Naomi's frustrating efforts to bring her wonderful story to print, I was interested. We met and discussed her book. I had never done fiction. I did a sample edit and re-write of some early chapters, and she decided to allow me to become her co-author. The rest, as they say, is history. It can be read in the pages of the *Chronicles of the Two Worlds.*

You began your collaboration on the *Chronicles of the Two Worlds* six years ago. Do you and Naomi work together the same way now as you did then? Has your working or personal relationship changed over time?

Naomi still delivers the initial plot and rough draft of the story. We review and discuss. Our roles may be reversed for certain chapters, certain characters, and certain action (I know more about police work than she does), but in all cases drafts are passed back and forth until we achieve unity. This unity is essential for the book not to feel as though it was written by a committee. It is essential also for consistent character development and coherent plot development. Artistic unity is the vital core of our partnership, and the years have strengthened it.

We follow the same protocols as we did in the beginning, but we have become more efficient in applying them. We don't need to ask as many questions of one another as we did in the beginning. We spend less time reassuring one another, and more time writing and editing. Finally, we are much handier with Microsoft Word, a form of Artificial Intelligence that will one day rule the world.

Many professional collaborators become friends. Some do not. We are in the former group. Over the past six years we have shared adventures in mountaineering, hiking, amateur radio, photography, and music (she plays the piano, I the cello). This sharing has drawn us closer and enhanced our ability to work together and speak clearly with one voice in our writing.

-Book Club Discussion-

1.   How would you feel if you were being groomed to be the Guardian? Would you agree to accept that role? Why or why not?

2.   How do you think Alexandra feels about not being with her parents?

3.   Do you feel that John and Mary Ward should have told Alexandra that she was adopted?

4.   Which characters do you identify with the most? Why?

5.   Is Euwen McConnelly a good guy or a bad guy? Why?

6.   Who in *The Successor* would you most like to meet? What would you ask them? What would you say to them?

7.   Do you think that Andronius Caledon did the right thing in leading the exodus into Second World? Why?

8.   If you had been magical at the time of the exodus, would you have chosen to leave First World for Second World? Why?

9.   If you could live in either world today, which would you choose? Why?

10.   What is the most important lesson Sigvardr teaches Alexandra? Why is it important?

11.   What passage in the book did you find very compelling or interesting? Why?

12. Which protector do you identify with the most? Why?

13. How do you think First World inhabitants would react if they learned about Second World?

14. If you could study any Cryptid in the Scotland Cryptid Preserve, which one would it be? Why?

15. Why do you think Bree decided to help Daniel?

16. Why do you think Bree's wand worked for Daniel?

17. Why do you think Elizabeth is hesitant to bring Daniel to Byrnhelen? Do you agree with her? Why or why not?

18. Does a part of *The Successor* or any of the characters remind you of your own life? Which part or characters? Why?

19. Do you have a favorite epigraph (quotes at the beginning of each chapter)? Which one and why?

20. If you could ask the authors three questions, what would they be?

-ABOUT THE AUTHORS-

Naomi Sawyer was born in Berlin during the Cold War; attended high school in Ansbach, Germany; and has traveled extensively in Europe, the Eastern Block, Mexico, and Canada. She is a freelance writer, the mother of three, and lives in Phoenix, Arizona.

Charles Sale is a retired law enforcement officer, writer, editor, and nature photographer. He lives with his wife, Teri, in Colorado Springs, Colorado.

-LIVE EVENTS-

Sawyer & Sale LLC can bring the authors to your live event. For more information or to calendar an event, email Sawyer & Sale LLC at sawyersale@gmail.com.

CPSIA information can be obtained
at www.ICGtesting.com
Printed in the USA
FSHW011938010319
56049FS